He curled his fingers around the side of my neck and slid th   to my jaw.

"You good?" he asked.

I swallowed. Then I

"Wanna be better?

My belly did a somers

Oh yes. I definitely wanted to

I pressed a hand to his chest and breathed,

He dipped his head and I held my breath as he held my eyes and glided the side of his nose along the side of mine.

Oh.

Wow.

He rubbed his thumb along my cheek and continued to stare into my eyes. I squirmed a little bit.

"What you want, Butterfly?"

He was making me ask. Why was that so arousing?

"I want you to kiss me."

Acclaim for Kristen Ashley and Her Novels

"A unique, not-to-be-missed voice in romance. Kristen Ashley is a star in the making!"

—Carly Phillips, *New York Times* bestselling author

"I adore Kristen Ashley's books. She writes engaging, romantic stories with intriguing, colorful, and larger-than-life characters. Her stories grab you by the throat from page one and don't let go until well after the last page. They continue to dwell in your mind days after you finish the story and you'll find yourself anxiously awaiting the next. Ashley is an addicting read no matter which of her stories you find yourself picking up."

—Maya Banks, *New York Times* bestselling author

"There is something about [Ashley's books] that I find crackalicious." —Kati Brown, DearAuthor.com

"Run, don't walk...to get [the Dream Man] series. I love [Kristen Ashley's] rough, tough, hard-loving men. And I love the cosmo-girl club!" —NocturneReads.com

"[*Law Man* is an] excellent addition to a phenomenal series!"
—ReadingBetweentheWinesBookclub.blogspot.com

"[*Law Man*] made me laugh out loud. Kristen Ashley is an amazing writer!" —TotallyBookedblog.com

"I felt all of the rushes, the adrenaline surges, the anger spikes...my heart pumping in fury. My eyes tearing up when my heart (I mean...*her* heart) would break."

—Maryse's Book Blog (Maryse.net) on *Motorcycle Man*

RIDE
STEADY

RIDE STEADY

A CHAOS NOVEL

KRISTEN ASHLEY

FOREVER

NEW YORK   BOSTON

Copyright © 2015 by Kristen Ashley
Preview of *Walk Through Fire* copyright © 2015 by Kristen Ashley
"More Pleasure Than Pain" copyright © 2015 by Kristen Ashley

All rights reserved. In accordance with the U.S. Copyright Act of 1976, the scanning, uploading, and electronic sharing of any part of this book without the permission of the publisher constitute unlawful piracy and theft of the author's intellectual property. If you would like to use material from the book (other than for review purposes), prior written permission must be obtained by contacting the publisher at permissions@hbgusa.com. Thank you for your support of the author's rights.

Forever
Hachette Book Group
1290 Avenue of the Americas
New York, NY 10104

www.HachetteBookGroup.com

Printed in the United States of America

First Walmart edition: June 2015
10 9 8 7 6 5 4 3 2 1

OPM

Forever is an imprint of Grand Central Publishing.
The Forever name and logo are trademarks of Hachette Book Group, Inc.

The Hachette Speakers Bureau provides a wide range of authors for speaking events. To find out more, go to www.hachettespeakersbureau.com or call (866) 376-6591.

The publisher is not responsible for websites (or their content) that are not owned by the publisher.

This book is dedicated to Mr. Robinson.
My junior high history teacher.
The coolest teacher in school.
A teacher who asked me out into the hall for
the sole purpose of telling me I was more than
I believed I could be.
I didn't believe you then, Mr. Robinson.
It's taken a lot of time, but I'm beginning to believe.
I thank God for teachers like you who see
what we do not see.
And take the time to set us on the
course of believing.

RIDE
STEADY

RIDE
STEADY

PROLOGUE

Stay Golden

AFTER HIS FATHER cuffed him, Carson Steele's temple slammed into the corner of the wall by the refrigerator. It happened so fast that, despite all the times it had happened, and there were a lot, he still wasn't prepared. So his hand came up to curl around the corner too late to soften the blow as the sharp pain spread from his temple through his right eye and into his jaw. Doubling that, his left cheekbone stung from the back of his father's hand slamming into it.

"Trash fuckin' *stinks*!" his father yelled. "What's the point a' you, boy? You good for nothin'?"

Carson had learned not to respond. Anything he said made it worse. He could defend himself and get his ass kicked. He could apologize and get his ass kicked.

Problem was, he could be silent and get his ass kicked too.

But his dad had a woman at their house, and even though they were both slaughtered on beer and vodka, if his dad had a woman (which he did surprisingly often, regardless that he was a jackhole, and not only to Carson), his father would have other things on his mind. This being the reason Carson hadn't been prepared for his dad to have a go at him.

When he turned from the wall, still holding on to the

edge and battling the pain, and looked into his old man's eyes, his dad just muttered, "Piece of shit. Good for *nothin'*. For fuck's sake, do somethin' worth somethin' in your sorry life, take out the fuckin' trash."

Then he moved to the fridge, opened it, nabbed a six pack, slammed it, and stormed out.

Carson went to the trash.

It was a third full.

His father was right. It stunk. Carson had no idea what the man threw in there, but whatever it was smelled lethal.

The same thing had happened last week, though. The garbage hadn't been half full, his dad tossed something in that smelled to high heaven, and unable to bear the stench, Carson took it out.

The minute he came back, he got open-palmed smacked across the face because "We're not made of fuckin' money, you piece of shit! I'm not a millionaire who can afford fifty trash bags a week, for fuck's sake! Wait until it's goddamned *full*!"

He couldn't win for losing.

This didn't bother Carson. He had a good memory, which sucked, seeing as every one of them wasn't one he'd want to remember.

He was used to losing.

He took the garbage out to the alley and tossed it in the Dumpster. As he was dropping the lid, he saw his neighbor roll up in his pickup.

The man slid his window down and stopped.

"Hey, Car, how's it hangin', bud?" Linus Washington asked.

Then Linus's eyes narrowed on Carson's face.

Linus was a big, black guy who'd lived next door to them for the last three years. Good guy, serial dater, but he'd had a steady woman for the last year. Carson liked her. She was pretty, had a smokin' body, but he liked the way she looked at Linus the best. Like he could do anything. Like if he went to the Pacific Ocean, raised his arms, and spread them wide, the sea would part.

Yeah, that's what he liked about her best.

Sometime recently, Linus had got on bended knee but Carson only knew that because his dad had told him she'd accepted the ring, then said, "Dumb fuck. Gettin' his shit tied to a woman. Stupidest thing you can do, boy, gettin' your shit tied to a woman. Learn that now, save you a world a' hurt."

He understood this coming from his dad. Carson's mom was beautiful. He'd seen pictures. That was the only way his mother was in his life. Stuffed in an envelope full of pictures shoved at the back of his father's nightstand. Pictures just of her, smiling and looking gorgeous. Pictures of her and his dad, both of them smiling, looking happy.

She left before Carson could even crawl. He had no memories of her. His father never spoke of her, except the constant trash he talked about women that Carson knew was directed at her.

He also knew better than to ask.

And last he knew that she left her baby before he'd even learned to say the word *mom*.

He could get this, if his old man knocked her around the way he did Carson.

He also didn't get it.

Not at all.

"It's hangin', Lie," Carson muttered, dipping his chin and turning toward their back gate.

"You wanna come over, get a Coke, watch a game?" Linus called before Carson could turn his back on him and their conversation.

"Got shit to do," Carson kept muttering, moving toward the gate.

"Bud!" Linus yelled.

Carson drew in a breath and turned back.

"Anytime you wanna come over and hang, my door's open. Yeah?" Linus said what he'd said before a lot.

"Yeah," Carson continued to mutter, knowing he'd take him up on that, as he had hundreds of times since the man moved next door.

This just wouldn't be one of those times. He didn't go over after his dad had a go at him. And the reason he didn't was right then written on Linus's face.

Linus was giving him a look that Carson read. He'd honed his skills at reading people, started doing it the minute he could cogitate. If he didn't, he'd have it far worse than he did from his old man.

Far worse.

But the look on Linus's face said he didn't know if he wanted to climb out of his truck and give Carson a hug or if he wanted to climb out of his truck, slam into Carson's house, and kick his dad's ass.

Sometimes he dreamed of Linus kicking his dad's ass. The man was built. He was tall. He'd wipe the floor with Jefferson Steele.

But most of the time, he dreamed of doing it himself.

He didn't because his dad kept him fed. He kept a roof over his head. He kept clothes on his back. He needed the jackhole.

When he didn't, things would change.

But he didn't court disaster for Linus. Linus was a good man. If he had a go at his dad, his dad would stop at nothing to put Linus in a world of hurt any way he could.

Linus didn't need that. The woman who looked at him like he could move mountains didn't need that. And Linus didn't need to give it to a woman who he looked at like the first day that dawned for him was the day he laid eyes on her.

"Take care of yourself, Car," Linus said quietly.

Carson nodded and moved to and through the gate, lifting a hand behind him as he did in a lame goodbye.

The goodbye was lame. *He* was lame. Weak. Pathetic. Of his own free will, walking away from Linus and into a filthy, stinking pit that held nothing for him but pain, violence, and neglect.

He hit the back door and heard it immediately. His father's grunts. The woman he brought home whimpering through each one.

Not the good kind of whimpering, the pained kind.

She was dry.

How the fuck his father could nail as much tail as he did and not sort that, Carson had no clue.

What he knew was the man was good-looking. He made decent money. He could be a charmer.

But mostly, he was a jackhole, and he only hid it long enough to get off. Therefore none of the women stuck around.

He would have thought they'd talk. Women did that shit. But apparently, when it came to his dad, they didn't.

Or maybe his dad was just that good of a player.

Moving swiftly through the house, avoiding going anywhere near the living room where his dad was fucking some bitch on the couch, he headed to his room.

He was sixteen but he'd already had four girls. The first one sounded like the woman his father was currently pumping on their couch. Those pained whimpers.

It wasn't good, fucking dry. He got off but it wasn't good.

It *really* wasn't good for her.

He'd learned with the second one that if he kissed her a while then paid some attention to her tits, things were a lot better *down there*. Wet and hot. Sweet. And it far from sucked, tonguing and toying with a girl's nipples. He'd got off, she hadn't, but the whimpers he got when he was doing her were of an entirely different variety.

Number three was where he found it. She'd shown him. He got her ready. He got off. But when he was done, she wasn't and she wanted to finish. So she took his hand and pressed his finger against her clit and moved it around, moaning and squirming and...*fuck*. So damned hot, he nearly came again on her leg watching her. In the end, he got her off with her help and Carson watched, thinking it was beautiful.

A miracle.

So number four got it all. After he made out with her forever, did shit to her tits and got her wet for him, he'd fucked her while he worked her clit, and she'd gone wild. It was magnificent. So good, he wanted to try other shit, using his mouth, his tongue, his hands, see what that would bring. She let him and the results were spectacular.

But after he gave that to her, she got clingy and kept calling and coming around and his dad gave him crap, not the good, teasing, my-boy's-becoming-a-man kind of ribbing.

Mean. Like the jackhole he was.

So even if Carson kind of liked her, had a good time with her, and not just when he was doing her, he scraped her off. He didn't need that shit.

And hearing his father's grunts and groans coming faster, as well as the pained cries and, "Jeff, hold on a second, honey," he decided he didn't need this shit either.

So to make a quick getaway, he grabbed what he did need, opened his window, climbed out, and took off.

Carson Steele walked a lot since his father got shitty for some reason, tossed Carson's bike in the Dumpster, and beat the snot out of him so he knew not to go out and retrieve it.

Now Carson had a job. He was saving up for a car. He

didn't care how beat up it was. The minute he could afford one, he was going to buy one.

First step to freedom.

He'd fix it up too. Linus was a mechanic, and sometimes when Carson was over at Linus's house he helped Linus in his garage, getting Linus tools as Linus tinkered with an old Trans Am he was fixing up to sell. He watched, Linus showed him things, let him do things, he learned.

Which was why Carson went where he went. Moving through the residential streets of Englewood, Colorado, he found Broadway and walked north. Block after block. He saw it from a distance: his destination. The American flag on the flagpole on top. The white flag under it with its insignia, the words around it, *Wind, Fire, Ride,* and *Free.*

His place, even if it wasn't his. It still was.

The only place he felt right, even standing outside the fence.

So he walked right to it and stopped when he hit the end of the fence.

He stood there. His body on one side, he craned his neck around and looked into the forecourt of Ride. It was an auto supply store up front on the street but they had a garage at the back.

And the day got better even as it threw Carson right into a yawning pit of hell.

That was because the cool guy with the dark hair and kickass goatee was working in one of the bays.

And he was doing it with his son right by his side.

The best.

And the worst.

Since Carson spent a lot of time watching, he'd seen that guy—and others, all members of the Chaos Motorcycle Club—around Ride, the store and the custom car and bike shop at the back, all of which they owned and ran.

The best and worst times were watching the goatee guy
with his boy.

His kid had to be Carson's age. Looked just like his old
man, like Carson looked like his.

But Carson would bet the three hundred fifty-eight dollars he'd saved that the kid he was watching was proud of
that fact, where Carson absolutely was not.

He'd seen them grin at each other, they did it a lot, and
Carson couldn't remember one single time he'd smiled at his
old man.

And he'd seen the goatee guy laugh at something his kid
said. Or he'd smack him on the shoulder in a way that wasn't
mean. Or, the best, he'd grab him by the side or back of the
neck and tug him close, swaying him around.

It was a hug. A motorcycle guy hug for his boy. Carson
knew it, even though he'd never felt anything like it. The kid
had done something his father liked. Or made him proud. Or
maybe it was just because he looked at his son and couldn't
stop himself from showing some love.

Right then, they were bent over the engine of a car, hood
up, one on each side, doing shit. Every once in a while they'd
look at each other and say something. Or smile. Or laugh.

Carson watched a long time. Until they quit and walked
through the garage, disappearing in its dark depths.

Probably they were off to some house Carson figured was
clean and nice and maybe even decorated good. They'd have
dinner together. Maybe with the pretty dark-headed girl he'd
also seen around who could be none other than that guy's
daughter and that kid's sister.

They'd get home and have dinner and that guy would ask
his son if he'd done his homework. He'd give him crap about the
girls he was dating. The good kind. The my-boy's-becoming-a-
man-and-I-like-how-that's-happening kind.

The kind Carson never got.

On this thought, he took off. Kept walking. Found a spot and dug the book out of the back of his jeans where he'd shoved it, and took the nubs of pencils out of his pockets. He sat with his back to a tree in the park, his ass to the ground, and flipped through.

Sketches.

His.

Drawings of Linus's bulldog, Ruff. Carson loved that dog. He looked like a bruiser, the way he waddled was flat-out hilarious, but he always seemed like he was smiling. As he would, the love Linus showered on him.

There were also drawings of Mrs. Heely's house.

She lived across the street and one down from Carson and his dad. She had an American flag on the flagpole, aimed high but stuck at a slant on the house at the top side of her front door, the edges tattered.

He mowed her lawn for money. He also did shit around the house for her because her son, and only child, was gone and so was her old man, so she didn't have anyone else to do it.

She was a great old broad. Made him cookies. Noticed when he was younger and alone because his dad was out carousing and would bring him over a plate of food, warm food, good food, with vegetables and everything. Sat with him while he ate and made him eat his vegetables and watch *Wheel of Fortune* with her and other shit before she'd hear his father's car in the drive. Then she'd put a finger to her lips, wink, grab his dirty plate, and sneak out the back door.

He'd asked about that flag. She'd said they gave it to her at the funeral after her son died "over there." She put it up and it stayed up, wind, rain, snow, sun.

She told Carson she was never going to take it down. It

would fly out there until she died. She didn't care how tattered it got. Beaten and worn. Faded.

"He would too, you know, if he'd been able to live his life," she said. "Age does that to you. All's I got is that flag, Carson. I didn't get to watch him be a man. Make his life. Grow old. So I'll watch that flag do it."

After she said that to him, Carson thought that flag was maybe the most beautiful thing he'd ever seen.

So he drew it.

Ten times.

He flipped the page and at what he saw, his throat got tight.

The flag might be the most beautiful thing he'd ever seen, but on that page was the most beautiful person he'd ever seen.

Carissa Teodoro. Cheerleader. Dated the quarterback. Long golden brown ringlets the color of honey, warm dark brown eyes, sweet little tits, tiny waist, long legs, heart-shaped ass. He knew. He'd seen it in her cheerleader panties when she flipped around.

The golden girl.

Half of the golden couple.

It was too bad her boyfriend, Aaron Neiland, was a total fucktard.

The guy was good-looking and his dad was loaded so he got it.

But he was still a fucktard.

Carissa wasn't. She smiled at him in the halls. She smiled at everyone. She was nice. Everyone liked her.

Carson did too. Carson wanted to make her whimper.

He also wanted to make her laugh. Throw her head back and laugh real hard, like he saw her do at lunch sometimes. Or at games. Or in the hall. Or whenever.

She laughed a lot.

He was glad she did.

Pretty girls like her who could be bitches but weren't deserved to laugh.

He turned the page in a notebook that was filled with drawings. Drawings of things that Carson thought were beautiful. Things that made Carson smile, inside, the only place he let himself do it. Things that gave him a little peace.

And he drew a picture of the goatee guy with his son working on the car.

Only when it was done—and he was sure his dad had either passed out or was in a decent mood because he got off—did he go home.

* * *

"A minute, Carson," Mr. Robinson called as everyone filed out of his classroom.

It was the last period. He was good to go home. He didn't want to go home but it was better than being at school. He hated school. Bells telling him where he was supposed to go next. Teachers telling him what (they thought) he was going to do when he got home. Rules about what you could wear, what you could say, where you could be, how you could act.

Totally hated it.

Still, Mr. Robinson was the shit. He made class fun. He dug teaching and didn't give a crap that everyone knew it.

Half the girls had a crush on him.

Half the boys wanted to be history teachers when they grew up.

Because he liked the guy, Carson walked to his desk.

"Yeah?"

As Carson was walking to the desk, Mr. Robinson got up and rounded it. That was another way he was cool. He didn't sit behind his desk like a dick with some authority and lord over you that way. He also didn't stand behind it like he had to have the desk between so you wouldn't infect him with high school loser-ness.

He got close. Man to man.

Respect.

Yeah, Carson liked him.

"You good?" Mr. Robinson asked when he stopped close but not too close. Friendly. Natural.

"Yeah," Carson replied, not asking why he'd asked because he had a bruise on his cheek and one on his temple so he knew why Mr. Robinson asked.

Carson didn't hide it. He never hid it. Everyone saw it. They always did.

He didn't really care. It was his life for now.

Then he'd be gone.

But only Mr. Robinson would call it out. School had started over a month ago, the first time he had Mr. Robinson's class, and the man had been giving him looks for a while.

Carson knew right then the teacher was done with just looks.

Mr. Robinson leaned a hip against the desk and put a fist to his other one. He then tipped his chin to Carson's face and dipped his voice quiet.

"Looks like something got rough for you recently."

"It's all good," Carson lied.

Mr. Robinson gave him a long look before he sighed.

Then he said, "Talked with some of your teachers."

Carson said nothing.

"Your grades are good, Carson, very good. Especially for a kid who only half the time turns in homework."

Carson had no reply to that either.

"You turned it in more often, you'd be on the honor roll," Mr. Robinson shared.

Carson had no interest in the honor roll.

He had an interest in saving for a car, then saving every

dime he could make, and the second he turned eighteen, getting the fuck out of Dodge.

Something moved over Mr. Robinson's face when Carson didn't reply. It was something Carson had never seen. He hadn't seen it so he couldn't get a lock on it. It could be pity. It could be sadness. It could be frustration. Whatever it was, it made Carson feel warm and cold at the same time.

"You're exceptionally bright," Mr. Robinson said quietly.

"Thanks," Carson replied lamely.

"I've been teaching seven years and not once have I come across a student with your capabilities."

What?

He didn't ask but Mr. Robinson told him.

"You think with both sides of your brain. You excel in shop. You excel in art. You excel in chemistry. You excel in trigonometry. And you excel in history. You do this simply by paying attention in class and making a half-assed attempt at studying when you're home."

Carson was a little shocked the man used the word *half-assed* but it only upped his cool factor.

"You have no test anxiety," Mr. Robinson went on. "Your teachers have noted you pay close attention and take copious notes in class. When you're there, you're there. We have you. Totally. I wonder, if you applied yourself, what that could mean."

"Not much, and it doesn't have to, seein' as alls I'm gonna be is a mechanic," Carson shared.

"I take issue with 'all you're gonna be,' Carson. A mechanic is a worthy profession," Mr. Robinson replied instantly. "Though, not an easy one. You have to study to be a mechanic."

"Know that," Carson muttered.

"I figure you do. And if you want it, you'll be a good one. But it would be a shame if you were a mechanic when you had it in your head to design cars, engineer them. Make them maneuver better. Safer. Or use different forms of fuel."

"Hardly got that in me, Mr. Robinson," Carson told him the truth.

"How would you know?" Mr. Robinson shot back.

Carson felt his body still.

"Usually, by your age, teachers can see where students are leaning," Mr. Robinson continued. "Where they have aptitude. Languages. Arts. Science. Math. Computers. Manual skills that are no less admirable than any of the rest. Some can show partiality to several of these. I've never met a student who shows gifts with *all of them*."

Carson shook his head, not getting why the guy was on about this crap. "Nothin' special about me, Mr. Robinson. Just a kid who likes history."

"No, you would think that, seeing as whoever puts bruises on your face or makes you take your seat at your desk slowly because your ribs hurt would make you believe nothing about you was special, Carson. But the truth of it is, they are very wrong, and so are you."

He wanted that to feel good.

But he wasn't the one who was wrong.

Mr. Robinson was.

He liked the guy. Respected him.

But they were not talking about this.

"We done here?" Carson asked and watched the teacher's head jerk.

"Carson—"

"I dig you give a shit, but none of your business."

"Car—"

"So, we done?"

Mr. Robinson shut his mouth.

It took a couple beats before he opened it again to say, "If you ever need to speak with someone, I'm here."

"No offense, your class rocks, you're the best teacher in the school, everyone thinks so, but I wouldn't hold my breath."

"That's a shame, Carson, because I can help."

Okay, enough was enough.

"Yeah?" he asked sharply. "Can you give me a ma who gave a shit enough to hang around to see me start crawlin'?" Carson asked.

Mr. Robinson's lips thinned, "I—"

"Or give me a dad who wasn't okay with leavin' me at eight to go out and get laid so the neighbor lady had to bring over food so I'd eat?"

Mr. Robinson's face turned to stone. "This is exactly what I'm talking about."

"Sixteen, almost seventeen, less than two years I gotta wait, Mr. Robinson. Been waitin' a long time to be free, now you wanna fuck that up for me?"

"If we spoke with the principal—"

"What? And get me in foster care? Make my dad pissed at me for more than just breathin'?" He shook his head again. "That shit gets out, it'll make all the kids pity me or say jack to me, which would not go down too good so other shit would go down and I'd get suspended or expelled. Dude, when it's over and I'm gone, I won't have much, but I stick with my plan, at least I'll have my degree."

"I see you've thought this through," the man remarked.

"Only thing on my mind since I was eight."

That and Carissa Teodoro. But she hadn't entered his mind until he was thirteen.

Mr. Robinson closed his eyes.

He felt that. He didn't like that.

Carson couldn't help him.

He had to focus on helping himself.

"I'll get through," Carson declared and the teacher opened his eyes. "Got neighbors who look out for me, so it isn't as bad as you think. Means a lot, you give a shit, but I got it under control."

"Then if you take nothing from this, take from it that you have a teacher who cares and will look out for you, too. More than just me, we all believe in you, Carson. So if you take nothing from this but that, it won't make me happy, but it'll be something."

"That means a lot too," Carson returned, his voice weird, like thick and gruff, a sound that echoed what he felt in his gut.

While Carson was feeling that and, not getting it, before he got a lock on it, Mr. Robinson swooped in for the kill.

"One day, Carson Steele, you're going to be a magnificent man. I don't know how that will be. You could be president. You could eradicate disease. Or you could be a master mechanic who builds amazing cars. But whatever it is, it will happen. I believe it. And one day, you'll see past what you've been taught and you'll believe it too."

Carson didn't share that he probably shouldn't hold his breath about that either.

Then again he couldn't. The thick in his gut was growing, filling him up like he ate way too much, but not in a way that made him need to hurl. In a way that made him want to take a load off, sit back, and just feel the goodness.

Since it was all he had in him, he just again muttered, "Thanks."

"My pleasure," Mr. Robinson muttered back.

Carson moved to the door.

"Carson?" Mr. Robinson called when he was almost out of the room.

Taking in a deep breath, he turned back.

"Don't forget this conversation," the teacher ordered. "Any of it."

Like he ever would.

"Got it," he confirmed.

Then, fast as he could, he took off.

*   *   *

Carson stood with his back to the pole at the bottom of the bleachers at the high school football field. He did this listening to the posse of girls sitting above him.

They had no clue he was there.

Freshman football game. One of Carissa's stupid, bitch, up-her-own-ass girlfriends had a brother who played.

But they weren't there to watch the brother play. They were there to say mean crap about the freshman cheerleaders.

All but Carissa. She didn't talk much. She smiled a lot. She cheered and kicked and flipped around better than any of the others. But she wasn't a talker.

But now, her friends had stopped saying bitchy things about the cheerleaders.

Now they were talking about him.

"I'm *so* gonna go there. Jenessa said he *rocked her world*," Brittney spouted.

"I would go there just 'cause he's hot," Theresa declared. "God, he wears jeans better than any guy in school."

"You guys are gross. He's a total loser," Marley stated. "He barely says anything. Just wanders around school, brooding. Doesn't have any friends. He doesn't even hang with the stoners or hoods. And he totally knows how hot he is and uses it to get into girls' pants. It's lame."

"I'm not gonna *date* him, just get laid by him," Brittney replied. "My dad would have a conniption if I brought someone like Carson Steele home. He'd get me, like...a chastity belt or something."

Peels of giggles.

Carson tipped back his head and looked up through the bleachers.

The girls were all turned to each other, not paying a lick of attention to the game, but Carissa was leaned forward, elbows on her knees, eyes to the field, mouth shut.

She wasn't even smiling. Definitely not giggling. And the graceful line of her jaw was kind of hard.

Fuck, but she was pretty.

"Jenessa said he," Theresa's voice lowered, but not by much, "*went down on her*. Like, put his mouth right between her legs and everything!"

"Totally gross," Marley murmured.

"Hard...*lee*," Brittney returned. "*God*, I'd *pay* him to go down on me."

"He'd take your money, seeing as he could probably use it," Marley told her. "Can the guy wear anything other than jeans and T-shirts?"

"I'll give him money if *he* gives it and gives it *good* and then goes on his way," Brittney shot back.

"I think I already weighed in on the jeans, but Marl, seriously, it would be a crime to put anything on that hot bod but one of his skintight tees. *Lush*." The last word out of Theresa's mouth was like a breath.

"You do know, he's a person," Carissa put in.

"What?" Theresa asked.

"Carson Steele. He's a person," Carissa announced.

"Yeah. A person of the male persuasion that Jenessa says has a really big dick," Brittney replied on a giggle that was met with Theresa's giggles.

"I'm sure," Carissa said coldly. "He's also really smart.

He's always getting picked for the Beat the Brains Team when Mr. Robinson does games in his class. He knows everything about history, so no one ever beats him. And he might not have a lot, but he's also got a job so he doesn't get given everything, which isn't a bad thing. At least that's what my dad says. And Theo and his jerk friends were being mean to that kid with all that awful acne and Carson just walked over to them, crossed his arms on his chest, and they scattered. Didn't say a word and they took off. That was cool, and it was a cool thing to do. And Theo and his friends don't do that kind of thing anymore, not if Carson is around."

"Does Aaron know you have the hots for Carson Steele?" Brittney asked bitchily.

"I don't have the hots for him," Carissa returned sharply, and Carson felt his gut lurch. "I just think he's a nice guy. And he doesn't deserve some girl pretending she's into him just to get in his pants. He's a person. He has feelings. And if you did that, Britt, that wouldn't be cool."

"Goody-two-shoes," Brittney muttered.

"Maybe, but I'd rather be that than be mean," Carissa fired back immediately.

"All right, calm down, I won't play with Carson Steele," Brittney replied.

Carissa didn't say anything. She looked back to the field.

"I need a Coke," Theresa decreed into the tense silence. "Does anyone else need a Coke?"

"Coke? Are you crazy? There are more calories in a Coke than there are in a piece of chocolate cake," Marley stated.

"That's not true," Theresa returned.

"I'll go. Get a diet. Anyone?" Brittney asked, rising from the bleacher.

"I could get a diet," Marley said.

They all rose, except Carissa.

"Riss? You wanna come?" Theresa asked.

"I'll stay here, save our seats."

Carson looked to the rest of the bleachers. They weren't even half full, and there was no one anywhere near the bitch girl crew.

"Okay," Theresa said quietly.

"Whatever," Marley muttered.

They took off.

Carissa remained.

He watched her lean further forward and put her jaw in her hand, her eyes to the field.

He wondered if she was thinking about him.

He figured she wasn't. She was cool, she'd had his back, but he would be the last thing on her mind.

He studied her, wishing he knew what she was thinking.

And as he studied her, knowing she had her eyes to the field but her thoughts somewhere else and they didn't look happy, suddenly he remembered about her sister.

Everyone knew about Carissa Teodoro's sister. It was a long time ago, but what happened was so ugly, no one forgot.

Freak accident. Tragic. Even his dad flipped out about it.

She'd been a little girl, riding around on her tricycle in the driveway. Folks were over at her parents' house. Not a big party but enough people a little girl got lost. A couple left, no one knew she was behind the car. They couldn't see her in their rearview, ran right over her. Crushed her to death. Right in her own driveway.

If that hadn't happened, the sister would be a freshman. If she followed in Carissa's footsteps, she'd be a freshman cheerleader.

He remembered his dad going on about it. Remembered it even if he'd only been about six at the time.

It wasn't something you forgot.

Looking at her from below, her face soft, her thoughts somewhere else, he figured she hadn't forgotten either, and he wondered if she sat at a freshman football game thinking her sister should be cheerleading. He wondered if it crushed her to think those things.

And he hoped she didn't because he didn't like the idea of her feeling crushed.

His eyes never leaving her, Carson wanted to call to her.

No, he wanted to go sit with her. Put his arm around her shoulders. Tell her how he felt that she took his back with the bitches who were so bitchy he didn't get why she called them friends.

He didn't do that.

He heard gravel shifting and looked from Carissa.

Julie Baum was headed his way under the bleachers, a smile on her face.

They were meeting there. A date.

Or the kind of dates Carson Steele got.

She wasn't going to introduce him to her parents either. Her folks thought she was at the game with her girls. Carson would buy her a burger, find someplace to fuck her, return her to her friends, and they'd take her home.

He'd get off.

She'd get off too.

Then she probably wouldn't think about him, except when she could arrange another meet where she could use him to get off and still do what she could to catch that football player's eye. The one with no neck that had a dad who was a surgeon.

Which was okay with him.

It was because, not including the no-neck football player, he would do the same.

*　　　*　　　*

Carson's boot connected with his dad's face and the man didn't even groan when his head snapped around.

Out cold.

Carson stared down at him, lifting a hand to wipe the blood pouring out of his nose from his mouth.

Then he spat on him.

He was two months away from eighteen. More than that from graduating.

But fuck it.

It was time to leave.

He'd never laid a hand on his father, but tonight was bad. The man had been in a rage. A frigging *rage* about a new oil stain on the floor of the garage.

Their house was old. There were so many stains on the garage floor, it was a wonder his old man noticed a new one.

But he did and he lost it.

And for the first time, Carson did too.

So he was done.

Carson was going to disappear.

So he didn't get his degree.

Shit happened.

He went to the bathroom and cleaned up. Then he went to his bedroom, changed out of his bloody tee into a clean one, and grabbed his bag. He stuffed everything he could get into it. After that, he went to the AC register, pulled off the face, and tagged the money he'd saved and the letters he'd written, preparing, getting ready for the day he would be free. He took that and anything that meant anything from his room (there wasn't much).

Done with that, he moved through the house and nabbed whatever he could that was worth something, including the jug of change his father was always filling. He even emptied his dad's wallet.

He put everything in the car he'd bought for five hundred dollars and Linus had helped him fix up. He then strode to Linus's mailbox and shoved in his letter. Across the street and down to Mrs. Heely's, he shoved her letter in hers.

Ready, he got in his car.

One more thing to do before he went and he was going to do it.

So he drove to Swedish Medical Center.

He knew why he'd snapped with his dad. Mr. Robinson was out that day and word got around. It shouldn't have. It was no one's business. But it did.

The man had lost a kid the day before. His wife, pregnant, had a stillborn baby.

And Carson thought that sucked. It sucked so huge, he couldn't get it out of his head.

That shouldn't happen to anyone, but never to a man like Mr. Robinson. If gossip was true, and he figured it was, they'd been trying for a while and getting nowhere.

And that was wrong. It proved the universe was fucked.

Because outside of Linus, Carson knew no man who'd be a better dad.

So it sucked worse for Mr. Robinson and the dead kid he lost.

Carson should have come out stillborn.

Mr. Robinson's baby should have come out bawling so he could have all Mr. Robinson had to give, which was a lot.

He went into the hospital, found where they did the baby stuff, and it took a while—nurses and doctors and other folks giving him looks as he hung around—but finally, he saw Mr. Robinson walk out of a room. He had his head down. Even if Carson couldn't fully see his face, he could still see the man looked wrecked.

Carson gritted his teeth.

Suddenly, Mr. Robinson's head came up. He stopped dead right there in the hall when he saw Carson.

Carson put everything into his face. Everything he felt for the man. Everything he felt for the man's dead kid, who wouldn't get a lifetime of knowing just how fucking lucky he was to have the seed that made him.

Then he lifted up his hand, palm out, and kept it there.

Mr. Robinson didn't move except to lift his hand the same way.

But Carson saw his eyes were wet.

He'd give him that. Any man before him, Carson'd think that was weak because his father taught him a long time ago just how weak it was for a man to cry.

He'd been seven when he'd learned that lesson, a lesson delivered with a lit cigarette.

It was not the first or the last time his father had used that method to deliver a lesson, but he'd not even so much as teared up since.

But Mr. Robinson made it different.

He made it strong.

Carson nodded once, dropped his hand, turned on his boot, and walked away.

*   *   *

In the hospital parking garage, he was opening the door to his car, thanking Christ he got that fake ID, which would mean he could rent a hotel room, when he heard a familiar female voice say, "Carson?"

His body locked, all except his head, which swiveled.

And he saw Carissa Teodoro coming his way.

Cute little skirt. Cute little top. Cute little cardigan. Cute little ankle boots. Tights on her slim legs. Honey ringlets bouncing on her shoulders. Eyes aimed direct at him.

But the instant she got a look at his face, she rushed to him, skidding to a stop on the opposite side of his door.

"Oh my God!" she cried. "Are you okay?"

Not her.

Anyone could see him like this but not her.

In the halls, after his dad went at him, he'd avoid her. Skip the classes they had together.

But there she was.

Fuck.

When he said nothing, she asked, "Are you...?" she looked toward the hospital then to him. "Are you going in to get checked out?"

"Did already," he lied. "I'm good."

"You sure?" she kept at him. "You look like you need an ice pack."

"I do," he told her truthfully.

"Didn't they give you one?"

He lied again, "I'll get one when I get home."

She stared at him and he had a weird feeling she knew he was lying.

It wasn't like they didn't speak.

She said "hey" whenever she'd catch his eyes.

She'd tripped down the stairs when she was a sophomore and he was close so he caught her. She'd laughed, told him she was a klutz, and thanked him for saving her from taking a header. In return, he'd told her it was no problem then he took off.

They'd had a substitute teacher once who was a scatter-brain and kept dropping the chalk, and Carissa caught his eyes in class and rolled hers.

She'd also been in front of him in line at Dairy Queen with her dad once when he was there getting Mrs. Heely a hot fudge sundae and she'd shared that Blizzards with Reese's Pieces *and* Cups were *the bomb*.

There was more, but not enough she'd know he was lying.

Still, she did, and he knew it when she asked, "Are you sure you're okay?" and he knew she wasn't asking about his face.

"You heard about Mr. Robinson?"

She did. He saw it move over her expression. Her obvious distress weirdly making her even prettier.

"Yeah," she said softly. "Sucks. He's totally awesome. He'd be such a good dad."

"Yeah," he agreed.

"So, you're upset about him?" she asked.

"Who wouldn't be?" he asked back.

"No one," she murmured, still eyeing him.

Totally didn't believe him. There was something more, but he wasn't saying what.

"I'm good, Carissa," he said firmly.

"If you say so," she replied doubtfully.

Her eyes strayed to his car. She opened her mouth but closed it and stared into his car.

He turned his head and saw what she saw. His bag. His stuff. Shit from his house.

He looked back at her just in time for her to curl her hand on his, which was resting on top of the open car door, seeming not to care his knuckles were torn and bloody.

"Carson," she whispered but said nothing more.

"I'm good, Carissa," he stated, and it came out firm but it also came out rough.

Because she was touching him.

God, just her hand on his felt good.

"You've never been good," she shocked him by saying. It was quiet but he could tell it was also angry. Her hand squeezed his carefully. "But you will be."

"Yeah," he grunted, feeling a lot, too much. Her touch. Her being that close. The knowledge that she'd paid attention to him like he did her. The warmth in her eyes mixed with anger and compassion.

No pity.

He knew why she was there. Her mother was sick. Some treatment that wasn't working. Everyone was talking about it. It wasn't looking good.

She'd lost her sister.

She was going to lose her mother.

And she still cheered their team to victory, took his back with her bitch girlfriends, was the most popular girl at school dating the most popular guy (who was still a dick and didn't deserve her), became homecoming queen with big smiles and was nice to everybody.

She didn't feel pity. She'd lived through a lot.

She felt something else, because she got it like he did. She got that life could seriously suck.

And that something else was something he liked.

Then again, he liked everything about Carissa Teodoro.

"Good stuff for you out there, Carson," she said, tipping her head very slightly toward his car, telling him he had her support. Telling him she agreed with what he was doing. Telling him she didn't think he was weak. Pathetic. A loser. Lame. Telling him she thought something else entirely. "Good stuff. A good life. A beautiful life. You'll get it. I know it. Because you deserve it."

Not knowing what else to say, he muttered, "Thanks."

"I'm picking up my mom, but after I drop her off at home, do you want...I mean, are you in a hurry?"

After asking that, she grinned at him.

His world ended.

Right there, his world was done. Because there was nothing that would be better than Carissa Teodoro standing a foot away with her hand warm on his, grinning up at him.

Nothing.

"We could go have a Blizzard before you go," she finished.

"Gotta get where I'm goin'."

It killed him, but that was his response.

This was because she was not his to have.

She was golden. Nothing beat her. She smiled through pain and made you believe it.

He'd just kicked his father in the face after beating the shit out of him because he was done getting his ass kicked for anything, much less something as stupid as an oil stain on the garage floor.

That was his life. That was him.

That meant he had no business having a Blizzard with Carissa Teodoro.

She didn't need the darkness that gathered inside him, bigger and bigger every day. Darkness he had to fight back so it didn't black him out.

She needed to stay golden.

And Carson Steele had no idea in that moment as the darkness swept through him that, in turning down that Blizzard, he'd made the biggest mistake of his life.

And he'd changed the course of hers in a way that he would have bled to have stopped it. Bled until he was dry so she could have better.

In that moment, in the parking garage outside Swedish, she was disappointed. She didn't hide it.

But she did curl her fingers tighter on his and lean in.

She smelled like flowers.

"Okay, Carson," she said softly. "Go after your beautiful life."

He cleared his throat, pulled his hand from under hers, and muttered, "Will do."

Her grin became a smile.

Then she proved him wrong.

His world hadn't ended a minute earlier.

It ended then, when she leaned in, going up on her toes, lifting her hand to curl it on his shoulder as she reached high to touch her lips to his cheek.

He stood stock-still.

"Later," she whispered into his ear, let him go, and turned. He watched, motionless, as she did that thing she did, skip-walking, her skirt bouncing side to side, her hair swinging, so full of energy and life even after losing her sister, even while losing her mother, she couldn't just put one foot in front of the other like normal people.

He watched her until she disappeared into the stairwell.

Then he changed his plans.

He didn't hightail it out of Denver.

He slept in his car. He went to school the next day, doing it late, walking through the empty halls, heading straight to Carissa Teodoro's locker.

And finally, he popped her lock and put an envelope with her name on it right at the front, propped on her books.

After he did that, he left.

In it was one of his sketches of her. His favorite because she had her head thrown back and she was laughing.

On the back he'd written, *You'll get a beautiful life too. Because you deserve it.*

He didn't sign it.

*   *   *

When Carissa Teodoro opened her locker and saw the envelope, she knew exactly who it was from.

And it made her smile.

Because she believed down deep in her heart that the cute, mysterious, smart, sweet Carson Steele was right.

She *was* going to have a beautiful life.

Losing her sister. Enduring her parents' mourning. Watching her mother fade away.

She'd earned it.

Didn't matter if she did, she'd work for it.

And she was going to get it.

But she wouldn't tell anyone, not a single soul, that she didn't really want it with Aaron.

He was great and all, but when it happened, *really* happened, she wanted it with someone like Carson Steele.

Someone who had earned it too.

No, she wouldn't tell anyone that.

Because she actually didn't want it with someone like Carson Steele.

She just wanted it with Carson.

He'd sketched her.

Even with her mom so sick and him having run away (she knew and she worried for him but she was glad he was finally getting away), that made her happy.

Because that said a lot.

That said maybe one day he'd come back.

And then it would happen.

*　　*　　*

She was very, *very* wrong.

CHAPTER ONE

Shop Window

Tack

Seven years later…

"It him?" Kane "Tack" Allen, president of the Chaos Motorcycle Club, sitting at the head of the table, asked the men sitting around him.

The table was made of shining wood at the edges, the middle of it Plexiglas under which was an old Chaos flag, the first of its kind, stitched by Hammer's old lady, a stripper who was good with a needle.

Hammer was in the ground. His old lady was a great-grandmother.

The flag remained.

The only ones at the meeting were the elders. The ones who'd been around when the man had been a kid hanging around their fence. The ones who saw. The ones who knew.

Tack knew the answer to his question before Dog answered, "Yup."

"Anyone know what took him so long?" Big Petey asked.

He got no answers.

Tack looked to the chair that had been vacated by Carson Steele.

Tack had fucked up years ago. He'd seen it in the man's eyes as he'd sat down across from him, among the brothers he wanted to make his brothers, casting his lot to become a recruit of the Chaos MC.

Nothing in those eyes but secrets.

Yeah, Tack had fucked up. They all had. They'd seen the kid hanging around. They saw him do it a lot. Too much.

They should have taken him in.

Shit was swirling, they didn't have the time.

Then he'd disappeared.

Tack hadn't forgotten. None of them had.

They all had their reasons for joining the brotherhood.

And they read those reasons years ago in Carson Steele.

Too late, Tack had looked into it. And he hadn't liked what he'd found.

This was why he turned his head, locked eyes with Brick, and asked, "Jefferson Steele?"

"Same house, three miles away, same asshole as ever," Brick answered.

"Our guy have anything to do with his old man?" Tack went on.

Embedded in his big, red beard, Brick's lips twitched. He knew what Tack saying "our guy" meant.

Tack had made his decision.

The vote would follow.

"Haven't been there 'round the clock, but from what the brothers have seen since he made his first approach, nope," Brick told him.

"You know where he's been?" Tack asked.

Brick shook his head.

"Brother," Hound cut in and Tack looked his way. "You want any info, you ask. He wants his patch, he'll tell."

"Don't make a man like that share his secrets," Tack muttered.

Hound nodded. He knew that to be true.

"Saw his work and it's fuckin' top notch," Hop put in, and Tack gave his brother his attention. "He can build bikes and cars like that, we should take him on as brother just for him to make us a mint."

"We don't take on brothers because they can build bikes," Big Petey stated.

"Then you haven't seen his drawings," Boz entered the conversation. "He could be a weak-ass runt still tied to his momma's apron and I'd vote him brother, he could do those builds. They're wild." Boz looked to Tack. "They're Chaos."

"Lucky for us, he ain't no weak-ass runt but looks like a man who'd carve your eyes out and do it smilin', you looked at him funny," High noted.

He wouldn't do it smiling, Tack thought. The man didn't smile. The man had a look about him that said he never had.

This troubled Tack.

And made him believe even more it was time to bring Chaos to Carson Steele's life.

Brothers.

Bikes.

Belonging.

And, if he was lucky, he'd find a bitch who'd lay to waste that shield Carson Steele had up and bring him bliss.

"More talk, or vote?" Tack asked the table.

"Got nothin' to say, he's got my vote," Hop said.

"Had my vote when he was watchin' from the fence," Dog muttered.

"He's in for me," Boz added.

Pete, High, Arlo, Hound, and Brick weighed in the same.

As it had to be, it was unanimous when Tack grabbed the gavel and lowered it.

"Preliminary vote done, call the rest of the brothers. The vote stays true, we got ourselves a new recruit," Tack announced.

Boz pushed back his chair, his hand to his pocket to grab his phone.

Brick leaned forward to nab the bottle of tequila. Men started shooting the shit.

Tack felt Dog's eyes and looked to the man sitting to his right.

"Warm, red blood flows in Chaos veins, brother," Dog said quietly. "That boy's got nothin' but ice. Stone cold."

"We'll see," Tack replied.

"We will but we got problems, Tack, the kind that get solved with loyalty, balls, and fire. Lived a fair bit a' life. Done a lot. Seen a lot more. Still, I'd check I had my blade *and* my gun, I ran up against that guy in a bad mood in a dark alley. So I reckon he's got the balls. But not sure he's got the other two in him."

"Time will tell," Tack muttered.

"Boy's got secrets," Dog muttered back.

"Boy's never had one thing in his life he wanted," Tack replied. "We're givin' him that. First time. He's twenty-fuckin'-five. First time, Dog. Now, we'll see how that plays."

"Brother's got dark in him he don't bother to hide, secrets he doesn't share. With the problems we got, Tack, that makes me uneasy," Dog stated.

"Had the vote, Dog, you had a problem, you should have opened your mouth," Tack returned.

Dog shook his head. "Saw that kid watch us, just like

you. Shoulda done something then. Don't have it in me to turn him away now."

"No one who doesn't have fire walks three miles to watch men work on cars, Dog. And he wasn't at that fence watchin' men work on cars. He was at the shop window, empty pockets, face pressed to the glass, starin' at what he wanted but couldn't have. I'll wager, to survive, he's banked that fire. We gotta help him direct it and make sure if it flares bright, it doesn't burn him out."

Dog held Tack's eyes. Then he nodded sharply and looked away.

The rest of the Club came in, had words, and voted.

It was unanimous.

Carson Steele was a recruit. A recruit that would shortly after be christened Joker.

And if he did his time, took his shit, proved his mettle...

He'd be Chaos.

*   *   *

It took him a year and three months.

And he did.

CHAPTER TWO

All I Wanted

Carissa

"AARON, REALLY, I'M in a bind."

I tried not to sound like I was begging. It didn't feel good to beg.

But he'd heard me beg and I'd learned begging didn't work.

"You bring Travis to my house in forty-five minutes or we've got problems, Carissa," Aaron said in my ear and then disconnected.

I stood there in the filthy grass on the verge, looking down at the phone, my baby boy at my hip, the crawling rush hour traffic of Denver on I-25 in front of me, along with my old, ugly, worn out, mostly kinda still red Toyota Tercel with its flat tire.

Aaron, my ex-husband, drove a black Lexus SUV.

Aaron, my ex-husband, had also just refused to come and help me change the flat tire even though I had our son with me and I was on a stupid interstate during rush hour traffic.

I couldn't believe this.

I should, with our history, all he'd done that I'd turned

a blind eye to and all he'd done that I eventually couldn't. Nothing should surprise me. And I was hanging on to a slim thread of hope that it still did. That I could be surprised. That I hadn't lost that ability. That I still believed that people could be decent. Even Aaron.

I hated to admit it but I figured I would soon lose the ability to believe Aaron could be decent. Especially after he just hung up on me.

I couldn't reflect on this.

My lip was quivering and I bit it to make it stop, but I didn't try too hard to hold back tears as I stared at my car.

I'd cried a lot the last year and a half. And I will admit, no matter what this made me, I often cried to try to get my way. This always worked with my dad. For a long time it had worked with Aaron.

A year and a half ago, it stopped working. At least with Aaron.

But I needed to cry. I had my little boy with me, his little fist twisted in the platinum chain of the necklace my dad gave me the Christmas after Mom died, his other hand banging my shoulder, completely oblivious (thank goodness) to our dire situation. I didn't know what to do with him if I tried to change the tire myself. I didn't think it was safe to leave him in the car. Traffic was crawling but I was still on a busy interstate.

What if something happened?

I fretted, bit my lip and blinked away tears as I ran through my options.

My dad was in Nebraska looking after my grandma. He, obviously, couldn't come and help.

He also didn't need added evidence that I'd made a hideous mistake spending ten years of my life at Aaron Neiland's side, eventually accepting his ring, his vows to honor me in sickness and health until death did us part (all lies, obviously). All this before finding myself pregnant with Aaron's child while he was cheating on me (again), this time with a model. *Then* me confronting him, after which Aaron told me we were through and he was marrying his model.

No, Dad didn't need that.

Further, I didn't have any friends. I'd never truly had any real friends, but I hadn't known that until it was proved true when Aaron and I fell apart and they (*all* of them) went with Aaron.

And I didn't have any time to make new ones. I had a baby. I had a full-time job as a grocery store clerk. And I had an ex-husband who was a lawyer who seemed, along with his father and all their colleagues, to have made it his mission to make my life a misery.

He was succeeding.

I knew what he wanted. He wanted me to step aside, give him my son so he and *Tory* could raise Travis, and Aaron could forget he broke my heart, shattered my soul, destroyed my dream, and ruined my life.

Aaron didn't like reminders of his failures. Due to his father being driven, and driving Aaron, my ex-husband did his best not to fail. But should that rare happenstance occur, he obliterated any memory of it so he didn't have any indication in his life that he was any less than perfect.

I was a flaw. I was a fail. I needed to go away.

I wasn't going to go away.

I just didn't know how I would do it.

After I got my divorce, I received a settlement (that I now knew was so small it was a joke) and child support (since Aaron's income was *far* more than mine) and nearly full custody of Travis (since he was only two months old at the time).

This was good.

It was good until Aaron took me back to court and made it bad. Since Aaron had been born into the good ole boys network of the legal world of Denver (his father being a judge), he'd managed to win (or connive) partial custody and a lowering of child support.

Then he took me back again and won half custody with no child support.

We'd been officially divorced for six months, the decree coming through two months after I pushed out our son (alone, since Dad was driving from Nebraska, and Travis came out quickly). In that time, I'd been to court twice and I knew Aaron was looking for any little thing that he could use to prove I wasn't fit to look after Travis or that I'd broken our arrangement so he could get me into (more) trouble.

I had long since run out of money for a lawyer. Dad sent a bunch but I stopped asking after the second trip to court. He worried about me. He was all I had left (except Travis), but all I could think about was that Travis and I were all he had left too and he'd been through enough. I couldn't drag him through this with me.

I could, however, get a new attorney.

The one I'd had was expensive and we'd gone over things before I had to let him go. It was clear he was concerned about his ability to defend me considering the firepower at Aaron's back.

But when I begged (and okay, cried), my attorney had told me I could pay installments.

However, they just racked up (I was still paying them off). I couldn't afford more. I needed a new car. Eventually, I'd need more than a one-bedroom apartment and preferably one that was in a *much* better neighborhood. I needed to find time and money to go to beauty school so I could learn how to do hair. I was good at hair. I had a natural talent. I'd spent a lot of time trying to figure out what I was good at, what I could do, and that was the only thing.

And stylists at nice salons made huge tips.

I needed huge tips.

I pretty much needed everything.

So I'd tried to find a less expensive attorney.

Not many were willing to take me on (this, I feared, was Aaron and his father's doing too), but I'd found one. And he'd be *really* less expensive, if, in his words with that oily smile on his face, I got down on my knees (repeatedly) while he battled Aaron for me.

I didn't need him to explain what getting down on my knees meant. I also didn't need to explain verbally why I got up from my chair in his office and walked out.

So I could get a new attorney, I just didn't like the way he wanted me to pay fees.

But right then, what I needed most was to change my tire, get back on the road, get my son to his father before it was too late and Aaron logged that on the list of things to use to make his ex-wife lose custody of her son and hopefully go away for good. After that, I needed to figure out how to get my tire fixed, or how to pay for a new one, and finally, get to my evening shift at the store.

I was just going to have to put my baby in the car and hope to God no one hit me or my vehicle.

I didn't have good thoughts about this. I hadn't had a lot of luck in my life.

Some of my bad luck was out of my control.

Aaron wasn't.

That was on me.

That was *my* fail.

And it was a biggie.

I looked into Travis's little baby face with his big pudgy

cheeks and his dancing eyes that had turned brown, like mine, like his granddad's, and he gurgled up at me, his little red lips wet and curved up, his little fist banging my shoulder.

Okay, so Aaron wasn't a total fail. He gave me Travis.

"We'll be fine," I told my boy on a squeeze.

"Goo," he replied.

I smiled. "Mommy can do this."

"Goo, goo, gah." Fist bump and twist on my necklace, pulling it hard against my neck.

I smiled bigger even though I still wanted to cry and started toward the car.

Then I heard a loud noise getting louder because it was getting closer.

I stopped and turned my head to the side.

That was when I froze.

I froze because I saw one of those bikers on his big, loud motorcycle riding down the shoulder my way.

And he wasn't one of those recreational bikers. I knew this at a glance. His black hair was very long, *too* long, and wild. He had a full black beard on his face. It was trimmed but not trimmed enough (as in, the beard being nonexistent). He had black wraparound sunglasses covering his eyes, glasses that made him look sinister (as bikers, in my mind, were wont to be). He was also wearing a black leather jacket that looked both beat up and kind of new, faded jeans, and those clunky black motorcycle boots.

He stopped as I held my breath. He turned off the motorcycle and put down the stand before he swung a long leg with its heavy thigh and clunky boot off the bike.

Travis squealed.

Letting go of my necklace, he twisted in my arms and was pumping his fists excitedly.

I started breathing, feeling my heart beat fast, as the biker walked toward me, his sunglasses aimed my way, then he abruptly stopped with a strange jerk.

He studied me, his face impassive, standing like he was caught in suspended animation, and I studied him right back.

I didn't know bikers. I'd never met a biker. Bikers scared me. They did this because they looked scary. They also did this because I'd heard they *were* scary. They had girlfriends who wore tube tops and they had knives on their belts and they drove too fast and too dangerously and got in bar brawls and held grudges against other bikers and did things to be put in jail and all sorts of stuff that *was* scary.

As these thoughts tumbled through my head, he came unstuck, started moving my way, and in a deep, biker voice, he called, "You got a problem?"

Travis squealed again, pumping his arms, then he giggled as the big biker guy continued coming our way.

And as he did, slowly, my eyes moved to the traffic. It was bumper to bumper, crawling along at what couldn't be over twenty miles an hour. Looking at it, I knew I'd stood there for at least ten minutes, on the phone, then not, baby on my hip, car with a flat.

And not one single person stopped to help.

Not one.

I turned my head back to the biker who was now standing three feet away, his eyes downcast, his sunglasses aimed at my baby boy.

He'd stopped to help.

"I . . . have a flat," I forced out.

The sunglasses came to me and I felt my head tip to the side when they did because I got a look at him up close.

And what I saw made me feel strange.

Did I know him?

It felt like I knew him.

I screwed up my eyes to look closer at him.

He was a biker. I didn't know any bikers, so I didn't know him. I couldn't.

Could I?

"You got Triple A?" he asked.

I wished.

"No," I answered.

He lifted a black leather gloved hand. "Give me the keys, stand back from the road. I'll take care of it."

He'd take care of it?

Just like that?

Should I let a biker change my tire?

Better question: Did I have any choice?

Since the answer to the better question was definite, I said, "I . . . well, that's very kind."

At this point, Travis made a lunge toward the biker. I struggled to keep him close but my boy was strong and he tended to get what he wanted, and not only because he was strong.

Just then, he got what he wanted.

The biker came forward, gloved hands up, caught Travis at his sides and pulled him gently from my arm.

He settled him with ease and a natural confidence that made my breath go funny against his black T-shirt and leather jacket clad chest and looked to me.

Taking them in, biker and baby, for some reason, that vision filed itself into my memory banks. The ones I kept unlocked. The ones I liked to open and sift through. The ones that included making cookies with my mom. The ones that included dad teaching me how to ride a bike and how he'd looked at me when I'd peddled away without training wheels, so proud, so happy. The ones that included the Easter before my sister Althea died when she won the

Easter egg hunt and Dad got that awesome picture of us in our frilly, pastel Easter dresses, wearing our Easter bonnets, holding our beribboned Easter baskets, hugging each other and giggling little girl giggles.

He didn't belong there. Not in those files. Not this biker.

But somehow, he did.

"Got the kid. Free hands, you can get the keys," he said and I knew how he said it that it was an order, just a gently (kind of) worded one.

"Uh…right," I murmured, tearing my eyes away from him still holding Travis, who had become mesmerized by the biker's beard and was tugging on it. Tugging hard. Tugging with baby boy strength that I knew was already a force to be reckoned with.

But the biker didn't yank his face back. His chin jerked slightly with the tugs but he didn't seem to care.

Not even a little bit.

His eyes just stayed aimed to me until I took mine away.

I dug in my purse that was looped over my shoulder and came out with the keys.

I did this just in time to see the biker had tipped his chin to Travis and his resonant biker voice asked, "You gonna leave any whiskers for me, kid?"

Travis giggled, punched him in the lips with his baby fist then tore off the biker's sunglasses.

I drew in a quick breath, hoping that Travis doing that wouldn't anger him.

It didn't.

He just muttered, "Yeah, kid, hold those for me."

Then he transferred Travis to my arms, took my keys and sauntered to my car.

He had the trunk open by the time I got myself together and took two steps forward.

"Uh...sir—"

His head twisted, just that, he didn't move a muscle of the rest of his body, and he said in a low rumble, "Stand back from the road."

I took three hasty steps back.

He returned his attention to my trunk.

"I just wondered," I called, juggling an active Travis, who was trying to get away since he clearly preferred leather and whiskers to his mommy, "your name."

"Joker," he answered, his hand appearing from the trunk holding tools, which he tossed to the tarmac with a loud clang. I winced as he went back in and pulled out my spare.

Joker. His name was Joker.

No, I didn't know him. I knew no Jokers.

And anyway, who would name their child Joker?

"I'm Carissa. This is Travis," I yelled as he moved around the other side of the car and I saw the back of his jacket. On it was stitched a really interesting patch that included an eagle, an American flag, flames, and at the bottom, the word *Chaos*.

Oh dear. He belonged to the Chaos motorcycle gang.

Even I knew about the Chaos biker gang. This was because when I was growing up, Dad got all his stuff for our cars at their auto store on Broadway, a store called Ride. Pretty much everyone did who knew about cars and didn't want folks to mess them around.

"They're bikers, but they're honest," Dad had said. "They don't have a part, they don't tell you another part will work when it won't. They tell you they'll get it, it'll be in in a week, and then it's in in a week. Don't know about that gang. Do know they know how to run a business."

As this memory filtered through my head, at the end of it, I realized the man called Joker made no response.

"This is really nice!" I called as he disappeared in a crouch on the other side of my car. The other side of the car meaning right by the traffic.

That concerned me. It wasn't going fast and I'd pulled so far over, my passenger side tires were in the turf and scrabble at the edge of the shoulder, but it was still dangerous.

He again didn't respond so I yelled, "Please be careful!"

His deep voice came back. "I'm good."

"Okay, but stay that way. Okay?" I shouted back.

Nothing from Joker.

I fell silent. Well, not really. I turned my attention to my tussle with my son and did my all to turn his attention from the biker he could no longer see but very much wanted to get to.

"He's busy, baby, helping us out, fixing our car."

Travis looked at me and shouted an annoyed, "Goo gah!" and then shoved the arm of Joker's sunglasses in his mouth.

I balanced him on my hip and tried gently to take the sunglasses away so Travis didn't get drool all over them or worse, break them.

Travis shrieked.

"We can't thank Joker for his help by breaking his sunglasses," I explained.

Travis yanked the sunglasses free from my tentative grip, and so they wouldn't break, I let him. He then brandished them in the air with victorious glee for a couple of seconds before bringing them down and shoving the lens against his mouth whereupon he tongued it.

I sighed and looked to where Joker was working, even though I still couldn't see him, and cautiously (but loudly, to be heard over the distance and traffic) shared, "Travis is drooling on your sunglasses."

Joker straightened, lugging my tire with him and tossing

it with a swing of his broad, leather-jacket-covered shoulders into the trunk (something he did one-handed, which was impressive), this making my entire car bounce frighteningly.

His eyes came to me. "Got about a dozen pairs. He fucks those up, not a problem."

Then he crouched down again.

I bit back my admonishment that he shouldn't use the f-word. Aaron cursed all the time. I found it coarse, eventually annoying, and finally ended concerned he'd use that language around our son.

I had no idea if he did.

But he probably did.

Instead of focusing on that, I focused on the fact that Joker seemed really nice.

Not seemed, he just was.

All the people who passed me, not helping, but he stopped.

Now he was changing a tire and, except for the time my dad made me do it so he could be assured I'd know how if the time came to pass when I'd have to, I'd never done it again. But I knew it wasn't a lot of fun.

He'd let Travis pull his whiskers, yank off his glasses, and even let slide the good possibility some baby he didn't know would break them.

I looked to the glasses and knew they were expensive. They said LIBERTY on the side. They were attractive yet sturdy. I didn't think he got them off a revolving rack.

And I didn't want him to stop, help us, and lose his expensive glasses, even though he was very nice and didn't seem to care.

"Please, baby boy, don't break those glasses," I whispered.

Like my eight-month-old understood me, he stopped licking the lens and shoved the glasses to me.

I grinned, murmured, "Thank you, my googly-foogly," took the glasses and bent into him to blow on his neck.

He squealed with glee.

Since he liked that so much, like I always did, I did it again. Then again. And since I didn't have anywhere else to put them, I shoved Joker's sunglasses in my hair so I could adjust Travis in order to tickle him.

He squirmed in my arms and squealed louder.

Goodness, that sound was beautiful.

No better sound in the world.

Not one.

I kept playing with my boy, and in doing so, I was suddenly unconcerned I was standing on I-25 with a biker from a biker gang changing my tire, and that soon I'd be handing my baby off to my ex and *Tory*, so I wouldn't have him for a whole week.

Right then, it was just Travis and me.

It had been just him and me for a year and a half, part of that time he was in my belly, the rest he was my entire world.

I'd wanted a family. After Althea died, I'd started wanting that and made it with my dolls, then my Barbies, then in my dreams.

That's all I wanted. All I'd ever wanted.

A husband. A home. And lots of babies.

I didn't care what it said about me that I didn't want a career. That I didn't dream of cruises or tiaras or being important, carrying a briefcase, getting up and going to a high powered job.

I wanted to do laundry.

I wanted to make cookies.

I wanted to have dinner ready for my husband and children when they got home.

I wanted to be a soccer mom (though, I didn't want a minivan, I wanted something like Aaron's Lexus SUV).

That's all I wanted.

I wanted to be a good wife and a *great* mother.

And again, I did not care even a little bit what people thought that said about me.

My mom worked. She'd worked even before Althea died. She'd worked after too.

I didn't mind that then. It made her happy.

But now, I wanted those moments back, the ones when she was at work. Those times she was away when I got home after school.

I wanted them back.

I wanted my dad to have them back.

And that was what I was going to give my husband. I was going to give my children the same.

That's all I wanted, to give my family that.

All I'd ever dreamed.

That dream had to change. Aaron killed it so I had to revise it.

So now it was just Travis and me, every other week.

That was my new dream and if I tried real hard, I could convince myself I was living it.

Even though I wasn't.

Not even close.

But I'd make do.

"Done."

My head jerked up and I saw Joker standing in the turf a few feet away.

"Looked at your tire, hoped it was a nail," he informed me. "It wasn't. It blew. Your tread is low on all of them. They all need to be replaced."

My bubble of joy with me and my baby burst as life

pressed into it, the pressure, as always, way too much for that bubble of goodness to bear.

I couldn't afford four new tires.

"Can't drive on that spare," Joker kept speaking, but he was doing it eyeing me closely. "Not for long. You need to see to that, soon's you can."

I stopped thinking about tires, my inability to afford them, and the absence of time I had to deal with it, and stared into his eyes.

They were gray. A strange, blunt steel gray.

It was far from unattractive.

It was also very familiar.

"Yeah?" he asked on a prompt and my body jolted because my mind was focused on trying to figure out how his eyes could seem so familiar.

Travis lunged.

And yet again, surprisingly Joker instantly lifted his now bare hands to my son and took him from me, curling him close, natural, taking that beautiful load on like he'd done it since the moment Travis was born.

Something warm washed through me.

"Yeah?" Joker repeated.

"Uh, yes. New tires. Don't drive on the spare," I replied.

"You go to Ride, I'll give them your name. They'll give you a discount."

And that was when something dirty washed through me.

The dirty was the fact that my car was twenty years old, faded, rusted, worn out, and probably only still working because God loved me (I hoped), and all that was not lost on him.

This was embarrassing.

And as that washed through me, more did. Suddenly, gushes of nasty poured all over me.

The fact that I hadn't shifted off the last fifteen pounds of baby weight.

The fact that I hadn't been able to afford highlights for the last seven months so my hair did not look all that great, the golden blonde streaks starting four inches down from my roots in a way that was *not* an attractive ombré.

The fact that I was dressed to go to work in a polo shirt, khakis, and sneakers, and not in a cute dress and cuter shoes.

The fact that he had expensive glasses, an expensive bike, a leather jacket, and he might be ill-groomed, but he was tall, broad, had interesting eyes, was nice, generous with his time, great with kids, and a Good Samaritan.

"You got time to do it and can hang," he went on. "I'll ask them to go over the car. Make sure it's good."

Oh no.

He was taking pity on me.

More dirty washed over me.

"No...no," I shook my head, reaching out to take Travis from him. It was a feat, Travis didn't want to let go, but I bested him and tucked my son firm on my hip. "I...you've already been very nice. I should..." I flipped out my free hand, "I have money..."

I trailed off and twisted to get to my purse, thinking the twenty dollar bill in it was not enough, but it was all I had. I was also thinking that I was unfortunately going to have to use my credit card to get gas.

"No need. Just get to Ride. Sort out that spare, yeah?"

I turned back to him. "You sure?"

"Don't want your money."

That was firm in a way that sounded like he was offended, something I really didn't want, so, hesitantly, I nodded. "You've been really kind."

"Yeah," he muttered. "Be safe."

And then he turned toward his bike.

He just turned toward his bike!

I couldn't let him just turn toward his bike and *walk away*.

I had no idea why but there was no denying in that second that I knew into my bones I couldn't allow the biker named Joker to walk away.

"Joker!" I called.

He turned back.

When I got his eyes, I didn't know what to do so I didn't do anything.

"Right," he said, walked to me and got closer than he had before.

Even as Travis tried to make a lunge at him, he lifted up his hand and I held my breath.

I felt his sunglasses slide out of my hair.

"Thanks," he murmured and turned back.

"Really, thank you," I blurted, this a hopefully not blatant effort to detain him (although it was an effort to detain him) and he again turned to me. "I don't know what to say. I feel like I should do something. You helped me out a lot."

"Get you and your kid off the side of the highway and get safe, that's all you gotta do."

"Oh. Yes. Of course. I should do that," I babbled.

"Later," he said and moved to his bike.

"Later," I called as he did, not wanting him to go.

I didn't understand this.

Okay, he helped me out and he was very nice about it.

And okay, I was alone. Like *really* alone. No family close by. No friends. No husband. New baby. New life I didn't like all that much (except said presence of my new baby).

And Joker stopped and helped me out, making a problem I would have had to sort into one of those now nonexistent times when I got to let someone else sort it and I could play with my son, even if that time was on the side of a traffic-clogged interstate.

That meant a lot.

But I didn't want him to go in a way that wasn't just not wanting to see the last of a person who did me a kindness.

It was different.

And it was frightening.

But what was more frightening was that he was on his bike and making it roar.

It was almost over.

He'd be gone.

And I'd be alone.

It wasn't that (or just that).

It was that *he'd be gone*.

I opened my mouth to yell something over the noise of his motorcycle and Travis hit me in the jaw.

I looked down at my son.

I needed to get him to safety.

And then get him to his dad.

I closed my eyes, opened them, and saw Joker jerk his chin in an impatient way to my car.

So I hurried there, opened the passenger-side door, got my son safely in his car seat, rounded the car, and got in.

Joker didn't merge into traffic until I did. He also didn't leave the interstate until I did. He followed me off the ramp to Speer Boulevard.

Then he turned off.

And was gone.

CHAPTER THREE

Down on Her Knees

Carissa

I LOOKED INTO the mirror and blocked out all thoughts but what I could see.

The dress wasn't bad. It was one size up from what I'd worn before Travis, but it was cute. It was a blushy-pink fake silk underneath with a chiffon overlay in blush with black butterflies on it. It had no sleeves but it did have wispy frills at the arm holes. It had a full, shortish, flirty skirt, pleats up the front of the bodice, a scoop neck with a little bow at the base, and another bow at the belt at the waist.

It hid my little leftover baby pouch. It also hid my larger-since-Travis behind.

I wore it with my amazing black sandals with a thin T-strap, big double-winged butterfly at the toe, and platform wedge with cork at the sides.

All this was cheap, not to mention, I'd bought it on sale, the only way I could afford clothes for me, clothes I needed since none of my old ones fit.

Still, it was cute. Or at least I thought so.

I'd done up my hair so it was fuller and the ringlets more

pronounced. I'd also given myself a new pedicure, elegant, understated ballet pink on my toes. I had on good makeup, slight drama around the eyes, but mostly pink and dewy. And I'd used my expensive perfume, something I rarely used, since it was almost gone and I couldn't afford to buy more.

I was ready.

Before I could think on what I was ready for, I rushed out of my bedroom and into another one of the three rooms that made up my apartment: the kitchen/dining bar/living room.

I grabbed the chocolate pecan pie with its homemade crust that I'd covered in cling film from the bar.

And again, before I could think, I dashed to my car and headed out.

It was two days after Joker had fixed my tire. I still had the spare on. I hadn't had time to deal with it, what with work, laundry, cleaning house, not to mention pedicure and pie-making.

Now, I was going to deal with it.

And give my thank-you to Joker.

This made me nervous, so I didn't think on it as I made my way to Broadway, down Broadway, and straight to Ride.

I was still not thinking on it as I pulled in and drove past the parking spots where you'd park if you were going into the store.

I headed straight to the enormous structure at the back that had three big bays.

The garage.

I drove right to one that looked mostly empty and stopped outside it. I threw open my door, threw out my cute sandaled foot and heaved myself out.

Before I could move to the back seat to grab the pie, two men came out from the bays. One was tall, dark-haired, lanky-(but hard)-bodied, carried a clipboard, and had eyes on me. The other was tall and stoop shouldered, was wearing greasy jeans and an oil-stained tee, and also had his eyes on me.

The greasy jeans guy was your normal, everyday guy.

The lanky guy was incredibly handsome.

"Hey!" I called on a little wave, a bright smile, and moved to them.

They both watched and, normally, this wouldn't make me feel strange. Dad had told me I was beautiful since I could remember. Mom had done the same thing. Aaron had said it so many times since we met and started dating when we were freshmen, I believed he believed it (until recently) and I believed in me.

I knew I wasn't ugly. More importantly, I knew back then I was loved.

Now, not so much.

Now, I was a size bigger (two in pants), had a baby pouch, a big bottom, and a husband who dumped me for a size 0 model. I also had grown-out highlights that didn't look great.

No cute dress or cute shoes were going to cover any of that.

I'd known appreciative glances. I'd had them since I could remember too.

Now, I wondered what both of those men thought, me, twenty-five (almost twenty-six), dumped, a single mom (not that they knew that but I felt like I wore that knowledge on every inch of me), climbing out of an old, worn-out car, wearing a flirty but cheap dress and cute but cheap butterfly shoes that at that moment felt stupid and, worse, desperate.

I should have worn jeans.

No.

I shouldn't have come at all.

"Yo," the lanky one called.

I got close. "Uh…yes, yo." He grinned. It was highly attractive. I ignored it and I carried on, "I'm Carissa. Carissa Teodoro. A couple of days ago—"

The lanky guy's head jerked and he interrupted me. "Joker's girl?"

I shut my mouth.

Joker's girl.

Why did that sound so nice?

"Yup, spare. Tercel. Joker gave us the heads-up. We're covered," the guy in the greasy jeans said and twisted toward the bays. "Yo! Someone come get this bucket! Joker's girl is here!"

I looked from him, mouth open to say something, to the lanky guy with the clipboard (thinking, seeing as he had a clipboard, he was probably someone with authority). But I didn't say anything because he was looking me up and down with attractive green eyes and his lips were quirked like something was amusing.

Immensely amusing.

"We'll need your keys," he stated when his eyes again met mine.

"I, well, yes, of course," I dangled them out in front of me while a man in coveralls jogged from the bay, heading our way. "I kinda have a financial situation." I shared my understatement. "So can you give me an estimate before you take care of everything?"

Both men stared at me like I was crazy before lanky guy said, "We'll get Joker to take care a' that."

I nodded and told him, "I have to grab my purse and something from the back."

Greasy jeans guy came to me, nabbed my keys, and said, "Get 'em, babe."

I looked to him, nodded agreeably, then rushed back to

my car. I leaned in deep and grabbed my purse from where it sat in Travis's car seat. Then I went to the back and got the pie.

When I closed the door and turned to the guys, I saw they were all leaned slightly to the right, heads tipped, eyes on my behind or, in the case of the lanky guy, my legs.

I felt warmth hit my cheeks and called, "Is Joker around?"

They all came to and looked to my face.

"She brought him pie," the lanky guy muttered.

"Fuckin' brilliant," the greasy jeans guy also was muttering.

"Does Joker even like pie?" the coverall guy was only slightly muttering.

But my heart squeezed.

Didn't he like pie?

Didn't everyone like pie?

Oh no! What if he didn't like pie?

"Does Joker like anything?" greasy jeans guy asked.

"I bet, today, he's gonna like butterflies," lanky guy noted.

"Today, *I* like butterflies," greasy jeans guy declared.

I cleared my throat.

Lanky guy's lips quirked again just as he jerked his chin to the right and said, "Compound."

"Sorry?" I asked.

"Joker's in the Compound, babe. Building over there." He swung his clipboard in that direction and then smiled a highly appealing but definitely meaningful smile. "Go right on in. He's not out front, someone in there will get him for you."

I looked where he was indicating and saw a large, long building that ran the entire length of the property from the back of the auto store to well beyond the garage. It had an overhang along the front, picnic tables under it (five of them, precisely), a big barrel grill to one end, and four kegs with taps looking like they were ready for use sat against the wall of the building, close to the grill. Last, there were a number of motorcycles parked in formation at the front.

There was also a set of double doors.

I turned my eyes back to the men.

"Thanks!" I called on another bright smile, ignored the strangeness they were making me feel and my inability to understand if it was a good strangeness or a bad one, and then I moved toward the Compound, carrying my pie in front of me with both hands, acutely aware they were watching me.

It was a long walk, and when I made it to the end, balanced the pie, grabbed the handle to one of the doors, pulled it open, and chanced a look back, I saw what I had a feeling I'd see.

Not a single one of them had moved, and their eyes were on me.

More strangeness invaded but even if it was quite a distance, they had to know I was looking at them. So I lifted a hand to wave before I slid through the door.

Only the coveralls guy waved back.

I rebalanced the pie in both hands, took two steps in, and stopped because I had to due to the fact I couldn't see a thing.

The place was dark. After the bright Denver sun, my eyes needed time to adjust.

This took time, neon beer signs finally coming into focus. Then more.

None of it good.

Tatty furniture. Pool tables. A long sweeping bar. Flags on the walls like the one flying over the auto store under the American flag. Pictures also on the walls. Harley-Davidson stickers, again stuck to the walls. It wasn't tidy. It wasn't even clean.

It was just scary.

"Yo!" I heard and turned my head right.

I had company.

At the curved part of the sweep of the bar, a man was standing, leaning into his arm on the bar. He had a goatee. He was large. He was rough but nonetheless very good-looking. He had a lovely redheaded woman in a dainty blouse and tight skirt in front of him on a barstool. He was standing very close to her. Although he looked firmly the manly biker yin to her girly classy yang, she clearly didn't mind this.

Behind the bar was another man with dark, messy hair, a mustache over his lip that also grew down the sides. A patch at the indent in the middle of his lower lip. An adorable baby younger than Travis tucked securely in the curve of his arm, an arm that was decorated in tattoos of dancing flames. And finally, an elegant, tall, stunningly beautiful brunette in the curve of his other arm (which also had flames).

Last, sitting beside the redhead was a black lady in a dress I might sell a kidney for if it was my style (it wasn't, it was chic, cutting-edge, and sophisticated, I was flirty, ruffles, and sometimes flowers, definitely butterflies, none of this I knew in a glance she'd ever wear, even upon threat of death). Her hair was coiffed to perfection. Her eyes were sharp in a way she could never play dumb and get away with it.

Those eyes, as were all the others, were on me.

And the remains of their fast food lunch was all over the bar.

"Hey!" I called and took several more steps in.

The men's eyes dropped instantly to my skirt.

The women's eyes moved directly to each other.

"I'm looking for Joker," I informed them.

The women's eyes instantly swiveled back to me.

"Say what?" the black lady asked, sounding like she was choking.

"Um...Joker." I lifted up my pie. "He helped me out a couple of days ago. I wasn't in the position to say a proper thank-you then. So I popped by to say it now."

The second I was done talking, I jumped when the goatee guy turned his head to the side and roared, "*Joker!*"

"Holy crap," the redhead breathed.

"This...is...*awesome*," the brunette whispered.

"Girl, get your butterfly ass over here," the black lady ordered. "I need to get a better look."

Disregarding this order, sensing his movement, my eyes skidded to the mustachioed man to see his head dropped. He was looking to his feet, but his shoulders were shaking.

The baby in his arm gurgled.

The door behind me opened. I turned to it and saw lanky guy entering.

He looked right to the bar. "Couldn't miss this."

With a deep biker voice (that was not as attractive as Joker's, but it was still attractive), that voice shaking like his shoulders, the mustachioed man replied, "Bet not."

I was confused.

"Sister," the black lady started and I looked to her. "I see either Joker didn't communicate the dress code to you or, better option, you chose to ignore it, struttin' your butterfly ass in here not wearin' a halter top and daisy dukes." She tipped her head to me. "Kudos to you. Be who you are. Bikers be damned."

The redhead and brunette started giggling.

I was still confused. More so now since there were three women among me and none of them were in halter tops and daisy dukes.

"Sorry?" I asked.

"*Joker!*" the goateed man roared again.

I jumped again.

"*What?*"

This came barked from the back of the big room, and my eyes flew there to see Joker striding out of a door that appeared to lead to a hall. He did this looking irate.

He also did this looking like a tall, dark, bearded, broad-shouldered, sinister biker.

And I liked the latter.

A whole lot.

My legs started shaking.

"Company," a gravelly voice declared.

Joker looked to me.

I nearly dropped the pie.

I held on and called a chirpy, "Hey!"

He kept striding in, his eyes glancing toward the bar then back to me. He stopped five feet away.

"I came in to, uh...take care of my tire like you said I should and I made you this." I extended the pie to him, both hands still under it, a smile I knew was tentative on my face. "To say thanks."

He looked to the pie. His expression said nothing.

But I was watching him looking at the pie and I again got that feeling I knew him, and not just because two days ago he changed my tire.

It was a weird feeling. A feeling that felt like it was rattling my memory banks.

But it was also tugging at my heartstrings.

I no longer could concentrate on that feeling, or get a lock on why I was certain I knew him, when he stopped looking at the pie and came to me, took the pie, walked to the bar, dumped the dish on it with no ado whatsoever and looked beyond me, to lanky guy.

"They dealin' with her ride?" he asked.

"Got on it immediately," lanky guy replied.

"Right." Joker turned his attention to me. "They'll sort you out."

"I...um. Okay," I replied.

"Pie's nice," he went on. "Brothers'll like it."

The brothers will like it?

Wasn't he going to have any?

Maybe he *didn't* like pie.

Darn it!

My phone started ringing in my purse when I said. "Well, that's good. But—"

" 'Preciate you comin' by," he cut me off to say. Then he looked to the bar. "Got shit to do."

I was struggling with my bag on my arm to get to my phone. I was doing this feeling a variety of things. All of them bad.

"Good to see you again, uh..." he trailed off just as my hand closed around my phone and my head jerked up when he did.

"Carissa," I whispered.

"Yeah, good to see you. Take care," he returned.

He'd forgotten my name.

That hurt.

It really hurt.

But...

Why?

To hide it, I looked to my phone as I heard a gravelly, "Joker."

But I wasn't listening because the caller was Tory.

Aaron had long since delegated communication about most everything to his fiancée. That *most everything* was always Travis, since that was now all Aaron and I had to talk about.

This was mean. It was also awful. And last, it was very much Aaron.

I hated it.

It wasn't nice, but I also hated her. She stole my husband. She got to spend every week with him and every other one living my dream, being a family with my baby. She drove a sporty Mercedes Aaron bought for her and was regularly in ads in the paper for local department stores or on TV commercials for local furniture stores, sitting in loungers and on couches, her long, thin legs always bare and stretched out.

She was beautiful. She had glossy dark brown hair that I suspected was glossy without product, which was irritating. She was taller than me by probably five inches. She had a natural grace. And even though I was not even close to over the hill, heck, I couldn't even *see* the hill, she was almost four years younger than me in a way that made me feel fifty years older than her.

Obviously, for these reasons and about a thousand others besides, I didn't want to take her call.

But she had my son.

So I had to take it.

"Excuse me," I mumbled, knowing probably no one was paying any attention to me. I took a step away, turned my side to the others, and put the phone to my ear. "Tory."

"Uh, hello, Carissa."

She didn't sound right.

My skin started tingling.

"Is everything all right?" I asked.

"Okay, don't freak. It's all good now. It's gonna be okay. Aaron didn't want me to call you because it's normal, it happens, the doctors say..."

My back shot straight and my heart clenched even as my

hand gripped the phone so hard, if I had any attention left to pay to it, it would hurt.

"The doctors?" I whispered.

"Yes, they say he's gonna be okay. But we had to take Travis to the hospital last night."

"*Hospital?*" I screeched, and again, if I had any attention left to pay to it, I would have noticed the feel of the room had gone alert.

"He's fine. Fine," she said hurriedly. "It was just croup. So little, working so hard to cough, it was scary but it's totally okay. The doctors took care of him. Sent him home. Aaron didn't want me to say anything, but I thought you should know."

My head was buzzing, my skin still tingling, my heart beating so hard I could feel it thudding in my chest as I said, "I'm coming to your house."

"No!" she cried. "No, Carissa, don't do that."

"He's my son!" I snapped. "He's been to the hospital, he doesn't feel good, so now I'm *coming to your house*." I looked up and said to the first person I saw, which was lanky guy. "I need my car. Immediately."

He was studying me but when I spoke, he jerked up his chin, turned, and jogged out.

"Carissa!" Tory called from my phone. "You cannot come here."

I was marching to the door as I hissed, "Stop me."

"Don't make me regret telling you this. If Aaron knows you're here without permission, he's gonna be pissed. *At me.* But you know it'll be more *at you.* And he'll go off on you, Carissa."

I had my hand to the door handle but I stopped at her words.

"No judge is going to take away my right to see my child when he's ill," I declared.

"Come on, Carissa," she returned quietly, gently, but

swiftly and resolutely. "By now you have to know his father knows a lot of judges and they golf together. They'll do whatever he wants them to do."

I closed my eyes and did it tightly, my fingers clutching the door handle even tighter.

I knew that. I'd learned that lesson, so far, twice.

"You can't come over here," Tory went on and I opened my eyes, staring unseeing at the door. "I don't agree with him keeping this from you. I wanted him to call you last night. He refused. He's at the office now, left Travis and me a little while ago to take some meetings at work. He said he's going to come back, work from home. I don't know when that'll be. I just know if you're here, he'll lose it. You know it too. I'm sorry this is the way it is, but we both know it's the way it is. I'm taking good care of Travis. The doctors say he's going to be okay. He's already better. He's being looked after. And when Travis feels better and Aaron's at work, I'll bring him to your store so you can see him. Okay?"

That's what I got.

That's all I got.

My son was sick and in order to avoid a lawsuit and have more of him taken away from me, a lawsuit I couldn't defend against because I couldn't afford an attorney, I had to wait for my ex-husband's young, beautiful fiancée to bring my baby boy to me at work.

I closed my eyes again, leaned forward, and didn't feel my forehead hitting the door.

"Carissa," Tory prompted. "Okay?"

"Okay," I whispered brokenly.

It wasn't okay.

Nothing was okay.

And worst of that nothing, my baby was not okay and I couldn't see him.

"Okay," she whispered back. Then, "I'm so sorry."

I really hated her, and right then I hated that she was making it hard for me to keep hating her even when she had my baby and I didn't.

I also hated what I had to say next.

"Thank you for calling me."

"If anything changes, I'll find a way to call you again. But he's good. I promise."

"All right."

"See you at the store tomorrow. Yeah?"

"Yes."

" 'Bye, Carissa."

"Goodbye, Tory."

She disconnected.

I kept my phone to my ear, my forehead to the door, my hand clasping the handle, my eyes squeezed tight.

"What was that?"

The words came to me in a deep biker voice I knew but they didn't penetrate.

My baby boy with his chubby cheeks and his granddad's eyes was sick without me.

The words came again. "What was that?"

They again didn't penetrate because as I stood there, I knew.

I had to do something. I had to put a stop to Aaron's mission of misery.

I had no choice.

"Carissa, what was that?"

"I have to get on my knees," I whispered.

"What?"

I pulled away from the door and looked to my side.

Joker was close.

"I was wrong. I don't need my car," I announced. "But

I'll wait in the office or go and browse the store. I'll just go on over to the garage first and let them know." I hauled open the door. "Enjoy the pie."

I didn't get out because Joker curled his fingers around my upper arm and pulled me back.

That got my attention, slightly, and I distractedly noticed the two other men (one still holding his baby) and three women in the room were all gathered close behind Joker and they were watching me.

I looked up into Joker's steel eyes.

"Is something wrong with Travis?" he asked.

"He has croup," I said, my voice flat. "I'm assured he's fine."

"Darlin', got my car here. While they work on yours, I can take you—" the black lady began.

I stopped her by shaking my head. "I'm not allowed at my ex-husband's house without his permission."

"Your kid's sick," the mustachioed man told me something I very well knew.

I straightened my spine and met his eyes.

"My ex-husband is an attorney. As was his father, before he became a judge. As was his grandfather, ditto the judge part. All of them in Denver. This means if he doesn't want me at his house, I don't go."

"You're fuckin' joking," Joker bit out and I looked to him.

"I am not," I stated curtly.

His hand tightened on my arm.

My eyes started stinging. "If you'll release me, I'll get out of your hair."

"What's it mean, get on your knees?" Joker asked.

Dirty water washed through me, and I felt an uncomfortable charge hit the air at his question.

I shook my head, pulling at my arm in his hold. "Doesn't matter."

"What does it mean?"

I could take no more.

I yanked out of his hold, leaned toward him, and shrieked, *"It doesn't matter!"* I threw out both hands, still screeching. *"Nothing matters! Nothing but him! Travis! That's all that matters!"*

Then I whirled, hauled open the door, and ran out.

"Joker, no. Red, go," I heard a gravelly voice say as I ran. Then, "Hop, lock 'im down. Red, *go.*"

I heard it.

But I just ran.

Tack

The door to the meeting room opened and Tack's eyes, along with those of the boys who were with him, went to it.

He watched his woman strut through.

Normally, he would take the time to appreciate this. It was a habit. He did it daily.

Right then, he saw the expression on her face and he didn't take that time.

He looked around the room. With Dog and Brick in Grand Junction opening up the Club's new store, he'd made Hop and Shy his lieutenants. Hop had been a brother for decades. Shy was newer. Hop was married to his woman's best girl, Lanie. Shy was married to Tack's daughter, Tabitha.

The room was rounded out with his son, Rush, as well as Boz, Hound, Speck.

And Joker.

"Where is she?" Joker clipped.

Tyra looked to Joker as she moved to her husband in his seat at the head of the table. Joker had been pacing under the watchful eyes of his brothers. Now he'd stopped, legs locked and planted wide, hands to his hips, secrets still behind his eyes, dark at the surface nearing to black.

But that black could disintegrate in a second. Tack knew it.

It would not ice over.

It would blaze hot in a way that could consume them all.

But especially a girl named Carissa.

Tack knew the minute he saw her that she wasn't just a girl in a cute dress with shoes that were as sexy as they were ridiculous that Joker helped change a tire.

This girl was something else.

"Elvira's taking her home," Tyra told Joker and looked back to Tack. "Hawk let her have the afternoon off. She's staying with her. Lanie took Nash and went back to work. She and I are going over to Carissa's after to hang with her and Elvira."

Tack nodded.

Tyra hefted her round ass in its tight skirt up on the table by his side and twisted her torso to the room but kept her eyes locked to her man.

He read them before she spoke. She'd been his woman a long time. She'd given him two sons. She'd given him a multitude of phenomenal orgasms. She'd given him her love. She'd given him redemption. She'd told him he turned her world to color. She made his life complete.

"Lenny wouldn't let her back on the road in that car," she said to Tack quietly, but the room could hear. "He said it's a heap. Tack, honey, Lenny says it'll take nearly four thousand dollars' worth of parts and labor to make it safe."

"Do it," he said shortly.

"That car isn't worth that," she replied.

"She gonna take a free car from us?" he asked.

"Not likely," she answered.

"Tell Lenny to do it."

Her lips curved up.

He knew what that meant. It meant he'd get her appreciation for his kindness for a girl he didn't know later.

He didn't do it for that.

But he was looking forward to it.

"What does get down on her knees mean?" Joker asked,
and Red twisted to him as Tack lifted his eyes to his brother.
"She tell you that?"

When his wife didn't answer, Tack glanced at her to see
her looking at Hop and Boz.

They were closest to Joker.

It was a warning.

Tack came alert.

She gave her attention to Joker. "She was really upset,
Joker. She shared a great deal."

"She share that?" Joker bit off.

"Yes," Tyra said quietly.

"And?" Joker prompted.

"Brother—" Hop started, beginning to unfold his body
from his chair.

"*And?*" Joker barked, his focus on Red.

"Her ex-husband is fond of filing motions. As part of
these motions, and him winning them, it means she doesn't
receive child support regardless that his income is more than
triple hers. Therefore, she's no longer able to pay an attorney's fees," Tyra answered.

"That isn't answering my question, Cherry," Joker said
like a warning.

Tyra's best girl, his daughter, some of her family, and
many of her friends called his woman Ty-Ty. He called her
Red. His brothers called her Cherry.

"She met one who expressed he'd like an alternate form of payment."

Hop and Boz got close. His son, Rush, not stupid, also moved to do the same.

They did it, but they knew Joker better.

He didn't lose it.

He got cold in the way the entire room felt a chill.

"Name," he whispered.

Tyra looked to Tack.

Tack looked to Joker.

"She'll give it to Boz and Hound. They'll deal with him," he declared.

"Oh no they won't," Joker replied.

"Who's she to you?" Tack asked.

"Not your business," Joker answered.

"Saw what I saw in my own club, Joker. Saw it, didn't like it. No mother should go through what I witnessed today. Saw you watchin' her go through it. Don't get it. Who is she to you?"

"Brother, not gonna repeat myself," Joker returned.

"We got two choices with this," Tack shot back. "We ignore it, which means we let a brother do what he's gotta do and not take his back, or we go all in. We go all in, we gotta know why we're doin' it."

"No one's askin' you to go all in."

"And you didn't sit in this room and throw in your name to earn your patch thinkin' you'd ever go it alone without your brothers at your back. So that means my two choices are bullshit. There's only one. Knowin' that, we gotta know, who is she to you?"

"No one."

It was a lie. Everyone in the room knew it. They didn't like it. But Joker wasn't done.

"Went to school with her. She was a cheerleader."

That wasn't a surprise.

"Remember, twenty years back, the kid on her trike who got crushed by a car in her driveway?" Joker asked.

The air in the room got thin.

They remembered.

"That was her sister," Joker finished.

"Fuck me," Hop muttered.

"Far's I know, lost her mother later too," Joker went on.

"High school friend you're lookin' out for?" Tack asked.

"She has no clue who I am," Joker answered.

Honey hair. Great legs. Fantastic ass. Excellent tits. Shining eyes.

Tack bet that fucking stung.

"Doesn't remember?" Tack asked.

"Wouldn't. And I'm glad. I'm not the kid she knew. She ain't gonna remember either."

That said a lot, and Tack didn't like what it said. But he had no choice. Joker wanted that, he, nor any of the brothers, could make another play.

"Where do you want the Club to go with this?" Tack asked.

"Make sure I don't get incarcerated after I make an attorney swallow his own balls."

Tack clenched his teeth to stop a smile before he went on, "Which attorney?"

"Strike that. Make sure I don't get incarcerated after I make one attorney swallow his own balls and another one do the same with his dick shoved up his ass."

"You did either of those, her ex has the weight behind him she says he does, she could feel it," Tack warned.

Joker's jaw flexed.

"Lotta emotion there for a girl who doesn't remember you," Tack noted cautiously.

"Her sister was crushed, man," Joker bit out, and Tack felt that. He had two young sons, a grown one and a grown daughter. He felt that deep in his gut. And he knew, God forbid, shit happened like that, his kids would feel it too. "And it's been a long time, but none of us ever forgets that high school kids are assholes," Joker kept at it. "The ones who aren't are just tryin' to make their way without sustaining too much damage. She wasn't either of those."

"A good girl?"

"Last person I saw in Denver before I ran away from my old man. She knew I was doin' it. Probably knew I was underage. Definitely knew I should do it. Kissed my cheek and told me I was gonna have a beautiful life."

There it was.

And it was more than Joker had ever given them. Out loud at least.

Joker's voice suddenly went quiet. "I have that life. What she wanted for me. Good around me. She doesn't. That shit ain't right. Now, that's all you'll get from me, brother. She's worth it. Carissa Teodoro doesn't lean against a door like she held all the joy on earth in her veins and it leaked out, not without retribution. That's what I know. That's what I'm tellin' you. That's what I'm doin'. The Club is either in it with me, or they're out. But that's what's happening."

He said no more.

He also didn't wait for an answer.

He stalked out.

Tack looked to his son.

"Rush, on him," he ordered quietly.

Rush nodded once and followed his brother.

"Baby," Tyra whispered and Tack looked to her. "There's a lot more to share."

"Why am I not surprised?" he muttered.

She didn't hesitate.

"She's hurting, Kane. She has a full-time job, it doesn't pay much, benefits are great, she likes where she works, but what income she has is eaten up by daycare expenses and paying off her old attorney. She's tight with her dad but he's in Nebraska. She won't tell him what's happening, is insistent he's shielded from it, and now I have a better understanding of why."

She paused and Tack nodded.

He understood too.

Tyra kept going, "Her friends migrated to the ex. You know she's got a shit car. She's also got a one bedroom apartment in a very bad part of town. And she's convinced, and it sounds like she isn't making things up, that her ex is carrying forward a strategy to take her son away from her and get her gone for good so he can set up house with his fiancée and forget she even existed."

"What's your take on this girl?" Tack asked.

"My take is, she lost a sister, a mother, her ex is fucking with her head, and she still puts on a pretty dress, walks right into a biker compound with a homemade pie and looks at Joker not like he rides astride a Harley but does it on a white horse. If she doesn't remember who he was from high school, it doesn't matter. She knows who he is now and went out of her way not to let him forget her. No girl dresses like that if she doesn't hope to get attention. She likes him. He made an impression, and he did it more than just being a good guy who stopped to change her tire."

She drew in breath.

Tack held her eyes and his silence.

She continued, "But she broke today, Tack. She is not a girl who gives a blowjob for legal services but she was going to do it. She loves her son. She's running out of options. She's running scared. And it's taking everything she has to keep those pieces together so broken doesn't become shattered."

"I know one thing about this, Red, if they're tight, her dad doesn't want to be shielded. Got a baby girl. I'd wanna know. 'Spect he does too."

"Her dad is in Nebraska looking after his mom, who's far gone with Alzheimer's, her grandfather has already passed, and her father doesn't have the heart to put her in a home."

Fuck.

"We gotta take her on," Tack murmured.

"You don't, Elvira's in a snit. This guy, her ex, has been a dick for a long time. Carissa just put on her game face and ignored it. Her fail, as she calls it. Elvira doesn't see it the same way. She's ready to blow. And that means she'll nag Hawk until he takes it on, and Hawk's messy."

Tack felt his lips curl up.

Elvira was Tyra's girl and Hawk was Elvira's boss. Hawk was a different kind of brother to Tack for a variety of reasons. And Hawk was a man who got things done and didn't mind how he had to go about doing that.

Tack looked to the room.

"Boz, Hound, deal with the man who thinks coercin' head for payment of legal fees is something he can do and convince him he's wrong."

Boz nodded.

Hound looked ecstatic.

Tack shook his head.

Tyra gave them the attorney's name.

They took off.

He looked to Speck. "Go with them. Make sure Hound doesn't kill anyone."

Speck shot him a grin and took off.

Tack turned to Hop. "We need whatever we can get on her ex and his father."

"They got judge friends, we got added problems to the ones we already got, Tack," Hop warned.

"You watch that girl listen to her replacement tell her she couldn't see her sick son?"

Hop's jaw went hard.

"Worth it to you that doesn't happen again?" Tack asked.

"Don't ask that shit. You know it is. But it's my job to point out where this Club is at," Hop returned. "And, bottom line, brother, this shit is bigger than we think it is, it's gotta go under the gavel."

He was not wrong.

"I'll find out," Hop carried on. "Then we'll know if we need a meet."

Tack lifted his chin. Hop took off.

Tack looked to his wife. "Feel like talkin' Big Petey into opening a daycare center?"

He heard her soft laughter. "He's already got two hooligans at his informal one."

"Pete likes babies."

It was then, her eyes got soft and they stayed on him. "I'll give him a call."

She hopped off the table and he enjoyed the show. Then she bent into him to touch her mouth to his.

He liked that too, but would wait to get more later.

She strutted her ass out, and this time Tack took the time to appreciate it.

Shy moved to him and took the seat beside him to his left, where he sat at meetings, a position he'd earned fast because he was smart, loyal to his brothers, and loyal to the Chaos family.

"Tab's friendly," he said.

Tab was Tack's daughter, the girl Shy had earned the hard way.

And Shy was right. Tabby was friendly and usually open to recruiting new sisters into her crew.

Tack looked at his brother and son-in-law.

"See if she's recruiting."

Shy nodded.

Tack looked at the door.

"Gone for her."

That was Shy. He was talking about Joker.

He would know. He had the love of a good woman, gave that back.

Tack knew too. He had the same.

He looked back to Shy. "Before shit went down, he was set on icing her out."

Shy held his eyes.

"Different cold wind blew, she got that call."

Shy didn't say a word.

"He doesn't keep his shit, Shy, he'll fuck things for her. And he doesn't open his eyes and see butterflies, he'll fuck things for him."

"I'll get on it with Rush."

"Yeah."

Shy nodded, pushed out of his chair and rounded the table behind Tack.

Tack watched the door close on him.

Then he let the thoughts in.

They didn't need this shit.

They were at war. They were currently in détente, but that could change in a blink. Benito Valenzuela had a plan, he wanted Chaos turf, and he wasn't going to sit on his hands for long.

They didn't need this shit.

What's it mean, get on your knees?

They were gonna take on this shit.

"Fuck," he muttered, put his hands to the arms of his chair and folded out.

He had a woman and boys to feed, TV to watch, a wife to fuck, and sleep to sleep.

That was where his head was at.

Tomorrow, he'd see.

CHAPTER FOUR

Tasted as Good on His Tongue

Joker

THERE WAS NO ring. Just cement and a throng of bystanders who got out of the way whenever the fighters got too close.

Bare feet. Bare chest. Bare knuckles.

Joker hit him with a right hook but knew even before he threw the punch the guy would take it and go down.

With a jarring thud, he did.

The crowd roared.

Joker just stood there, staring down at him, taking deep breaths and flexing his fingers.

There was no referee. There was just a promoter, a sleaze named Monk who had a legal business running a local night-club. But for this business he took bets and had a few of his bruisers act as crowd control and bouncers, ousting anyone who showed who didn't lay down a bet.

So he waited until Monk wandered toward him, grabbed his hand, and lifted it.

The crowd again roared.

Joker tore his hand from Monk's, not liking the little weasel touching him, and he turned away.

He didn't look to the cinderblock wall, where he knew Rush and Shy were leaning, watching the action through the crowd. His brothers knew he fought underground. Rush and Shy weren't the first to come and watch him. Hound was at nearly every fight.

No. He looked to the girl he'd clocked earlier, jerked his head, and she grinned huge, immediately moving toward the door.

Then he walked to his shit, tugged on his tee, socks, and boots and grabbed his cut. He went to Monk's boy and got his pay. He shoved the envelope in his back pocket, shrugged on his jacket, and after that, enduring claps on the back, bumps to his arms and ignoring anyone who tried to stop him, he pushed to the door and out of it.

Up the steps and into the alley.

She was at his bike.

They wouldn't have company. He was one of the last fights of the night, but everyone stayed until the end. There was blood to be drawn. Sweat to be leaked. Money to be won. Or lost. No one would leave.

Even if there was, he didn't give a shit. And she was a fighter groupie, she wouldn't either.

"Hey," she whispered when he got near and she shifted closer to his bike.

He let his lip curl and grunted. "Wall."

She looked disappointed but he didn't give a fuck.

She might have been disappointed but she moved right to the brick wall of the alley.

She stopped, facing him. Joker jerked his head once in a no.

He watched her face change when she understood him, not disappointment, far from it.

Then she turned to face the wall, putting her hands up to it.

He moved in behind her and yanked up her short jean skirt.

He looked down at her bare ass.

Commando.

He didn't know that's the way she played it, but the girl she was, he could guess.

Carissa wouldn't go commando. Not ever.

He put Carissa out of his head and gave the girl the absolute minimum of what she needed to get her ready. He heard her greedy moan when he was done doing that and kicked her feet further apart.

She tipped her ass.

He unzipped, freed his cock, expertly dealt with the condom he pulled out of his pocket, drove in, and fucked her against the wall, barely touching her, just enough to send her over the edge.

He pushed her there with her making a lot of noise, especially when she took the fall.

Joker didn't make noise, not even when he planted himself to the root and shot hard.

And that was the only time he gave her something, but he did it because he couldn't stop it. Bending his neck to rest his forehead on her shoulder as the release of coming followed on the heels of the release of beating the shit out of someone.

He rushed his recovery, pulled out, yanked her skirt down, and growled, "Get gone."

She turned to him, wanting more.

They always wanted more.

"Jo—"

"*Gone.*"

She took in his face, his tone, nodded, and rushed away.

Leaving the spent condom in the alley, not doubting for a minute it joined others of its kind, Joker went to his bike. Then he rode to the Compound.

It wasn't a surprise when he went in that Rush was sitting

at the bar, Shy behind it. He'd seen their bikes outside before he walked in.

Unlike Joker, Rush had his own place, didn't stay at the Compound often, usually only after a party. Shy had a sweet crib with Tab, and Shy just had Tab, so unless Tabby was with him, he never took a bed in the Compound.

He also knew Tack had set them on him. Both had seen him fight, neither of them came often, but they were there that night for a different reason.

They were in the Compound right then for that same reason.

Shy took the bottle of tequila that was in front of him, poured a shot, and sent the glass skidding down the bar toward Joker. Joker nabbed it, shot it, and even if he didn't want to, moved to his brothers.

He liked them both. But he wasn't in the mood.

When Chaos took him on as a recruit and he found out that Rush was a recruit with him—and remembered the guy, knowing he was Tack's son, Rush being the kid Joker used to watch with his father at the garage—he didn't think he'd like him.

Joker knew it was jealousy, but he didn't care. The guy had everything worth anything all his life, and Joker had none of that shit.

It didn't take long for him to learn to like him. Rush was solid. He was smart. He was loyal to his brothers. He loved his sister and had the balls to show how much. Same with his dad, even if they butted heads. Same with his stepmom and half-brothers. He could be funny. He was honest, spoke his mind, was an alert, aware, prepared partner when they were on patrol, and he was an excellent wingman when they were out and Joker was in the mood for a fuck that didn't happen against the wall of an alley.

Shy was one of Tack's lieutenants. He'd been a full member longer than Joker or Rush. He was a lot like Tack, which was a lot like Rush. Loved his Club, loved his brothers, loved his woman, and not in that order. Tabitha Allen Cage came first for her husband Parker "Shy" Cage. The road to full member included eating a lot of shit from the brothers, cleaning up puke and other crap that was even more vile, stocking shelves in the store, proving loyalty and smarts on patrol, and learning Chaos history.

Shy hooking up with the one and only Chaos princess was not popular. You could fuck whatever pussy you wanted, as much as you wanted, take any old lady you wanted, treat her like you wanted, it was your business.

But you didn't do that to family.

Shy wasn't just fucking her, though, and the rock resting against the band she had on her finger proved it. It got to the point where it was almost her or his brothers. He made it clear if it got to that point, he picked her.

It was a surprise decision. But it being Tabby, the brothers made it clear it was the right one.

Joker made it to them, leaned into the bar, and put his shot glass down.

Shy filled it up.

"Thanks, brother. Won two large on you tonight," Rush muttered.

Shy jerked up his chin. "And I added to my stash for Tab's next set of earrings."

Joker said nothing. He just shot the tequila.

It felt good his brothers bet on him, but then again, they'd be stupid not to. He'd been on the underground circuit a long time, well before Chaos. Had a stash of cash in a safe in his room in the Compound that he'd been adding to for years, all earned fighting.

He never lost.

He was a natural talent. He'd had years of learning how to take abuse and remain standing. He also could read an opponent. And he had a lot of incentive to beat the shit out of anyone who raised their fists his way.

"Boz, Hound, and Speck took care of that attorney," Shy told him.

Tack, as always, sent the right ones. Hound was a lunatic. Boz wasn't far behind. But Speck would keep their shit straight.

They'd make their point though. It was just that Speck would keep it from being messy.

He put the glass down and Shy again filled it.

He didn't lift it before Shy started talking.

"Think you get what went down today, Cherry, Lanie, and Elvira took your girl firm into the fold."

Not his girl.

Carissa Teodoro would never be his girl.

Joker stayed silent but looked into Shy's eyes.

"Shit like that, girl like that, they're mother henning all over the place," Shy went on.

Not a surprise. He wasn't sure he got why Elvira, who worked for a man called Hawk, a man who was undoubtedly a badass, but his business was nebulous, was so tight with the Club. Hawk was tight with Tack. There was a reason and Joker had learned that history too. But Elvira lingering... he had no clue. She wasn't their people, and by that he didn't mean black, he meant biker.

But she fit. She was hilarious.

And she didn't take shit or let any of her sisters take it either.

Tyra and Lanie were more quiet about it, but they were the same.

Joker said nothing, just threw back the shot.

"What I'm sayin' is," Shy's voice dipped quiet when Joker's hand dropped. "She's in the fold, brother, and shit gets around. Shit like, you fuck another fighter groupie in an alley, that could get to her, and your girl..." He shook his head. "That'd damage her."

Joker finally spoke.

"She's not my girl."

Shy's brows shot together. "The woman brought you pie."

She did, and he wanted to taste it. Not since Mrs. Heely looked after him did he have that. Not until the old ladies at Chaos threw barbeques and the boys did their hog roasts and anyone found any reason to party, which happened often, and people would bring good food they made to eat.

He wanted to taste the goodness Carissa could put in a pie. There probably was a lot. So much that pie could win awards.

But by then, that pie lying around, he figured his brothers had decimated it.

Joker stopped thinking about the pie and changed the subject, asking Shy, "You sure you wanna be the person to tell me who I can fuck?"

"You can fuck biker skank, fighter groupie, mix 'em up, I don't give a shit," Shy replied. "I'm just sayin', you take the path that leads to her, you wanna keep butterflies in your bed after you get them there, the days of empty pussy are done. I figure you know that, seein' what Tack has with Cherry, Hop with Lanie, me with Tab. I'm just sayin'."

Joker grabbed the bottle himself and poured another shot.

After he took it, he again looked to Shy. "Not lookin' to put butterflies in my bed. But even if I was, she's not like that, so I wouldn't get her there."

"Dress was cheap, brother, same with the shoes. But it was all she had. She put 'em on, did up her face, her hair, and trotted her ass into a den of bikers to bring you a pie. You want butterflies, at this point, you gotta crook your finger. You wanna keep 'em, you gotta be smart."

"You don't know Carissa," Joker told him.

"I know no bitch makes pie for a man she doesn't have in her sights," Shy returned.

"Again, you don't know Carissa," Joker fired back. "She's a good girl. I did her a good turn. She's not the type to let that stand without payback. That's it."

"She the type to trick herself out before she does it?" Rush entered the conversation. "I didn't see her, bro, but word flies. She coulda gone to Tessa's Bakery and got you some cupcakes. But she made you a pie and tricked herself out to deliver it."

"Jesus, fuck, who gives a shit about the pie?" Joker bit off.

"You should," Shy said quietly. Before Joker could return, Shy went on, "You're settled. You've got your patch. You do your thing. You got your brothers' backs. But it's not lost on anyone, man, that you are here and you still aren't. You give what you need to give to your brothers to keep you here and that's it. You want this family, same's we all do." He flipped out a hand. "You earned your place in it. We know it means something to you. But outside what you need to give, you don't give back jack."

Joker didn't like that shit.

"You got a problem with me havin' my patch?" he asked low.

"I got a problem with a brother I like, a brother I respect, a brother I see reachin' for somethin', he gets the dregs, and he's good with that," Shy answered. "You haven't told me, which is part of the problem, but my guess is, whatever

family you had sucked. I get that. My parents were murdered, lost the family I liked, got stuck in one I hated. So I
found one that worked for me. You found one that worked
for you. Time for you to go all in, Joke. And time for you to
stop accepting the dregs, reach for what you deserve, and
take hold of butterflies."

Joker turned to Rush. "Does it hit you," he glanced to
Shy, "either a' you, that this shit is whacked?"

"What shit?" Rush asked.

"This chat," Joker answered tersely. "I'm not feelin' it.
It's none of your fuckin' business, and I'm not good with you
makin' it your business."

"Then that tells us you've never had anyone around that
gives a shit enough to make your business theirs so they can
do their bit to lead you to happy," Rush retorted.

Joker clenched his teeth.

"Just to lay it all out," Rush kept at him. "You can tell
yourself, brother, that you don't wanna catch butterflies, and
that might work for you. That might stop you from takin'
a shot at gettin' what you want. I hope like fuck it doesn't.
That's up to you. This chat is part about us doin' what's right
by you and doin' what we can to open your eyes. You wanna
keep 'em closed, your call. But in the meantime, while the
Club wades in to Carissa Teodoro's problems, you keep your
shit sharp. You were actin' like a caged lion today, Joker,
ready to go for the throat of anyone that got in your way. She
didn't ask for it, but the Club's all in because they know what
you're denying. She's something to you. Since she's something to you and you're family, she's family. So, while the
brothers and the old ladies sort her shit, you got one job. Not
fuckin' that up."

"No one asked the Club to wade in," Joker pointed out.

"You did, by puttin' her name in at the garage and tellin'

the boys to give her VIP on a fuckin' twenty-year-old Toyota Tercel," Shy stated. "You can deny that too, but I wouldn't waste the effort. We saw her. We saw you. We know."

Joker had had enough.

"We done?" he asked.

"I hope you're not, but I'm guessin' we are," Shy answered.

Joker grabbed the bottle, didn't bother pouring, but threw back a long slug.

He slammed it down on the bar, and without looking at either of them, prowled to the back hall.

He went to his room, turned on the light, and put that conversation out of his head.

He might have thought about it. He might have considered butterflies.

But he didn't.

Because she didn't remember him.

He thought she did, out on I-25 when he first got close, recognized her, and she peered up at him with those big brown eyes. He thought there was something there.

Then there wasn't.

It happened again after he was done with her tire. He was sure she recognized him.

Then she didn't.

In fact, when he first approached her, she looked like she didn't know whether to scream or run away.

It was low to pretend he didn't remember her name that day. He saw her hurt. Fuck, he *felt* it. And he wouldn't do that kinda shit again.

But that was as far as he'd go.

Her life was fucked and that sucked. Her kid was cute. Unlike her, he didn't mind bikers, and he looked like her, which was good since her asshole ex was an asshole and that shit was written all over him. Joker was not going to stop the Club from taking her back. Seemed she needed good people in her life, and it was about time she had them. She'd never been good with that, a sworn member of the bitch girls without having the number one quality needed for that crew, being a bitch.

But she'd get her shit sorted. If she was looking to get laid, she'd find that too. With her bigger tits and sweet round ass, all that fucking hair, those eyes, she was the one who just had to crook her finger.

And when she was ready to find a man who wanted butterflies in his bed and wanted to keep them there, she'd find that too. Not a problem.

It just wasn't going to be him.

If she'd given him a smile and said his name, anytime it hit her while he was changing her tire that she remembered him, maybe.

But that was also doubtful.

He couldn't deny it sucked, she didn't recognize him. He couldn't deny that took a bite out of him. But he wasn't surprised.

Carson Steele was gone. The only place that name existed was on his license. He was Joker. He knew since he'd last seen her that he'd grown taller. He knew he'd put on more muscle. He didn't shave and hadn't cut his hair in years so that wasn't the same either. And he'd seen a lot, done a lot, fucked a lot, fought a lot since then. He was not the kid she knew.

But bottom line, Joker only did empty pussy, and he didn't foresee a day that was going to change. There was no denying what Tack had with Cherry, Hop with Lanie, Shy with Tabby was good. That was as clear as it could get. They got what they needed in their beds and their lives, and they didn't fuck around in letting their women know they appreciated it.

But Joker was not Tack, Hop, or Shy. No matter he turned his back on the name given him, he was Jefferson Steele's son.

And he always would be.

He took Shy and Rush's point that he didn't give back to his brothers, and they were right. That shit had to change. This was solid. It was good. It was real. It was his. He'd gone for it. He'd earned it. Finally, he had a family, one he wanted.

And maybe it was time to let back in other good things in his life.

But he was giving Carissa Teodoro the only thing he could give her.

And that was the only thing she'd get from Joker.

He moved into the room, shrugging off his cut. He was tossing it to the end of the bed when he saw someone had put Carissa's pie on the nightstand. Shoved the change, army knives, condom wrappers, and empty beer bottles out of the way and laid it there, fully intact, plastic wrap still on.

Like he couldn't stop himself, he walked right to it, tore back the wrap and dug his fingers in at the side. A huge piece covering his curved fingers broke off in his hand.

He lifted it and shoved as much as he could get in his mouth.

And went still.

Every punch he'd landed. Every kick. Every time a man went down at his feet. Every time he'd sunk his cock into tight wet. The moment Kane Allen told him he was a Chaos recruit. The day they handed him his patch.

None of it tasted as good on his tongue as that pie.

Fuck.

He sat down on the edge of his bed and ate the rest from his hand, licking his fingers.

Then he dug in and ate more.

When he was full and a third of the pie was gone, he smoothed the wrap back over it, went to the bathroom, took a shower and washed sweat and blood from his skin, the residue of used condom and empty pussy from his cock.

When he was done, he wandered back to the room, turned out the light, fell into bed, and slept with his stomach full of Carissa Teodoro's chocolate pecan goodness.

And when he woke up, he had the rest for breakfast.

CHAPTER FIVE

I Had This

Carissa

I SAT AT my kitchen bar looking with tired, puffy eyes at the items I'd laid on it.

My eyes were puffy because Tyra and Lanie had come over with dinner last night to join Elvira and me and they'd stayed awhile. They'd been sweet and supportive in a genuine way that I regrettably had little experience with, which was also why I didn't quite trust it.

Still, I'd given it to them. Everything.

Althea dying.

Aaron asking me out in high school, and since he was rich, cute, and a good football player, my acceptance, catapulting me into the popular kids, a place where I'd never really felt comfortable, but I'd stayed.

Mom dying.

The gossip that said Aaron had had sex with my supposed best friend Marley when we were juniors, doing this because I wouldn't put out. But he'd stuck with me for some reason, even though I didn't put out until the day before he took off to Massachusetts to go to college.

I also shared I ignored that gossip.

And I told them that, when he was still in the dorms his freshman year and I'd gone to visit, I'd overheard his friends snickering about a girl named Katie and how they had a plan to keep her away from Aaron while I visited.

I shared that I ignored that as well.

I also told them about Aaron saying he couldn't live without me our first summer back, so against my father's wishes, I quit UC, moved to Cambridge, got a job at The Gap and an apartment with four other girls. I tried to get into a school out there, but between struggling to pay rent and Aaron, I didn't succeed.

I further told them about the time when Aaron was in graduate school and he broke up with me for three months and dated a fellow student.

I then shared that he'd come back on bended knee, ring and everything, and we'd gotten married in a huge wedding that Aaron's mother decreed we *must have* that my father paid for but clearly didn't enjoy. And this was not because he was giving away his little girl but because he wasn't a big fan of who he was giving her to. Then I'd gone back to my job, now manager of The Gap, while Aaron finished law school.

And I'd shared we'd moved home after he graduated, home being a house that was waiting for us to move in to, seeing as his parents had given it to us for our wedding.

I'd taken a part-time job at an exclusive boutique that paid little but, regardless, they expected me to wear clothes that cost a fortune (theirs, and they only gave a ten percent discount). This employment was something Aaron's mother decreed was "acceptable" before we started our family, upon which I would quit and take care of said family (the first part I didn't agree with, the second part I did).

Aaron took his position as a junior associate in his

father's old firm, which was his grandfather's old firm, which meant, even though both of them left it to become judges, their name was still on the letterhead. And even though Aaron was a junior associate, they were fast-tracking him to partner. Giving him meaty cases. Putting him as second chair to the big names in the firm so he could learn from the best.

All of this meaning he worked brutal one-hundred-and-twenty-hour weeks, which I knew now was not true because a number of those hours he was wooing and winning Tory.

And last, I'd shared that having Travis was Aaron's idea. I might not have used it in a while, but I did have a brain, which meant I had an inkling things with my husband were not right. I would never have brought a child into that.

But he was all about us, our future, our family, making strong stronger (his words), one of those times I did not get—and got it less now that it was over—when he was so devoted to me it didn't seem real.

Maybe because it wasn't.

But it was beautiful.

So I again turned a blind eye and gave in, quitting my job when I started showing, and shortly after ending up in hell.

I told them all that and more.

So I'd cried a lot. Lanie had cried with me. Tyra teared up a few times.

Elvira just looked angry.

If she wasn't so funny and friendly and nice, she would scare me. Luckily, she was all those things (but also scary).

They left and now my eyes were tired because after they did, even though it felt good to get it out, share it with people who seemed to care, I didn't sleep.

I didn't because I didn't want to do bad things God would frown on (seriously) to keep Travis.

Not unless it was a last resort.

And it wasn't.

Not yet.

That was why I'd put out the stuff on my bar.

The platinum necklace with the quarter-carat diamond pendant Dad had given me. The pearl and diamond earrings my grandmother gave me to wear to my wedding. The emerald and diamond tennis bracelet Aaron's parents gave me when we'd become engaged. The gold bangles Aaron bought me for Valentine's Day every year (which also was our wedding anniversary—cliché, now embarrassing, what with me being a hopeless romantic with emphasis on *hopeless*).

And my engagement and wedding rings.

I would start with selling the useless stuff Aaron and his folks gave me and then move on to the others when needed.

And I'd find an attorney who would take my case, be ruthless, get me the child support that *Travis* deserved, and make it clear to Aaron I was not going anywhere.

If that ran out, I'd find other ways, selling the furniture I got in the divorce that I had in storage (well, Dad did, since he paid for the unit) being one of them.

And if it came to it, I'd get on my knees.

I was just going to exhaust all my other options first.

But I wasn't going to lose my son.

On this thought, there was a knock on the door and I looked to it.

I didn't need company and I couldn't comprehend how I'd have any. No one visited me.

But I'd left my car at Ride and I had a day shift at the store. I needed to take the bus. I'd looked up the route and one dropped off about three blocks from the store. But I had no idea how long it took. My normal commute was twenty minutes but I'd added on another thirty just in case.

I needed to get going.

I slid off the stool and went to the door. I looked through the peephole, saw coverall guy from Ride was standing outside (again in coveralls), and with some confusion, I opened the door.

"Hey," I greeted, ready to tell him he could have called with the estimate. I hadn't exactly given him my number, but Tyra was office manager at Ride and I'd given it to her.

He spoke before I could.

"Car's downstairs."

He held out my keys and my hand automatically lifted to take them.

He dropped them in my palm and continued talking, "New tires. New tranny. New plugs. New shocks. New exhaust. Oil change. Oh, and new wipers. Boys filled the tank and detailed it too. You're all good."

I blinked at him. "Tranny?"

"Transmission."

Transmission?

What on earth?

Those cost a fortune.

"Transmission?" I whispered.

"Yeah."

"I . . . uh, asked about an estimate—"

He interrupted me, "On Ride."

"Sorry?"

"No charge. Ride is covering it. Means Chaos is covering it. You don't owe anything."

How?

Why?

What?

He looked behind him, then to me. "Later," he said, and without waiting for my farewell, or one of the many other things I could have said, he jogged down the open air walk that ran outside our apartment building.

I watched and was about to call out to him when my phone rang. He was already at the stairs at the L to the building and I had a phone ringing so I closed the door, locked it, and hurried to my phone on the kitchen bar.

The display said *Unknown Caller*.

I took it anyway.

"Hello?"

"May I speak with Carissa Teodoro?" a businesslike woman's voice asked.

"This is she."

"Right, hold for Ms. Howard, please."

"Sorry? Who?" I asked.

"Ms. Howard. Of Gustafson, Howard and Pierce. Hold please."

Oh no. I didn't like this.

Did Aaron find a new way to make trouble for me?

Gustafson, Howard and Pierce sounded like an attorney firm. I didn't need any more of those in my life, except the one selling off Aaron's false tokens of love was going to buy me.

"Ms. Teodoro," a more businesslike woman's voice said.

"Uh...yes," I replied.

"Right. Hello. I'm Angelique Howard, but my clients call me Angie."

"Well, okay," I got in before she kept speaking.

"I received a call from Mr. Allen this morning so I'm introducing myself before I send you back to my assistant. She'll take the details of your last attorney so we can contact them to get your files. When we get them, I'll go over what's been happening with your former husband and construct a strategy."

I didn't know what was going on so I started with the easiest part first.

"Mr. Allen?" I asked.

"Yes. Mr. Allen. Kane Allen. Operating manager of Ride Auto Stores and Custom Design. We're on retainer with them, and my specialty is family law. So I'll be taking care of you."

I didn't speak because I couldn't.

She didn't need me to. She wasn't finished.

"Once I see what's going on, I'll ask Leanne to contact you and we'll set a meeting so we can meet face to face and talk about what we're going to do going forward. Are you all right with that?"

No. I wasn't. Mostly because I had no idea what was happening.

"I, well, I have to admit, Ms. Howard—" I began.

"Angie."

"Right, Angie," I said quickly. "I have to admit, I don't know what's going on."

"Mr. Allen didn't speak to you?"

He didn't. I wasn't even sure I knew who he was.

"Not really," I replied.

"Okay, then, Chaos is utilizing their retainer agreement with us to look into what Mr. Neiland has been doing to you. I'll say from the little I've heard that it sounds suspicious. To be honest, though I think this is something that won't surprise you, Neiland and Belkirk have been around so long, they started the good ole boys network in Denver and they enjoy their status as founding members. Which, I'll share, I find annoying. Thus, I'm going to enjoy digging into this one."

"I—"

"So, to end, it's all in good hands. Just tell Leanne where we can get your files and I'll start."

"Well—"

She spoke over me. "Nice meeting you, even on the phone. Have a good day."

I heard nothing until I heard the first voice come back and say, "Hello again, Ms. Teodoro. I'm ready to take down the information about your old firm."

"I think I need to speak with Mr. Allen first," I shared.

"Right. Okay. You do that. In the meantime, give me your last attorney's details. Angie is raring to go on this and she's had me clear her afternoon to do it."

Clear her afternoon?

This afternoon?

"Okay, then perhaps I should speak with Ms. How...I mean, Angie again for a moment," I tried.

"She's already on another call."

I drew in a deep breath.

"Ms. Teodoro, sorry to rush you," Leanne said when I took my time doing that. "But Angie wants these files by this afternoon so I have to get cracking. Your old attorney's name?"

I let out that breath, telling her my old attorney's name.

"Good man," she muttered. "Not as good as Angie. Okay!" she cried brightly. "We're on it. Have a lovely day, Ms. Teodoro."

She didn't wait for me to share that sentiment. She disconnected.

I stared at my phone, wondering how they even got my number.

Then I thought Tyra. Or Lanie. Maybe Elvira. We'd shared numbers last night. Maybe that was it.

I felt something biting into my palm so I lifted it and looked to it.

My car keys.

New tranny.

I looked to the door.

Kane Allen. Operating manager of Ride Auto Stores and

*Custom Design. We're on retainer with them, and my spe-
cialty is family law. So I'll be taking care of you.*

Kane Allen, Operating Manager of Ride Auto Stores and
Custom Design.

And Joker was a member of the Club that ran said business.

Something unpleasant slid through me. And after yesterday, baking the pie for Joker, having him set it aside like
it meant nothing, the call from Tory, my son being sick, my
mortification in front of five people I didn't know (and Joker)
caused by me shrieking like a lunatic, breaking down in front
of three women I also did not know, all that Aaron was doing
to me, I didn't cry (again). I didn't feel mortified (again).

I got mad.

There was nothing I could do about that mad. Not right
then. I had to get to work.

And I was hoping Travis would feel well enough that
Tory could bring him in to see me.

After that, I'd do something about that mad.

Definitely.

*   *   *

Four hours later, Tory did bring Travis. I was at my register
and I saw them come in.

My heart leaped. My boy looked pale but he also looked
right to me, stretched his arms my way, and screeched
(hoarsely).

He wanted his momma.

My heart warmed as my throat tickled.

My manager, Sharon, who was lovely and who also knew
about Travis being sick (and some about Aaron being a jerk),
let me finish with my customer and take my lunch.

My grocery store was LeLane's. It was a gourmet food
market. It had all the things normal stores had, like mustard

and sour cream, but they were much more expensive. It also had a bunch of other stuff normal stores didn't have, like live lobsters, a cheese case that would make any Frenchman sigh with delight (I guessed, I'd never met a Frenchman), and the like. They had six of them in the Denver area, one in Boulder, one in Fort Collins, two in Colorado Springs, and two in Pueblo.

It was family owned. They took care of their customers and employees, and they did the latter by giving great benefits, being nice about when you took your hours (for instance, they did their best to let me work days when I had Travis so I didn't have to pay extra for after-hours daycare), and they paid relatively well.

But they were expensive. They also had employee discounts, but I didn't use them. Unless Travis was consuming it, I went generic all the way.

Tory, however, didn't blink at shopping at LeLane's. Which was what she did to pass her time while I fed my boy and spent time with him in the break room.

When my thirty minutes was up, I hid my despair from my son and trudged out.

Tory was waiting for me by her Mercedes.

"Can I strap him in?" I asked.

She nodded and moved away from the passenger side door, but did it opening it for me.

I put him in, gave him tickles, made him giggle, then kissed him right on his wet, open lips.

That made him grab my hair.

I fought back tears. "See you in a few days, sweetie pie."

"Goo gah!"

I grinned at him, kissed his mouth again, then his cheek, his head, and having to get to work but preferring to endure torture, I pulled away.

I looked to Tory. "Thanks."

"I'm glad you got time with him."

I tried not to pay a lot of attention to her but right then I did.

She looked strange. Not haughty (which wasn't often, but it happened). Not happy (which was often). Not indifferent (also often).

Troubled.

I didn't ask. I didn't want to know. But if I had to guess, she might be twenty-one and slim and beautiful with an up-and-coming attorney in one of the most established, wealthiest firms in Denver as her fiancé, but what was happening with Aaron and me couldn't escape her.

I was hardly older than her and I'd been replaced. Then shoved to the ground. Then kicked when I was down. And last, kept from my son when he was sick.

If she didn't hold Aaron (and she wouldn't, she'd be me in a few years), my guess was it was beginning to dawn on her she could face the same.

It was unkind, but that wasn't my problem.

My problem was I had to leave my son, go to work, and after work, go to Ride.

"Thanks again and take care of yourself," I mumbled, closing the door on my son, giving him a finger wave and a big smile through the window while he stared up at me, looking like he did when he was about ready to start crying.

"Yeah, you too," Tory replied as I turned quickly and rushed back to the store.

*　　*　　*

Four and a half hours after that, I turned into Ride.

I again didn't park in the parking spaces by the store. I also didn't park at one of the big bays of the garage.

I parked outside the Compound in the open space by the line of bikes.

I grabbed my purse, threw out my navy Converse-shod foot, pulled my khaki-clad bottom out of the seat, and slammed the door. I settled my purse on my shoulder and marched to the double doors of the Compound.

I threw one open, entered and blinked quickly against the sudden dark, still walking in, my eyes going to the bar.

It came into focus and I saw it was my lucky day.

Among four other men, Joker was sitting there.

"Yo, babe," one of them called.

"Yo," I replied haughtily, my eyes never leaving Joker. Then I didn't waste a second. "Joker, I'm sorry to bother you again, but can I have a word?"

"Travis okay?" Joker asked instantly.

It was sweet he asked and it was sweet it was instant.

But I wasn't in a sweet mood.

"Yes, I saw him at lunch. He's pale and has a bit of a cough still, but he's fine. Now can we speak?"

"Aren't we speaking?" he asked.

"In private." It came out almost as a snap.

At that moment, I felt the mood and looked to the other three men. None of whom I'd met or seen. All of whom looked curious, and didn't hide it, and immensely amused, and didn't hide that either.

The latter was the mood in the room.

That also didn't embarrass me.

It didn't make sense either. I didn't find anything funny.

"Why don't you take her to your room, Joke?" one of the guys suggested.

"Yes, let's go there," I agreed.

There was a truncated guffaw, which was truncated when I looked to the man who was emitting it. He pressed his lips together, but the minute he did, his eyes got huge, like biting back his humor was going to make his head explode.

"Hall," Joker said and I looked to him.

"Sorry?"

He was off his stool and jerking his head toward the back. "My room's off the hall."

"Right," I said shortly, straightened my shoulders, and I very well might have flipped my ponytail as I whipped around and marched to the door that Joker had come out of yesterday. I did this not knowing that my marching had a lot of bounce associated with it. But I felt the eyes, so I did it very much knowing they all followed.

I made it to the doorway and heard Joker direct, "Left."

I went left.

"Stop," he ordered when I was two doors down from the end.

It wasn't surprising it was a long hall considering it was a long building. But it was surprising the number of doors off it.

I stood outside one that was open and peered in.

It wasn't big, it wasn't tiny.

What it was was *filthy*.

I swallowed.

I sensed Joker close and looked to see he was standing on the opposite side of the door waving an arm toward the room.

I marched in.

He came in after me.

"What's on your mind?" he asked as I was turning and saw he was closing the door.

"Your room needs to be cleaned," I announced.

"What?" he asked.

"Your room," I threw out an arm, "it needs to be cleaned."

"I'll get my maids on that," he muttered, then asked, "Is that why you needed to speak in private?"

I shook my head, restraightened my shoulders, and declared, "I have a new tranny."

His brows shot together. "Say again?"

I jerked a thumb to myself. "I have a new tranny."

He shook his head. "I don't get it."

"A new transmission."

"Know what a tranny is," he stated.

"I have one," I told him.

"Know that too. We don't deal with Tercels but the boys got a lock on one, loaded it up in yours last night."

"Why?" I asked.

"Why?" he parroted.

"Yes," I snapped. "Why?"

"'Cause you needed one."

"I'm sure I did," I retorted. "That still doesn't explain why I have one." Before he could say anything, I added, "A *free* one."

He leaned slightly back while crossing his arms on his chest.

It was then I noticed his chest was rather well-defined—as could be seen through his tight, black T-shirt—and his arms were even more well-defined. The biceps bulged and his forearms were all sinewy.

"You got a couple grand to lay down on a new transmission?" he asked and my gaze shot from its sudden rapt contemplation of his arms to his eyes.

"If I had a couple thousand dollars to lay down, as you put it, on a new transmission, I'd buy a new car," I returned.

"And that would be a good call," he muttered.

I ignored that. "But at this moment I don't need a new car since I have a new transmission, new tires, new wipers, an oil change, it's a far sight cleaner than this room and smells like pine."

"What? Did you want new car smell?" he asked and I stared.

Then I cried, "No! I didn't want my car detailed. For *free*."

He shook his head. "I don't get your problem, Butterfly."

I ignored the nickname, which was definitely cute and made me feel nice, and declared, "I'm not a charity case, Joker."

"I know that," he returned.

"Then why do I have a spick-and-span car that runs better than when I bought it and a new attorney that's taking my case through retainer with the Chaos Motorcycle Gang?"

"Club."

"Sorry?"

"We're a club, not a gang."

"There's a difference?"

"Absolutely."

I shut my mouth since his answer was so firm, it was granite.

He didn't keep his mouth shut.

"Listen, you might have an idea about bikers. And in some cases, that idea would be on the mark. In the case of Chaos, boys here, they don't like women to get jacked around by assholes. You lose it in our common room when you're gettin' jacked around by an asshole, and a kid's involved, then their old ladies take your back, they're gonna wade in. The Club waded in. That means you got people lookin' after you. My advice, don't bounce in here with your attitude and get shitty about it. Let 'em do it. You fight it, they'll still do it and you'll lose the face you're tryin' right now to save because you'll have no choice but to give in."

"That's ridiculous," I declared.

"That's Chaos," he retorted.

"They barely know me. In fact, outside of you, none of the men actually do," I told him.

"Don't matter. You walked in with homemade pie. You strutted your ass right onto Chaos with homemade pie for a brother who did you a good deed. Then you got kicked in the teeth by your ex. No good woman gets kicked in the teeth on Chaos without retribution. He's gonna feel our displeasure, and that's just the way it is. Again, don't fight it."

Although something about that made me feel something that was not unpleasant in the slightest, still, I couldn't let it go.

"That's slightly insane."

"That's our world," he returned. "We claim you, you're ours. No goin' back."

I shook my head in confusion. "You've claimed me?"

"I haven't. Chaos has."

That didn't feel pleasant. It kind of hurt.

"Listen," he kept going, "I saw the way you looked at me when I stopped to deal with your tire. That's the way a lot of people look at my brothers and me. They make assumptions. They judge. You mighta done that for a second, but then you let that go. After that, you showed here, and I'll tell you straight up, unless they want auto parts or a custom ride, no one shows here. Definitely not with pie. Not unless she's a biker groupie, a girl who gets off on rough trade, or a woman fit for the life of an old lady who's throwin' her hat in the ring. And none of those bitches bring pie. We judge right back and that would be, we judge people who judge us or live narrow lives or have sticks up their asses. But people who open themselves to our world without bullshit coloring it, we let in. You met Elvira. She's one of 'em. Now, you're another. Anything threatened Elvira, every man who has a patch would throw down to protect her. As insane as you think that is, yesterday, you became Elvira but in a cute butterfly dress and sexy shoes."

He thought my dress was cute.

And my shoes were sexy.

Wow.

"I had my son with me and I was in an uncertain situation," I stated, feeling the need to explain my first reaction to him, which unfortunately he didn't miss. "Any man who approached us when we had our flat—"

"I hear you. I get you," he interrupted me quietly. "You still did it because I'm a biker."

That was true, regrettably.

So there was nothing else to say but what he deserved to hear.

So I said it.

"I'm sorry."

" 'Preciated. Now, we done?"

His curtness was both annoying and upsetting.

Further, I wasn't done.

"I don't judge you," I told him. "Or your people. They're all very nice."

"Glad you think that way seein' as you're adopted. Now, we done?"

No, I wasn't *done*.

"As lovely as you're all being, I'm uncomfortable about taking help from people I don't know."

"Get over it."

I waited but that was it.

Get over it.

"I'm not sure I can," I shared.

"Try harder," he replied.

I stared at him.

Then I glared.

He watched one turn into the other and the second it did, he muttered, "Fuck, we're not done."

"No we aren't!" I yelled. "Your people practically bought me a new car and got me free legal counsel!"

"Carissa, do you know what a retainer is?" he asked.

"Yes," I snapped.

"Then you know this Club gave that firm a shit ton of money to be at our service. Luckily, we don't need them often, so they sit on our money and do fuck-all. It's no skin off our nose and actually is a good thing they're doin' somethin' to earn that pay."

This made sense so I let that go, for now.

"You shouldn't curse," I admonished sharply.

His head jerked back. "Seriously?"

"I'm a lady. It's rude."

"You are a lady but I'm a biker and I do what the fuck I want," he shot back.

"Do you speak like that in front of Tyra?"

"You've known her a day, Butterfly. She's got a mouth on her too."

Women often cursed so he was probably right.

I tried a different tack. "Do you speak like that in front of your mother?"

His face went hard and he pierced me direct through the heart with his reply.

"Don't have one. Never did. She took off before I could crawl. So no. I don't. 'Cause I never got the chance."

I fell silent, feeling it deeply, but not believing it because I couldn't fathom it.

Travis was scooting around like a crazy boy. Which would mean Joker's mother left before he was Travis's age.

"How could that be?" I whispered.

"You know," he replied bitingly, uncrossing one arm and jabbing a finger my way, but his next words caused no harm. Far from it. "That right there is why Chaos has thrown down for you. That look on your face. Those words outta your mouth." He crossed his arm back on his chest. "You got no clue how a woman could do that to her kid. We know that your kid needs that kind of woman in his life. Fuckin' let it go and fuckin' let us help, for fuck's sake."

"That's three f-words in one sentence," I said quietly.

He threw out both hands. "Who gives a fuck?"

His response was funny and I wanted to laugh. I really did.

And I didn't remember the last time I laughed at anything that wasn't something that Travis did.

"Now, are we fuckin' done?" he asked.

"No," I whispered my answer.

"What now?" he clipped, planting his hands on his hips.

I watched him do this.

His knuckles were all scabbed. But his fingers were long, not graceful, but handsome. They were a working man's hands. They'd be rough. I could even see grease stains around the nail beds.

Something about that caused something to happen inside me.

My focus shifted from his hands to his crotch. His jeans were faded. The area around his crotch more faded.

Up I went to a black belt with silver rivets in it that had seen some wear, the length beyond the clasp dangling from a belt loop to the side in a supple way, the leather not close to stiff.

Up his flat belly to his wide chest and broad shoulders and bulging arms.

And up to his long black hair that looked thick, messy, had a lot of wave and brushed his shoulders. His beard wasn't bushy, it was trimmed, but it was about two days away from being unkempt.

He was tall.

He was annoyed.

I felt the latter because he was the kind of man whose mood altered a room and I understood this because I was right then experiencing it. But I also knew it wasn't just that or that we were the only ones in the room and having the conversation that was making him annoyed so of course I'd be feeling it.

It was him. He had that kind of power behind his personality.

I shifted my eyes to his.

Steel. A strange flat color that seemed impenetrable.

And suddenly I had a new dream. One that didn't involve motherhood, cookies, doing laundry, and being a soccer mom.

One that centered around penetrating the impenetrable.

"So? What?" he prompted irately.

At his words, I flew across the room.

He had the chance to go back on a boot but that was all he had before my body slammed into his, my hands went to either side of his head and I lifted up on tiptoe as I yanked him down.

Then I pressed my lips hard against his.

A breath later, something strange happened.

Strange and wondrous.

His arms closed around me, and if I could think of anything, I'd worry about the state of my ribs.

But I couldn't think of anything because his tongue spiked into my mouth and my world changed.

My entire world.

I didn't have a dead sister.

I didn't have a dead mother.

I didn't have a lonely father looking after his mother, who was addled with Alzheimer's disease.

I didn't have an ex-husband, who I once loved who I thought would cherish and protect me and help me build my dream, but now was making my life a misery and trying to take my son away from me.

I had *this*.

All of it. All the biker named Joker gave me by holding me so tight it was a pain that hurt so good and who was invading my mouth with his tongue in a way that stated clearly he could do it for a lifetime and never get enough.

My hands left his head so I could curve my arms around his shoulders as I pressed closer.

In return, one of his hands slid up my spine. He pulled out my ponytail holder and drove his fingers into my hair, cupping the back of my head, tilting it one way while he slanted his the other. He deepened the kiss in an intoxicating way while his other hand glided down and cupped one cheek of my behind.

That felt *good*.

He shuffled me back.

I went with him.

We kept kissing.

Then he turned quickly and we were falling.

He landed on his back on the bed. I landed on him but barely had the opportunity to experience the dizzying beauty of the long length of his hard frame under mine before I was given more beauty when he rolled me and I had the weight of his hard frame pressing mine into the bed.

His hand left my bottom and went up, fingers yanking at my navy LeLane's polo shirt, pulling it from my khakis, and then I had its heat, skin against skin.

I was right.

His hands were rough.

It felt so miraculous, I whimpered against his tongue.

The instant I did, he was gone.

I lay on the bed, blinking up at him as he stood over me, a biker god with long, messy hair, a beard that made the skin around my mouth sting gloriously, his chest rising and falling in a way I wanted to *feel*, the steel of his eyes closed against me.

"Joker—" I whispered.

"Took that too far. That's on me. You don't try that shit again, it won't happen again. But you try it again, what happens will be on you."

I had the highly unusual and electrifying desire to try it again and again and *again*.

"You need to get laid, do me and my brothers a favor, find it off Chaos. And you throw Chaos's help in our face, that's your call," he clipped. "But you do that shit, you're a fool."

He said not another word.

He turned on his boot and stalked out, slamming the door behind him.

CHAPTER SIX

Free

Carissa

"WHAT THE FUCK?"

I looked up, tossing a ringlet back that had escaped the red bandana I had tied (rather adorably, I thought) around my head to hold my thick mess of curly hair back, and saw Joker at the doorway to his room, looking unhappy.

The ringlet fell in my eye.

Joker's eyes narrowed on it.

"What the fuck are you doin'?" he asked when I didn't answer his opening question.

"That's twenty cents," I returned.

"Hunh?" he grunted.

"Regular curse words are a nickel," I told him. "*Bad* curse words are a dime. Everyone knows the f-word is a bad one and since, starting now, you're paying me every time you curse, that's twenty cents you owe me." I shook my hair, bandana and all. "I'll give it to charity or something. The way you cuss, we'll probably be able to build a homeless shelter in a week."

He didn't look any less unhappy when I finished talking but he did take two steps toward me.

"Carissa, what are you doin' in my room?"

It was the day after my kiss with Joker. A day where I thought of nothing but Joker...and that kiss. A day and a sleepless night where I thought long and hard about it and made a decision.

I wanted more.

There were a variety of reasons for this.

He was handsome. He wasn't my type, but really, who knew what my type was? All I'd had was Aaron, and I'd found Aaron was definitely the wrong type for me.

So maybe Joker *was* my type.

He was also nice. Sure, he cursed constantly and in the beginning he'd seemed thoughtless about my pie, but he and his friends had done a variety of good things for me, all of them huge. But it started with him, which meant *he* started it.

Further, once he'd prowled out after our kiss, I'd seen the pie plate in his room on his nightstand.

The *empty* pie plate.

So he *had* liked my pie.

And last, there was that kiss.

Truthfully, the rest could go away and the kiss could remain and it was so good, I'd still want more.

He acted like he could take me or leave me, but even if I'd only ever kissed Aaron, I'd kissed him a lot and we'd *never* (not ever) shared a kiss like that.

I didn't know what was holding Joker back. I may only have had Aaron as experience but there was no way to miss Joker had been into that kiss. A woman throws herself in your arms and you don't want that, you push her away. You don't stick your tongue in her mouth, redefine her world, and shuffle her straight to your bed.

He liked it as much as me.

But I didn't care what was holding him back. I was just going to do whatever I could to put a stop to it.

I looked around his room that now had a stripped bed, four pillowcases full of dirty clothes, a box filled with bottles to recycle, and two huge black trash bags filled with trash. Then I looked down at me, wearing my red Converse, my cuffed boyfriend jeans with the holes in the knees (and up the thighs), my cute tee that declared my devotion to Betty Boop, and the Windex and used paper towel in my hands.

After that, I looked to him. "I'm cleaning your room."

"For fuck's sake, why?" he bit out.

"That's thirty cents," I returned disapprovingly.

He didn't respond. What he did was lean his torso slightly back, wrap his fingers around his hips, and scowl at me in a scary way that again got me talking.

"Yesterday, you were right," I informed him, lifting my chin. "I would be a fool not to take what you and your friends are offering. It's extraordinarily kind, *too* kind, but I'm in a pickle. A *bad* pickle. I need help. I have no friends. My dad is in Nebraska taking care of my gramma, and I don't want him worried about me. And my options are limited. But bottom line, I'm concerned about my son. I'm concerned about his father's behavior, a father who would be raising him and clearly doesn't know right from wrong or how to be respectful. Now, I have to do everything I can to make certain my son has a good upbringing, that being from *me*."

I lifted the Windex bottle and jerked a thumb at myself on the "me" and kept talking.

"So I'm taking you up on your offer," I declared. "However, the generosity of it makes me uncomfortable, so I'll be doing what I can to give back. And since you started all this, you're up first. You need your room cleaned because no one should live like this." I threw out the Windex bottle. "So I'm cleaning your room."

"I don't want you to clean my room," he returned.

"I didn't want people I don't know to offer assistance I need. And further I didn't want to have a life where I was in a position that I was forced to take that assistance no matter how embarrassing my needing it was. But we can't always get what we want," I retorted.

His scowl got scarier. "What's happenin' to you is not embarrassing."

I held his eyes and quieted my voice. "You're wrong about that, Joker."

His jaw flexed.

I cleared my throat and straightened my shoulders, taking us back to the point. "But I'm taking it and doing that. I'm also giving back. With you first."

"You're not cleaning my room," he declared.

I shook my head. "Too late. It's half done."

That wasn't exactly the truth. His room was really filthy. I still had a lot of work to do. Also, I had to cart his stuff to the Laundromat but I had a shift so I'd have to do that the next day. Therefore, I wouldn't be completely done until tomorrow.

"I don't want you goin' through my stuff," he kept at it.

I felt warmth creep up my neck but I ignored it and what he said, and returned, "Speaking of your stuff. I found an envelope full of money in a pair of your jeans that were on the floor in the bathroom. It's there." I motioned to his dresser. "And I'll, uh...commend you on your obvious commitment to safe sex. Though, the unwrapped prophylactics are now in the drawer of your nightstand, not scattered among the wrappers on top. Easier access since you won't have to sort through the wrappers to find a new one."

At that, he looked fit to be tied, or fit to tie *me*, and he leaned slightly toward me.

"That right there is why—"

"I'm doing it, Joker," I whispered. "You can be all scary and scowl at me and get angry, but I'm doing it. I'm doing whatever I have to do to feel better about what you're all doing for me. I have to." I drew in breath and finished, "And I'm asking you to let me."

His jaw flexed again.

I watched his jaw flex, thinking two things.

One, for some reason, I found that appealing.

Two, I didn't feel even a little bad about lying by omission by not including the fact that I was there to do other things as well. Those including being around him, attempting to flirt with him, and doing everything I could to get him to kiss me again and/or ask me out on a date (with that last, I was hoping for *and*).

Of course, I did want to give back to him and the Club. Definitely.

It was just that I wanted other things too.

We stared at each other, and this lasted a long time. Long enough for me to have a strong urge to end the staring contest by running to him and throwing myself in his arms, but this time, not allowing him to let me go.

Unfortunately, when I was just about ready to do that, he broke the contest, asking, "My clothes in those cases?"

"Yes," I answered, lifting my hand with the paper towel in it, palm out. "And I'm doing your laundry and I'm not taking any guff from you about it."

"You got a washer and dryer at your house?"

"No, I'm taking it to the Laundromat."

He went scary again. "Butterfly, you are not *payin'* to do my laundry."

"I absolutely am," I returned.

"You gotta do it to make your shit feel better. Do it. But there's a washer and dryer here. Off the side hall, at the back."

"That's thirty-five cents," I told him, not sharing my relief that they had a washer and dryer. That would save me tons of time, not to mention money.

He crossed his arms on his chest. "You do know with this shit you're pullin' that no way in fuck I'm ever gonna stop and help a woman change her tire again."

"That's fifty cents."

He stared at me.

Then he turned on his boot and stalked to the door, muttering, "Fuck me."

"Sixty cents!" I yelled at his back.

But he was gone.

I stared at the door, wondering how that went.

There were no kisses or even heated glances (outside angry heat, but that didn't count). He didn't even act like he was talking to a woman he'd kissed (thoroughly) just the day before.

That was bad.

But he'd given in relatively easily to me cleaning his space and doing his laundry.

However, this could be so he wouldn't have to be around me in order to fight about it.

That would also be bad.

But it could be he liked the idea of me hanging around because he liked the idea of me being around. It also could be, since he obviously didn't have anyone to look after him, and didn't look after himself, he liked the idea of someone doing that.

Before I could make my decision about which it was, good or bad, I focused on the door I was staring at distractedly.

One of the men who'd been sitting with Joker at the bar

the day before was standing in it. He was older than Joker. Stockier. He had slivers of gray in his dark brown hair that was shorter than Joker's but still messy. He had what I was approximating as nine weeks of stubble, also silvered with gray.

He also had his eyes on me.

"Uh, hi," I called.

"Hey," he replied.

"I saw you yesterday but I didn't introduce myself. I'm Carissa."

"High."

"Um..." I tipped my head to the side, wondering why he was greeting me again. "Hi."

"No, babe. That's my name. High. With a *g* and *h*."

"Oh!" I grinned at him. "*High*. Right, hello, High. Nice to meet you."

He didn't return that sentiment.

He gave me a look that made me brace and said in a quiet voice, "Don't give up."

I felt my head jerk in confusion. "On Joker's room?"

"On Joker," he stated.

I felt my eyes go round.

He disappeared.

* * *

The next day, I walked to the door of the Compound wondering if I'd made the right decision.

I'd come before my shift at LeLane's, and after I did what I had to do, I had to go straight to LeLane's. So I was in my LeLane's uniform of polo, khakis, and Converse (though, LeLane's didn't require Converse, that was my nod to style because everyone knew Converse rocked).

Joker had mentioned he'd thought my dress was cute and my heels were sexy. I didn't have an excess of cute dresses and shoes (well, I did, but none of them fit me anymore), but I was a cute-dress-and-heels type of girl. I had more than just the butterfly one that fit me.

But this was me. The new me. A single mom, grocery store clerk in khakis and Converse. And if he asked me out on a date and eventually kissed me again, this would be the woman he'd be kissing.

I hadn't been about me. Not for a long time. Maybe never. I had been coasting in life for so long, I actually didn't know who *me* was.

I just knew right now most of me was being a mom and a grocery store clerk.

So the LeLane's uniform it was.

I threw open the door and kept walking in as my eyes adjusted to the dim.

They'd just done that when I heard, "Fuck, you movin' in?"

I turned my head right and saw Joker at the bar with three other people. One was the lanky guy from the first time I'd been there. The other two were a man and woman. Both looked about my age. Both looked a lot like the goateed man I met the first time I was there. They had to be brother and sister. Though, she was with the lanky guy. I knew this by the casual way his arm was flung around her shoulders.

They all were outside the bar, Joker was behind it.

"I believe the tally is now seventy cents," I returned.

Joker put both hands to the bar, spread wide, leaned his weight into them, and dropped his head.

He was handsome even in a pose of frustration.

"Seventy cents?" the girl asked, and I stopped taking in Joker's handsome and looked to her.

"He owes me a nickel for every curse word, a dime for every *bad* one," I explained.

At my explanation, without hesitation, the girl burst into

laughter. It took a moment for the two guys to process it, in fact, they looked so surprised by this, I wasn't sure they were going to process it. But once they did, they joined her.

Joker lifted his head and glowered at them before he turned that glower to me.

"Clean sheets, clean clothes, Butterfly," he stated irately. "So you're here today why?"

I stopped by their huddle and I did it with my gaze on him.

"First, would you introduce me?" I requested.

"Shy, Tab, Rush," he said shortly and rudely. "Now why you here?"

I ignored his rude introductions and looked to the group.

"We didn't officially meet. I'm Shy," lanky guy said, also ignoring Joker's rudeness.

"Hey," I replied.

"Tab," the girl said. "Tabby, Tabitha, take your pick."

I nodded, smiling, "Lovely to meet you. I'm Carissa."

She smiled back.

"Rush," the last one said. "Tab's my sister. Tack's my dad."

I nodded again. "Right, I can see the family resemblance. Lovely to meet you too."

He smiled as well.

I was already smiling.

"Yo," Joker called and I looked his way again. "You wanna answer my question?"

I put my hand on the bar. "I'm getting the impression you don't want me here."

"Seein' as yesterday you went through my shit, *all a' it*, I'm just needin' to know what to brace for today," he replied.

"I hardly need to clean your room every day, Joker," I retorted.

"Least there's that," he muttered.

"I'm actually here to meet Big Petey," I shared. "Tyra

phoned and said he looks after her sons and might be willing to take on Travis at a reduced rate to what my daycare center charges."

"Reduced," Rush muttered and my eyes went to him.

"Yes," I confirmed. "It'd help out a lot. Daycare is very expensive."

"Big Petey loves kids," Tabby told me. "Ty-Ty is my step-mom, and Ride and Cut are my baby bros. Pete looks after them all the time. He loves it. They love him."

I had to admit, that was a huge relief. I needed a break on the daycare center fees and therefore was there to explore that option, but I had to admit to some trepidation about what biker childcare would entail.

Though her little brothers' names surprised me. They shouldn't have, considering the ones I'd heard before, Joker, High, Shy, Rush, etc., but they did.

"Just so you're prepared, Butterfly, *reduced* means *free*," Joker said.

I looked to him. "Sorry?"

"Reduced would be free," Shy reiterated. "You can offer, but Pete won't take your money."

Not this again.

"But—" I started.

"Don't fight it," Tabby said in a soft voice that had a tone in it that got my total attention. "He's old enough to be a grandfather, but his daughter died before she could give him grandbabies. He loves kids. Loved his daughter. It messed him up losing her, as it would. But it wasn't helped that when he lost her, any chance of his legacy died with her. He's a woman's man, and I mean that in the sense you would guess I mean, but also in the sense that he's a man with one child, that child was a girl, he loved her to pieces, and she's gone. He'll like you. He'll wanna help out like he'd wanna help his daughter if she needed it. And if he offers it, you can give him lip for a while, but accept it. You're doin' more for him than he is for you. Seriously."

My voice was also soft when I replied, "That's very sad. And I thank you for sharing it. But he really would be doing more for me than I would for him."

"Not to be blunt, babe, but you have a live son, he has a dead daughter. Do you think that's true?" Tabby asked.

I looked into her eyes a moment, feeling my heart twist at her words, before I whispered, "Point taken."

She grinned. "Good."

"How's the car runnin'?" Shy asked.

I turned to him and smiled brightly. "Good. Thank you for that. It was really—"

"Don't mention it," he cut me off, firm but gentle.

I shut up.

"When you get your kid back?" Rush asked.

"Monday," I answered.

"We're havin' a thing here, Compound, Saturday night. You're welcome," he told me and my world lit.

A thing, I was guessing, meant a party.

A party that Joker would likely attend. And no one could be surly at a party.

"Really?" I asked excitedly.

I would have sworn I heard Joker make a noise like a swallowed grunt but I ignored him.

"Yeah," Rush answered over Joker's noise.

"That'd be so cool, you could come," Tabby said. "It gets rowdy but it's a great time. And we girls need to let our hair down, you hear me?"

I heard her, she was right in front of me.

But after I heard her, it hit me and my world went dark.

"I work the afternoon shift. I don't get off until late."

She grinned again. "Babe, this is a biker party. It'll go until everyone is hooked up or passed out. Come whenever."

I had a feeling their rowdy would be well beyond my rowdy since I'd never really done rowdy. But I also hoped Joker would be there, and in a party mood, so I was going to have an open mind and I was most definitely going to show.

"Do you work every day?"

I turned my head to Joker since he asked the question.

"Yes," I replied.

"*Every* day?" he pushed.

"Yes," I repeated. Then explained, "Mostly. See, my manager, Sharon, is super nice. She tries to schedule me for as many days on as she can when Aaron has Travis, so I can have my days off when I have him so I can save on daycare and I want to spend my time with him. And in return, I take afternoon and evening shifts when Travis is with his dad because people prefer day shifts."

"So when you don't have your kid, when do you have a life?" Joker asked, sounding strangely annoyed. Or more annoyed than he already had been.

"My life is Travis," I answered and something moved over his face that I didn't like, knowing about what his mom did to him. But I did my best to ignore it since he likely wouldn't like me to make note of it, especially in company, and kept speaking. "And anyway, it's only eight and a half hours a day, so it isn't like I'm always there. Except the over-time," I mumbled the last bit. "Everyone can use it and Sharon's fair, but she throws a good amount my way because I need it."

He stared at me, still looking annoyed, and I stared back, not annoyed even a little bit.

I wasn't because you didn't get annoyed for a girl you

didn't like and possibly want to ask out on a date which would end in a kiss (I hoped).

So as he stared at me, I stared back. I also smiled brightly.

His eyes dropped to my mouth and he looked even *more* annoyed.

My smile got bigger as my belly felt warm.

At that point, the door to the Compound opened and I unfortunately had to look away from annoyed-biker-handsome Joker toward the door.

"Hey, Pete!" Tabby cried to the man lumbering in.

I said nothing.

Instead, I made the instant decision that, if he would look after Travis, I'd let him.

This was not because he had on a beat-up leather vest over a black T-shirt that had been washed so many times it was gray. It was also not because his jeans were faded, too big on him (which was a feat, he was not a small man), and had stains on them, though the jeans were clean. It was further not because he had a very long goatee, stubble on his cheeks, bushy sideburns and a mass of lead-gray hair pulled back in a ponytail at his nape. Lastly, it was not because he had a gut that shouted *I love beer!*

No, it was because he had kind eyes and a face that lit up when those eyes hit Tabby. The overall look might be scary to some, but to me, he looked like Biker Santa Claus.

"Hey, darlin', how you doin'?" he called to Tabby.

"I'm good, Pete. This is Carissa."

Big Petey trudged to me and did it with a grin and beefy hand lifted my way. "Figured you were. Hey, girl."

I took his hand. Its calloused warmth closed around mine firm but not hard.

Yes, I was going to let him look after my son.

"Hey," I replied. "Nice to meet you."

He gave my hand a squeeze before he let it go and leaned into the bar. "Your asshole still got your boy?"

I assumed correctly by the a-word that he meant Aaron. "Uh, yes, until Monday."

"Bummer, darlin'," he muttered.

"Agreed," I muttered back.

He gave me a grin. "Tyra keeps her boys with her in the office a lot but I also got 'em a lot so your li'l bugger'll have company."

"Uh . . . is that too much for you?" I asked.

"I'll amend," he declared. "Tyra keeps her boys with her in the office a lot and her old man likes their boys with him a lot, so I have 'em a lot but not *a lot* so your boy will have company but also he and me'll have alone time."

"I think it's important he socialize," I told him.

"He'll get that, seein' as Ride and Cut's brother and sister come 'round to see 'em and every brother and their old ladies in this Club ain't exactly introverts. It'll be good."

"It sure sounds like it will," I agreed.

"Gotta see your kid takes to me and you're good with how. We'll set it, you bring him here when you got him again. Me and him'll have a meet and greet."

I smiled. "That sounds excellent."

He smiled back.

"Now about pay—" I started but stopped when he lifted his hand.

"Talk about that later," he said.

"That later bein' never," Tabby muttered behind my back and Big Petey winked at her.

Oh boy.

"No, really, perhaps we should—"

Pete looked to me. "Talk about that later, darlin'," he said unbendingly but gently and finished on, "Yeah?"

I took him in, thinking about his daughter and Tyra, who didn't strike me as a woman that would leave her kids with just anyone, and I said, "Yeah."

That was when his eyes moved around my head and then he turned, leaning further into the bar, saying to Joker, "Like your girl, Joke. Pretty. Sweet. Wild hair means wild side." He looked back to me. "We bikers like it wild."

I fought against the pink I felt creeping into my cheeks as Joker said to Pete, "Don't be an asshole."

"I think that's seventy-five cents," Tabby put in.

Big Petey ignored that and asked Joker, "How'm I bein' an asshole?"

"You know," Joker clipped, looked to me, jerked up his chin, ignored everyone else, and prowled along the bar and right out the door.

I thought that was rude.

Looking around, I saw none of my company felt the same way. They all clearly thought it was amusing.

I took heart in that (although I was a little concerned—if bikers liked it wild, that was not me) and announced, "I have to get to work. It was really cool meeting you all."

"Give me your number," Tab said. "Maybe you and your little guy and me can go have lunch some time or something."

I loved that idea!

"Great!" I chirped.

We exchanged numbers. We all exchanged goodbyes. Pete and I made a date of when to meet again with Travis. And I took off.

I scanned the massive expanse of tarmac outside the Compound, looking for Joker.

He was nowhere to be seen.

This unsettled me, because really, I should give some

thought to why he seemed to want to avoid me at the same time he seemed to be interested in me.

But now was not that time. I had to get to work.

So I got in my car and headed to LeLane's, thinking that I could roll that question around in my head for ages but I'd never get an answer. The only one who had that answer was Joker.

Maybe I'd ask him. Maybe bikers liked honesty and straight talk.

And driving to LeLane's, that's what I decided.

At the party, I'd ask Joker what was the deal.

And hopefully, after we got whatever it was straightened out, he'd ask me on a date.

Thinking this thought meant I walked into LeLane's smiling.

*   *   *

The next day, while I was in my bathroom getting ready for work, my phone rang.

I looked to it, saw it was Tabby, so I answered it.

"Hey, Tabby."

"Hey, babe. How's tricks?"

"They're good, I think."

She laughed.

I smiled at the phone.

She quit laughing and said, "Listen, every girl needs to know what she's getting into on a night out. And since I'm guessin' you've never been to a biker party, I thought I'd call and give you the skinny."

That was nice.

It was also surprising. I'd never had anyone do that for me.

Of course, when I'd had friends and we went out, we'd always dressed to the nines, hit swank bars, and drank martinis or the like, so I knew what I was getting into.

And in that moment, it occurred to me that I'd never thought that was much fun.

I liked the dressing up part, but I'd never liked martinis. I always made a face when I'd take a sip because I didn't think they tasted good. And I wasn't a big drinker so one would have me tipsy in a way that wasn't fun. It was more like I just wanted to go home, get into comfy clothes, and stretch out in front of the TV.

Further, the goal for the evening was mostly my girl-friends picking up guys or them saying catty things about every other woman at the bar. Since I had a guy (then), I was odd man out on the first part. And I'd never liked the second part. It was mean.

This made me feel unsettled because all of a sudden, it made me wonder why I went out with them at all when I'd never really had any fun.

I'd long since wondered why I'd had the friends I had, all the way back to high school, when I didn't feel I fit in with them, but especially when they dumped me after Aaron did.

Even though I'd wondered, I'd also not come to any conclusions.

"So," Tabby continued, taking my mind off these things, "first of all, biker bitches aren't big on lots of clothes and by that I mean they show skin. But you dress however you're comfortable. Casual, though. You might feel weird if you show up all dolled up."

"Okay," I agreed.

"And since Ty-Ty and Lanie are home with their kids, so the only folks you'll know are some of the boys, who might be otherwise engaged, and me, I'll text you when Shy and I get there so you'll know you have someone to hang with."

Again, super nice.

"Thanks, Tabby."

"Don't mention it," she said. "Also, kinda anything goes and privacy is sometimes not an issue. Just so you know."

"Uh...what?" I asked in confusion.

"Makin' out, bein' loud, groping, smokin' pot, you name it, it could happen," she explained. "You're not into something, the family is what it is because everyone in it wants the freedom to be just that, so no one will push anything on you. But you should know."

That was nice too. A little frightening, I wasn't big on marijuana (though I'd never tried it; still, I didn't intend to). But it was still nice.

So I again said, "Thanks," to Tabby.

"We girls gotta look out for each other."

That wasn't my experience.

Nevertheless, I said, "Right."

"Okay, I gotta go. I'll text you when we're there tomorrow and I'll see you there. Yeah?"

"Yes, and thanks again."

"No probs, babe."

"See you later."

"Yeah, later, Carissa."

She hung up.

I put my phone on the counter and stared at it, feeling a variety of things.

First, I was a little afraid. A biker party would be something all new to me, and I had a feeling parts of it would be shocking, parts of it I wouldn't like. But all of it would be Joker's world, and I liked Joker, so I had to be brave and non-judgmental. Things might get crazy, but my experience so far was that, surface and deep down, these people were good people. They accepted me how I was; I had to do the same.

I was also more than a little nervous. Joker would be there and, again, I liked Joker. But he seemed at odds about how he felt about me. And I'd never had to try to catch the eye of anyone. I caught Aaron's eye when I was fourteen and that was it. It wasn't that I was out of practice, I'd *had* no practice. And I liked Joker enough it meant a lot that I could beat down that shield he had up for whatever reason. I just had no idea how to go about doing that.

Further, I was a little confused. Mostly about why I barely knew this man but all of this seemed so important to me. Very important. More important than, rationally, it should be.

But last, and most, I was excited. Things had been terribly lonely since I lost Aaron. Joker's question about when I got to live my life had hit home. I had no life. I had my son and I had my work and I had my worry about what was going to hit me next.

But I *had my son*. And I wasn't teaching him anything that was good if I taught him life was narrow. If I taught him that life was about sacrifice, not about living. If I had nothing but him to make me happy, rather than just being happy all around with things to do and good friends to do them with.

So I was excited. I was excited I suddenly had places to be, things to do, and people to do them with.

And I was excited to have exciting things to think about.

Those things being Joker. How his beard felt against my skin when he was kissing me. How he tasted. How tight his arms closed around me. How I wanted to know what his hair felt like (I should have taken that shot when I had my arms around him, but his shoulders felt so lovely, I didn't). How I wanted to know what was behind that guard he had over his eyes. How I wanted to know if he liked my pie.

And being mostly excited, for the first time in so long I couldn't remember the last time (outside having Travis), I was happy. I had a spring in my step. I had something to look forward to.

And it felt good.

*   *   *

I felt terrible.

This was a disaster.

An utter, complete *disaster*.

And I wasn't talking about the disaster that was me assuming, since it was a party, the done thing was to bring something when absolutely no one brought anything. So I'd looked like an idiot when I strolled in with two bags of Le-Lane's fresh tortilla chips and a huge tub of their signature guacamole (that was handmade to order at the deli counter).

Although that was embarrassing, the chips and guac were all gone and I hadn't even been there an hour.

"Girl, you want a fresh one?"

I turned my head from my wounded contemplation of Joker with the big-haired, tube-topped, ultra-mini-miniskirted brunette at the pool table (I just *knew* biker babes wore tube tops!).

Joker was not smiling and flirting. But he was still flirting. I knew it. I knew the way she sashayed around him and gave him knowing looks and rubbed up against him every chance she got and licked her lips after they'd take a shot of whatever they were shooting.

I'd been at the party for forty-five minutes. I got there after my shift, rushing home and changing clothes because Tab had texted to say she and Shy were already there, so I'd gotten there pretty late (or late for me).

And when I got there, the party was in full swing. There were a lot of people there, *lots* of women, other bikers from different clubs (if the patches were anything to go by), and it was what Tabby said it would be. The music was loud. The people were loud. There was making out. Groping. Flirting. Drinking. Shots thrown back. And smoking, including the marijuana variety.

In this mess, although Tab found me right away and got me a drink, Joker hadn't even looked at me.

Not once.

I looked to the guy behind the bar. I'd just met him and he'd told me his name was Snapper. He was in the Rush/Shy/ Joker age group of the Club. Currently, he was acting as one of several bartenders (though they didn't seem to have an official one, guys went back, girls went back, you wanted it, you got it or you asked whoever was back there to get it for you).

I had my hand around a warm beer and my seat on a stool, my eyes locked to Joker, and Tabby had left to go to the bathroom.

So I was alone.

Again.

Even at a big biker party.

"Sorry?" I asked him, the fact he'd spoken to me belatedly processing through my thoughts.

"Fresh," he said, tipping his head to my plastic cup that was not even half-drunk. "Toss that warm shit and I'll get you a cold one."

"Um..." I couldn't answer because I couldn't think.

I could only hurt.

Why did I hurt?

Why did I even come?

Joker, it was now clear, didn't want me.

Maybe he kissed back whoever kissed him. He was a guy. Guys probably did that. And it was obvious from the used condom wrappers that he had experience. Maybe he was just a good kisser because he'd had a lot of practice.

But I had in no way given him the impression I wanted it to stop.

He'd stopped it.

I was taken from my thoughts again when Snapper pulled my cup out of my hand, threw it (and its liquid contents) in a trash bin, and grabbed a fresh plastic cup. Then he went to one of the three kegs behind the bar and pulled me a new one.

He came back and set it in front of me.

"Thanks," I mumbled, and as I did, I took that opportunity to take him in fully.

He had light blond hair, long and pulled back in a slipshod bun at the back of his head. He had light blue eyes and blond lashes, the both of them together unusual and attractive. He had blond stubble on his cheeks, but I knew he shaved (though, apparently infrequently) since the whiskers at his chin were a lot longer than the rest so I figured when he was feeling in the mood to be neat, he just wore a goatee. He also had nice cheekbones, very white teeth that probably seemed whiter due to his tanned skin, and a straight nose.

"You the one with the kid?" he asked and yet again that dirty washed through me.

I dropped my eyes to my beer, lifting it, and before taking a sip, replied, "Yeah. I'm the official Chaos charity case."

I put my cup to the bar, still looking at it, but didn't continue to do this as I had planned, along with feeling sorry for myself and finding a time when I could tell Tabby I had to go (that time being soon), because I felt a fist gentle under my chin, lifting it.

My eyes went to Snapper's.

"We all fall on hard times," he said quietly, removing his fist from my chin. "It's just lucky for you that you fell in the right direction."

"That's one way to look at it," I told him.

"Only way, babe," he returned immediately. "We are who cares about us."

I felt my brows draw together. "Sorry?"

"You weren't worth the trouble, we wouldn't make it."

That was so nice the dirty washed out of me and I couldn't help but smile. "That's sweet."

He smiled back. "Maybe. Still true."

"That's also sweet."

He kept smiling and offered, "Want a shot?"

I shook my head. "No. I shouldn't. I'm driving."

"You get blotto, I'll put you on the back of my bike, take you home."

"I, well…that's nice, but my son comes home the day after tomorrow and I have a lot to do as well as a shift at work. I probably shouldn't be hungover."

"Your call," he muttered.

"Though I've never been on the back of a bike," I shared and he focused on me.

"No shit?"

I shook my head.

He grinned and he took his time doing it. "Then fuck that beer. Best high of your life, bein' on a bike. I'll take you out."

My disaster of a night started looking up. "Really?"

"Absolutely."

I looked toward the pool table and saw in the short time my attention had been diverted, Joker and his brunette had stopped playing and now Rush was playing with some redhead.

Rush's girl wasn't in a tube top. She was in a Harley T-shirt and tight jeans, much like me. Minus the Harley tee—mine was a girl-fit Broncos babydoll tee—and also minus the tight jeans. I had on jeans, just not tight, except at the bottom where every pair of pants seemed to be tight these days.

I scanned the room and saw Joker was gone altogether.

So was his brunette.

My heart squeezed.

"Yo!" I heard Snapper call and I looked to him to see he was looking beyond me. I turned around and saw Tabby was heading toward me and Snapper. "I'm takin' Carissa out on my bike. You wanna look after her purse or put it in Shy's room or somethin'?"

At his request, Tabby's gaze immediately cut to the pool tables. When she took them in, for some reason, her face got hard before she softened it and looked back toward us.

"Not a problem," she said, stopping at us. "Go. Ride."

"Never been on a bike," I told her and her face split in a big smile.

"Then go. *Ride*." She leaned in to me. "Beware, wind in your hair, moon on your skin, you'll fall in love."

I wasn't sure that was a good thing. I'd fallen in love with something I couldn't have, and if I fell in love with the wind in my hair and the moon on my skin, without someone to give that to me, I couldn't have that either.

But to heck with it.

Maybe this would be the only bike ride I'd have in my life.

And maybe the kiss Joker gave me was the only fabulous kiss I'd ever get.

And maybe my dream of having a family or the other dream of getting behind the steel guarding Joker's eyes was lost to me.

But I was still breathing.

So I'd take what I could get.

Tabby put her hand on my purse, which was lying on the bar. "Got this. Have fun."

"Thanks," I whispered.

She winked at me.

I looked to Snapper. "Let's go."

"Meet you at the end of the bar, babe."

"Right!" I chirped, jumped off my stool, threw Tabby a smile, nabbed my jacket that I was sitting on and bounced to the end of the bar.

When I got there, Snapper had pulled on his leather jacket. He grabbed my hand and guided me out the door and to his bike. Then he got on his bike before instructing me on how to do the same.

The bike roared, he backed out on an angle, and we glided over the tarmac of Ride.

He pulled out onto Broadway and I got it.

The wind in my hair.

The moon on my skin.

The leather of his jacket in my nostrils.

The solidness of him under my hands at his waist.

We got close to the onramp of I-25 and he shouted, "Hold on!"

"Sorry?" I shouted back.

"Hold on!" he yelled, taking one hand off the grip and using it to pull my hand from his waist and around to his stomach.

He put his hand back on the grip and we turned up the ramp, going faster, faster, *faster*, the wind whipping my hair and biting into my skin. I curved my other arm around him, put my chin to his shoulder, drew in air and leather, and I got it.

Instantly.

That *it* being why this was the life for a biker.

No encumbrances. You wanted to smoke pot, you smoked it. You wanted to wear a tube top, you wore it. You wanted to drink shots, you drank them. You wanted to make out hot and heavy on a couch in a room filled with people, you did it.

You wanted to live, you lived.

You wanted to be free, you got on your bike and rode in the moonlight.

You did not drink martinis you didn't like. You did not take a job your mother-in-law thought you should have. You did not take guff from your ex, not ever.

You did what you wanted.

You were free.

In all that was happening to me, all that I was feeling, all the disappointment of that night and the bizarre devastation I felt that the first time this happened, me on the back of a bike, I would have preferred it be with Joker...right then, for that moment, I let it all go.

I let it go, held on to Snapper and I let myself feel it.

Feel something rare and beautiful and overwhelming.

Feel something I knew for certain I hadn't felt in my whole life.

Free.

CHAPTER SEVEN

He Gave Me You

Joker

JOKER SWUNG OFF his bike and headed to the Compound, his mind consumed—as it had been since that shit happened—with the vision of Snapper touching Carissa's face, of Carissa smiling.

He'd ridden a long time. Long enough to get that crap out of his head.

But it hadn't worked.

He put his hand to the door, pulled it open, and was not surprised to see that the party was over. The music was low, the common room had a few bitches and bikers passed out on couches, but mostly the room was cleared. It was early the next morning, the rest had either hooked up and already sent their bitches home, were still with their bitches in their beds, or they'd passed out.

"Dick move."

Shy's words sounding from his right made Joker turn his head that way.

His brother's eyes were on him and one look, Joker knew the man was pissed.

Jesus, what now?

"Say again?" he asked.

"She came for you," Shy bit out. "And right in her face, you hooked up with Stacy. Dick move, Joke. Fuck. Seriously."

Joker stopped well down from where Shy, Tab, and High were congregated at the bar, High inside, bottle on the bar in front of him with glasses at the ready, apparently doing shots.

High engaged in this activity was not a surprise.

High had not been at the party. He had an old lady and kids. He liked to be around his kids, so it was rare, unless it was a family thing, that he partied.

Not the same with the old lady, the liking to be around her part.

Chaos history stated High and his woman had never been tight. He'd knocked her up and done the right thing for their kid, the wrong thing for High. Since then, it had never been copasetic. Joker knew her and she didn't have old lady in her. It was rare she'd show at anything related to Chaos, sending her kids to the family shit but not showing herself, and she put up with her man so he'd put a roof over her and her kids' heads.

So it was frequent when High's kids were asleep that he'd leave the woman behind in a home that was far from happy, come to the Compound, and throw a few back.

He quit thinking about High and focused on Shy.

"She get home okay?" he asked.

"Do you give a shit?" Shy returned, and Joker felt his frame come alert.

He was not doing this again.

"Think I made this clear the other night, not your business who I fuck," he returned. "But, just sayin', Stacy was ridin' the edge of smashed, the bitch has no problem drivin' in that state, and so she wouldn't fuck herself up, or someone else, I took her ass home. Then I took a ride. I didn't hook up with shit."

Shy visibly relaxed.

"She likes you," Tab said softly.

She was right.

Carissa definitely liked him.

Then again, Carissa didn't know him, so Tab was also wrong.

"She likes havin' people in her life who give a shit," Joker returned.

"There a reason you got a block about this bitch?" High asked.

Joker didn't do this. He didn't share.

He looked to High.

High didn't share either. High was a hard motherfucker who kept himself to himself.

But High had once laid it out to Joker over vodka and brotherhood that home was no good. It made him miserable. And worse, he was worried the mask was slipping and his kids could read it.

Joker had been shocked as shit when the man shared. He'd also felt grateful. His brother giving him that said a lot about how he felt about Joker, and Joker didn't miss any of it.

And he'd decided it was time to do this.

So he said, "I'm not that guy."

"What guy?" High asked.

"The guy she needs," Joker answered.

"How do you know?" Shy asked.

Joker looked to him. "Because I don't like butterflies. They're beautiful, but they're delicate, and I don't got it in me to handle anything with care."

"Maybe you're wrong," High noted.

"And maybe I got a life that proves I'm right," Joker returned.

"You can't know unless you try," Tabby put in.

"And chew her up in the meantime?" Joker asked and shook his head. "She doesn't need that shit."

None of them had an answer to that and he knew why.

They knew he was right.

"She's home safe," Tabby told him. "She texted me when she got there. But before she took off, she went for a ride with Snapper."

Fuck.

Joker clenched his teeth, pushing the thought of Carissa wrapped around his brother on his bike to the back of his mind, where, for her sake, he'd put their fucking unbelievable kiss—and the fact she'd laid that on him, not the other way around—doing that hoping like fuck, if she wanted to find a man to get her off, she took that shit off Chaos.

"Good to know she's safe," he muttered, tipping his chin to them and moving away.

No one stopped him so he went to his room, took off his clothes, and fell into bed.

He laid in bed and as he did it, he smelled the fading scent of fabric softener on his sheets.

So he did it thinking of Carissa.

And he didn't sleep.

*   *   *

The next day, Joker rode his bike onto the cement that made up the forecourt of the two-bay garage. The place was a mess, cars everywhere, tires stacked all around, the large square-paned windows of the office dirty, one cracked and held together with tape. He saw the doors of both bays up, cars in each, men working on them.

Taking it in, Joker knew it wasn't rundown because it was rundown. It was rundown because they had so much work, they didn't have time to straighten it up.

He liked this.

He parked, swung off his bike, and stood by it, eyes on the bays.

He'd come. Finally.

Now the man had to come to him. He didn't know why, but he figured it had something to do with Carissa. She'd been around him more than once, took his tongue, whimpered into his mouth (and Christ, he had to bury that shit as well, that whimper alone had him near to losing control and ripping her clothes off), and still, she didn't know who he was.

This had to go a certain way.

If it didn't, he'd get on his bike and leave it behind.

All of it.

Forever.

He saw a man come to the end of the bay, wiping his hand on a rag.

"Yo, bro! You need something?" he yelled.

Joker didn't reply. Just stood by his bike, cut on—the patch on the back he had no clue if the man had seen. But if he had, the guy would know he was dealing with Chaos, and how he handled that would tell the tale. Joker also had his arms crossed on his chest, shades covering his eyes, which were aimed at the bay.

"Dude, seriously, you need something?" the guy shouted.

Joker didn't move.

The man stared at him, swung his head to look behind him, then his eyes came back to Joker. A few beats later, a big black guy came walking to the end of the bay.

There he was.

The owner of this establishment. The man who'd bought it five years ago and made it thrive.

Joker braced.

The man looked at him, and even from a distance, Joker could see him looking harder.

He felt his insides draw tight.

Then Linus Washington's face broke into a big smile and he hooted, "Holy *fuck*!"

Joker felt his body loosen as Linus started to jog, heading Joker's way.

"Holy fuck! Car!" he shouted as he jogged. "Jesus! Fantastic!"

He made it to Joker and didn't hesitate before snaring his hand, holding it firm in his, and moving in to bump chests and round Joker with an arm, pounding him on the back.

Joker closed his eyes behind his shades and returned the gesture.

Linus broke free but left their hands gripped between them, shaking them back and forth before he finally let Joker go.

"Christ, good to see you. Fuck me." His eyes tipped down and up and his smile stayed steady. "You look good."

"Same, Lie."

Linus accepted the comment by lifting a hand and clapping him on the shoulder.

"Where you been, Car?"

"Around and about. Came back just over a year ago."

The smile stayed in place even as he stated, "Well, kiss my ass, dickhead. Over a year and this is the first time you come to see me?"

"Not big on visiting the old 'hood," Joker told him. Then he went on to lie, "Just found out about your place, decided to swing by."

It was a lie because Joker had known about Linus's garage even before he approached Chaos to join their ranks.

But back then, he wasn't ready.

He didn't know why he was ready now. He just was. So he'd rolled with it.

"Don't live in that 'hood anymore, bud. Got me three kids. I look at my woman, she gets pregnant. And Kamryn wasn't big on raisin' our crew in a two-bedroom house. We moved to Littleton four years ago."

Joker studied the face of a happy man and said quietly, "Glad for you, brother."

"Not as glad as me," Linus replied just as quietly. "You gotta come meet my kids, Car. Two boys, in the middle, a girl. Apple of her daddy's eye. And my boys," his chest puffed up, "tough. Love their momma, make their old man proud."

Joker nodded.

He liked that too.

"Kamryn?" he asked.

"Woman gets prettier every day," Linus told him. "Don't know how she does it. Tell her I think she's got voodoo. She just laughs and falls on my dick. Six weeks later, she's pregnant. That's my life."

"Heard worse," Joker remarked.

"Bet you have," Linus said low.

Joker rounded that and asked, "Mrs. Heely still at her place?"

The joy slid out of Linus's face and Joker again braced. "Kam got her a new place a year back. Assisted living, so it ain't like it's a shithole where you go to die. What it is is life. She just got old, found it harder to get around, took a fall. Luckily, she and Kam and the kids had planned to do something that day. Kam found her. Got her sorted."

"Shit," Joker muttered.

"She worried about you," Linus told him. "You took off, that asswipe didn't do dick. Mrs. Heely marched over there, givin' him shit about how her boy was dead, his boy was alive and breathin' and a good kid, and how your old man was good for nothing. Shouted and carried on so much, had to go over and get her outta there. No tellin' what your dad would do if he lost it. Even with an old lady."

That was the fucking truth.

"You should go see her, Car. She'll be freakin' beside herself, you show."

Joker drew in breath before he made his decision and nodded.

"Tell me where she is, I'll drop around."

Linus grinned at him.

Then his eyes fell to Joker's jacket and bike before coming back to his face.

"Found yourself a place to belong?"

Joker nodded.

"You good there?"

"Got brothers. The good kind. Don't know what to do with them. But they're patient with showin' me the path."

"Like that, Car," Linus murmured.

"Joker, Lie," Joker corrected. "Left the boy I was at my dad's house. I'm him on paper only. Now, I'm Joker. It's a better fit for me."

Linus held his eyes. "I get that." He tipped his head to the side and his lips curved up. "Find yourself a good woman?"

"A few."

Linus's lips turned down. "Mean a certain kind, son."

"Know what you mean, and no."

"You're young," he muttered.

He didn't feel young, but he still was.

That didn't change who he was and how he intended to live his life, and no good woman would be a part of that. But Linus didn't need to know that.

"You're at work," Joker said. "I'll leave you alone. But give me Mrs. Heely's details, I'll go 'round."

"Sure thing," Linus said, turning and inviting, "Come to the office. Gotta call Kam to get it."

Joker followed him.

Linus spoke while he walked.

"Not shittin' you, Car...I mean, Joker. Want your ass at my table. Kam'll wanna see you too, and I want you to meet my kids."

Joker made another decision.

"I'll be there."

Linus gave him another smile.

Ten minutes later, he left with Mrs. Heely's address, Linus's number in his phone, his in Linus's, and after another back-pounding hug.

He rode off seeing Linus standing outside the bay, still smiling.

Joker didn't smile.

But that didn't mean he didn't feel good.

*   *   *

"Oh my goodness gracious!" Mrs. Heely cried, her hands going straight up in front of her before she reached further, slapped them on either side of his head, and didn't let go. "Carson!"

She'd just opened the door and, like Linus, she knew exactly who he was.

She shook his head side to side. "Oh my goodness gracious! Goodness! What a fantastic surprise! I can't believe it! I simply can't!"

"Yo, Mrs. Heely," he greeted.

She dropped her hands and narrowed her eyes. "Yo? What kind of greeting is 'yo,' Carson Steele?" Before he could answer (not that he was going to), she kept at him. "And when was the last time you got a haircut? Or had a shave?"

"Like it like this," he told her.

"You look scruffy," she returned. "You're a handsome boy. You shouldn't hide it under all," she circled her finger two inches from his face, "*that.*"

"You gonna let me in or make me stand outside your door for the next hour, ridin' my ass?" he asked.

She rolled her eyes, pretending to be pissed even when she wasn't. He knew. He saw her mouth quirk.

He also knew because she used to do that when she'd give him shit and mean it, but not.

He'd missed it, but he didn't know that he had until right then.

"Your language. Always did my head in with your language. I blame your father." She pierced him with a glare. "For *a lot* of things."

He didn't have a chance to say anything, she stepped aside.

"Get in here," she ordered, waving her hand at him and moving inside. "If I knew you were coming, I'd have made cookies. Since I didn't, you get Chips Ahoy or Oreos. I think I also have some Nilla Wafers."

Fuck, but it felt good to know some things didn't change.

"May have escaped you, darlin', but I'm not eight anymore," he muttered, coming in behind her and closing the door.

She whirled on him. "I'm not either. I still like my cookies."

He stared at her.

She rolled her eyes again and flounced through the small living room to an even smaller kitchen.

Joker followed, not liking what he saw. Not that it was a pit, just that it was small. She'd filled it with stuff that was familiar to him, made it hers. But it wasn't like the house she'd lived in that just *was* her, becoming that after she'd spent decades of her life living in it.

And there was no flag outside the door.

"Where's the flag?" he asked carefully as he hit the kitchen.

"We have a clubhouse where all of us in God's waiting room go to experience such thrills as bingo and movie night, with every movie they show being PG. I told them about the flag. They let me fly it out there," she answered, grabbing all three brands of cookies, dumping them on the counter, and shuffling to the fridge to get out the goddamned milk.

He nearly smiled because the last glass of milk Joker drank, she'd poured it.

"Good you still got it in your sights," he told her and she looked to him after pulling down a glass.

"Never let it out of my sight, sweetheart."

Joker fought back swallowing against the lump suddenly clogging his throat.

She poured him milk.

After she did that, she slid it along with the cookies toward where he was leaning a hip against her counter. "Where you been?"

"Here and there," he answered, reaching for an Oreo. He gave her his eyes. "Home now."

"Good, Carson," she said softy.

"Not Carson. Known as Joker, Mrs. Heely. Left my father's son behind."

She nodded, surprising him with her easy acceptance of

that, her eyes moving to his cut before lifting again to his, "Found a home."

"Yeah, and brothers."

"Hear some of those motorcycle boys can raise Cain," she noted. "Hear some of them take care of their own."

"I got both."

She grinned. "Reckon that's good."

"It is," he assured her.

"Missed you," she whispered, blindsiding him. The look on her face, her tone, the suddenness of it, taking it in, his insides shredded. "Worried for you, bad. Missed you, worse. Thought about you every day and—"

He shut her up by shoving the Oreo in his mouth and pulling her in his arms.

She wrapped hers around his middle and pushed her face in his chest. She was tough, though, and he wasn't surprised when she got a lock on it and didn't lose control in about the time it took him to chew and swallow the cookie.

But when she tipped her head back, she said, "God took my boy. Then He gave me you."

That was when his insides started bleeding.

He stared down at her wrinkled face. A face he remembered from since he could remember. Her hazel eyes bright with wet.

He had no clue.

Fuck.

No clue.

But he should have had one. She'd given him a million of them.

His voice was gruff when he began, "Mrs. Heely—"

She shook her head. "We won't go on about that. You're here. You're healthy. You're strong. You've found where you fit. I'm happy. If you needed to leave to find that, then it's good. But this time, for this old woman, would you stay around awhile?"

Joker gave her a squeeze and it again came out gruff when he said, "Not goin' anywhere."

She pulled her arms from around him to rest her hands on his chest.

For his part, Joker did not let go.

"Good," she whispered before she slapped him twice on the chest with both hands and pulled out of his hold. "Now, eat your cookies and tell me everything. And don't leave anything out, even if it's juicy. I've been telling the folk around here about you for a year. We all need to get caught up, and we're sick and tired of PG."

"You do know I'm not tellin' you shit that's juicy," Joker replied.

She tossed him a look. "I'm older than you, you'll hardly shock me."

"Wanna bet?" he asked.

"Try me," she shot back.

And that was when it happened.

Joker's lips twitched.

It wasn't big on the outside.

But it still was huge.

*   *   *

Joker pulled into the parking lot and saw immediately that Carissa's Tercel was one of the best cars there.

He stopped, idled and looked around.

Four stories. L-shaped. All brick. All flat. Outside walkways made of cement. Ugly iron banisters. Same for the stairs, a set at the front, a set in the bend of the L. Not one thing there to make it look anything other than what it was. Cheap apartments for those unlucky enough to have to live there.

And he saw a few of those unlucky enough to have to live there.

A man and a woman hanging out on the walkway by the railing, second floor up. The man was smoking, the woman looking like she was giving him shit, the man looking like he was about two seconds away from doing whatever he felt he had to do to make her stop.

An old lady on the bottom floor, head tipped back, housecoat on, feet in slippers, watching them, probably so she could share what she saw wide. But she was doing it in a way that Joker knew she'd seen it before. From the couple. From others. And she'd seen a fuckuva lot more.

A couple of kids hanging around the cars, looking like they were up to nothing, but whatever that nothing was, was no good.

Joker looked to the third floor, scanned, and saw the numbers he was searching for, the middle one hanging upside down.

Apartment 323.

Carissa's place.

He felt his mouth get tight as he pulled his phone out of his pocket.

His thumb moved over the display and he put it to his ear.

"Brother," Tack answered.

"Where are you?"

"It's Sunday. Where would I be?"

At home, with his woman and boys.

"Need a word," Joker told him.

"How quiet does this word have to be?" Tack asked.

"I could come to you. You share what I have to say with Cherry, your call. But outside that, quiet."

"Where are you?"

"Nowhere good."

"Don't wanna make you haul your ass up here, don't wanna haul my ass to the city. So, help me out, Joke. Where's halfway?"

"Morrison Inn," Joker told him.

"Thirty," Tack replied and disconnected.

Joker shoved his phone in his pocket, glanced at Carissa's apartment, knowing she was there because her car was and figuring she was up there alone, killing time until her boy was back.

He wasn't about to take the steps he knew she had to take, lugging up her kid, lugging groceries, to knock on her door to make her less alone.

He just had to settle in the knowledge that sometime tomorrow she'd have her boy back.

So she'd be okay.

Or as okay as she could be.

He rounded the lot and drove out of Denver and into the foothills to hit Morrison Inn.

He had a beer in front of him on the bar when Tack walked in.

He waited until Tack had his own beer before he started.

"Heard word the renters at Tyra's old pad gave notice."

Tack had the beer to his lips, his eyes to the bar, when he replied, "Heard true."

"Want you to offer it to Carissa."

Tack's eyes came to him.

"Give her some bullshit about how Tyra bought it years ago, mortgage low or paid off or whatever. I don't give a fuck," Joker told him. "I'll find out what she's payin' now. You throw a couple hundred on that so she can't read the bullshit. Whatever's the difference, I'll pay the rest."

Tack took a pull and put the beer down but Joker wasn't finished.

"Also need a lock on some info."

"That would be?"

"A man named Robinson. Wanna know where he is. Wanna know how he is."

"Wanna tell me who he is?" Tack asked.

"Knew him once. Good man. Last I knew, he'd taken a hit. Lost a baby. Wanna make sure life for him has turned around."

Tack studied him a beat, he did this with some intensity, Joker withstood it, then Tack said, "Need more than Robinson."

"I'll get you what you need."

Tack nodded, looked away, nabbed his beer and took another sip.

He kept his gaze to the back of the bar when he said, "Not my usual thing, tellin' a man where to put his dick, but word is, I'm not the only brother who's payin' attention and there's a sweet piece available. A piece only open to you and you're not taking."

Fuck, not this.

"I'm not havin' this conversation again."

Tack looked to him. "You can break the cycle."

Joker felt his brows snap together. "Say again?"

"Seen you fight. Worked out next to you. You don't smoke. Never asked. Now I'm askin'. How'd you get those cigarette burns on the insides of your arms?"

Joker leaned away.

Tack put his forearms to the bar but did it sliding them an inch toward Joker, his eyes never leaving his brother's. "Joke, your story to tell when you wanna tell it. Your story to keep if you don't ever wanna tell. Thought you had secrets. Way you're holdin' back with this girl, think I'm wrong. You don't have secrets. You got demons."

"I had a shit dad," Joker bit out, surprised it came out, but not uneasy about it.

With what he'd done that day, the time had come.

Something lethal slid through Tack's features. "He burn you?"

"And other shit, yeah."

"Jesus Christ," Tack hissed, looking back to his beer.

"Long time ago," Joker told him.

"Boy at the fence."

"Hunh?"

Tack looked to him. "Know you, brother. Known you more than a year. You're the kid at the fence."

Joker said nothing but he felt that deep in his gut.

"He burned you," Tack's voice was tight. "And I let you stand at that fuckin' fence."

The last person's fault that shit was was Tack's.

Joker started to tell him that. "Tack—"

Tack cut him off, "Your scars, your call, but we know him. We know where he lives. And we know how to put the hurt on him. You say it, your brothers roll out."

Joker shook his head. "He isn't worth your time."

"You fuck around with this girl, let her slip through your fingers, you're wrong. 'Cause that's not on you. That's on him."

"I'm doin' right by her."

"That's where you'd be wrong."

Joker closed his mouth.

Tack took another pull on his beer and looked to the back of the bar. "You're not alone. We all got it in us. That seed we don't wanna grow. The one we gotta stop 'cause if we don't stop it, it'll turn us into our old man." He looked back to Joker. "Every brother you got that feared that seed killed it, Joke. They found Chaos, they broke the cycle."

"Rush didn't," Joker pointed out. "Brother doesn't have to."

"Yes he does," Tack stated firmly, a statement, in a way, that Joker got. Rush and his dad didn't see eye to eye on a lot of things, mostly in regards to the direction of the Club. They also didn't keep that a secret.

Tack kept going.

"You're the next generation, Joker. Right now, the most important brothers in our Club are the ones who are layin' down the path of where we'll take the generation *you* recruit. A path, by that time, if you stay on the right one, will build a foundation that I hope like fuck nothin' ever shakes. The ones who been around, we picked careful. Now *you* gotta pick careful. Shy'll lead that, and Rush has his ideas. But we'll see what Rush brings to the table. Shy harnessed wind. If you harness butterflies, I'll be a lot less uneasy."

Joker didn't get it. "Shy harnessed wind?"

Tack jerked up his chin. "My girl looked outside the family, coulda been gone on the wind. There's the life she was headin' for and then there's the life we lead. The life we lead is important to me, and I didn't like losin' her from it. Shy brought her back."

It was then, Joker got it. Tabby had been engaged to a physical therapist who did not come close to living the life. The man died in a car accident.

Then came Shy.

Tack didn't wait for him to confirm, he kept talking.

"Figure your father didn't give you this so I will. A man is defined many ways. One of those is the woman he picks to be at his side."

"Says a lot," Joker muttered, turning to his own beer, and before taking a sip, finishing, "Seein' as my ma left my dad before I was old enough to focus."

"More important than that is the woman who chooses to

take a man's side," Tack stated on the heels of Joker's words, and Joker looked back to him. "You wouldn't have your cut if any one of your brothers thought you weren't defined as Chaos. But your old man chose the kind of woman who would clear out on her kid, that defines him. Your ma cleared out on her kid, that defines her. You get your shit together and explore what's on offer right now to you, you've already beat that 'cause you know what's on offer does not have that shit in her."

It was time to share.

So he did.

"It's me protecting her, Tack."

"Against what?"

He leaned toward his brother and hissed, "Demons."

Tack held his gaze and whispered, "He beat you bad."

"Wasn't worth shit."

"Him?"

"Me."

"Brother," Tack slid further his way. "He planted that seed."

"I know. Doesn't mean it didn't take root."

"You fear the dark." It was a statement.

A correct one.

"She doesn't need dark," Joker told Tack something anyone knew just taking one look at Carissa. "She never shoulda had it and she's had a lifetime of it. What I got in me gets loose, it'll engulf her."

"You gotta find a way to set it free."

"How?"

"God's honest truth?" Tack asked.

"Absolutely," Joker answered.

"If your brothers haven't brought you to that revelation, then you gotta sink your cock in cute, sweet, wet, butterfly pussy."

Joker leaned back.

"I'm not shittin' you, man," Tack told him.

Joker again said nothing.

Tack studied him before he remarked, "You think I'm whipped."

Joker made no reply. He wouldn't disrespect a brother like that, especially not Tack.

But he did think that.

Absolutely.

Tack grinned and took a pull from his beer.

After he dropped it, he said reflectively, still grinning, "Maybe I am. Though, the way I am and the woman holds that whip, it's a good thing to be."

"Right," Joker started and got his brother's gaze back. "I go there, she's got a kid. Her ex fucks with her, and he'll fuck with her, man, and I lose it, then where will she be?"

Tack's face drained of amusement. "That right there is what you need to get."

"What?"

"She is what I think she is, all you'll need to do is take one look at her, and it'll check."

"It'll check?"

"Do you think I'd do fuckin' anything to harm my woman?"

Joker felt heat hit his throat.

"My kids?" Tack pushed.

"No," Joker forced out.

"She is what I think she is, it'll check."

"What if it doesn't?"

"Then she isn't what I think she is."

"She is," Joker stated inflexibly and Tack stared at him a beat before he burst out laughing.

Joker did not laugh.

Then again, he never did.

But at that moment, he didn't think fuck-all was funny.

Still chuckling, Tack said, "Jesus, Joke, you already know your path."

"I also know hers, and it isn't the road to bein' a biker's old lady. Fuck, Tack, she was a cheerleader."

Tack again lost his hilarity and speared Joker with his eyes.

"Now, brother, if you don't think you're good enough, the life you lead is good enough, the family you can give her is good enough, then we got a much bigger problem."

"Don't read that shit into it, because you know it isn't there. You also get me. There are women built for the life. There are women who take it on. But she deserves a white picket fence, Tack."

"Then give her one. No law says a biker can't live behind a white picket fence."

Jesus.

Shit.

Shit.

He felt that burn in his throat too. So bad he had to suck back a long pull to douse the flame.

Tack lifted up from the bar and turned fully to Joker.

Then he laid it out.

"That motherfucker, he taught you to think you were garbage. You took that on. You were a kid. You had no fuckin' choice. But he was wrong, Joke. And the only person who doesn't get that shit is you. Get it. Get over it. Get your head outta your ass. And find what you deserve. Find some fuckin' happy. If it isn't this girl, it isn't. But whatever it is, I want it for you. Your brothers want it for you. Their old ladies want it for you. The only one who isn't lookin' for that for you is *you*."

Joker turned away, lifted his beer, and took another tug.

"Your call not to let that sink in," Tack said, and Joker felt him move to drain his beer and slide off his stool.

But he wasn't done, and he left his kill shot for last.

"Now, not many people on this earth I would rather sit and have a beer with. But, see, my woman is up the mountain with my sons. And you got my love, Joke, I got all the time in the world for you. But straight up, I'd rather be up the mountain watchin' my kids tear my house apart and my woman struttin' around thinkin' that shit's cute when it's not than down here with you, watchin' you wallow in shit that's history. You know how I feel about my Club. Think about that."

Kane Allen was a wise man and a strong one, so Joker thought about it.

And Joker thought about Rider and Cutter and the fact that Tack was not lying. Those boys were hoodlums and neither of them had reached double digits yet.

He then thought about Tyra, her tight skirts, her ass in those tight skirts, the class act she was from top to toe, and the fact that the only man on earth she'd let tap her ass was sitting next to him.

And then he thought that he did not want to be the kind of man who wallowed in history. But he was thinking he was.

And last, Joker thought all of that was something to think about.

"Go," he muttered, throwing back another swallow and not looking at his brother.

"Tyra will reach out. We'll get Carissa in that house."

Joker gave him his eyes.

Tack kept going.

"I see I didn't sort your shit, and that troubles me, but they're your terms to come to, you choose how you do it. Now you need time. But you need this again, Joke, I'm at the stool next to you. I'll repeat it until I can't talk anymore. I'll do it as many times as I have to until you get it. That's what you mean to me. So now, I'm goin'. But you need me back," he tipped his head to the bar, "that's where I'll be."

Then, after taking out his wallet, throwing some bills on the bar, and clapping Joker on the shoulder, Tack strode out.

Joker watched him go.

Then he finished his beer.

He ordered another one.

Well, kiss my ass, dickhead. Over a year and this is the first time you come to see me?

God took my boy. Then He gave me you.

You need me back, that's where I'll be.

These thoughts in his head, Joker took his time over his second beer.

When he was done, he put the empty bottle on the bar, went out to his bike, home to the Compound, and right into a clean room.

With mostly clean sheets.

CHAPTER EIGHT

Feeling Lucky

Carissa

"I THINK HE likes you," I said to Big Petey through a smile.

Though, with the way Travis, who Big Petey was holding, was trying to gobble up Pete's nose, I would say it was more like love at first sight.

It was Tuesday, late morning, and I was standing at the bar in the Chaos Compound next to Big Petey, who was on a stool and had just taken hold of my son.

"Ooo, he's so cute. I remember the days when they were all warm, squiggly, bundles of goodness," Tyra, standing behind the bar, cooed.

Pete avoided having his nose amputated by baby teeth and gums and did this slanting his head and blowing a loud raspberry on Travis's chubby cheek, making my baby giggle and squirm more, which made me smile bigger.

Once he did this, Pete turned to Tyra and ordered, "Don't get any ideas, woman. Your man is already saving up, not for future college tuition, for future bail money. He don't need no more headaches in the form of hooligans."

I looked to the two dark-headed boys currently wrestling

around on the floor of the Compound, grunting and giving it their all, something Tyra was ignoring, so I guessed it was normal, and thought Pete was not wrong.

"Tack would give me ten more kids if I wanted them," Tyra returned.

"Definition of crazy in love," Pete muttered, turned his attention back to Travis and advised gravely, "Learn early, little man, find an ugly woman so she'll bend over backward to do your bidding, not a pretty one you'll break your back to do hers."

"Pete!" Tyra snapped.

He looked again to her. "What?"

Tyra glared.

I kept out of it but only because Travis had yet to learn how to understand English.

Fortunately for Big Petey (or maybe Tyra), at that moment, a loud crash sounded in the room and I looked to see that Rider and Cutter had knocked over a chair.

But they were still wrestling.

I looked at Tyra. "Uh . . . is this normal?"

She stopped glaring at Big Petey and looked to me. "I'm an only child, but Tack has a brother he hasn't spoken to in years."

That didn't answer my question, but she wasn't done.

"He said they really never had anything to do with each other. All the way back since they were young. He also had a sister."

I didn't think the past tense of that last bit was a good thing, but I didn't get to react since she kept going.

"He said they were in each other's faces all the time. But he adored her. He also said that Tabby and Rush were constantly going at it from kids to teens. And they're super-close." She looked to her sons. "My boys are always together, sometimes wrestling or arguing, sometimes not. Whatever this is will mean something else later. Knowing that, I let them be."

This was food for thought should I be lucky enough to give Travis a sibling.

I was chewing on that notion when the front door opened and I twisted my neck to see Tack sauntering through. As he shifted around the back of the bar and came our way, he gave a chin lift to Pete, a nod to me, and a smile to his wife that made my heart flutter in a happy way for Tyra.

"You talk to Carissa?" he asked.

"No!" Tyra cried. "Shoot! With her showing with Travis, I got caught up in baby and forgot."

"Talk to me about what?" I asked.

Tack made it to Tyra as Tyra looked to me. "Tack and I still own my old place. We rent it out for extra cash. And our renters gave notice about a week ago."

I didn't know why she was telling me this, so when she stopped talking, I said, "Okay."

"Thought you might wanna have a look at it," Tack said.

"I—" I started but only got that far.

"A little house," Tyra stated and at that, my heart thumped.

Travis and me in a little house?

How wonderful would that be?

"Two bedrooms," she went on.

Two bedrooms?

Heaven!

"I redid the kitchen when I was there, which was a while back, but it's still nice," she kept going. "And we put new carpet down in the whole place and repainted after the renters before these and our current renters have only been in there a few months. So it's really nice."

"I, uh . . . I . . ." I stammered.

"We need someone in it we can trust," Tack told me. "The ones leavin' jacked us around. Jumpin' their lease early 'cause they had a kid, got pregnant, need a bigger place. The ones before them got a puppy, didn't tell us, didn't pay a pet deposit, puppy messed the place up. Which bought new carpet and paint and a pain in our ass. Not worth the hassle of gettin' in the faces of a couple buildin' a family. But need someone steady. Regular. In the family, meaning *our* family, who we know'll take care of the place."

I would definitely take care of their place.

Though, I'd likely have to start selling plasma (and then some) to afford it.

"Well—" I began.

Tyra cut me off again, "Six hundred dollars a month."

My eyes got big.

Six hundred a month?

That was only a few hundred more than what I was currently paying for the not-so-great place I was raising my son.

A deal!

She took in my big eyes and added swiftly, "Plus free cable." When I didn't speak because my excitement made me mute, she threw in, "And electricity paid."

"I, uh...a *house* for six hundred dollars?" I finally got out.

"It's nice. Really nice. In a good neighborhood. And you said you weren't real big on where you're staying," Tyra said by way of answer.

At this point, Tack was holding out his phone. "Scroll, girl. Those are pictures. We can take you 'round whenever. Place'll be open at the end of the month, which means a week."

I took his phone and I scrolled through the photos. They weren't big on the phone but I could still see the place wasn't nice.

It was *very* nice. Clean and attractive with personality.

Not something that cost six hundred dollars a month.

And here it was again.

This wasn't a deal, it was a steal.

And I'd be the thief.

Darn.

I gave Tack back his phone, saying, "That's really sweet but I couldn't."

"Why not?" he asked.

"Because you can get more out of it if you rent to someone else," I explained what he well knew.

"Yeah, and we can get more headaches with dogs and lease jumpers and shit like that," he returned.

"Not to mention, the expense of placing an ad in the paper," Tyra put in.

I didn't know how much ads cost but I did know that whatever they cost didn't cover what they weren't making if they rented their place to someone who could afford it.

"And we don't go through a management company," Tack added. "So we gotta go through applications, pay for credit checks, drop shit to do showings. It's a pain in the ass. You take it, we don't have to do any a' that shit."

Okay, well, I could imagine that none of that was fun, not to mention it had to be time consuming and pricey.

"When's your lease up?" Tack pushed.

"It's month to month. Where I am, they know not to try for anything over six months. Tenants are pretty transient," I told him. "Once I did my first six months, they went month to month."

"Notice?" he asked.

"I'd have to check but I think it's a week."

"Give it. We'll get you in. Boys'll help. First up, Tyra'll show you around so you know it's where you wanna be."

I already knew it was where I wanted to be. Me, Travis, a clean, nice little house that was *not* in my current neighborhood. It was where I wanted to be.

But taking advantage of them wasn't who I wanted to be.

I opened my mouth to reply, not knowing how to turn them down, but I didn't get a word out.

The front door opened again, all eyes went to it, including mine, and I shut my mouth as this time my heart skipped before it squeezed when Joker strode in.

Unfortunately, my ride with Snapper had worn off by Sunday morning. I knew this when I woke up with a strange ache that had Joker and his brunette written all over it. Luckily, I had work to take my mind off of it and Travis back so the ache went away when my little boy again filled my life.

But even with work (and Travis) I thought of pretty much nothing but Joker, and I'd come to the realization that it wasn't Joker's fault. He didn't lead me on. He didn't give any indications (outside of returning that kiss) that he was interested at all.

So it was all me.

Still, it had hurt.

And seeing him right then, the ache came back.

I felt it settle in as Joker did much the same as Tack when he entered, except he came around the outside of the bar, and after giving lifts and tips of his chin to the others in the room, his eyes came to me.

"Butterfly," he muttered.

Another heart squeeze.

Nicknames, obviously, were a biker thing. Joker's parents hadn't named him Joker, for sure. And Shy wasn't Shy, Tabby had told me Saturday night his real name was Parker. Same with High, Snapper, and the rest (though I didn't know their real names, I just knew what Tab referred to as their Club names).

That said, Ride and Cut were Tyra and Tack's kids' names, but shortened from Rider and Cutter.

So a nickname was the thing with biker clubs.

Still, I wished *butterfly* had a different meaning.

As I was wishing this, Joker sauntered right past me.

And he did this to go straight to Big Petey.

And he did this so he could firmly pull Travis from Pete's arms, lift him up so they were face to face, and ask, "How goes it, kid?"

Taking that in, I suddenly had trouble breathing.

Travis screamed with glee and latched on with both hands to Joker's beard.

Joker pulled him forward like he was going to give him a kiss, but he didn't. He just touched his forehead to Travis's before he dropped him down, making Travis lose purchase on his whiskers. He then tucked Travis's little tush in his hand, settling his back in the curve of his arm, and turned to me.

"All good?" he asked.

Although I wasn't certain about his question, at that moment, Joker holding my son right in front of me, all was definitely good.

"Uh...yeah," I mumbled.

Then, in order to remain sane, I tore my eyes from Joker and saw that Big Petey had his head dropped to look at his lap, but I could see the side of his face and his lips were turned up.

I cast my gaze behind the bar and saw Tyra looked like she was trying not to laugh. Her eyes were on Joker, and they were dancing.

Tack was also looking at Joker, and his lips were curved up as well, but he was also shaking his head.

I didn't know what any of this meant, and I didn't give it any time to figure it out.

I couldn't.

Because I didn't know what to do.

Or say.

What I did know was that that ache had both intensified and lessened. The contradiction couldn't be real, but it was and I knew it because I could feel it.

"You tell her about your place?" Joker asked and I turned my eyes back at him to see he was addressing Tack and Tyra.

"Yeah," Tack replied. "She's movin' in at the end of the month."

I opened my mouth again and again didn't get anything out before Joker spoke.

"Good. It's safe, Carrie, and clean. It's also close to LeLane's."

My body locked.

Carrie?

I stared at him and the ache was gone.

Then something he said hit me.

"It's close to LeLane's?" I asked.

"Your store. Only maybe five, ten minute drive away," Joker answered.

In my life, five, ten minutes was a far sight better than twenty. Not to mention, I'd save on gas money. Not thousands of dollars, but every savings meant something to me.

Further, I absolutely intended to pay Big Petey something for looking after Travis, but I knew whatever that was would probably not come close to what I was paying my daycare center. Travis's center was awesome, but it was expensive.

My current rent was super cheap. But paying whatever I was going to pay Big Petey, which would be less than what

I was currently paying for daycare, would more than likely cover the additional it would cost to live at Tyra's old place.

And bottom line, where I lived was noisy. It wasn't safe. It wasn't attractive. It wasn't well kept. It was too small. And I lived on the third floor. Since I was no way in heck going to leave my son in my apartment while I carried up groceries (or whatever) that meant I had to climb two flights of stairs repeatedly, carting up whatever I had to cart up along with Travis. And that was a pain in the behind.

All this meant I had no choice but to accept their kindness. Again.

Maybe, when I became a stylist, Tyra would let me do her hair for free and let me do this for eternity.

I looked from Joker to Tack and Tyra. "Can we arrange for Travis and me to look at it tomorrow? Say, after I get done with my shift?"

Tyra's face lit up. "Sure thing."

"Notice today, though, babe," Tack ordered.

I nodded.

"Yo," we all heard.

I looked the other way, leaning to the side, and saw Snapper in nothing but long shorts and gym shoes, carrying a ribbed white tank top in his hand, his rather well-defined chest on display (and covered in a sheen of sweat). He was heading out of the doorway that led to the side hall and also to what I'd learned on cleaning day was a meeting room, a workout room, some locked doors I didn't know what they were, and a laundry room.

"Hey, Snapper," I called and his eyes came to me before he smiled.

"Yo, babe."

I reached and grabbed Travis from Joker (doing this avoiding his eyes). Travis latched on to my hair right away but I didn't feel it (I had a tough scalp seeing as he did that a lot and my scalp had no choice but to toughen up). Once I had him, I walked to Snapper.

"This is my son, Travis," I declared and looked down to Travis. "Travis, this is Snapper. He took Mommy on a ride on Saturday and it was really nice."

Travis gurgled, staring at Snapper while trying to eat his own fist.

"Yo, little bro," Snapper said quietly, lifting a hand toward Travis, which meant Travis lost interest in eating his fist, wrapped his baby fingers around Snapper's index finger, and yanked that into his mouth.

He barely got it wet before Travis was no longer in my arms.

He also no longer had hold of Snapper's finger.

He was held high against Joker's chest.

Travis didn't mind, and I knew this when he commenced slapping Joker on his bearded cheek then fell forward and licked black whiskers.

That made the ache come back, but through it, I felt surprise at Joker's maneuver.

In fact, I was surprised he'd done it the first time with Big Petey (though not as aggressively).

And I was so surprised, I was about to say something.

But then I felt it.

The tenseness in the room.

It was then I *saw* it.

Even with a baby sucking on his beard, Joker had his eyes locked to Snapper and he was not looking at him with motorcycle brotherly love.

I wanted to take a step back.

I wanted more to snatch my son and *then* take a step back.

But the heaviness of the situation was not lost on me and I sensed any movement would not be a smart idea.

So I stood still and waited.

Luckily, the wait didn't last long.

Strangely, it ended with Snapper saying low, "I get it."

To which Joker rumbled lower, "Good."

I felt my eyes get big even if I had no earthly idea what was happening.

Travis gave up lapping at whiskers, declared, "Bee, bo, bah," and yanked Joker's hair.

Joker ignored it and kept scowling at Snapper.

"Brothers, last day of the month, clear it. Need men to move Carissa into Tyra's old place," Tack announced through the thick air.

Snapper stepped back, glanced at me, and said, "I'm in." He lifted his tank top my way. "Good to see you, babe. Your kid is cute."

After that, he strode off without me being able to say anything.

I looked up to Joker, not knowing if I wanted to yell, stamp my foot, demand an explanation, or laugh hysterically.

I did none of these things.

Joker still had Travis held high but now he had his head turned to him.

"Know you don't got any, little dude, but it'll grow and I kinda like my hair where it is."

Travis emitted a "Dee dah," and slapped Joker on the mouth.

That mouth twitched.

Okay.

Enough.

"I'm going to the mall," I announced.

I mean, when your life was in turmoil, what else did a girl do?

I had no money to get anything at the mall, but Travis loved it. He was social and was dedicated to charming anyone who came within two yards of him. He needed those opportunities, and they weren't afforded when we were stuck in our tiny apartment.

So the mall it was.

I reached toward Joker and quickly averted my eyes when his came to mine.

I grabbed my boy just as Tyra declared, "Awesome! Ride and Cut and I'll come with. I'll call Elvira."

I settled Travis against my body as I turned to her. "Doesn't Elvira work?"

"Hawk has a time-off-for-shopping policy," Tyra told me.

She said this and I knew she meant it because her head was bent and her thumb was moving over her phone.

I watched, thinking that I wanted to work for whoever this Hawk was.

"I'll be at your house an hour before you gotta leave for shift tomorrow," Big Petey said to me, heaving himself off his stool. "You can show me the ropes before you go."

"Thanks, Big Petey. That'd be great," I replied.

He lifted a hand and plodded out.

"Ride, Cut, quit tryin' to kill each other and get your asses over here," Tack ordered, making me think Tyra should instigate her own cursing levies since her boys were old enough to understand the English language.

"Later, Butterfly," Joker muttered and my eyes went to him just as my heart again flipped.

"Uh, later, Joker."

He gave me a look that said nothing, firm behind his wall of steel, then he sauntered to the back hall.

"Elvira," Tyra said into her phone. "You. Me. Carissa. My boys. Carissa's Travis. Mall and lunch. Thirty minutes." Pause, "Which mall do you think? See you there." She looked to me and smiled. "Let's roll."

I hadn't been shopping with girlfriends since before I got pregnant.

I had no money for trifles, a higher rent coming up, a hefty debt still to pay my old attorney, and non-monetary debts racking up to new friends.

Even with all this, lunch and the mall on the horizon with women I liked, I... could not... *wait*.

So I didn't.

Me and Travis *rolled*.

*　　*　　*

"If you don't get that," Elvira started, standing, bouncing, and holding my son to her while holding his hand so he couldn't smack her with it (anymore). "I'm gettin' it for you."

"And I'm getting the other one. The tank with all those rectangular sequins on it," Tyra declared.

We were in the handicapped dressing room of a store that I'd never been to.

All of us. Including Rider and Cutter, who had proved through a mannequin incident in a previous store that they needed constant vigilance.

And I was standing in front of the mirror in my jeans and a tube top.

It wasn't your average, everyday tube top.

It was a muted forest green in a smooth, stretchy, but tight knit. It had a thin turnover lip at the top and a seam under the breasts. And it went down my midriff and lower, to tuck into my jeans.

It was a *classy* tube top.

And I couldn't believe it with my bigger breasts, but it looked really cute.

Further, Tyra was right. I'd also tried on a black tank that had rectangular silver sequins stitched in an amazing design on the front, and although that wasn't my normal thing either, it still looked fabulous.

It looked biker babe.

But biker babe chic.

I stared at myself wondering if I'd ever have the nerve to wear such a top.

Then I thought about Joker with his brunette and I wished I could afford it.

On that thought, my phone rang.

"I'm on it," Tyra said, sitting on the shelf bench, before she dug into my purse, which was on the bench beside her.

I felt a little hand slap my thigh and looked down to see Cutter standing there, his head tipped way back, his mother's green eyes in a face reminiscent of his father on me.

"Pretty," he said.

Well, there was another vote.

I smiled at him. "Thanks, honey."

"Says unknown number," Tyra stated and I turned to her to see she had her arm extended, phone toward me.

I grabbed it, took the call, and put it to my ear.

"Hello?"

"Ms. Teodoro?" a woman that sounded familiar asked.

"Yes."

"Hold for Angie, please."

Oh. My attorney.

I heard a click and then I heard, "Ms. Teodoro?"

"Hi, Angie. Please, it's Carissa," I corrected.

Or Carrie.

Or Butterfly.

But those were Joker's.

I looked back to the tube top, thinking maybe I *could* afford it, if I could talk Sharon into giving me some overtime next week.

"Just wanted to touch base, tell you we got the files, and I've been over them. I'll transfer you back to Leanne to set up a meeting but I wanted to ask you about breastfeeding."

I stopped thinking about tube tops and my eyes unfocused as I gave my attention to Angie.

"Sorry?"

"Breastfeeding. There's a note in your attorney's file that says that Mr. Neiland refused your breast milk during his visitations with Travis and started your son on formula without discussing this with you. Is this true?"

It was, but I tried not to remember it because at the time I'd been so hurt, and so angry, I'd phoned my attorney and told him all about it.

That being that, in the beginning, when Aaron had Travis for only short periods of time, the fact that I breastfed him wasn't an issue. I just pumped extra and handed it over when I handed over Travis, and, if needed, I would drop more by his house.

But when Aaron won half custody, it was harder for me to keep up with supply and demand, meaning I couldn't hand over a week's worth at one time. This meant that I had to pop by Aaron's house more often, but also, because I worked and I couldn't be at Aaron's beck and call, Tory would have to come by my place or the store to get more milk.

Therefore, this had gone on for two visitations before they stopped setting up pick-up times for more milk, which obviously made me worry.

Then at the end of his time with Travis, Aaron handed my son back to me, telling me he was no longer feeding Travis my milk, but formula. He also declared it was better for Travis if I stopped breastfeeding and switched to formula, essentially ordering me to do so.

Now, I wasn't the kind of woman who wanted to breast-feed until my kid was five.

But I was the kind of woman who wanted to give my child the kind of nurture and connection he could get only from me until it was a healthy option to stop doing it.

So, of course, I refused. My times feeding Travis were *mine*. They were *beautiful*. There was no way to describe how significant that connection was, and I had no intention of giving it up.

Unfortunately, Aaron's decision had a variety of ramifications.

The first being, since I was tossing a lot of milk down the drain once the freezer filled up (and had to take breaks from work to pump), this became onerous and disruptive, rather than necessary for my son's nurture.

Still, I would have continued doing it, but then it came clear that Travis was having trouble coping with the constant change. He'd already suffered nipple confusion when the back and forth was happening between my breast and Aaron needing to use bottles. Not to mention just having to endure the back and forth between his mommy and daddy.

But then Travis started spitting up more, having trouble returning to the nipple when I got him back, was cranky and slept fitfully, and in the end, he wasn't gaining weight the way he should.

Since Aaron flatly refused to put him back on my milk, I had no choice but to switch to formula.

And heartbreakingly, Travis's feedings steadied, he was in better spirits, slept peacefully and looked healthier.

At the time, I'd been devastated, the experience made worse by learning precisely how powerless I was about what happened with my baby.

So it also terrified me.

"It's true," I answered Angie. "He demanded I switch from breast milk to formula, and although I refused in the beginning, Travis had issues with the change, Aaron would not hear of accepting my milk, so I had to relent."

I heard Tyra gasp but I didn't turn to her. I stayed focused on Angie.

"It says in your custody agreement that matters of health and well-being are to be decided equally between you and your ex-husband," Angie told me, something I already knew.

"That may be so, but that's not Aaron's way of doing things," I shared. "If he wants to do it, he does."

"That couldn't have been easy on you or your son," Angie noted.

"It absolutely wasn't," I confirmed. "On either of us. But Aaron has little concern about what's easy on me or, apparently, Travis. In fact, just last week Travis had croup. Aaron took him to the hospital, and he didn't inform me he did. His fiancée shared with me after the fact, but Aaron didn't contact me at all. I requested to see my son, but this was refused. I saw him two days later, but only because Aaron's fiancée snuck him to my place of work so I could spend thirty minutes with him."

There was heavy silence before Angie said, "When you speak to Leanne, please make our meeting as soon as you possibly can, Carissa. There are a number of motions I could file. In the meantime, I'll think things over so I can fully discuss our strategy options going forward during our meeting."

"Can you give me a hint?" I asked, my heart thumping.

"Of course," she answered. "First, there's no way the financial support you can provide your son should not be augmented by your ex-husband. The discrepancy between your earnings is vast. Second, even though your marriage was not very long, your settlement, considering proceedings started when you were pregnant, was outrageously low. There is no way you could set up an appropriate home for your son and yourself with that kind of money. Your husband more than has the means to have helped provide you with that, not only through his earnings but also the trust fund that opened to him when he turned twenty-five, and two rather substantial inheritances that he's received in the last four years."

She took a breath before she continued and I kept listening hard, my heart still hammering in my chest because she sounded on the ball and raring to fight. I hadn't had anyone but me in my corner for so long, it was a thrill to have someone who knew what they were talking about finally helping me fight.

"Also, your ex-husband by signed agreement does not have the right to make unilateral decisions of the magnitude of ceasing breastfeeding. And last, regardless that it was croup, and I assume, as well as hope, your son is feeling much better, any illness should be reported to an ex-spouse. It's an unparalleled hardship that you weren't informed of his ailment nor granted access to him while he was ill. From what I understood from Mr. Allen, this situation was sketchy at best. Now, understanding it fully, it's far worse. I'm fighting mad, Carissa. I just hope you are too."

"I am," I whispered, my heart thumping faster, because she didn't sound fighting mad.

She sounded incensed.

"Then please, make a meeting with Leanne as soon as is convenient. I'll stay late if you have to work. I'll instruct Leanne about that. Take care, Carissa, and I hope to see you soon."

She transferred me. I spoke with Leanne. We set a meeting the next day after I got off work and I disconnected, then stood there in a cute tube top, staring at my phone.

I did this thinking maybe, just maybe, finally there was hope.

"Your ex made you stop breastfeeding?"

I stiltedly turned to Tyra at her question.

She was staring up at me, her eyes bright with tears, though, from the look on her face, I didn't know if they were tears of camaraderie of a mother done wrong or tears of fury.

"Yes," I told her.

"Oh my God," she whispered. "I *totally hate* your ex."

"I hate him too!" Rider cried loyally.

I forced a grin at him but said, "That's sweet, cutie, but you really shouldn't hate people."

"You should if they're mean," Rider returned.

Now, how could I argue that?

"Tyra, notice," Elvira stated, and at her tone, my eyes went direct to her.

At one look, I saw Elvira wasn't feeling upset about a mother done wrong.

She was just flat furious.

"Your man's got T-minus a month to sort that jackass, then I'm settin' Hawk on him," she warned.

"Vira said *ass*!" Cutter shouted, though why he'd point that out when his father said the same and he hadn't uttered a word, I didn't know.

I also didn't ask.

This was because Tyra said, "We're on it, Elvira."

"You better be," she snapped then looked at me. "Tube top and tank. And I saw a cute dress out there you're gonna try on, girl. I don't care what you say. And if it looks as cute as all that," she pointed a finger at me, "I'm gettin' all of it for you." Her upraised hand snapped into a palm out position when I opened my mouth. "No lip," she ordered. "Not lost on me you're a sister whose current circumstances say you can't treat yourself, and no sister of mine who looks that good in that top, that tank, and probably that dress you're gonna try on doesn't get a treat. Comes around goes around. That's life. You'll have your shot. Now it's my turn."

Then, taking Travis with her, she flounced on her deep purple suede stilettos out of the dressing room.

I looked to Tyra.

"You'll learn Elvira's ways and bow to them like the rest of us," she informed me.

I had a feeling I would.

"And she's right," Tyra continued gently. "You need a treat, Carissa. You'll enjoy it, but trust me, as much as you do, she'll enjoy giving it to you more."

I felt a stinging in my eyes and bit my lip that had started quivering. Since I had to do that, I didn't answer.

I just nodded.

She kept hold of my gaze and kept talking gently. "You're going to be okay."

"You're all helping a lot. Too much," I replied, my voice quaky.

She stood and got close. When she did, she placed a hand light on my cheek and leaned toward me.

"We've all had our times. And if we're lucky, we've all had people that took our back during those times. You've been unlucky, honey. But your luck has changed. Roll with it."

I stared into her eyes.

And with lips again quivering, I nodded.

Thirty minutes later, we all left the store, me pushing Travis's empty stroller (Tyra had ahold of him now), and in it was a bag that held a cute tube top, an awesome tank, and a fabulous petal-pink sleeveless tee dress with a boat neck, blousy top, and side-ruched skirt that wasn't exactly me.

But it was perfect.

Better, it was a treat. And I hadn't had one of those in a *long* time.

We had lunch at the food court while Rider and Cutter terrorized all the children in the play area.

And I ate, chatted, and even laughed...feeling it.

Feeling it like I felt it when I was riding with Snapper.

But this time, that first-time feeling wasn't feeling free.

It was feeling lucky.

CHAPTER NINE

You Like Mexican?

Carissa

IT WAS AFTER lunch and more shopping that included Tyra buying me a pair of really neat big hoop earrings with a webby thing in the middle but mostly included Tyra and Elvira amassing five shopping bags each.

It was also after Tyra spoke with her renters and they let us come around so I could view her home.

It was better than I could imagine just looking at it on a small phone screen.

In real life, it was a dream come true.

But now, it was dinnertime and I was back home, someplace I didn't want to be and someplace I was thrilled would not be home for long.

I had my son at my hip, my purse and Travis's diaper bag over my shoulder, my shopping bag in my hand, my foot lifted to take the first step that led to many—steps I would soon not have to climb when I got home with my baby (and there it was, me feeling even more lucky)—when I heard, "Yo."

I turned, stopped dead and stared, unfortunately with mouth open, at Joker sauntering to me.

What on earth?

"What are you doing here?" I asked as he made it to me.

"Got him," he muttered, and before I could make a move to stop him, he grabbed Travis.

Then before I could say a word about that, he spoke.

"Here to check your place. See how many trucks we need to move your crap."

Crap was not a great word, but it wasn't worth a nickel, so I let it slide.

And *disappointed* was not exactly the right word for the emotion I was feeling that he was just there to check out my place to see how many trucks they needed, but for my peace of mind I didn't think too hard on what the right word would be.

"Well, okay," I mumbled.

He stood there.

I stared up at him.

"Butterfly, haul your ass up there," he ordered.

That was worth a nickel.

"Another five cents," I told him.

He shook his head then jerked it to the stairs.

I sighed and moved that way.

I climbed. Travis and Joker climbed behind me.

I walked down the walkway. Joker with Travis walked with me.

I opened the door and entered my apartment. Joker brought Travis in after I did.

He closed the door and looked around.

I did too.

The single bonus of Tory (outside her having enough human kindness to inform me my son was sick and then bring him to see me) was that she wanted to redecorate my house after Aaron kicked me out of it. Something Aaron let her do. Therefore I got most of the furniture that used to make its home in a much nicer place.

This meant what Joker was seeing was incongruous.

That being a beautiful, expensive, comfortable fawn suede sectional that ate up nearly every inch of space and surrounded a fabulous, large, heavy, carved, square coffee table and faced a massive media center including a big flat screen TV that took up all the wall space with none to spare.

The attractive rush-seated hardwood stools at my bar didn't belong to the place either. Nor did the countertop appliances and kitchen paraphernalia that were all expensive because they were top of the line. All this was given to us during our engagement party, my shower, and our wedding, and those gifts were mostly from Aaron's parents' friends.

And last, there were the accoutrements, heavy silver frames (that now did not hold pictures of me and Aaron over the too many years we were together but instead held pictures of Travis, Travis and me, Travis and my dad, or my dad, my mom, and Althea), expensive decorative knickknacks, and a Bose dock that I didn't get in the divorce decree. I filched it. But luckily, Aaron either didn't notice or was so busy having sex with a barely legal model and making my life a misery he didn't have the energy to fight to get it back.

Joker couldn't see my bedroom suite, which also took up the entirety of space in my tiny bedroom, especially with Travis's crib and changing table shoved against a wall.

I'd even gotten the comforter and sheets. All that was magnificent, elegant, even regal.

As it would be.

I'd picked the comfy sectional.

But Aaron's mother had chosen our bedroom furniture.

Plus I had the storage unit my father paid for (saying he needed it for his stuff but I'd been there, he had two boxes stored there, the rest of the space was taken with the leftovers of my marriage). It held my dining room table and the guest bedroom furniture from one of our *four* guest bedrooms.

Something I intended to sell should I have needed to.

Now I didn't and would be able to use it (or most of it) when I moved into Tyra's house.

More lucky.

"See the asshole left you with somethin'," Joker muttered.

"Nickel," I snapped.

He looked at me, ignored my snap, and stated, "Thinkin' we need more than a coupla trucks."

"That would be useful," I confirmed. "I also have a dining room set that it would be great if you retrieved from my dad's storage unit."

"We'll take care a' that," he stated, and instead of nodding, shaking my hand, wishing me a good night, handing me my son, and walking out the door, he walked toward my kitchen, around the bar, and to the fridge. He then asked, "Thoughts on dinner?"

I stood where I was and stared at him. Then I stared at the fridge door when he mostly disappeared behind it.

I was still staring when he straightened, looked down at Travis, who was studying the wonders of the inside of the fridge with rapt baby attention, and asked, "Spaghetti?"

Travis looked up at him and replied, "Guh."

"Yep. Sounds good to me," Joker replied, disappeared behind the fridge door and came back out with a package of hamburger meat. His eyes came to me. "Skillet?"

"Uh…"

"Dah!" Travis declared.

Joker looked to him then at me. "When does he eat?"

"Now."

"You do him. I'll do spaghetti."

Okay.

What was happening?

"Um...Joker—"

"Drop your bag, Butterfly, and get your kid," he ordered.

"Are you having dinner with me?" I asked.

"Yeah, after I cook it," he answered.

I didn't know what to make of that so I asked, "Why?"

"Why not?" he asked back.

I had no answer to that.

Fortunately, he gave me more.

"I'm here. It's dinnertime. You need to eat. I need to eat. You feed your kid. I'll make shit to feed you."

I liked the idea of dinner with Joker. What I wasn't so sure about was why Joker wanted to have dinner with me.

Maybe he was just being friendly.

Maybe he was just hungry.

I didn't ask.

Instead, I shared, "I think the tally now is eighty-five cents."

He shook his head and then he gently shook my son as a message to me.

"Get your kid, Carrie."

Carrie.

Three people called me that.

But it started with Althea.

When she was little, she couldn't say Carissa and instead said *Cah-ree-ree* which morphed into Carrie.

My parents called me that back then too.

When we lost Althea, they stopped.

No one had ever shortened my name to Carrie again. In fact, except for calling me "honey" sometimes, "beautiful" others, and "baby" when we were having sex, when he stopped calling me Riss ages ago for whatever reason, Aaron had had no other sweet nothings or cute nicknames for me.

The return of Carrie should have brought up bad memories. Maybe even hurt.

But it didn't.

No, I liked Joker calling me Carrie.

"Babe, kid," he said impatiently.

I jumped to, got rid of Travis's bag and my purse, moved into the kitchen, and grabbed my son.

This commenced both Joker and I moving around, me putting Travis in his highchair and getting his baby food ready and Joker taking off his jacket, tossing it on a stool, then opening and closing cupboards, grabbing stuff, and starting to get our dinner ready.

I pulled the highchair around to the stools, sat on one, and started feeding my son.

I did it while also watching Joker. So I saw him season the browning meat with salt, pepper, and dried basil. I also saw him peruse my meager spice collection like he was looking for something.

"What do you need?" I asked.

"Red pepper flakes," he answered.

"I don't have those."

He turned to me. "Don't like a kick?"

"I do. I just..." I shrugged. "Actually, I just eat what I eat as long as it's fast. I don't spend time on it because I don't have that time or the energy."

There was that, of course, but also dried red pepper flakes cost money and were unnecessary, thus they were not in my cupboard.

His jaw flexed and he shut the door on the spices.

I concentrated on feeding Travis, who was banging his fists, one that had a set of humongous plastic keys in it, against the highchair tray.

But I did this talking.

Or, maybe, semi-interrogating.

"You know how to cook?"

"Yeah."

"Self-taught?"

"Learn or earn."

I looked to him, loaded baby spoon in the air. "Learn or earn?"

He kept his eyes to the spoon he was using to push around the meat. "Learn or earn my dad bein' pissed. He liked his food. I learned to make what he liked 'cause I wasn't big on the consequences."

I drew in breath to calm the tumult of feelings his disclosure caused and forced my tone to nonchalant, like I was asking the weather, when I noted, "So, no mom, and your dad wasn't all that great either."

"Hitler wasn't all that great. My dad was a dick."

My gaze shot to him. He must have felt my horror because he looked at me.

"Relax, Butterfly. It's a joke." He held my gaze. "But my dad was a dick."

I nodded, thinking he didn't want me to make a big deal of it, even though it was a very big deal, so I looked back to Travis.

Only then did I say softly, "I'm sorry, Joker."

Joker didn't reply.

Okay.

He was being forthcoming. He wasn't avoiding me. In fact, he was doing the opposite. He also seemed taken with Travis. Not many men (I assumed, I hadn't tested this theory)

wanted to hang with single mothers *and* their babies. They
certainly didn't claim said babies at every given opportunity.
Not if they only intended to be friends. Or, essentially, bum
a meal.

And he was calling me Carrie.

Hope flared and I made a decision.

It was time to explore.

I cleared my throat and shoved strained peas into my
boy's mouth.

He spit them out, I scooped them up and shoved them
back in, saying ultra-casually, "So, that pretty brunette you
were with on Saturday. Is that your girlfriend?"

"Stacy?"

Her name was Stacy.

Ulk.

"I wasn't introduced."

Travis banged the keys against the tray.

"Not a girlfriend."

My heart leaped.

Joker continued, "Decent woman. Until she gets slaughtered. Then decent goes out the window seein' as she has no
problem gettin' behind a wheel when she's shitfaced. She got
that way Saturday, knew that shit would go down, so I took
her home."

The hope started burning so bright I didn't check it when
my head snapped up and I asked, "That's it?"

Joker looked from the hamburger to me.

"That's it, Carrie," he said gently.

He said it *gently*.

And he was looking at me in a way that told me he
wanted me to believe those words.

"Oh," I whispered.

I said no more.

Joker didn't either.

But we stared at each other across my kitchen and the new way he started looking at me made my skin start tingling.

"Moo mah!" Travis cried.

My head jerked down to him. "What, baby?"

He banged the keys against the tray. "Gah!"

"Did you just say 'moo mah?'" I asked, meaning, did my son just call me Mommy?

He banged the keys and kicked out his feet.

He wanted more peas.

Well, he didn't want more peas. He wanted to be done with peas so we could get to the peaches.

I gave him more peas but after I did, I looked back to Joker, and I knew when I did, I was smiling brilliantly.

"I think that was my first *Mommy*," I shared with glee.

"Sounded like that to me," Joker agreed.

But I was staring at him feeling even more glee.

Because for the first time since I'd met him, he was grinning.

He wasn't biker handsome.

No.

He was biker *amazing*.

I wanted to get up and jump up and down, for a number of reasons.

Instead, I shared, "I think that's early."

"Kid's a genius."

I smiled bigger.

"He's gonna say somethin' else, you don't fill his belly," Joker warned.

I looked down at an irate Travis. "Sorry, googly-foogly."

"Bah, bah, bah!" he snapped.

I grinned at him and gave him more peas.

Joker opened a cupboard and grabbed a box of spaghetti.

And I sat on my stool, in my dinky apartment filled with its magnificent furniture, yet again experiencing something new. Another something I hadn't felt before Joker rode up the shoulder of I-25 and into my life.

Normal.

Average.

A woman feeding her child while a man worked in her kitchen to feed them.

The way it should be.

The way I'd always wanted it to be.

The only thing I really wanted for me.

And my baby.

*　　*　　*

I sat on my couch, feet up in the seat, knees to chest, arms around my calves, eyes on the TV, nervous as could be.

This was because my son had a belly full of baby food and formula, and not long after, decided to call it a night.

He was in his crib in my room.

And I had a belly full of spaghetti Joker served me, and not long after, he decided we were going to watch TV.

So we were sitting on my couch, watching TV.

During dinner, conversation hadn't been free-flowing, mostly because Travis curtailed it, as was his wont. But things had been pretty easy.

Until Joker had invited himself to camp out in front of the television and then did just that.

I'd gotten Travis down and joined Joker.

Now I didn't know what to do.

Men could be friends with women, this was true (though I had no men friends, still, it was true, I'd seen it on TV).

But could bikers be friends with women? Were they

the kind of guys who hung out for dinner and TV just because?

It was my understanding, though it hadn't been confirmed, that Joker lived at the Compound. And he didn't have a TV in his room. There was one behind the bar in the common area, but not in his room.

Maybe he just wanted a comfy space to lounge. A change of scenery.

Or maybe he liked me.

But lounging, he was doing. Feet up. Boots still on. Ankles crossed. Heels resting on my coffee table. He was slouched down, not far from me, arms out and resting on the back of the couch. His hand was so close to my shoulder, it felt like it was hovering there, aimed to strike.

This meant I was so wound up, so unsure, so nervous, I didn't even know what we were watching.

Actually, to all that, I was also trying to control my mouth from opening and asking what was happening at the same time control my body from hurling itself in his arms.

In other words, I was a wreck.

What I should do was ask.

I liked him.

He was (maybe) giving indications he liked me.

I should know. I should be a big girl and put it out there. Just grab the remote, hit mute, turn to him and say the words, "Joker, what's happening here?"

Easy.

So why couldn't I do it?

I swallowed.

Then I bit my lip.

After that, I took a deep breath.

It stuck in my throat when Joker's hand, poised to strike, struck.

It did this by capturing a lock of my hair then twirling it around his finger.

I forced myself to breathe and do it steadily so he wouldn't hear me hyperventilating.

Okay, that felt nice.

Okay, did male friends of females twirl hair around their fingers?

No.

They couldn't.

Could they?

Afraid to move so I didn't lose his fingers playing with my hair, I slid my eyes to the side. I couldn't see him fully but I could see he had his attention on the TV.

Okay, now, what did that mean?

I had to know. I couldn't sit there a moment longer and not know.

"Joker?" I called and immediately cleared my throat because it came out croaky.

"Yeah, baby?" he asked distractedly.

But I froze.

Okay, male friends did not call females *baby*. Not the warm, intimate, albeit distracted, way he just said it.

I felt a tug on my hair and that tug, no matter how light, shot straight over my scalp, sizzled down my neck, and exploded at the heart of me.

"Carrie?"

Slowly, I turned my head and saw him looking at me.

He looked relaxed. He looked comfortable. He looked at home.

He looked amazing.

"What you need, Butterfly?" he muttered.

I knew what I needed.

I didn't tell him.

Not verbally.

I dropped my feet, twisted, planted a hand in the couch and launched myself into his arms.

Those arms closed around me, and right before my mouth would hit his, fear saturated me when he seemed to be coming up out of the couch like he intended to push me away.

But he wasn't.

He was coming toward me so he could skate his arm down my back, over my bottom, to hook around the backs of my knees. He curled his other arm around my back as he dragged me across his lap then dropped to his side, taking me to my back in the couch.

And it was his mouth that hit mine.

The second I had it, I wasted no time. I opened my lips in invitation and drove my fingers in his hair.

It was thick, springy, *thrilling*.

His tongue swept into my mouth.

I had it back.

Thank God, I had *him* back.

I held his head to me as I pressed up and he kept kissing me.

He shifted so my thighs were no longer draped over his lap, stretching out beside me and also on me.

And he kept kissing me.

I rolled into him, pressing my body the length of his, keeping a hand firm in his hair so he wouldn't leave me as I trailed the other hand down his back.

And he kept kissing me.

He yanked my shirt from my jeans and dove right in, his rough calluses grating up my skin, causing shivers to erupt along their path, a path that took him up my side.

I pressed closer.

Joker kept kissing me.

Then up my ribs.

I held tighter.

Joker kept kissing me.

To under my breast.

I went still.

Joker swept his thumb along skin, the very tip a whisper against the curve of the underside of my breast.

I whimpered.

A cell phone rang.

Joker broke the kiss but didn't pull away.

He shoved his face in my neck.

I didn't even try to hold back my whispered plea.

"No, no, no."

"Shit, shit, *fuck*," he growled.

"Joker?" I called tremulously.

He lifted his head and I held him even tighter as he shifted his hand out of my shirt and reached to his back pocket for his phone.

I was holding him tighter because I liked him on me. I liked what we'd been doing. And I didn't want him to let me go or what we'd been doing to stop.

But mostly, I was holding him tighter because he was looking me in the eyes and his were not blunt steel.

They were a sheet of blazing *molten* steel.

"Hang tight, Carrie," he murmured before he turned his head, looked at the phone, and clenched his jaw. I heard a beep, the phone was at his ear, and he said, "Bad fuckin' timing."

I closed my eyes.

But I didn't let him go.

I opened them when he said, "I didn't forget. But I got two hours before I gotta be there."

I watched. He listened.

Then he grunted, "Fuckin' Valenzuela."

Valenzuela?

"Yeah. I'm at Carrie's. It'll take me twenty." Pause and then, "Carissa." Another pause before, "Right. Later."

I heard a beep and he looked at me.

"You have to go," I said quietly.

"*Have to* bein' the operative words."

Wow, that was sweet.

I smiled.

His eyes dropped to my mouth and he made a sound like a groan.

That made me quit smiling and blurt, "What's happening here, Joker?"

His eyes came back to mine. "You like Mexican?"

My head jerked on the couch.

"Uh…yes."

"You work tomorrow?"

I nodded. "Day shift."

"Right, what's happenin' here is, tomorrow, Travis is in a high chair at Las Delicias while I feed you the best *burritos chicharrones* in Denver."

I melted underneath him.

A date.

He was asking me (and Travis!) out on a date.

I could wear my tube top!

Suddenly, I stopped melting.

"*Chicharrones* are essentially fried hunks of bacon fat," I shared.

"So?"

"Well," I proceeded cautiously and a little mortifyingly, "I haven't lost the last of the baby fifteen."

"And I like it," he announced.

I blinked.

"So in an effort to keep it as I like it, you get *chichar-rones*," he finished.

I loved *chicharrones*.

I mean, they *were* essentially bacon and everything even minutely bacon was amazing.

I loved it more he liked me as just me.

"Okay," I agreed, beginning to melt again. But the melting stopped when I remembered. "Oh no. After work I have to go meet my new attorney."

"Burritos after I take you to meet your attorney."

After he took me.

I smiled.

His eyes again dropped to my mouth.

Then his lips did and he kissed me, sweet but brief.

He lifted his head and said in a way I knew he didn't want to say it, "Gotta go, Butterfly."

My reply came out the same way. "Okay, Joker."

He knifed off me but did it grabbing my hand and yanking me up with him so I was on my feet.

He didn't let go of my hand as he pulled me to the stool. Only then did he release me so he could nab his jacket and shrug it on.

But he claimed my hand again when he took the four steps to the door. He pulled it open, turned to me, and pulled me in front of him.

I tipped my head back just in time for his hand to curl light around my jaw.

"When's your appointment?" he asked.

"Six," I answered.

"Distance to the office from here?"

"It's closer to work."

"Right. I'll come and get Travis, pick you up at work, take you there, then dinner."

"You'll need Travis's baby seat."

"Leave it for Big Petey."

I nodded.

His fingers pressed in and I automatically went up on my toes.

It was the right move since his head was bending toward me.

He touched his lips to mine, his whiskers brushing the skin they'd sensitized earlier, making my knees go weak so I had to reach out my hands and catch his T-shirt at his belly.

He ended the touch too soon but when he lifted his head, his rough thumb glided over my cheek as his steel eyes moved over my face.

"So fuckin' pretty," he murmured and it was a wonder my body didn't jerk out of his hold so I could twirl with glee.

"Thank you for dinner," I whispered and he looked into my eyes.

"No problem, Carrie."

I smiled.

His thumb rubbed over my lower lip before the pads of his fingers dug in lightly and he let me go.

I was proud I held it together and stayed steady rather than losing his touch and teetering.

"Later, Butterfly," he said.

"Later, Joker," I replied.

He moved out the door but looked back, doing it over his leather clad shoulder, a sinister biker who had a light touch, a molten look, a way with babies, and a talented mouth.

I put one hand to the edge of the door and lifted the other one to do a quick wave.

His mouth quirked, he shook his head, then he looked away and disappeared around the door.

I wanted to watch him walking away.

I didn't.

I closed the door, locked its three locks, turned my back to it, and smiled at my massive furniture.

Then I brought both hands up and clapped them together in front of me, softly but repeatedly.

After that, on a skip-hop launching me that way, I went to go check on my baby.

Joker

No, no, no.

With Carissa's sweet plea playing in his head, Joker parked at the end of the line of three bikes, swung off his, and moved into the dark alley.

Halfway down, close to a Dumpster, he saw Speck, Boz, and Hop circling two whores.

All eyes were on him.

His eyes were on the whores. "Early night?"

"Heidi needs to talk to you," Hop said, sounding impatient.

Then again, he would be. His old lady was fucking beautiful. And their new baby was a quarter of Hop's world, the rest of that made up with his other two kids and his woman.

He did patrol like they all did.

Then he got his ass home.

Tonight wasn't his night for patrol, though. He was there because he had a way with whores.

But these whores, or one of them, was Joker's.

Joker looked to the blonde, jerked his head, stopped moving their way, turned, and retraced his steps.

He heard her heels following and gave her his side when he stopped and waited for her to get to him.

When she did, she got close.

"I'm fucked, Joke."

"Babe, you're a whore workin' for Valenzuela. You pulled me from somethin' I was seriously into doin' to give that shit to me?"

"I'm pregnant."

Joker clenched his teeth and looked to his boots.

"Benito is gonna *freak*," she hissed.

He looked to her. "You know whose it is, or you get knocked up by a john?"

"No way a client. Protection only. It's my boyfriend, Brent's."

"And Brent says...?" he prompted.

Her face went hard. "Brent says it isn't his."

"You sure it is?"

Her face went harder and her eyes turned to stone. "Yes," she snapped.

"You keepin' it?" he asked.

"Hardly," she bit out.

"You're tellin' me this because...?"

"Gonna find a buyer."

He stared.

"Which means I'll be outta commission," she stated. "Which means you're gonna have to find some other stupid bitch to narc on Benito."

Fuck.

"And don't even bother askin' me to stay close anyway," she went on. "Benito found out I'm knocked up, he'd scrape me off and I'd be lucky he does that before he beats the shit outta me. So I'm takin' off to avoid the beatin' the shit outta me part. This'll be a sweet gig. If I find buyers, heard they pay doctor's bills. Pay for an apartment. Feed you. Get you clothes. And give you wads of cash."

Allowing his lip to curl, he did it wondering if he would

have been better off if his mother had sold him to some couple who was desperate for a baby.

The answer to that was probably.

"Doin' you a solid by givin' you a heads-up," she told him.

"You couldn't've shared this with Hop?"

"I only talk to you."

She did. He had no clue why. Except she'd tried it on with him a couple of times, looking to replace Brent, who had zero balls and a meth habit, with a man whose cock she hoped to suck to get her out from under the thumb of a lunatic.

Her problem was, Joker might fuck empty pussy, but he didn't fuck greedy pussy.

"Got a lock on another girl we can turn?" he asked.

"Maybe, for one large."

Yep.

Greedy pussy.

"You give a name, she gets us solid info, you'll get your bonus."

She nodded.

"Now, you're here, I'm here, you got anything for me?"

"I think Benito is saving the best for last. He's still concentrating on the Ruiz patch."

This, they knew.

Benito Valenzuela was a pathological drug-dealing, porn-producing pimp who saw an opportunity when a couple of major players in Denver shifted out of the felonious into something that increased their life expectancy.

He went with it, claimed turf, did it easy, and got himself a complex that he was unstoppable.

He also got himself a mission.

Take over Denver.

All of it.

Including Chaos, the five-mile area surrounding Ride

that Chaos decreed was free of drugs and whores. They decreed it but they also made it so by patrolling—brothers going out every night to keep their patch clean.

They'd been scuffling with Valenzuela for a while. Chaos attention turned to other issues. Valenzuela's attention turned to other turf. But they'd had skirmishes, including invading a porn set to free Tabby's junkie best friend who was paying her debt to Valenzuela by making her film debut.

Valenzuela did not take this kindly.

Since then, he'd been dormant where Chaos was concerned, doing his usual, sending dealers and whores into Chaos, causing headaches, but nothing extreme.

But the extreme was coming. Every member of the Club made it their purpose to know everything they could know about Valenzuela through every means available.

He hadn't forgotten Chaos.

Their problem wasn't just him. It was that with each move he made, he got more money, which meant more firepower.

No one was unstoppable.

But part of the past and future Joker had learned about his Club included learning that Valenzuela had once been a nuisance.

He was now a viable threat.

There was a day when Chaos would have moved at any time during the past few years to neutralize this threat.

But Tack had guided the Club from hostile negotiations that led to aggressive takedowns that could get bloody for all concerned to defensive maneuvers that centered solely on their patch.

If Valenzuela threatened them directly, the Club would move to take him down.

Until then, they kept their shit clean and their families safe from blowback.

This was the beef Rush had with his father. Because even if Tack had pulled the Club out of maneuvers that started antagonistic and led to violent, Tack was still set on doing whatever they had to do to keep their territory clean.

Rush felt the Club should leave the policing to the police.

Until that moment, Joker hadn't given a shit what the Club did. Whatever it was, he was all in.

But standing in an alley with a whore instead of exploring the many ways he wanted to make Carissa Teodoro whimper on her couch, he now had an opinion.

And until that moment, Joker didn't understand why Tack didn't work out his beef with his son.

But standing in that alley the day after he made the decision he should have made years ago in a car park outside a hospital, he got it.

Because Joker was standing in an alley with a whore. What he was not doing was exploring the ways he could make Carissa whimper, something he didn't know where it would lead, he just knew where he wanted it to go.

And Tack had led his Club away from a dark path through blood then vengeance to clean.

He'd earned his scars.

Now his newer brothers, who had not walked through fire to turn Chaos around, were the future of the Club. They needed to prove their grit and earn their scars.

Tack would someday step down.

And the Club would be at the mercy of what he left behind.

But Tack knew you couldn't lead without knowledge. You couldn't demand respect without earning it. You couldn't understand without experience.

Fuck, the man had it going on.

"You alive in there?" Heidi called.

He focused on her. "Need you to grab your friend and get off our patch."

"Same drill," she mumbled.

He didn't confirm because it was a waste of breath. She was right. Chaos didn't allow whores on their patch. She'd been told more than once. So had her friend.

"Get me the name of your replacement before you disappear," he demanded.

"Whatever."

He studied her a beat before he advised, "Girl, you get loose, you take a desperate couple for a ride by dangling precious in their faces, you stay loose. Get the fuck outta the life."

"Nothin' else I know how to do," she returned sharply.

"You got a brain. Learn," he shot back.

She saw her shot, and as usual, she didn't hesitate to take it.

She moved in to him, the hard shifting out of her face, something false she didn't know rang that way shifting into it.

"You could take that ride with me. I'd share the proceeds and stay outta the life for a decent guy."

Joker stepped back. He didn't say anything; he let his actions do his talking.

She tipped her head to the side and whispered, "Sure you can do better?"

He'd have had to think about that question the day before.

Nine years ago, he'd known the answer down to his gut and it wasn't a good one.

Right then, the touch of Carissa's soft skin still on his hand, the feel of her fingers against his scalp, the vision of her corny wave goodbye burned in his brain, he still wasn't sure about the answer.

But he was leaning a different way.

"Take care of yourself, Heidi," he said to end it, even in saying it, knowing she would. She'd do anything to take care of herself.

Even sell her baby to do it.

"Got no choice, Joke," she replied.

She moved off, got her girl, and they took off.

His brothers joined him.

"Not a big fan of hangin' in an alley with pussy for hire waitin' for the queen bee to get her favorite subject to stand attendance," Boz declared irately.

"Not the queen bee," Joker shared. "Bitch is pregnant. She'll vanish by daylight. But she says she'll arrange a replacement."

"We holdin' our breath for that?" Speck asked.

"I wouldn't advise it," Joker answered.

"I'll think on it," Hop stated. "I come up with one I think'll be open for an approach, we'll plan."

Hop looked to Joker.

"You on tonight with Rush?"

"On my way back to the Compound to team up," Joker confirmed.

Hop nodded and said, "Home." Then he took off to go there.

Without beautiful women in their beds and kids under their roofs, Boz, Speck, and Joker moved down the alley toward their bikes a lot more slowly.

"You ever trust that bitch?" Speck asked.

"She didn't come up with much, but she warned us where Valenzuela would turn his attention, and her intel was rarely wrong," Joker answered.

"You think she'll clear out before she sells out to Valenzuela, playin' both ends?" Speck asked.

Joker shook his head. "She doesn't know jack about us so she's got nothin' to give. She's stupid enough to share she shared, she'll be in the morgue by morning. Heidi might not be much, but she ain't stupid."

Speck didn't reply.

They mounted their bikes but before they went their separate ways, Boz called, "Sharp on patrol."

And when he said it, Joker felt it.

Something new.

On patrol, Joker didn't give a shit what went down. He did what he had to do for his Club to protect what was theirs.

But right then, he knew he'd be sharp on patrol.

Not that he wasn't before.

Just that, should the uncommon happen and things got ugly, he was going to make certain it didn't get ugly for him.

And Joker had plans tomorrow night he was no way in hell going to miss.

CHAPTER TEN

I Drink Beer

Carissa

"IF WE GET a judge who's buddy-buddy with either of the Neilands, I'll ask that he recuse himself. I've no idea if he will. But if he doesn't, it sets him up for appeal."

It was the next evening and we were in the conference room at Gustafson, Howard and Pierce—Angie, Joker, Travis, and me. And Angie was explaining her strategy, which was essentially to obtain child support, revise custody so my very young son spent most of his time with his mother, as it should be (according to me, and now Angie), and lastly, to do her best to slap Aaron and his father on the wrist, hard, for what they'd been doing to me.

A strategy I agreed with wholeheartedly.

She kept talking.

"I'm actually surprised the judge you had didn't recuse himself. He's known to have a longstanding close relationship with Judge Neiland."

That was something I knew. Heck, the man had come to my wedding!

I didn't have a chance to share this before Angie continued, "Your last attorney is very good, but my feeling is that he didn't ask a judge he knew should recuse himself to do so because it would set him up for the man's displeasure. Judges have long memories. They're supposed to be objective, but they're also human. If they don't recuse themselves, they don't like to be asked. They also don't like threats of appeal. I don't have the same problem as your former counsel. They know that, and that should work in our favor."

I wanted to jump across the table and kiss her.

Instead, I just smiled at her before I turned my head to Joker, who was sitting beside me.

It was then I wanted to kiss him.

This was because Joker was feeding Travis, who was sitting happily on his thigh.

It was Travis's dinnertime. We couldn't wait for Las Delicias and a high chair. My boy needed his food.

And Joker told me I needed to focus.

So when we settled in, I focused on Angie and Joker focused on my son.

Now, with surprising ease, he was shoving carrots in Travis's mouth, the jar on the table in front of him, his attention on Travis, but I knew he was listening to Angie.

Taking him in, I thought he'd never been more handsome.

"I already have paralegals working on the motion we'll be filing," Angie continued and I looked back to her. "We're hoping to do that tomorrow, latest the next day."

"That'd be great." I gave her my understatement.

"I'll warn you that usually, as a first step, counsel would approach opposing counsel to try to negotiate things like this outside of court. However, I think we're beyond that at this juncture."

I nodded. "I agree."

She nodded back. "Now, if Mr. Neiland does or says

anything that makes you angry or uncomfortable or that you find questionable in any way, you document it. Starting with what happened with Travis and his croup last week. Dates. Times of phone calls. What's been said. Et cetera. Everything you can remember. You also report it to me."

I nodded.

"I have high hopes for this, Carissa," she told me. "It's unconscionable what's been going on. My gut feeling is that if we don't have the luck of the draw with which courtroom we land in, it will simply mean your circumstances will take more time to change. But I'll do everything in my power to deal with this swiftly."

"I don't know what to say," I replied. "Thank you."

She grinned. "Don't thank me. I'm getting paid. But regardless, I love my job. But when I get this kind of case, I *love* my job."

I was glad about that. I liked her. She seemed nice *and* bullheaded, and in this instance, both worked for me.

Still.

"Thank you anyway," I returned.

"My pleasure," she said then looked to Joker and back to me. "Feel free to use this room to take care of Travis. But I've got a few more things to do before I go home. So if you don't mind, I'll leave you."

"Of course not. Please go. And thank you for your time," I said.

She nodded to me, did the same to Joker and moved out.

I looked to Joker and wheeled my plush leather chair his way.

"She's amazing," I whispered excitedly.

"Club's not gonna retain morons," he replied, any bite to his words nonexistent since his lips were curled up very slightly.

It might have been a very slight curve, but I'd take it.

I looked down to Travis then to him. "You want me to finish?"

"Got it."

He certainly did.

"We can finish with the carrots and give him the yummy pears at LD," I said.

"Right."

"You're good at that," I observed carefully, because I didn't want to seem to be prying.

I still wanted to know. The man was a biker. As far as I knew he had no children (something, even at this early juncture between us, I would hope he'd already have shared with me). But he was very good with them.

"Long time ago, rented a room in a basement," he returned easily. "Woman needed the money. She had a man who was a dick. Gone more than he was home. She had kids, one was a baby. She worked. She also jacked down rent if I helped out. I needed her to jack down rent, so I helped out."

That explained that.

"That was nice," I noted.

"Her kids were the bomb."

That was nice too.

"She probably appreciated it," I told him, though even though I didn't know her, I still knew there was no *probably* about it.

"She did. Then she got deep in meth. I was gone by then but, last I heard, her kids were in the system."

"Oh no," I whispered.

He juggled Travis, jar, and spoon to scrape the last bits out and muttered, "Way of life."

"Not life like I know it."

His head didn't move but still, his eyes came to me.

"No."

That one word was low. It was meaningful. I wasn't sure I got the meaning. I just knew I liked it.

Travis gurgled through the last bite of carrots while Joker ordered, "Almost done. Pack up. Let's hit the road. I'm fuckin' starved."

Ugh!

"You're almost at a dollar, Joker," I shared, still feeling hopeful and riding the happy wave of watching Joker feed Travis, but nevertheless annoyed.

"You do know I'm never gonna quit bein' me," he remarked, tipping the spoon into the empty jar and lifting Travis's bib to wipe his mouth.

"You do know that Travis maybe said his first word last night. Since it was *Mommy*, that made me happy. His second word being the f-word would not do the same."

His eyes came to mine. Then I made a quiet sound of surprise when his hand shot out and caught me behind the head, something he could do seated since I was bent over Travis's diaper bag, which I'd dropped into my vacated seat.

After that, he pulled me to him so my mouth was on his.

He gave me a hard, short kiss.

"Bah buh bah!" Travis squealed.

Joker released the pressure on my neck just enough for me to move back an inch.

He looked into my eyes.

His, I couldn't read. That didn't mean he wasn't telling me something. I just didn't know what it was.

What I did know was that the guard was gone. I wasn't shut out by steel.

I just didn't know what to make of it now that I was in.

Then he let me go without giving more and I shifted out of his way as he straightened from his chair.

We packed up. We got Travis sorted. Joker yanked the diaper bag out of my hand and slung it on his shoulder even though he still had Travis in his arm. And off we went.

We did this in his spacious dual-cab truck. He'd picked me up at work. The "red wreck" (what Joker that night had christened my car) was to remain behind. I was off the next day. Joker told me he, or "one of the brothers" would be around in the morning to help me retrieve it.

So it was a proper date, him picking me up and everything.

Okay, he'd picked me up from work, brought my son with him, and we'd started our time at an attorney's office talking about battling my ex, so it wasn't a normal date, but it was still a proper one.

This made me happy.

Travis was snug in his seat behind us, babbling at nothing, and I was watching Denver slide by and smelling new car smell.

"So, you didn't get pine," I remarked.

"Say again?"

"Your car. It's obviously just been cleaned and you got new car smell," I said. "Not pine."

"I got new car smell 'cause this isn't a clean car. It's a new car. Bought this truck today."

I went still.

But only for a moment.

Then I woodenly turned my head his way.

He had a bike. That I knew.

But that day he had a date with a single mom who had a baby with a car seat.

So now he had a dual-cab truck.

Joker stopped at a red light and looked at me.

And when he did, I watched by the lights of a Denver city night as his face got soft.

It was a vision of beauty.

"Like a whole lot the way you're lookin' at me, Butter-fly," he said softly. "But I got a bike and we don't live in Arizona. We can get weather. Used to be, weather was bad, I needed to get somewhere, I had to borrow someone else's vehicle. That gets old. I had to get you and your boy to dinner, but that doesn't mean the time wasn't ripe."

I heard it all, but most especially the *I had to get you and your boy to dinner* part, so I just smiled at him brightly.

He shook his head, looked forward, and we went when the light was green.

He drove and, while he did, I wanted to hold his hand. I wasn't sure we were at that place but I was sure I wanted to do it and badly.

The problem was, he drove with his wrist, that wrist being the right one draped over the steering wheel. Therefore, I couldn't grab his hand.

Also, I had some concerns about this since the truck was large and probably more easily maneuvered if his fingers were wrapped *around* the steering wheel.

I didn't say anything since he promptly wrapped them around said wheel in order to parallel park outside Las Delicias.

We went in. We got one of their side half-oval booths. They gave us a high chair. We ordered. I gave Travis his pears then some Cheerios for him to play with, eat, and toss around. Finally, Joker and I ate.

All day, I'd been looking forward to this like it was Christmas Eve.

But I hadn't been on a first date since Aaron took me miniature golfing over a decade ago.

And Joker was *so* not Aaron it wasn't funny.

So all day I was also nervous like crazy.

But I shouldn't have been. Somehow, things between Joker and me were just easy. Conversation flowed.

And I wasn't the one making it flow.

He talked. Mostly about the Club, and that was mostly about his brothers, who he clearly respected and even cared a lot for.

He told me all their Club names. He told me all their real names (the only weird spot was when I asked his, he didn't answer, and it seemed he was acting like he didn't hear me but then again, he probably just didn't hear me). He told me about their old ladies. How long they'd been in the Club. About Ride, the store, the garage, and the new store they were opening in Grand Junction, which meant they were already looking for new recruits since all Chaos members did their "time" in Denver before they moved on to other branches, like Fort Collins, Boulder, Colorado Springs, and soon-to-be Grand Junction. He also told me he designed and built some of their custom builds.

"Workin' on one," he'd muttered. "Show it to you and Travis next time you're on Chaos."

I wasn't really into cars.

But I couldn't wait to see his.

At my gently probing questions, he also told me about himself and he did that easy too.

No hesitation.

He shared that he was an only child (which, with his parents, was probably good, though for him in that mess, it was sad he didn't have at least one person to love and love him back). I found out he was only a few months older than me. He explained that he did live at the Compound because "no reason to pay for some crib when I got a life where all I need is a room" (I also found this sad, but didn't have time to dwell).

I liked that he was easy. It wasn't like he went on and on,

sharing deeply, opening a window to his soul, trusting me with his hopes and dreams.

But it was a first date and I didn't think that was what you got on a first date. However, he wasn't closed and secretive like his eyes made it seem like he would be.

I'd take easy. In fact, I ate it up because I found I wanted to know everything about Joker. So when he gave me easy, I didn't push for more. I let him say what he had to say and didn't probe further. With as easy as he gave me, I knew it would come, so there wasn't a reason to push.

This meant (in my mind) that by the time we were finished eating, the date was a smashing success.

Or I thought it was.

Joker finished his meal before I did since I'd spent quite a bit of time during the meal seeing to my baby. So I took my last few bites of my burrito *chicharrones* while Joker had a drowsy Travis against his chest, Travis's head drooping on his shoulder.

That was when I looked up from my nearly clean plate and gawked because Lee and Indy Nightingale, the famous Denver couple who had their story told in the *Rock Chick* books, were walking from the back of the restaurant, heading our way.

I couldn't help but stare because they were famous but also because, frankly, Lee Nightingale was even more gorgeous in person. And in the pictures of him I'd seen in the paper, he was *fabulous*.

And just like Joker when he was with Travis, since Lee had a redheaded little girl held to his chest, resting her cheek on her daddy's shoulder, he was even *more* gorgeous.

Not to mention, Indy Nightingale was a knockout. As was the Lee Nightingale mini-me who was holding her hand and walking at her side.

I forced myself to stop gawking and was about to kick Joker under the table when Lee Nightingale looked toward us, tilted his head and stopped.

"Joke," he greeted.

Oh my gosh! Lee Nightingale knew Joker!

"Lee," Joker replied.

First-name basis!

"Hey," Indy Nightingale said and I looked to her to see she was addressing *me*.

"Hey," I replied, hoping it was casually.

She grinned. "Your baby is cute."

I knew that already but I still said, "Thanks. Your kids are too."

She kept grinning.

"You wear it well."

This came deep and easy from Lee and I looked to him to see he was aiming a drop dead gorgeous smile chock full of amusement Joker and Travis's way.

"Don't piss me off. Carissa fines me every time I cuss," Joker replied.

I got warm inside.

"Does that work?" Indy asked me curiously.

"Not so far," I answered.

"I figured," she mumbled.

Suddenly Lee went all business. "Tack called. I'm on your gig. I'll have results in a day or two."

"Appreciated," Joker replied.

Lee nodded.

"This is Lee and I'm Indy, by the way," Indy said to me. "And these are our offspring, Callum and Suki."

Like I didn't know. Everyone in Denver knew them. Though I didn't know about Callum and Suki.

"I kinda know who you are," I admitted.

"That figures too," she said with a not-a-problem smile.

I smiled back then did my bit. "Like Joker said, I'm Carissa and that's my baby, Travis."

"So cute," Indy repeated.

"Yeah," little Suki muttered sleepily. "Cute baby."

I grinned at her.

Lee turned to me. "Carissa, nice to meet you and sorry to make it short but we gotta go. My baby girl needs her bed."

So *totally* gorgeous.

I turned my grin to him. "Nice to meet you too."

"We'll leave you to it," Lee said. "Later."

Lee gave chin lifts, Indy waved, Callum gave a distracted hand flick (totally a mini-me), and Suki just gave a small wave goodbye.

When I was sure they were gone, I turned to Joker and hissed enthusiastically, "I can't believe you know Lee Nightingale."

"He's tight with the Club."

How cool!

"Is he as awesome as he seems to be?" I asked.

"If by awesome you mean he's a supreme badass and so good at his job it's kinda scary, then yeah."

I sort of meant that.

I smiled and shared, "Bad-A is a nickel, sweetie."

When I was done talking, I pulled in a sharp breath.

I did this because his eyes went semi-molten in a way that the banked heat in them warmed my skin.

Joker didn't address what was behind his molten look.

He murmured quietly, "He's mostly asleep, Butterfly. He isn't hearin' anything."

"Still."

"And a badass is a badass. There's no other word for it."

I had to give him that.

"Whatever," I muttered, grabbing one final chip, dipping it into LD's famous salsa, and eating it. I sucked back my Sprite then Joker and I did the whole packing up, carting out, loading up the vehicle drill.

But doing it, something that was just a part of life became something new that I liked, sharing the chore with Joker.

He took us home and again commandeered baby and diaper bag, leaving me only with my purse to haul up the steps, another break for which I was extremely grateful.

But I was again nervous.

Travis was out. Since the breast milk/formula change he'd turned into a good sleeper. And when he was done for the evening, in most cases, he stayed that way.

That meant he'd get a sleepy diaper change then into his PJs and finally into his crib.

After that, I'd be alone with Joker in my house with my huge couch.

Yes, I was nervous but in a way I liked the feeling.

My stomach had butterflies. My lips had a smile playing at them. My night had been great.

I hoped it was about to get better.

I just knew (like the night before) I'd have the novel feeling of going to bed looking forward to the next day.

And I was thinking all this when Joker took the last step and rounded the stairwell with me on his heels.

Suddenly I crashed right into his back because he'd stopped.

"Is everything—?"

"Company," he growled.

His dire tone made me look around him and that was when my heart stopped beating.

Aaron, still in one of his fabulous work suits, was standing at the railing outside my door. He was bent to it, hands curled around it, but his head was turned and his eyes were to us.

I stood unmoving.

Surprisingly, this wasn't because I thought a visit from Aaron at my apartment that he hadn't been to for months and months was a bad omen (I did, and Tory, if you can believe, did the Travis swap with me when they returned him, and Aaron never came to my door when I brought him to them).

No, I did it because I couldn't believe what I was seeing.

No again.

I couldn't believe how what I was seeing had changed.

Aaron was handsome. He'd been a handsome young man who'd turned into an exceptionally handsome adult. He had dark hair that was thick and shiny and healthy. He had unusual colored blue eyes that were sharp and interesting. He had a strong jaw, a high forehead, and beautiful lips. And he was tall, slim, and lean, with nice broad shoulders.

He wore a suit amazingly.

I'd never tired of looking at him. Even when I wondered at some of the mean things he did or said in high school. Even when I was turning a blind eye to the things he did to me. It didn't matter what turmoil my thoughts were in that I was pretending didn't exist, I'd take one look at him and again fall in love.

But right then, he wasn't close but I saw him standing there, confident, his bearing holding authority, and he did nothing for me.

He seemed bland. Bland and ordinary. An attractive stranger in a really nice suit. You might look at him twice, but once he was out of sight, he'd be out of mind.

Or at least my mind.

It was gone.

Like magic.

But something else was there.

And after all these years and all that had happened, that was magical too.

What it was was fury.

He hadn't seen me in months and he thought he could show at my home on a Wednesday evening out of the blue?

Not likely.

And he needed to know that.

Immediately.

I stormed around Joker in order to bear down on Aaron and share my thoughts.

I didn't get far because Joker caught my hand.

"Steady, Butterfly," he muttered.

I drew in breath and looked up at him. He lifted his brows.

I watched the brow lift realizing he was right. I didn't need to go off half-cocked on the walkway.

I could do it in my living room.

I nodded and whispered, "Steady."

Steady.

That was what I needed. In a life that had felt out of control from the moment my parents' friends crushed my baby sister in our driveway until a few days ago, through my own fault but sometimes not, I had not had steady.

I needed steady.

I was getting there.

And Aaron wasn't going to take that from me.

Joker carrying Travis, the diaper bag, and holding my hand, we walked to Aaron.

"This is a surprise," I said when we got close.

Aaron was staring at Joker.

"Would you like to say hello to your son's mother?" I asked.

"Do I know you?" Aaron asked Joker, his gaze intensifying.

"No, you don't," I answered curtly before Joker could.

"This is a friend of mine. Now, I'm sorry, did I miss a call or text telling me you'd be visiting? Something our custody agreement, by the way, notes specifically I should expect."

Aaron finally stopped examining Joker and looked to me. "No."

"Is there something I can help you with?" I offered.

"We could not do this on the walkway, Carissa. That'd help," Aaron replied.

"I'm afraid I'm not a big fan of you being in my home," I returned.

"Carrie," Joker said low.

I jerked my head back to look up at him.

He shook his head once.

I understood what he was communicating to me.

We were filing a motion and I had to be a good girl, not a jerkface like Aaron. I didn't need to give him any ammunition like he'd been handing me.

"Come in," I mumbled, letting Joker's hand go to dig in my purse. I got my keys and let us in.

I moved around turning on lights, and when I was done, I saw Aaron just inside the closed door, Joker with Travis asleep on his chest by the bar.

"Can I hold my son?" Aaron asked Joker.

Joker looked right to me.

When he did, my only thought was, *honest to goodness, I could love that man.*

"It's okay," I said quietly.

Joker didn't look like he liked it, but he moved to Aaron and transferred a still-mostly-asleep-but-blinking Travis into Aaron's arms.

"Hey, buddy. Hey, my little guy," Aaron cooed when he got his son.

I watched him do this and it happened again.

I used to hate that. I'd hated that he loved Travis that much. I'd hated that he was (probably) a good father. I'd hated that he didn't give all that to Travis *and* me.

But right then I didn't hate it.

I didn't care about it at all.

Because Joker fed my son his carrots and carried him up the stairs. And further, he let him lick his beard, pull his hair, and a lot more. He liked doing it too.

And now Travis also had Big Petey. And Tyra. And Elvira.

Not just me. No longer just me and a grandpa a state away.

My son had more.

We didn't need Aaron.

Travis and I were building our own family.

"I can imagine this is nice for you, Aaron, having a moment with your child outside our normal schedule," I remarked. "But it's late, he needs his crib, I worked today, and I'm tired. So if you've come by for that, please wrap it up so we can get on with our night."

My ex-husband settled our son to his shoulder and looked at me.

Yes, interesting blue eyes.

But just interesting.

"I deserved that," he said softly.

I felt the banked fire in my belly start to rage.

He was never nice to me. These days, he was never *anything* to me.

I held back the fire and replied, "I see. You know about Gustafson, Howard and Pierce."

Aaron let a flinch show. "The attorney community is—"

I shook my head. "Honestly, not to be mean, but I don't care. I didn't lie when I said I was tired. We just had dinner. I have things to do before tomorrow. Can you please explain why you're here so you can leave and I can do them?"

He glanced at Joker then back to me. "I had hoped to speak to you one on one."

"That's not gonna happen," Joker put in on a subdued growl.

Yes, oh heck yes, I could love that man.

"And who are you, exactly?" Aaron asked Joker.

"That his business?" Joker asked me.

Gosh, I wanted to kiss him.

"I should know who's spending time with my son," Aaron pointed out, his deep voice that once could lull me into believing just about anything verging on a snap.

"This is a friend of mine," I said quickly and got Aaron's eyes. "He's called Joker and we're…" I paused and put it out there, "dating."

"*Dating?*" Aaron asked incredulously.

And hurtfully.

"You lost interest in me but that doesn't mean the entirety of mankind did," I returned.

"Of course not, you're beautiful," Aaron spat and I blinked. "But you've got a job and a child to raise."

"Seeing as you work so much, I'm surprised you forgot," I shot back. "But you also have a job. *And* a child. Not to mention a fiancée."

Aaron scowled at me before he took in a visibly deep breath, ran his hand through his thick, shiny, dark hair, and rearranged his features.

"I didn't come here to fight," he shared when he again focused on me.

"I'm glad you mentioned that, because we still haven't established precisely *why* you've come here," I returned.

"If you have issues, Carissa, we should work them out one on one," he declared.

I stared.

Then I looked to Joker. "Is he kidding?"

Joker held my eyes then his roamed my face.

After he did that, he smiled at me.

Right out. Blinding and beautiful. Strong white teeth stark against his thick black beard and everything.

It was all I needed.

I turned back to Aaron. "You don't take my calls."

"I will in future."

"Will you share with me my son is ill in future too?"

His face turned to stone.

Tory was going to get it but I didn't care.

Regardless, I noted, "You shouldn't be angry with her. She did the right thing. One hundred percent. The person who didn't was you. She's not his mother. But you *are* his father and it should have been *you* who shared that with me."

"So you hired the most expensive firm in Denver to handle your hissy fit?" Aaron fired back.

Gustafson, Howard and Pierce were the most expensive firm in Denver?

No.

Wait.

My *hissy fit*?

"You took my son to the hospital, Aaron," I said, voice trembling with fury.

"It was just croup," Aaron blew it off.

"You took my son *to the hospital*, Aaron," I repeated.

He shook his head. "This is not the point. The point is, you cannot afford that firm."

"No," I volleyed. "The point is, you're terrified I'm going to use what little bit of money I have battling you by using attorneys that aren't scared of the mighty Neiland network and you'll have to pay their fees as well as the child support you should be giving Travis."

"If you want money, Carissa, you just have to ask," he retorted.

"Who? Tory?" I returned. "Since you refuse to speak to me, that is."

His mouth got hard.

"You created this situation, Aaron. And I know how it pains you, and you're my son's father, so it gives me no pleasure to point out that you've instigated another fail. You thought since you played me and mistreated me for years that I'd roll over for you. But you're no longer dealing with a girl who lost half her world by the time she was eighteen and therefore held on to all she had left with all she had in her. You're dealing with a mother. That's an entirely different breed. So I'd advise you change your tactics *and* your goals. Because your current fight is a fight there is no way *in hell* you can win."

"I don't want to hurt you anymore, Carissa," he said gently.

What a liar.

He didn't want his epic fail to bloom out of control and damage his reputation.

"Then reach out to my attorney," I suggested. "We can meet to rearrange our agreement so it's more beneficial for our son. But that will happen with my attorney present. Where it won't happen is in the late evening in my living room during a meeting that was meant to be an ambush. Now, please, give me my son and leave."

Aaron stared at me. He did this a while. Too long. So long I could actually feel Joker losing patience.

I was right there with him.

Then Aaron said, "You've changed."

"That happens when a girl dreams of nothing but being a part of a happy family and her husband cheats on her and then kicks her in the teeth. *Repeatedly.* If she can pick herself up, she learns, and that girl turns into a woman who'll fight, scratch, and die before she's brought low again."

"I still wish you'd speak with me *alone*," Aaron coaxed.

"Think we went over that," Joker stated.

Aaron looked to him. He did it angrily at first but then he did it strangely. Not with anger, more like focus, like he wasn't looking at him but he wanted to put his finger on something and couldn't find it.

But really, I was done.

"Aaron, my son," I prompted.

My ex-husband turned his attention back to me.

Then he got close and that was when I felt Joker get tense.

But Aaron stopped and I watched as he bent his neck to kiss Travis's baby head.

"'Night, little guy," he whispered.

Ugh.

Carefully, he transferred our son to me, and once I had him, I cuddled him close.

Aaron looked at me.

"You look good, Carissa," he murmured.

Another lie. I didn't. Unfortunately, on my first date with the handsome biker Joker, I was in my LeLane's uniform, my hair in a ponytail, and my makeup was ten hours old. There hadn't been time to change into my tube top.

But I was *totally* wearing my tube top when I met Aaron with our attorneys. He might be shocked but I didn't give a hoo-ha. He could kiss my behind.

"Goodnight, Aaron."

He stared into my eyes.

I sighed and allowed myself to look bored.

"'Night, Riss," he whispered.

Ugh again.

He hadn't called me Riss since high school.

Jerkface!

I said nothing.

Aaron turned from me, gave Joker an unhappy look, and moved to the door.

Joker sauntered there as well and didn't hesitate to shut and lock it the minute Aaron stepped outside.

"I need to see to Travis," I announced when he turned my way. "I don't have any beer or anything but grab whatever. Turn on the TV. Take a load off. I'll be out in a bit."

"You need to write that shit that just happened down, baby. We'll go over it together to make sure you didn't miss anything. And then you call it in to Angie tomorrow."

"Right. We'll do that after Travis is down."

Joker was studying me closely. "You okay?"

"I'm fabulous," I told him. "He's scared and he thinks he can play me. But I'm done with his games. I just want him to sort himself out so I can take care of my son the way he deserves and get on with my life."

On that, I turned away and headed to the bedroom.

So it was unfortunate I missed Joker staring after me, at first disbelievingly.

Then he was smiling.

*   *   *

I was camped out on the couch.

No, correction.

I was camped out on Joker who was stretched out on his back on the couch.

There had been no making out, which was disappointing.

But when I came back from putting Travis to bed, Joker and I sat at my bar as I recorded Aaron's visit.

Done with that, we headed to the couch, Joker going before me. So when I moved in front of him, he'd grabbed my hips and pulled me to the cushions, him on his back, me on him, me mistakenly tensing in a good way, thinking he was instigating a make out session. But that had been all he did.

I liked the way he kissed. I wanted more.

But something about this was (almost) better.

Part of that better was that Joker sensed this—and not a hot and heavy make out session—was what I needed.

Most of that better was that this was exactly what I needed even though I didn't know I needed it because until then, I didn't really know it existed.

To veg out in front of the TV, relaxing, mind clearing, body melting, Joker's fingers gently teasing my ringlets, his hard body warm and strong beneath me, his breath coming steady and easy.

Just that. Just us. Just nothing.

Nothing taxing.

Nothing exhausting.

Nothing annoying.

Nothing upsetting.

Okay, so also nothing exciting.

But I found lying on Joker that I liked this kind of nothing.

It wasn't the same as having nothing when you were alone.

It was vastly different.

And I liked that different a whole lot.

"You drink beer," I mumbled, my voice quiet and kind of sleepy because I was the same.

"Is that a question or a statement?" Joker's deep biker voice vibrated under my cheek.

"It's a statement."

"Then I'll confirm. I drink beer."

I grinned against his chest. "I'll get some in."

"I'll bring some."

"I can get it."

"You know what I like?"

"Uh . . . no."

"Then I'll bring it."

I'd allow that but only because if it was in my fridge, I'd see it so I could replenish it when it ran out.

"That question mean I'm comin' back?"

He wanted that.

I did too.

I melted deeper into him and pressed my cheek into his chest.

That was part of my answer.

The rest of it was, "You're way more comfy than my couch."

His fingers stopped playing with my hair so they could tangle in it.

That wasn't part of his answer, it was his whole one.

It was also a good one.

"Did good with that asshole tonight, baby," he said, the vibration in his chest a soothing rumble. "Didn't hold your own, you bested him."

I loved it that he thought that. *Loved it.*

And I loved it that I did that. I was proud of myself. Another new feeling that I liked.

"Thanks, sweetie," I mumbled.

His other arm stole around me and he gave me a light squeeze.

Minutes passed before he asked softly, "You goin' to sleep, Butterfly?"

"Do you mind?"

"Fuck no."

He liked me there.

I liked that because I liked me there too. Right there. Doing nothing with Joker.

"One dollar and five cents," I muttered, blinked, blinked again, felt something shaking, but it felt good.

So I fell asleep and missed that something being Joker's long, hard, warm, strong biker body...

Laughing.

CHAPTER ELEVEN

What You Need

Carissa

I WAS JOSTLED gently before I settled, but I settled blinking.

I didn't know where I was, though when my eyes finally opened it all came to me.

I sleepily pushed up on my forearms in the cushions and lifted my head to see a pair of jeans clad hips rounding the arm of my couch.

I looked up and over the back and saw a messy-haired, drowsy-eyed, phenomenal biker.

"Sweetie?" I called, and he looked down at me.

The second he did I became a puddle of goo on the couch.

"Hear him fussin'," he said softly.

I stared.

Joker disappeared.

I pushed up to sitting and was on my feet when Joker walked in, carrying Travis, who was rubbing his face on Joker's black T-shirt at the same time clenching it in his little fist.

I stared again as I became a new puddle of goo, but this time standing.

I pulled my goo together, walked to Joker, and grinned at him before I got close, put a hand on my son's back and whispered, "Mornin', baby."

Travis rubbed his face again, lifted his head in a wobbly way then gave up and planted his cheek on Joker's chest.

Total goo.

My boy loved his mommy, and he loved getting morning snuggles from me.

But he definitely liked Joker too. I knew this because he was happy where he was and not reaching out to me.

I found I liked this. All of it. I liked that Travis liked it, and I liked that Joker liked giving it.

I leaned in and kissed Travis's head.

"Want 'im or want first turn in the bathroom?" Joker asked.

My gaze lifted to his. "What do you want?"

"I'm easy."

He was.

I just didn't know how he could be. He'd had a crappy life and now he belonged to a club of bikers.

But he was definitely easy.

"I'll take him," I offered, moving my other hand to Travis. "You go first."

We did the baby transfer. Then we took our turns doing morning stuff in the bathroom. While Joker did his, with practiced ease balancing my baby, I made coffee.

We had our mugs and Joker was behind the bar, I was on a stool as Travis shook away sleep in my arms, when Joker asked, "What's on for your day?"

"Gotta get my car," I murmured as Travis made movements I read so I slid off the stool and bent to put him on his tush on the floor.

I went and fetched a variety of things from a basket in

the living room area. I brought him his selection of toys and Travis stared at them, still shaking off sleep but also deciding.

"Get you that," Joker said and I looked to him. "After we get your car, you need to do laundry? We can take it to the Compound."

He'd said *we*.

I liked that but I shook my head. "I do that kind of thing when I don't have Travis so I can be with Travis and not with him in a Laundromat."

"Groceries?" Joker went on.

"Same," I told him. "We're good."

He nodded and looked over the bar as Travis leaned forward, pressing his baby hands into buttons, making noise on the toy keyboard. He enjoyed the sound. I knew that from experience, but it was confirmed when he tipped back his head and giggled.

I grinned at my son as I thought about it, decided what I wanted, so I went for it.

I looked to Joker. "Are you, uh . . . busy today?"

His gaze went from Travis to me. "Nope."

"Wanna, maybe . . . spend the day with Travis and me?"

His lips curved up. "Yep."

And again I was goo.

"Travis needs breakfast and bath. I need a shower. And then—" I began.

"Got the first two covered, you take care a' you."

The idea of a shower that wasn't necessarily quick for the purpose of getting clean and getting out so I could rescue my child from his secure place in a jumper seat or because I had a million things to do when my son wasn't with me was a promise of heaven.

"His baby tub is in—" I started.

"Get me what I need, Carrie, then I got it."

I tipped my head. "You sure?"

"Been a few years, but you're not gonna be on the moon. I run into problems, I know where to find you."

In the shower.

I felt goose bumps spread on my skin.

Then I nodded.

After that, I got him what he needed and gave instructions on how to make Travis's cereal and do his bath. Then I laid out a new diaper and my boy's clothes for the day, got my own stuff, and hit the shower.

I didn't luxuriate in it. I didn't hurry.

But I'd been right.

Knowing Travis was in good hands and I could just take care of me was heaven.

* * *

"It looks...interesting," I said, struggling with Travis in my arms. We were in the bowels of the garage at Ride, and Travis wanted not to be in my arms but crawling all over the new and interesting things around him while charming the pants off of all the men working.

It was after we ran the errand of picking up my car. It was after Joker treated me to a big breakfast. A breakfast that was yummy and filling, but punctuated with me calling Angie with my report as well as me contacting my landlord to give him notice that I was moving out.

Angie made note of the Aaron visit and did it with glee, knowing like I did that they were worried.

My landlord informed me my notice was not one but two weeks, but regardless, the first of the month was coming up and I had to pay the whole month, or when I vacated, I'd sacrifice my security deposit.

This wasn't the greatest news, and when I shared it with Joker, it didn't make him look happy either.

But he had no verbal response and I decided to figure it out later, not wanting to ask Tyra and Tack to wait a month but also not wanting to lose my shot at that house.

We now were at Ride, looking at Joker's "build."

But to me, it seemed like a bunch of scrap metal laid out on a garage floor. There were shapes. I just wasn't a car person so I couldn't put them together.

Joker sauntered to the wall, where there were a number of holders jutting out where you'd put papers and files. He pulled a folder out of one and came back.

He flipped it open and turned it to me.

"This is what it's gonna be."

I stared because in the file was a sketch of the coolest car I'd ever seen. There were subtle hints of color shaded on it (canary yellow and fiery red). But it was the lines forming Joker's vision that enthralled me.

"Did you draw that?" I asked.

"Yeah."

I looked up at him, surprised and also humbled by what appeared to be a remarkable talent.

"That's, well . . . it's totally amazing."

He flipped the file his way and looked at it. "Not my best. Not my worst."

If it wasn't his best, I wanted to see his best.

"Would you show me more?" I asked and his eyes came to me.

"You're interested, yeah," he answered casually.

"I'm interested," I said softly.

This time, Joker stared at me and I watched, standing as still as I could with Travis fighting my hold, doing it mesmerized.

Again, the steel of his eyes was not a guard against me.

Those eyes were working, and I knew down deep they were working in a good direction.

But he said nothing.

"If it's private," I said quickly, "you don't have to share it with me."

"Sell this shit, Carrie. Not private."

I nodded.

He flipped the folder closed.

"Can I look at it again?" I requested.

His attention came back to me before he flipped it open and I again looked at it.

It really was amazing. I could see it framed. The car was probably going to be fabulous, but the sketch was a thing of beauty.

But suddenly, looking at it, something struck me. I cocked my head and kept looking, that something tugging at me.

"Just a car, babe," Joker muttered before I could get a lock on that thing.

I looked again to him. "You're very talented. I mean, really. If whoever eventually owns the car doesn't own that sketch, you should frame it and sell it."

That got me smoldering steel, a look I could read, a look that I lost when Joker got close, bent in, and touched his lips to mine.

They immediately dug in, pushing hard, scraping my bottom lip against my teeth because Travis got upset, screeched, and hit both our cheeks with his baby fists.

Joker broke away and I looked to Travis, noting, "He needs to roam free."

"He can roam free in the office. It's practically child-proof," I heard Tyra say.

I turned in the direction of her voice to see her walking toward us. "Hey."

"Hi, honey," she said as she stopped close. She looked

to Travis, lifting her hands. "Hey, cutie. You wanna wreak havoc in Auntie Ty-Ty's office?"

Travis lifted his arms, launched his baby body her way, doing this shrieking.

That meant yes.

She caught him and said to Joker and me, "Take your time. We'll be close."

Without another word, on her sexy heels with her tight skirt and lovely blouse that didn't seem to fit in with a garage, she strutted away, up some steps, and disappeared through a door with my baby.

"Got more sketches in my room."

I looked back to Joker.

Sketches in his room.

I wanted to see sketches.

I more hoped that Tyra would look after my son for a half an hour while Joker took me to his room on the pretense of showing me sketches but in reality to make out with me.

"Awesome," I whispered.

The whiskers around his mouth twitched as he threw an arm around my shoulders and guided me out of the bay, heading us toward the Compound.

*   *   *

Joker did not make out with me.

He showed me sketches.

He was right. Some were better than the one I saw, some not quite as astounding.

But they all were stunning.

*   *   *

I stood beside Travis's crib, looking down at him, waiting for nothing.

And he was finally giving me nothing after an unusual hour where he had trouble falling asleep.

It might have been our busy day and the fact he'd had to nap in places that were unfamiliar that made him have trouble finding nighttime sleep.

It might have been that he clearly liked Joker and didn't want to fall asleep when he had his new biker buddy around.

Whatever it was, he was down and I could finally join Joker in the living room.

I left my bedroom, swinging the door so it was open by a crack to drown out the light but I could still hear him if I needed to.

I moved into the living room, announcing in a hushed voice, "He's down."

"That took a while," Joker noted.

"It did," I agreed.

"That usual?" he asked as I rounded the couch.

"No...oh!" I cried out because I got close and Joker's hands shot out and caught me at the hips.

I fell into him as he guided the fall, my bottom toward his lap.

It was a busy day but not an exhausting one. Still, I didn't mind ending it by stretching out on top of Joker on my couch and watching TV.

However, I found in short order that I wasn't going to stretch out on top of Joker and watch TV.

Joker was going to stretch out on top of *me*, and I had a feeling from the look in his eyes that, although the TV was on, we would not be watching it.

It was a feeling that made me happy.

When I was on my back in the couch and he was pressed the length of my side, I looked into his eyes, feeling the pulse beat hard in my neck.

"Hey," he whispered.

Oh.

Wow.

"Hey," I whispered back.

He curled his fingers around the side of my neck and slid them up to my jaw.

"You good?" he asked.

I swallowed. Then I nodded.

"Wanna be better?"

My belly did a somersault.

Oh yes. I definitely wanted to be better.

I pressed a hand to his chest and breathed, "Yes."

He dipped his head and I held my breath as he held my eyes and glided the side of his nose along the side of mine.

Oh.

Wow.

"So fuckin' pretty," he murmured.

"Joker," I replied huskily.

He rubbed his thumb along my cheek and continued to stare into my eyes.

I squirmed a little bit.

"What you want, Butterfly?"

He was making me ask.

Why was that so arousing?

"I want you to kiss me."

He did another nose glide and kept hold on my eyes as he added the tip of his tongue sliding along my lips.

That already made me better. So much better, a whimper slithered up my throat.

Instantly, his gaze fired, he slanted his head, and he kissed me.

I rounded him with my arms, pressed up, and kissed him back.

This commenced a make-out session on my couch that included some lovely groping, and for me, lots of shivers, melting, and whimpering.

Joker again had his hand up my top and he did the thumb slide at the underside of my breast, sweeping up to take in the side, and that felt so good, I was done making out.

I wanted more.

I didn't have my head together to know how much more, but I did know I wanted him to stop teasing and at least slide into second base.

I also didn't know how to tell him that, but my body did and it didn't delay. On a deep mew, I freed my leg from its tangle with his, rounded his thigh with my calf, and slid the most intimate part of me against its hard length.

The minute I did, his hand came out of my top. He twisted his arm behind him to hook his fingers around the back of my knee, holding it there, but he also broke the kiss.

"Okay. We're done."

At his surprising declaration, I blinked right before I tightened my hold on him.

"What?" I asked.

"Carrie," he said gently as I forced myself to focus. "That offer, straight up, I wanna take it, right now, on your couch. But, gotta tell you, baby, that what this is isn't that. It isn't me fuckin' you for the first time on your couch. I want what you're offerin', but I'm not gonna give it to you. Not that way. When we get there, you'll get it the way you deserve. The right way for the girl you are."

"I, um...I, well..."

I trailed off because I was still in the throes of a certain mood at the same time (slowly) processing what he said.

And it was incredibly lovely.

However, my certain mood was urging me to urge him to take things further on my couch.

"When Travis is with his dad and it's you and me so I can focus on just you and you can give that back to me, we'll go there," Joker said. "Meantime, we'll work up to it."

"You're very good at working up to it," I told him, because he was.

Aaron and I had had our times. There was a period where those times were frequent and so good I didn't know there could be better. Those times became infrequent and then they became not so good.

But just making out with Joker was better than *any* time with Aaron.

I stopped thinking of that and started falling back into that certain mood when I saw the humor in Joker's eyes as he muttered, "I'll keep you in check."

"Well, okay," I agreed, mostly because it didn't seem I had a choice.

"Now we'll watch TV."

I wasn't a huge TV watcher. I liked to read mysteries (though the odd romance here and there worked).

But right then I had absolutely no interest in TV.

Nevertheless, with no other option open to me, I said, "Okay."

"Then I'm gonna go, Carrie. You need a good night's sleep in your bed."

I hadn't really thought of it until then but the best night's sleep I'd had in a long time was the night before on the couch. Or, more accurately, on Joker.

I didn't share this.

Again not by choice, I said, "Okay."

Joker didn't move so I didn't either. What we did was

stare at each other, which made me feel strange and suddenly uncomfortable.

Until he said, "I like you."

Of its own volition, my hand fisted in his shirt.

"In a way I wanna do this right," he went on. "For you and for Travis."

Okay, I could get on board with *that*.

"I like you too," I told him shyly.

"Got that when you rubbed that heat against my thigh."

I felt my face burst into a different kind of heat.

Then I felt Joker's body start quaking and saw his mouth in a full blown smile.

"The pink is cute, Butterfly, but no need for it. That shit was hot."

"Um . . . good," I muttered.

"Cute and hot. Only bitch I know who can pull that shit off."

That certain mood left me, as did my mortification, and I immediately started glaring. "First, Joker, I'm not a bitch. And second, our day was so nice I didn't share my running tally, but I do believe you've racked up a debt of twenty dollars and seventy-five cents."

"That's the cute part," he returned instantly.

"Stop flattering me at the same time irritating me."

"Cute, hot, and can hold her own against a biker or a stick-up-his-ass suit, that also being cute and hot."

I decided not to reply, just glare.

"You ready to watch TV?" he asked.

"Whatever," I muttered.

He gave me another grin that I refused to acknowledge I liked, dipped his head, touched his mouth to mine, then let my leg go and shifted us so his back was against the back of the couch, I was tucked in front of him, and we were spooning facing the TV.

It felt lovely.

Which was annoying.

*   *   *

On my first break the next day, I went to the little square locker in the staff room at LeLane's where I kept my purse.

The night before, Joker left my house around the time my eyelids started drooping. He did this guiding me to the door by my hand, giving me a soft kiss goodnight, then leaving.

Now I was back at work, Big Petey was at my place with Travis, and I was wondering what was next.

I was also hoping, since Joker and I exchanged numbers, that right then I'd find out what was next because I wanted whatever was next with Joker really badly.

As I extricated my purse, I bit my lip, wanting there to be a text or a voice message from him, even if it was just to say *hey*, which would tell me he was thinking of me. After what he said the night before about treating me like the girl he saw me to be, I didn't want him to be one of those guys who played games in order to play it cool.

I got hold of my phone and hit the button at the bottom to illuminate the display.

There was a text that said, *Get a break, call me.* And on the top it decreed it was from Joker.

My heart got light and my thumb flew over the screen. In no time I'd dialed Joker's number.

It rang three times before, "Yo, Butterfly."

My heart got lighter.

"Hi, Joker."

"You're up for it, I could hit your house tonight with Chinese takeaway."

It was not an exaggeration to say that after the bills were paid, my budget for laundry, food, gas, and limited sundries was reached (as it always was), that at the end of the month I had six dollars and fifty-five cents to carry over to the next month. And if anything came up, which it did frequently, I had to use my credit card. As I could only pay the minimum monthly payment, the balance never went down and, alarmingly, nearly every month went up.

This hadn't always been the case. In the beginning, when I had child support, I had some room to breathe. When I lost that, Dad had helped, but I'd stopped taking his money because it made me feel guilty. He was still working. When he had to go and help Gramma, he'd lucked out when his company transferred him. But he was paying a lady to watch Gram during the day; he didn't need the added burden of me.

So things had grown tight to the point where I'd scaled back on absolutely everything that wasn't Travis related.

There were no lunches at the mall. There was no Las Delicias. There was no Chinese takeaway. Not for me. Not for so long I didn't remember the last time I had Chinese.

In other words, Chinese takeaway sounded *great*.

Joker bringing it to my house and eating it with me sounded better.

"That sounds perfect."

"Six, your place?" he asked.

"Yes," I answered.

"Text me what you like. I'm hittin' Twin Dragon."

"You got it."

"Your day good?" he asked.

It wasn't. It was just a day.

Now it was a good day.

I didn't know if I should tell him that.

Then I decided I should tell him that.

"It was normal. It just got better."

That got me silence and I worried I'd given too much too soon before he murmured, "Like that, Butterfly."

Not too much too soon.

Phew!

"Right, gotta let you go," he told me.

I didn't want him to but I only had fifteen minutes and I needed some of it to freshen up in the bathroom.

"Me too."

"Later, Carrie."

"Later, but, um...Joker?"

"Yeah?"

I drew in breath.

Then I told him. "I hadn't been in a restaurant for six months, which was the last time Dad came to visit. I haven't had Chinese takeaway for longer than I can remember. And I love Mexican *and* Chinese." I took in another breath through my nose and said, "Thank you for giving those to me. It means a lot."

"Baby, it's just food."

"Maybe to you, but it's a treat for me."

He was again silent and I was again worried I shouldn't have told him that before he stated, "Your ex is a total fuckin' asshole."

I would use different words but he was right.

"It'll get better, once I figure out how to go to school to be a hairstylist and then find a salon, clients, and start to get tips," I assured him.

"Right." His word sounded far from assured.

"But, also, it's already better because I met you."

"Rule," he stated instantaneously.

His strange word made me blink at the lockers. "Sorry?"

"Rule. You can't be like that on the phone. You can only be like that when I can kiss you."

I lifted a hand and pressed it to the cold steel of my locker, leaning into it because my knees suddenly wouldn't support me.

"You hear me?" he asked.

"Yes, Joker."

"Right. Six. Text me what you like to eat. Later," he stated tersely.

"Later, Joker."

He rang off.

I took my phone from my ear and stared at it before I smiled at it and this was before I pumped it in the air three times happily.

Then I texted him my favorite Chinese selections, put my phone in my purse, locked my locker, and went about my business.

*   *   *

Joker's hands in my hair pulled my head up which meant pulling my lips from his.

"We're done."

No! He still hadn't even gone to second base!

It was after Chinese takeaway. After Joker played on the floor with Travis for a while, this consisting of Joker lying on his back in the narrow floor space available to him between couch and wall, allowing Travis to crawl all over him while giggling (this, incidentally, also made me gooey). It was also after Joker gave him his bottle while I futzed about. And last, it was after I put him down.

We'd been making out. It was hot and heavy. I'd just performed a miracle by forcing Joker from on top of me to our sides then maneuvering myself on top.

If he wasn't going to go to second base, *I* was. So I'd gotten my hands up his shirt. His skin was silky. It was also blazing. And maybe best of all, it covered what could only be described as supple steel.

I couldn't get enough. Of that. Of his hair. Of his tongue. Of his manly biker smell. I'd even run my lips over his beard to kiss his earlobe and the second I did it I wanted to do it again.

I could feel him hard against my belly through his jeans. I liked that feel.

How could he say we're done?

"Just a little longer," I cajoled, deciding now was a good time to run my lips over his beard again.

"Carissa," he growled. "No," he finished inflexibly.

I looked at him and blurted my lie semi-desperately, "You don't know me, Joker. I'm actually a floozy."

He burst out laughing.

It was the first time he did it. It was deep and sumptuous and hearing it was a multisensory experience, all of it good.

But it still peeved me.

"That's funny?" I asked.

He focused on me. "Got here with food, were you in your LeLane's shirt?"

"No," I snapped, though I had no idea why he asked that question at this point in our conversation, and not only because he knew the answer.

"No. You got home and changed into a shirt that had more ruffles on it than anything I've ever seen."

"It's cute," I retorted, worried he didn't think the same.

"It is. So are you. It *is* you. My Butterfly in her wings. What it isn't is what a floozy would wear to lure her man to fuck her on her couch in front of the news."

It was safe to say he was correct, however I didn't confirm that verbally.

"I didn't say I wanted to go all the way," I told him. "I just don't wanna stop."

"Carissa, you feel that against your belly?"

I bit my lip because I did.

"Do me a favor," he said to finish.

He had a good point, a very good one, I was being selfish and I needed to cool it for his sake.

I looked away, feebly pushing away, suddenly embarrassed.

Joker rolled so I was trapped against the back of the couch and ordered, "Look at me."

"This is embarrassing," I told his throat.

"Don't know how. Not a man who has you in his arms would think anything about you wantin' more of him than that he's fuckin' lucky." His words made my eyes lift to his. "You're honest about that and don't play games, that's even better."

"You really think that?"

"Yeah. I'm still not fuckin' you on your couch. Not now. Not the first time." He grinned at me. "Maybe the third."

I pushed at his chest and did it again weakly but this time I did it for a different reason and I did it slightly grinning.

After I did that, I curled my fingers in his shirt and bent my neck so my forehead rested at the base of his throat.

His next words sounded against the top of my hair. "Next week, I'll take you to a nice dinner. You can dress up. We'll do it up right. Then I'll give you what you need."

"That'd be nice," I whispered, and it would. It made me nervous but it also made me excited that I had a variety of things to look forward to: a nice dinner, a chance to dress up, a night with Joker...and what I needed.

It was safe to say Aaron dumping me at my age was a hit to my confidence. Then again, if that happened at any age, I suspected it would be.

I was never a girl to strut her stuff, but I was a girl who knew from Aaron's attention I had some stuff. After Aaron, I figured I didn't.

A handsome, manly man like Joker liking me, obviously attracted to me, wanting to spend time with me, and wanting to give that to me *while* respecting me was brilliant. It gave that back, the feeling that I might just have some stuff. And that meant a lot to me.

Just like everything Joker made it seem easy to give to me meant a lot.

"Now, it sucks, but I got plans tomorrow night," he continued.

That did suck.

"Next day, you're off?" he asked. I nodded, my forehead moving on his chest then I tipped my head back and caught his eyes. "You want, we'll do something."

"I want," I said quietly.

He wanted it too. He didn't lock that away behind his eyes. He gave it right to me.

And it felt like a gift.

He leaned in, touched his lips to my nose, my mouth, then he shifted and slid them along my cheek to my jaw.

He settled back beside me and caught my eyes.

"Now, I gotta go home, Carrie."

Bummer.

"All right."

He gave me a squeeze, and before I wanted it (way before) we were off the couch and on our feet. He took my hand and did the getting his jacket and going to the door taking me with him drill.

He cupped my cheek, brushed his lips to mine, and gave me his, "Later," but this time, he added, "I'll check in tomorrow."

"Okay."

"'Night, babe."

"'Night, sweetheart."

His face got soft before he moved into the walkway and out of sight.

I sighed, closed the door and put my back to it.

I wondered what his plans were the next night.

Then I decided to ask when he checked in the next day.

After that, I went to my room, took off my ruffly blouse and my jeans, hit the bathroom, washed my face, brushed my teeth, and went to bed.

I lay in the massive king with its gazillion thread count sheets thinking, without the promise of Joker being part of my day, I didn't have as much to look forward to tomorrow.

I still looked forward to tomorrow.

And especially the next day.

But mostly the night next week where I got to dress up, have dinner with Joker...

Then get what I need.

CHAPTER TWELVE

Chaos Is Pussy

Joker

THE NEXT MORNING, Joker stood at the sink in the small bathroom that was attached to his room at the Compound and looked at himself in the mirror.

He'd fucked up, and if he didn't sort it out soon, he knew he'd be fucked.

There was no doubt Carissa liked him. There was no doubt what they had was going somewhere, and this was because there was no doubt he was going to take it there.

The problem was, to do that, she'd eventually need to know his name.

Then she'd know *him*.

He did not like to think about how that shit would go down.

And he knew she recognized him, as did her ex.

More than once, he saw her studying him in a way where she wasn't just looking at him. In a way he had to cover that shit, take her mind off it, lead her away from a realization that would be uncomfortable for both of them.

In a way that in part was now on him.

It was Joker who pretended he didn't know her name. It was Joker who knew the beard, the hair, the bulk, the life he led, the easy openness he was giving her was not the Carson Steele she once semi-knew from high school. It was Joker who was deliberately guiding her into seeing Joker, and not Carson Steele. It was Joker who knew he had to give it to her. It was Joker who knew he should.

So it was Joker who was playing a game.

Carissa was not.

If it was him, some bitch played it like that, he'd walk away and not look back.

But Carissa was steady.

It was whacked, but with all that had happened to her, she had it going on.

There was nothing in her fridge or cupboards that had a brand label, not even the fucking ketchup, and she didn't seem to care.

Not to mention she had a kid, it was her first kid, but she handled him and the responsibility of having him not like he was her first but like he was her fifth.

And as he remembered it, unlike her friends, back in high school she wasn't rolling in it, but her family was comfortable. She'd had nice clothes. She drove a used but decent car to school. She didn't seem to want for anything.

Now, it was not close to the same.

Last, her ex came from a family who *was* rolling in it, and still looked like he was far from hurting. But Carissa lived in a jacked apartment with generic shit in the fridge and stuff all around that reminded her of her failed marriage and all she lost and she didn't seem to give a shit.

What mattered to her was her son. He didn't eat generic. He didn't wear cheap clothes.

And that was all she needed.

So maybe, if she could roll so easily with all that had happened to her, if Joker explained, she'd get it and he wouldn't lose her.

He just had no fucking clue how to tell her.

"Joke?"

He looked toward the door and then went to it to see High standing just inside his room.

"Yo."

High jerked up his chin and asked, "Heidi touch base with you?"

Joker shook his head. "Nope."

"Fuck," High muttered.

Heidi's departure meant the Club was uneasy. The woman didn't give them much, but at least they had a clue where Valenzuela's attention was leaning. Now they didn't have that.

"Hop's lookin' into turnin' one," Joker shared.

"Yeah. He spoke to one, she refused," High briefed him. "He's gotta be careful. The more he approaches, the more it opens it up to one of them givin' that to Valenzuela."

Joker had no reply because what High said was true.

"Pisses me off we hand cash to these bitches, they give us a shade above dick and the cloud remains," High muttered. "We need to get proactive with this shit."

High had not been totally on board with Tack's change in direction with the Club. But then they'd all learned the hard way with the extreme shit that went down with Cherry years ago that they needed to focus on taking each other's backs, not fighting within the ranks.

That didn't mean High was the kind of man who preferred sitting around with his thumb up his ass.

"It'll eventually play out one way or another, brother," Joker told him.

"Yeah, and it'd be good that happens now rather than when I'm in the position of havin' to stick a Valenzuela soldier with my knife, doin' it from my wheelchair in a nursing home."

Joker grinned at him.

High's head jerked as he caught it.

Then he crossed his arms on his chest and asked, "Things good with your Butterfly?"

Joker leaned against the jamb and held his gaze. "Mostly."

"Not lettin' you in her pants?" High asked.

Joker nearly laughed.

Never in his life did he think he would be in the position of putting the brakes on a hot little piece, especially that piece being Carissa.

But he was.

He didn't share that with High.

He just said, "That's not it."

"What is it?"

"We went to high school together. We knew each other. Now, she doesn't remember me," Joker told him.

"Got that part of the story from Rush," High replied.

"I haven't enlightened her."

High nodded even as he noted, "Also got from Rush she digs you."

"She does, but, brother, I'm into her in a way that will hold for a good long while. She's gotta know me. A woman played this scenario the way I've played it with Carrie, she'd see my back."

High's focus on him deepened. "I take your point."

"I gotta come clean. I just don't know how."

"You mean you don't know how without pissin' her off so she takes off."

Joker nodded. "That's what I mean."

"This is what I know, Joke," High said, and his sudden change in tone made Joker brace. "You gotta be the man you are. You can't be anything else. And she's gotta get the man you are and want him, nothing else. To give her any shot at doin' that, you can't hold back who you are. Any of it. Then it's down to her. She wants the man you are, fuck-ups and all, she sticks. She doesn't, you don't want her."

Joker matched his tone when he confided, "I've wanted her since high school."

"Why, 'cause she's got a great ass?" High fired back.

Joker felt his jaw clench and through his teeth he replied, "Not even close."

"Then come clean," High returned. "You read somethin' in this woman that she's the one for you. You saw it in her all the way back then. She might make it tough on you, but if she's that girl and you're it for her like she is for you, this will be a bump in the road, but then you'll ride steady."

"Yeah, me and her and her ex who's suddenly interested in reconnecting," Joker muttered.

"Now that shit's yours," High declared, lifting a hand and stabbing a finger Joker's way. "Word is he's done her wrong in a way he's not a man. You take care of your babies even if your ex is a bitch and you gotta do it through her. You eat that shit for your kids. His ex ain't a bitch and he's eatin' model pussy and hangin' his baby momma out to dry. Her ex is not a man, you'll have no problem takin' him down however that needs to be done."

"Carissa isn't the type of girl who would dig the way a biker would make his point by pissin' around his patch," Joker pointed out.

"That's not what I mean," High replied. "What I mean is, not a lotta women want a limp dick in their bed, no matter the way that limp dick comes, he's rollin' in it or whatever.

You are not that man. She sees that, she'll put up with him because her kid shares his blood, but that's all he'll be to her. You man up for her and her kid, you'll be the rest."

He hoped like fuck that High was right. About all of it.

His phone in his back pocket rang and when it did, High asked, "You good?"

There it was. That was it.

His brotherhood.

That was why he joined. That was what he wanted.

It was just that, until recently, he hadn't availed himself of all they could give.

Another fuck-up that he wouldn't perpetrate again.

"Good, High. Thanks, brother," Joker murmured, pulling his phone out of his jeans.

"Right, then later," High returned and took off.

Joker looked at his phone, took the call, and put it to his ear.

"Tack."

"Yo, Joke. Lee called in. Got a lock on your Robinson."

Joker moved to his dresser, where there was now a bowl with his change in it. Change that used to be scattered everywhere, even on the floor.

He grinned and replied, "What'd he give you?"

"Teacher, like you said he was before. A high school in Highlands Ranch. Tenured. Married. Pays his taxes. Five years into his current mortgage—"

Joker cut him off. "I dig that Nightingale was thorough, but I don't need to know that kinda shit."

"Clue me in. What do you need?" Tack asked.

"He got a family?"

"Married. Once and still. They been that way for eleven years," Tack told him.

"No kids?"

"Lee didn't mention kids."

"I'll call Lee."

There was a pause before, "Got it."

"And Tack?"

"Yeah."

"Thanks," he muttered, grabbing his wallet and shoving it in his back pocket, loading the chain onto his belt.

"Anything, Joke," Tack muttered back and disconnected.

Joker picked up his keys, shrugged on his cut, and moved to the door, his attention back to his phone, his thumb moving to Nightingale's contact.

He listened to the rings long enough he figured he'd get voicemail before Lee answered on, "Joke."

"Lee. Callin' for some follow up on Robinson," Joker told him.

"What do you need?" Lee asked.

"He got kids?"

"Nope."

Fuck.

"How thorough were you?" Joker pushed.

"How thorough are we usually?"

He had everything.

"I know he and his wife lost a baby eight years ago. Wanna know where that led."

"They're still married."

"Need more, Lee," Joker said quietly. Having walked through the building, he was pushing through the front door to the Compound.

"Retained enough to report to Tack. Don't know specifics of the file. I'm out of the office. Hang on, I'll patch in Shirleen."

Shirleen was Nightingale's receptionist, and Shirleen used to be one half of a formidable aunt and nephew team that dealt dope in Denver. Shirleen and her nephew pulling out of that shit years ago opened it up for Valenzuela to wreak havoc.

Regardless of the consequences, it took balls, huge ones, for Shirleen to do that. He'd met her. He liked her. Because of that and because she was fucking hilarious, said it like it was, and had been a cold-as-ice drug dealer that hid a heart of gold, a heart she let shine now, it was impossible not to like her.

Suddenly Shirleen piped in. "This better be good. My nails are wet."

"Shirleen. Got Joker on the line. Need you to pull up the Robinson file," Lee ordered.

"You're lucky clickin' on my mouse don't mess up my new manicure," she muttered.

Joker stopped by his bike and grinned at his boots.

"File up, need direction," Shirleen stated.

"Medical records. The wife," Lee told her.

"What am I lookin' for?" she asked.

"Babies," Joker told her.

"Scanned the file already, son. Man's got no babies," Shirleen confirmed unnecessarily.

"Attempts at getting them," Joker clarified.

"Oh. Right. Hang on."

Joker waited.

Lee waited.

Shirleen came back. "Three miscarriages. A stillborn, which breaks my heart. Another miscarriage. More of Shirleen's heart breakin'. Looks like after that, they gave up. Hang on again."

Joker hung on, but he did it feeling his entire chest squeeze.

"Another file. Luke just added it this mornin'," Shirleen said. "They adopted. Momma pulled a fast one, took their money to keep her all good during the pregnancy. Handed over the baby, they had him ten days and she changed her mind. I'm scannin' as I'm talkin' but what I see, seemed the girl was legit. She was young and scared. Took one look at her baby, changed her mind. Her prerogative. Still breaks my heart yet again for your guy and his woman."

"Jesus Christ," Joker hissed.

"That what you need?" Lee joined in.

It was. It wasn't what he wanted, though.

"Yeah."

"You wanna share with us why you want that shit on this guy?" Lee asked, and Joker knew it wasn't a request. He also knew Lee wasn't big on sharing in-depth information about a man that was good on paper with a random curious biker.

"He was my high school teacher. He looked out for me. Last time I saw him was at the hospital after his wife lost their stillborn. I'm lookin' to reconnect, wanted to be sure he was good before I did that."

"Well, my guess is, he's not," Shirleen gave her opinion.

Joker stared at his bike as the thought came to his mind at the same time his lips moved. "I'll pay, owe a marker, don't give a shit, but need you and your boys on another one."

"That would be?" Lee asked.

"Whore. Named Heidi. Last name is Smith, which means her last name ain't Smith. She was in Valenzuela's stable. She dropped off radar a few days ago. I need her found."

"This through Tack?" Lee asked carefully.

He asked carefully because he knew the Club had issues with Valenzuela. He also knew that Tack and his brothers were working it alongside the crew of brothers Tack had outside the Club. Namely Hawk and two cops named Mitch Lawson and Brock Lucas. The Nightingale boys were not in that, and Joker knew by the way he asked the question that Lee didn't want them to be.

"This is me," Joker answered.

"Need you to explain, man," Lee told him so Joker explained.

"Heidi Smith dropped off radar a few days ago because she's knocked up, Valenzuela would rough her up if he knew, and she wants to be healthy because she's lookin' for a buyer for her baby."

"Oh Lordy," Shirleen breathed.

Lee said nothing.

"You'll get on that?" Joker prompted.

"I get you, Joke," Lee said quietly. "Says a lot about you what you're lookin' to do for this man. But he and his wife have been through hell. They don't need a prostitute lookin' for a payday fuckin' with their lives."

"Some young girl might change her mind one look at her baby, Lee, but do you think a bitch like Heidi would take Chaos for a ride?"

Lee was silent a beat before he said, "I get you."

"You'll find her?"

"Fuck yeah, we'll find her," Shirleen agreed for Lee.

"Jesus," Lee muttered.

"I'll give it to Luke. No, Vance. Whatever. We're on it," Shirleen declared.

"You heard her," Lee added, sounding pained.

"Keep tabs, send me an invoice. Or accept a marker. Whatever, it's done," Joker told them.

"We'll sort it out," Lee replied.

"Right. Great. Thanks." Joker swung his leg over his bike and finished with "Later."

He got their laters, disconnected, and was about to put his phone in his back pocket when it rang in his hand.

He brought it back around, looked at the screen and smiled at his bike grip.

He put it to his ear. "Yo, Butterfly."

"Hey, Joker," Carissa replied, but her voice sounded funny.

"Everything okay?" he asked.

"Uh...I just got a call from Angie."

Fuck.

"Your ex?" he prompted when she didn't continue.

"No, though she did share that Aaron's attorney reached out to her to set up a meeting."

"You gonna take that?"

"Angie advises I should. Test the waters. So she's doing it."

She said no more.

"Okay, then what's the problem?" he asked.

"Well, she also told me that she contacted my landlord and demanded he fax a copy of my lease to her."

Good.

Joker had called Angie's assistant the day before. He was glad she didn't delay.

"And?" Joker pushed.

"Well, I haven't had the time to dig out my rental agreement, but Angie took a look at it. Apparently, my memory isn't faulty and I was right. Notice is just a week."

Thank fuck.

"She then called him to ask why he gave me erroneous information," she went on. "He told her the terms of the agreement had changed and I'd been informed of that in writing. She asked for my signed acceptance of that change and when he said he was having trouble locating it, she told him I'd be out at the end of the month. She also explained I'd have photo evidence to the state I left the apartment in, and if there was any issue with the return of my deposit, I'd see him one last time. In court."

Joker was glad about this too, but he was cautiously glad since he couldn't get a read on her tone.

So he asked, "This is good, am I right?"

"Considering I was gearing up to take the crushing blow that I had to inform Tyra and Tack that they should put their place on the market because I didn't think it was fair they had to wait a month with no rent and I couldn't give them a month's rent and pay for this place, yes. It's good."

Joker laid it out, "Not sure I'm readin' good from you, Carrie."

"Then you're not reading me," she replied quietly. "This was you."

"It was," he confirmed, still cautious.

"You looking out for Travis and me."

Joker said nothing because he finally got his read.

You man up for her and her kid, you'll be the rest.

Yeah. High was right.

Carissa continued, "I don't know whether to cry or do cartwheels, but I can't do either because I'm at work and I can't mess up my mascara because I didn't bring the tube with me and they might get mad at me because I'm pretty sure cartwheels are a health and safety violation."

"It's not that big of a deal. My take, your landlord wanted to take you for a ride. He didn't. You probably woulda eventually looked at your lease and questioned it. It would be a headache, but my Butterfly doesn't take shit. You woulda got in his face. Just saved you that hassle, Carrie."

"You did," she agreed. "I appreciate it and I don't know how to express that appreciation."

He knew how she could do it but that would wait until after they went out on their date next week.

"I could wash your bike," she suggested.

"The only thing you have to do with this bike is when I

put your ass on the back of it. You don't wash it. You also don't do payback. It isn't necessary. We're new, but if we wanna do this right, this is how we start, Carissa. You're in the position I gotta take your back. We get beyond new, there'll be a time you return the favor. It's just what it is. Roll with it."

That bought him nothing.

So he called, "Carrie?"

"I wanna cry and do cartwheels again," she told him, voice clogged.

He grinned and said nothing.

He heard her clear her throat before she went on, "That's all the good news. The bad news is, I've lost important days of packing so I need to get on that pronto. And to top that, we have two cashiers down with the flu. Sharon needs me to take a shift tomorrow."

He didn't want her to take a shift tomorrow. He wanted to have another day with her and her boy, this time packing boxes.

But he figured she needed that shift. She probably got paid dick but more was better than less, even if it was more of practically nothing.

"Right. Dinner and me helpin' you pack boxes tomorrow?"

"Yes," she said quietly.

She wanted that.

Fuck yes.

"I'll bring shit and I'll cook."

"I hope you won't be cooking shit."

He started chuckling at the first cuss word he'd heard from her ever.

"It'll be good shit," he said through his laughter.

"Whatever," she said, sounding amused.

"Okay, Butterfly. Give Travis a cuddle from me, yeah?"

A soft, quiet, "Yeah, sweetie."

Sweetie.

No old lady called her old man *sweetie*.

Joker fucking loved it from Carrie.

"Right, tomorrow," he said.

"Tomorrow, Joker. Can't wait."

And he fucking loved that she gave him that. No bullshit. She couldn't wait and she told him so.

He shared his feelings about that by dipping his voice when he said, "Later, baby."

"'Bye."

He waited for her disconnect before he shoved his phone in his back pocket, started his bike, backed it out, and took off.

*   *   *

"I had hoped you'd visit a barber before you showed for a family dinner," Mrs. Heely said after Linus's wife, Kamryn, opened the door to their house and Joker had walked in.

"I think you look wonderful," Kam said quietly, coming up to his side, touching his hand lightly, then reaching up and kissing his bearded cheek.

He looked down at her and caught the soft smile in her gorgeous face. Linus was a good-looking man, but he still scored with Kamryn Washington.

"You're an enabler," Mrs. Heely sighed.

"Pipe down, woman, and give me a hug," Joker ordered.

Her eyes lit, her face lost its fake irritation, and she moved to him and into his arms.

He closed those arms around her and bent to kiss the top of her head.

She smelled like she always smelled, a few days ago and way back when she brought him dinner.

He wondered if her son liked her smell and figured the guy had never thought of it. He also figured if he thought he'd lose it, he'd think of it and like it.

Like Joker.

"Buddy!" Linus boomed.

Mrs. Heely pulled out of his arms but Joker didn't let her get far. He kept her close with one arm around her shoulders.

"This menace is Jackson," Linus stated, his hand on the head of a kid who was studying Joker curiously, until his father gently swiveled his head around and he started grinning and rolling his eyes back to get a look at his dad. "This is Tyler." Linus let his boy go and bent deep to touch the head of a little one sitting on a step, eating from a bowl of grapes. "And this," Linus went on, twisting and hefting up a pretty little girl who was hiding behind her daddy. "Is Candace. My little Candy." He looked into her face and ordered, "Say hi to Daddy's friend, Joker."

She did a quick wave then tucked herself closer to her father.

"Joker? Like Batman?" Jackson asked.

"No, son, he's a good guy," Linus answered.

Jackson had a look on his face that said he didn't comprehend this but he was trying.

It was funny and Joker wanted to crack up watching him.

But he didn't.

Because he was taking it all in.

The house was a newish build, on a small lot, but that didn't mean it wasn't huge. It was also nice. Clean. Decorated. All about Kam's colorful, stylish personality...and family. And Linus, with his beautiful wife, his three healthy, cute kids, the man of the family standing among all he built, the most important things in life. Woman. Kids. And the home you could give them.

He took this in glad as fuck Linus had it.

But he took it in thinking for the first time in his life that he wanted this.

Just this.

Gorgeous woman. Cute kids. Clean home decorated in the warmth his woman wanted to give their family.

"You gonna stand there starin' at me, or you gonna take off your jacket and drink some of your old friend's beer?" Linus asked.

Joker let Mrs. Heely go to shrug off his jacket, answering, "Beer."

"Now that introductions are complete, Linus, would you like to share how you feel about Car...Joker's lack of grooming?" Mrs. Heely asked.

Linus turned laughing eyes to the woman. "Respect, Mrs. Heely, but even when he was a kid, he was good-lookin'. He could have hippie hair and still be that way."

This said a lot coming from Linus, who might work in a garage but right then he was dressed well. He'd always cropped his hair close to his head with clean lines razor-sharp all around and straight up took care of himself.

"I disagree," Mrs. Heely snapped.

"He'd be cuter with shorter hair," Candace piped up shyly.

"There's a girl with taste," Mrs. Heely declared, moving forward and arriving at Linus in a way it was impossible to misunderstand what she wanted.

Linus didn't misunderstand it. He put his daughter down and Mrs. Heely claimed her immediately.

Taking her hand, she moved her up the steps from the living room that led toward the back of the house and a big, open kitchen, saying, "We girls gotta stick together, Candy. Now, let's go help Mommy with dinner."

"Okay, Momma Heely," Candace replied.

"That's my cue," Kamryn muttered and he looked to her. "So glad you're here, Carson."

He nodded.

She moved into the house.

"Bud," Linus called. "Beer."

"Yeah," Joker replied and moved toward him thinking next time, he'd bring Carissa and Travis.

That being after he told her he was Carson and he could quit dicking around and give it all to her so she knew what she was getting, the man he was, how he came to be that man.

And then they'd see.

*   *   *

After dinner with his friends, Joker was walking into the Compound when his phone rang.

He looked right, saw some of his brothers hanging out with beer, shot glasses, and a bottle of vodka. He headed that way while he pulled out his phone.

"Beer or shot?" Rush called.

"Beer," Joker muttered, looking at his phone.

He didn't know why he took the call. He didn't want to talk to the man, and he no longer had any reason to talk to him.

But in the end he was glad he did even if it was the beginning of an uncertain end.

It started with him putting the phone to his ear and saying, "No reason for you to call me."

To which Monk replied, "Got my fighters, a basement full of bloodthirsty motherfuckers, and bets taken on my main draw. A main draw whose ass is not here."

"Told you when you texted me days ago, Monk, I'm out."

He had told Monk that. He got Monk's text about the next fight the day he decided to make his play with Carissa.

The money he made on fights was good. Good enough he

had a whack and could buy a truck with cash without hardly making a dent in it.

But he also got paid a brother's cut of Ride, which wouldn't make him a millionaire, but it was substantial. He didn't need to fight anymore.

Not to mention, any good fighter knew when to quit. Bare fists, if he was lucky, he might have a couple more years in him. But if he had a woman like Carissa in his life, he had no business taking those punches.

"You can't just be *out*," Monk replied as Joker stopped by his brothers at the bar.

"Fuck me. Apologies. Did we sign a contract and I forgot?" he asked.

"No, Joke, but you're my main fuckin' draw. You can't just pull out," Monk returned.

That was a lie. Monk had two monsters who always fought after Joker. They played that crowd like the pros they were, total carnage.

And Joker never threw a fight, as Monk had asked him to do repeatedly so they could both cash in on it. This meant Joker was a sure thing. Since entering the circuit in Denver, he was undefeated.

So he was nowhere near Monk's main draw. What he was was a fighter who people liked to watch, and bet on, and win, and Monk put up with that because they won on Joker, so they had money to bet on the monsters who came up after him, fights on which they could lose their cash.

"I can. Did. Done," Joker replied.

"Fuck me. Pussy."

Joker felt his spine snap straight.

"Say again?" he whispered.

"All of you. Chaos pussies. And it's not a surprise. Everyone is sayin' it. Your leader and his lieutenants are so whipped by their bitches, been led around by their dicks so long, it's a wonder they have any dicks left. You eat enough pussy, fuck enough pussy, you *become* a pussy. That's what's happened to Chaos. Chaos is pussy."

"All right," Joker said slowly, feeling the vibe in the room shift as his brothers felt the anger coming off him in waves. "You've got five seconds to assure me that I didn't just hear what I just heard."

"You heard me," Monk hissed. "I already took bets on you, motherfucker. You leave me high and dry, that's... just...*pussy*."

Joker hung up on him and turned his attention to the men with him.

Rush, Hound, Roscoe, Boz.

"What the fuck was that?" Roscoe asked.

Joker told them, finishing on, "Monk has three bouncers and a guy who looks after the money. They can fuck a man up, individually and collectively. Knowin' that, who feels like takin' a ride?"

It didn't surprise Joker that every man felt like mounting his bike.

And they all did.

*   *   *

It would seem Joker was going to give one last show to Monk and his bloodthirsty crew.

It just wasn't the show Monk wanted.

Hound had two bouncers down before they were five feet into the room, clearing the way for Joker to make a direct line to Monk.

Rush took out the third bouncer.

Boz was holding back the money man with the point of his knife.

And Joker was bent over Monk, who'd long since lost his feet, holding him by the collar and pummeling his fist into the bloody, swelling flesh of his face.

Before Monk passed out, Joker stopped, yanked him to within an inch of his face and demanded, "Tell me again that Chaos is pussy."

"J-Jo—"

Joker punched him again.

Monk made a moist noise that sounded like it came from his nose *and* throat.

He jerked him back and ordered, "Tell me again, motherfucker. Say it. Chaos is pussy."

Monk shook his head.

"Good," Joker spat. "Now, you're fucked up because I was havin' a good night, settlin' in, gonna down a few beers with my boys, and your bullshit put me on my bike so I couldn't do that. What you said, though, that's somethin' else. That's about Chaos, not me. And that means long-lasting retribution."

Another moist noise from Monk, this full of fear as he tried to pull away.

Joker shook him viciously then held him still and stated, "Valenzuela does not rule this fight, and he doesn't 'cause you had me fightin'. He's not ready for his round with Chaos, so he's steered clear. Now, he's gonna get word there is no Chaos at this fight. What's that gonna mean for you?"

Another noise of fear before, "Do-don't, Joke, he—"

Joker cut him off, "You ran your mouth. I gave you a chance to take that shit back. You didn't. Now you pay."

"I-I'll give a c-cut to Chaos," Monk offered quickly. "Buy peace."

"I'll share that with Tack. He gets finished eatin' his woman's pussy, brings that to the Club, we'll get back to you," Joker bit out, reared back, and landed a powerhouse punch that had worked for him numerous times in the past.

A man like Monk, it destroyed him.

And his now-fractured cheekbone.

He was out.

Joker dropped him and straightened, turning to Rush, who was speaking to Monk's only man left standing.

"We didn't make our statement and you consider payback, think again. You don't come up with the right answer and we see you when we don't wanna see you, shit's gonna get ugly."

The guy looked around at the four men on the floor, only one of whom was groaning and trying to push up, two had stab wounds from Hound's knife and were groaning, but not trying to push up, and it didn't take a mind reader to know he considered shit already ugly.

Their message conveyed, Roscoe stated, "Let's ride."

They all moved out, and even though the crowd had pressed close, they didn't waste time getting the fuck out of the way.

They were at their bikes when Joker looked to Boz. "You want me to call this in to Tack?"

"I'm on it," Boz answered.

Joker nodded.

They mounted.

Then Chaos rode.

Tack

In the dark, Tack sat on the side of his and Red's bed, talking into his phone.

"No. All good. But I want the brothers gathered in the morning."

"You got it, man," Boz replied. "Later."

"Yeah, later," Tack said, took his phone from his ear, hit the button, and tossed it on his nightstand.

Then he slid the fingers of one hand through his hair, followed instantly by the other hand, and he left both at the back of his neck while he rested his elbows to his knees.

Chaos is pussy.

That could not stand.

He felt Tyra slide her hand from the small of his back up his spine before he felt her position, on her knees, those knees spread, the insides of her thighs pressed to his hips. He felt her front hit his back as her lips touched his hands at his neck.

"Talk to me," she whispered. "Is everything okay?"

"Yeah," he replied and it was no lie.

It was.

For now.

His brothers sent a message. The right one. And they didn't fuck around doing it.

But it wasn't enough.

It was time.

And he fucking hated it.

Tomorrow, they'd go over what happened, what was said, what was done, and what they'd be doing.

Tack's new message would be to anyone else who thought that shit.

It would also be to Valenzuela.

Chaos was claiming more territory. They were going to clean it up. They were going to keep it safe.

Once the Club voted, no longer would Chaos be five miles around Ride.

It would be ten.

Valenzuela held firm positions to the north, east, and west.

He would retaliate.

But it was time.

The Club would meet, then Tack would sit with Hawk, Brock, and Mitch. Mitch was going to lose his mind. Lawson wasn't a straight arrow, but he was as straight as they came. Tack and Brock were working this to bring an end to Valenzuela that would not mean blood but would mean jail time, dismantling Valenzuela's operations in a way it would decimate him.

But that shit took time.

Too much time, apparently.

"Kane, you're kinda scaring me."

He lifted and twisted, dropping his hands and curling his fingers around her thigh.

"Boys had some trouble tonight, they neutralized it. Not happy about the trouble they had, but they took care of business," he told her. "But, Red, you gotta know, something's comin'. There was never any way to stop it, but the time has come for us to stroll out to face it. And what's comin', you gotta brace."

"Baby," she whispered, sliding a hand around his side to his stomach.

"It'll all be good," he promised.

"I know it will," she replied.

Zero hesitation.

Just, *I know it will.*

That was his wife. The mother of two of his sons.

His dream woman.

He tipped his head back and he didn't need to do more. She gave him her mouth.

He twisted further to take her to her back on their bed.

Then she gave him everything else.

CHAPTER THIRTEEN

That Hasn't Changed

Carissa

I SAT ON a barstool at the Chaos Compound, wondering how I was remaining seated seeing as I was so exhausted I could barely think, when Tack strolled in.

As usual, his eyes went right to Tyra, who had commandeered Lanie and Hop's baby boy, Nash, and was bouncing him, cuddling him and cooing to him.

"Jesus, woman, every baby that gets within ten feet a' you you claim. Do I gotta knock you up again?" Tack asked her.

She gave him eyes that were easy to read.

Tack read them. I knew this when he looked to the ceiling and muttered, "Fuck me. This rate, I'll live in a kid-free zone when I'm eighty."

"Like you don't love it," Tyra returned.

Tack took his eyes from the ceiling and gave them to his wife.

He, too, was easy to read.

He loved it. But he loved more giving her what she wanted.

I started to feel warm just watching them together as Tack looked to the bar and asked, "What the fuck?"

"Carissa cleared out the day-olds at LeLane's bakery," Lanie said, a half-eaten cream puff suspended three inches from her mouth. "And everyone knows day-olds at LeLane's are better than fresh everywhere else."

This was true.

As much as my Chaos friends said I didn't need to do anything for payback, I still needed to do something for payback.

And today was moving in day so I *really* needed to do something for payback.

Tack and Tyra's renters were out a few days early so the boys were going to get my stuff out of the storage unit and my apartment.

Tomorrow would be filled with me unpacking, cleaning my old place and doing the chores I didn't do when Travis was around but now needed to do because I hadn't done them in a week.

And then Travis and I would finally be in a nice place. The kind of place you'd want to give your baby.

I couldn't wait.

I still wanted nothing more than to curl up somewhere and take a nap.

This was because the flu had hit the cashiers at LeLane's and was now sweeping through the store. It was not the twenty-four hour flu. More like the ninety-six hour flu. Another two cashiers had gone down, a produce guy, two butcher boys, and a floral technician. It was all hands on deck at LeLane's and I had hands, so they used them. I'd taken extra shifts, double shifts or shifts and a half.

This would be awesome normally. I was racking up a ton of time and a half.

But I also had my son. I didn't mind working like that when he was with Aaron, but I hated doing it when I had him.

Not to mention, I had boxes to pack and all sorts of stuff to do, like find time to make a half a dozen calls to switch over utilities.

So I'd been on the go for days, sorting things out on breaks and lunch, forcing myself to pack at least five boxes before calling it a night, thus getting minimal sleep and dragging myself out of bed and getting on the go again.

Just to say, if I never packed another kitchen up *in my life* I'd be happy. It seemed like nothing but all the stuff was hidden behind the cupboards. When you had to take it out, wrap it up and box it, it seemed like it could fill ten kitchens.

Because of this, I hated to admit it, and tried my best not to, but when I handed Travis over to Aaron the day before, I'd actually been relieved. I needed a break any way I could get it. And I'd been so preoccupied with the move, I hadn't really noted that it was Aaron I handed him over to. He'd answered the door. He'd also tried to engage me in conversation, taking a close look at me and asking if I was all right.

I'd allowed this (though I didn't share how I was doing) since he needed to know I was moving so I told him that and that I'd text my new details to him. Then I'd bent in, given my boy a kiss, and took off, my mind filled with what I had to do next (a shift) at the same time battling the desire to crawl into the backseat of my car and sleep for a week.

Not surprisingly, Joker noticed the toll all this was taking and stepped in, bringing Chaos with him. Big Petey, Joker, and once Tabby and Shy looked after Travis while I worked. And after Joker saw me nearly fall into a box, losing my fight against sleep, Tyra, with Lanie and Tabby, came over to finish packing the boxes when I was at work.

So, obviously, buying a bunch of cream puffs, éclairs,

mille-feuilles, and petit fours at half off because the customer who'd ordered them hadn't picked them up, plus my extra twenty percent employee discount, was in order.

It had already been in order but it was currently *more* in order.

And luckily, due to my next paycheck being augmented, I could actually (mostly) afford it.

LeLane's still was in the throes of the flu epidemic, but the two cashiers who'd first gone down were back, which meant I had two days off.

Two days off where I'd be moving stuff in, unpacking it, doing chores, and running errands.

I couldn't wait to live in that house.

But I needed another day off.

Or three.

I was dead on my feet.

Or, more aptly, dead on my behind on a stool at Chaos.

I was also faking it. I was getting to know these people, and if they got one whiff I was struggling, they'd kidnap me, take me to the nearest luxury hotel, lock me in a room, and only disturb me to send up a massage therapist and, maybe, a skin technician.

"Babe, this is cool," Tack said, and I focused on him to see him tipping his head to the bar laden with pastries but he was looking at me. "Unnecessary but cool."

I pinned a bright smile on my face as I contradicted, "Necessary and the least I could do."

He grinned.

Boz, with a ring of chocolate stuck in the long whiskers around his mouth, declared, "Never stepped foot in that store. Thought they were up their own asses. They got éclairs like this, I'm goin' every day."

Bonus, I'd bought LeLane's a new customer.

He shoved the second half of his fourth éclair in his mouth and I turned my bright smile to him.

"Shee-it! What the fuck?" I heard hooted by Hound (who was at the other end of the bar, annihilating the petit fours).

After that I heard a catcall and a low whistle.

And finally, Boz shouted, "Fuck me. Joke cleans up *good*!"

That made me grin genuinely though I didn't understand the reaction to Joker since I hadn't seen him yet. Still, any promise of Joker in my vicinity would make me grin and do it genuinely.

Joker had told me he had something to do that morning and would come and get me around nine thirty. I told him I had something to bring to the Compound so I'd meet him there.

Now he was there.

And that made me happy.

Until he came into view.

That made me freeze.

It was him. I knew it was. I could see his eyes. The color of his hair. His usual faded jeans, tee, and leather jacket.

I could also see his face.

All of it.

He'd shaved.

He'd also had his hair cut. It was trimmed at the sides, not a crew cut or anything, but a lot shorter, messy and long-ish on top but not as long as it used to be. It still fell over his forehead, but not like before.

He had a very nice jaw.

He even had attractive ears.

And last, he did not look like him. Even if he still did.

No, he now looked like a boy I once knew. A boy grown up.

Carson Steele.

His eyes fell on me and his lips moved as he kept coming toward me.

"Hey, Butterfly. You ready for today?"

I didn't answer.

I was busy staring.

This couldn't be true.

I kept staring wondering how I could miss this. Wondering how this could be real.

But I hadn't missed it. The very first time he got close on the shoulder of I-25, I knew I knew him. And later that first meeting, I'd felt the same way. And again and again, repeatedly.

I knew that I *knew*.

But I couldn't put my finger on it because he'd changed. He had the years since we'd last seen each other written on his face, in every inch of his frame.

But it was more. The hair. The beard. The bulk on his body. The way he held himself. The way he dressed. The company he kept.

Carson Steele had been a loner.

Joker had a band of brothers. A huge family of good, kind people.

Suddenly, it occurred to me with blinding clarity that Aaron had sensed the same. That was why he'd studied Joker so closely. He'd even asked him if he knew him!

And last, Joker knew *me*. He'd known who I was the second he approached me on I-25. He'd gone completely still, staring at me.

He *knew* me.

Then.

And *since*.

And he didn't say anything. I told him my name, and he didn't say he knew me and I knew him.

He didn't *say anything.*

Why didn't he say anything?

He'd even pretended he'd forgotten my name!

"Carrie?" he called when he stopped close.

"Why didn't you say anything?" I whispered, looking deep into his eyes.

They hadn't been blunt steel back then. He was too young to have had time to build up that guard. Every girl in school could read the tortured brooding of the mysterious outsider who was Carson Steele right from his eyes. Every girl had wanted to soothe his savaged soul.

Every girl in school.

Including me.

It was then I knew. I knew in the single most humiliating moment in my life why he'd done what he'd done.

Back in the day he'd liked me. He'd smiled at me. He'd been cool with me. He'd given me chin lifts. And that awful night when I saw him beaten up (again) and set on running away, he'd given me his time.

And so much more.

That more being the next day in my locker when he gave me beauty.

And hope.

Hope that had died but I'd felt it, knowing that he'd taken his time to get to my locker and give that to me.

So it wasn't that he'd wanted to make a high school mean girl pay (though, I wasn't a mean girl, I just hung with them so I was guilty by association, still, Carson Steele was smarter than that).

No.

It was because he felt sorry for me. The cheerleader. The homecoming queen. The quarterback's girl. Reduced to nearly nothing, stranded on the side of the road, in her twenties and divorced with a baby, no friends, no family, no money, a horrible car, cheap clothes, a job at a grocery store.

He felt sorry for me.

"Say anything about what?" he asked, taking me out of my abysmal thoughts.

And in doing so, making that humiliation burn so deep, I knew if I didn't let some of what I was feeling out, it'd destroy me.

Therefore, I shrieked, "*About anything, Carson Steele!*"

His head jerked. His face changed. And the air in the room went flat.

Then he lifted a hand to me.

I scrambled, knocking over the stool. It fell with a crash and I nearly went down with it, but thankfully I kept my feet as I moved to get away from him, screeching, "*Don't you touch me!*"

"Carrie," he whispered.

"Out," I heard Tack order.

"I haven't tried a cream puff," I heard Boz reply.

"*Out!*" I heard Tack bark.

I vaguely sensed the room emptying but I was too busy backing up and focusing on Joker.

And my burning mortification.

"I can't believe you," I hissed.

"Listen to me—" he started.

"*No!*" I screamed. "You pretended you forgot my name. *You didn't forget me!*"

"Carrie," he said gently, moving cautiously my way. "Baby, take a breath and listen to me."

"Why?" I snapped. "You're sharp, *Carson.* You knew when I first saw you I recognized you!" I yelled. "But you didn't say *a word.* You let me introduce myself and you didn't say *a word.*

You did all this," I threw out a hand, "because you felt sorry for me, and you didn't say *a word.*"

"Carissa, seriously, *listen to me,*" he growled as I moved, rounding into the room to make my way to the door and escape, doing this as he stalked me.

"I didn't get it," I threw at him. "No one is *this* nice. Day-care. New house. Legal counsel. Too much. Too nice. *Too easy.* I didn't get it," I bit out. "Now I get it."

"Carissa, goddamn it, you need to shut up and *listen to me,*" he clipped.

"No, I don't," I retorted, making hasty decisions because I needed an end to this. I needed this over. I needed to escape the burn threatening to end me. I'd endured enough, too much. I could take no more. "I'll explain to Tyra and Tack about the house. I'll get some money to Big Petey. I'll sort the rest out. But no more Carissa Charity Case for you, Carson Steele. I'm leaving!"

I declared this, my heart breaking, my insides reduced to ash twisting in the flames, and I charged wide of him to get to the door.

He moved quickly, catching my upper arm in a firm grip and striding purposefully toward the back of the Compound, taking me with him.

I scurried to keep my feet under me as I was forced to walk backward, doing this shouting, "Take your hand off me!"

"Shut the fuck up," he ground out.

"Do not talk to me like that, *Carson Steele,*" I yelled. "Take your stupid hand off me!"

He didn't. He dragged me down the hall, pulled me in his room and then propelled me further with his hand on my arm pushing me then releasing me as I fell backward three steps and he slammed the door.

"*Let me out!*" I shrieked.

"Wanted you," he replied. "In high school, I wanted you. So bad, my life went to shit, like it went to shit every single *fucking* day, to give my head some peace, I'd draw you."

I snapped my mouth shut as my stomach squeezed so hard, I thought I'd be sick.

He kept at me.

"Last person I saw before I left my fucked-up life, meant everything that it was you. Years later, saw you again, you didn't know me."

Oh no.

"Carson," I whispered.

"That fuckin' hurt," he forced out in a way I knew those three words cost him.

A lot.

Too much.

Yes, I was going to be sick.

"I—"

"Didn't know who the fuck I was," he finished for me acidly.

"I did," I told him. "I just didn't completely recognize you and you didn't share when I introduced Travis and me."

"You're right," he shot back. "I didn't. Think on that, Carissa. You had a life where you got nothin' you wanted, but still, you were fool enough to want a guy. You liked him. He was nice to you and you used him to give you peace from the shithole you called a home and the jackhole you called a dad. You saw him again, he didn't know who the fuck you were, what would you do?"

Unfortunately, I saw his point.

More so seeing as he was a man, a *manly* man, a manly *biker* man who not only wouldn't take kindly to that type of thing but also wouldn't like to admit it hurt.

Not to mention, all he said about his home, his dad, using me to bring him peace killed me.

Sadly, thinking all this, I didn't reply, so he had his chance to keep going.

"Now it's been weeks where me, my brothers, their women have taken your back, looked after you, looked after your boy, *you* notice *your* fuck-up and you lay that charity case shit on me?"

"That was—"

"Fucked-up and ugly," he finished for me again.

He was right.

"I was surprised," I defended myself feebly.

"Yeah, me too. Surprised the homecoming queen had it in her *ever* to remember I existed."

Okay, wait.

That blow was low.

He was right. I'd messed up.

But I didn't deserve that.

"Joker, of course I'd remember you," I said carefully.

"Yeah? Had my tongue in your mouth, your hands up my shirt, looked into my eyes beggin' for more, Carissa, and that shit didn't happen."

Oh no.

Absolutely *not*.

"Your hair is different!" I retorted sharply.

"So's yours," he fired back.

This was true. It was longer. As was his.

Still.

"You had a beard."

"You have a baby."

Darn it!

"You're a biker!" I cried.

"You're a grocery store clerk," he returned.

He was too much!

"It's been years!" I yelled.

"Yeah, it has," he whispered ominously.

But I knew what he meant.

It had been years and he still knew me.

He didn't get the same.

But even if he was right, his reaction was *wrong*.

"Okay, you're right. You're absolutely right. And I'm sorry, Joker," I hissed. "I'm sorry I didn't recognize the boy I crushed on and did it *huge* back in high school. Honestly, I don't know how I didn't. Though, you know, I may have had a few things on my mind, say, a flat tire and a crappy apartment and an ex-husband whose sole desire seemed to be making my life a misery. But I still don't know how I didn't. Especially considering the fact that, almost right away, I started crushing on the man you became even *bigger* than I'd crushed on you back then."

I finished talking and did it breathing hard, so focused on what I was saying I didn't notice his expression change.

But then I noticed his expression had changed.

"What?" he whispered.

"What what?" I snapped, still feeling many things, including anger.

"You crushed on me?" he asked.

I stared for a second and did it hard before I threw up my hands and returned, "Like you didn't know."

"I didn't know."

I leaned into him and hissed, "Baloney."

The ominous whisper was back with his, "Be careful, Carissa."

"About what?" I asked crossly. "Every girl had a crush on you and you pretending you didn't know that is laughable. You totally knew."

"Not about you."

"So you knew," I pushed.

"Not about you."

"Oh my gosh!" I cried, narrowing my eyes at him. "You cannot believe for one second I believe you. Every time I saw you I smiled at you. Once I even *tripped* so I could *fall into you* so you'd *catch me*, for goodness sakes! I couldn't *be* more obvious!"

His body went completely still but I wasn't done.

"And honestly, the last time I saw you, I asked you out on *a date*. I knew you were leaving. I figured you had to do what you had to do. And I admired you having the courage to do it. Still, it was my last ditch effort to get you to notice me. I knew you had to leave but I wanted you to do it hopefully thinking of me so if you came back, you'd remember me and—"

He cut me off. "Shut up."

"No!" I shouted.

"Shut up, Carissa, now," he growled.

I shut up and I did this because of the way he was looking at me.

Suddenly I didn't feel the burning pain of humiliation.

Or anger.

I felt burning but it wasn't pain.

It was something else entirely.

"You had him," he said so quietly I barely heard him.

But I heard him and I understood him.

"If you'd given me a sign, the smallest clue, I would have let him go so I could have had my shot with you."

Joker stared at me.

I let him until I could take no more.

"Please don't be mad at me," I whispered.

Joker didn't reply.

"Please," I begged.

Joker said nothing. He just kept staring at me in that way that made me think he *was* saying something, I just wasn't sure I understood it.

But I had a feeling. I wasn't certain I was right but it was too important not to take my shot.

So I took my shot.

I rushed forward three steps and threw myself at him hoping with everything in me that he'd catch me.

But this time, he didn't catch me. He didn't close his arms around me and kiss me.

He also didn't push me away.

He bent, grabbed hold of me, lifted and swung me to his side. Then he took several long strides and tossed me on the bed.

As I landed, I sucked in breath, which was good since he fell, landing right on top of me.

That was when he kissed me.

And I kissed him back. Hard. Wanting him. Wanting Joker. Wanting Carson Steele. Not believing I had them... both.

So I was not about to let go.

Lucky for me, I knew with the way his hands were moving on me that this time, he wasn't going to let me go either. He wasn't going to stop.

This was it. Him and me. Joker and Carrie. Carson and Carissa.

Connecting.

Finally.

I wanted that. I wanted that more than anything I'd ever wanted—except my baby to be happy and healthy and my sister and mother to be alive—but it was a close fourth.

And that said a lot.

So I went for it. I gave it my all. I didn't want him to come to his senses and realize he was still mad at me for not recognizing him. Or realize we were in his bed in the Compound, not at my place after a special date. Or *anything* that might make him stop.

I wanted this to happen now. I wanted to show him how I felt about him back then.

But more, I wanted to show him what he meant to me now.

And I wanted that so badly, I messed it up.

Completely.

It started after he got my T-shirt off. I immediately pulled his off and went right in, mistaking my aim and slamming the top of my head hard into his jaw. So hard he grunted and reared back.

We were both sitting up, but I was bent to him, so I lifted away and whispered, "Sorry."

His eyes found mine, he drove his hands into my hair and pulled my mouth to his. Then he took us back down and it was all good.

It might have gotten better.

But instead it got worse when he had me on my back, was thrilling me with his tongue in my mouth, and he *almost* slid into second base, his rough, calloused hand *so close* to my breast I could feel the phantom of ecstasy I just *knew* it would bring, so I sucked his tongue too hard into my mouth as I dragged my nails up his side.

He broke the kiss and jerked away from my touch.

Humiliating.

Totally.

"I—" I began, feeling heat in my cheeks that had nothing to do with what he'd been doing to me.

"Relax," he whispered.

"Okay," I whispered back.

He bent to me and kept kissing me.

Then he kissed other parts of me. I liked it so much it was unreal. It took me out of my head and firm into what he was doing to me.

That was when I *loved* it, my body showing him by pressing into him, whimpers gliding up my throat, my hands moving on him feverishly to take in the warm, sleek hardness that was him *everywhere*.

He did things to my breasts that Aaron had done but I didn't think of Aaron because Aaron was forgotten with the way Joker did it. It totally obliterated Aaron's memory.

I knew why.

There was more feeling behind the touch, the taste, the sensations. More passion. More experience. More talent.

More everything.

I felt it. I sensed it. I *loved it*.

Then he drifted down, his lips moving over my belly, his hands to the button of my jeans.

Once he had it undone, he shoved up to his knees, straddling me, and dazedly I stared up at him.

I missed the beard.

I loved the hair.

Gosh, he was amazing.

That face. Those eyes molten and staring down at me. His face hard and handsome.

His chest...

I tensed as he unzipped my zipper and shifted to yank my jeans down my legs.

That did not thrill me because his chest was all I could see.

And his arms.

Perfection. Cut collarbone jutting shoulder to broad, defined shoulder. Bulging biceps. Prominent veins lacing his inner and outer forearms. His ribs were delectable ridges.

The boxes of his abs were deep and distinct. And he had tattoos that I couldn't take in fully with everything that was happening, but they still were fascinating.

Then there was the V.

The V.

The muscles around his hipbones delineated in sharp relief leading into the waistband of his faded jeans.

He wasn't amazing.

He was flawless. He was every woman's computer wallpaper. He was three-story tall billboard ads.

He was dazzling.

And I was not.

"Joker," I called as he pulled my last Converse off.

His head turned to me.

"I—" I started, gliding my hands over my belly, all that had gone before lost. Lying in his bed, all that was me with all that was him, I wanted nothing but to get up, get dressed, and get away.

I didn't want him to see me.

"Don't," he whispered.

I shook my head. "I don't think—"

He looked away and tore my jeans over my ankles.

"Joker!"

He surged over me, up on one hand in the bed beside me, arm straight, his eyes sheets of liquid steel.

"Do not," he growled.

"I'm not sure—"

His hand hit me palm flat between my breasts and glided down.

"You want this," he stated.

I had.

Now I wasn't sure. I'd conked him on the jaw, scratched him too hard, nearly sucked his tongue down my throat, and

I had a baby belly (not to mention a baby behind which, fortunately in my current position, he couldn't see).

His hand kept going, relentlessly shoving between my arms that were surrounding my stomach to hide it from him.

"I want this," he kept talking.

I wanted to believe that.

"You're flawless," I whispered.

His hand slid into my undies, his finger dipping deep, dragging hard against my clit. I lost all thought as his touch made my back arch right off the mattress and my hands shoot up, fingers curling into the waistband of his jeans. My eyes closed and a moan tore up my throat.

"So are you," he muttered gruffly, dragging his finger back and doing it harder.

"Oh my," I breathed.

"Yeah," he ground out, pushing, dragging, circling.

Oh *my*.

"Joker," I panted, unconsciously lifting my knees and spreading my legs to give him better access.

"Fuck yeah, Carrie," he groaned as he shifted so he was no longer straddling me but positioned between my legs.

"Don't stop that," I begged, opening my eyes, trying to focus on his, pressing into him, feeling it building, all he was giving me, and doing it squirming. "Please."

He didn't do as I asked. He dragged his finger hard against my clit again and buried it inside me.

Oh *yes*.

My neck arched back, my head pressing into the pillow, my eyes closing again as I pushed down into his hand and moaned, "Okay, you can stop the other, stick with this."

"Anything you want, Butterfly," his voice came at me, thick but amused as he pulled his finger out and thrust it in. He did that awhile, I rode it awhile, writhing, panting, exhilarating, then he pulled out and thrust in two fingers as his thumb came to my clit.

My body jolted and I took one hand from his jeans to wrap it around his wrist to keep him precisely where I needed him to be.

"Oh God," I breathed, my eyes opening, "Yes. That. More of *that*."

"Yes. That," he grunted, his voice no longer amused and now so thick, it felt like a hot touch, coating me. "More of that."

I tried to take in the expression that went with his tone but I couldn't. I was close and spiraling closer very, *very* quickly.

"You ready for me, Butterfly?" he asked.

I'd never been more ready.

"Yes," I panted. "Yes, now, Joker. *Please.*"

I lost his fingers but I didn't lose the feelings because of the hot, violent, delicious way he tore my panties down my legs.

I gasped and felt his weight bearing into my left hip as I heard a drawer open and him order, "Help me out, Carrie."

I didn't know what he wanted and I opened my eyes to see he had the edge of a condom packet between his teeth. He was still up on one hand in the bed but no longer pressed into my hip.

His eyes were consuming me.

With dumb luck, since I was so far from thinking it wasn't funny, it hit me that to use that condom, he needed to be freed of his jeans.

And I needed him free of his jeans.

Immediately.

It was so hot, so unbelievably *amazing* to stare into his eyes as I unbuttoned his jeans, yanked them down to his hips and felt him spring free, hard and ready for me, I'd never forget it, that moment after he'd given so much to me, knowing I was about to get all of him.

"Thanks, baby," he muttered.

"Hurry," I pleaded.

Joker hurried. His eyes keeping mine captive, it took him no time at all to deal with things. Then I felt him guide himself to me and nudge through my wetness.

"Yes," I whispered.

"Ready?" he whispered back.

This was Joker.

And me.

Joker.

Carson Steele.

Oh yes. I was ready.

I nodded. "Absolutely."

He slid inside.

My head again went back as I moaned, "Oh yes, *yes*, sweetheart."

He started moving, suspended over me, slow and steady but with his leverage, *deep.*

Oh *yes.*

"More," I begged.

"Wrap your legs around my thighs," he ordered.

I did as told.

"Now just take me."

I opened my eyes as he pulsed between my legs, far away but still close, connected. I lifted my hands and grasped onto his waist.

"Lift, tilt, move with me, Carrie," he instructed, his voice now rasping.

I lifted, catching his rhythm and moving with him.

Oh gosh. *Much* better.

"Yes," I panted.

"Yeah," he grunted. "Hold on, baby."

I grasped him tighter with my fingers at his waist and my legs around his thighs.

When I did he went deeper. Faster.

"*Yes,*" I moaned, my fingers digging in hard.

His free hand roamed my belly, down and in, as in *in*.

And that was it.

"*Yes!*" I cried, my fingers clawing at his waist, my legs tightening so much that I lifted my hips off the bed and he pounded inside me as it scored through me, blazing heat like I'd never experienced, long and hot and wild and beautiful in a way I thought it would last forever and I wanted it to as Joker kept taking me.

"God. Fuck. *Fuck,*" he grunted, his finger no longer manipulating my clit but moving so he could clamp his hand around my hip, keep me stationary and drive deep. "Fuck," he whispered. "*Fuck,*" he groaned and reared inside me.

I opened my eyes, holding on, and saw his neck bent, his head down, as he thrust one last time and stayed planted inside, and I knew, even if it was silent, that he had what he'd given me.

I lay under him, breathing heavily, clasped to him like I never wanted to let him go (and thinking I actually didn't), glorying in the feel of him filling me, watching with what could be nothing but utter glee as the shudders of his orgasm shifted through his powerful body as the fragments of the glory of mine whispered through mine.

And I kept watching, committing him to memory, as his fragments left him.

Not a second later, he lifted his head and said, "Be back," pulled out of my hold, rolled away, got to his feet and that was when I watched him walk to the bathroom, adjusting his jeans.

I stared at the open bathroom door where he'd disappeared and I did this for only a single second before it struck me.

I'd conked him on the jaw. I'd scratched him too hard.

And he'd had to *instruct* me.

I'd been married and my husband had a healthy sex drive. The mood came over Aaron a lot. Sometimes, the mood even came over me, and until the end, Aaron was happy to accommodate me (as I was him).

I'd just had great sex, the kind I'd never had before, so in reality I'd just discovered what great sex was.

But I'd thought what Aaron and I had was great.

Now I knew it wasn't bad, sometimes. Most of the time it was what it was.

But it had never been great.

And I knew right then that was because of me.

I wasn't great.

I wasn't even good!

I wasn't anything.

With Aaron I didn't care. I had a feeling I understood better now why he replaced me, but I still didn't care.

With Joker...

I shut my eyes.

Oh no.

A new burn of humiliation blazed through me as I moved in a frenzy on the bed, searching for my panties.

I saw them dangling off the side. I snatched them up, bent and shoved my feet through. Collapsing with my back to the bed, I lifted my hips and pulled them up, my mind whirling around and around.

Joker had started out kissing and caressing, but in the end he'd barely touched me.

He'd just done the deed, taking me with him, giving me

glory, giving it to himself (without my help *at all* and maybe it wasn't glory—he hadn't even grunted—maybe it was just a perfunctory bodily release).

He'd been going through the motions to get it done.

Yes, oh yes.

Humiliating.

I thought being the Chaos Charity Case was bad.

This was worse.

I rolled off the bed, frantically grabbing my jeans. On my feet beside the bed, I bent over. One foot in, then the other one, I tugged them up.

And collided with a hard body behind me.

Fingers curled around my hips.

"What you doin', baby?" Joker growled in my ear.

"I have to leave," I whispered, pulling out of his hold only to find myself yanked back and again crashing into his body.

But this time his fingers didn't curl around my hips. Two strong arms locked around my belly.

"You have to leave?"

It was another growl but this wasn't a semi-curious, post-sex growl.

This one sounded borderline angry.

"Yes." I struggled against his hold.

"Why?" he asked, quelling my struggle with frightening ease.

Then again, I now had very intimate knowledge through vision *and* feel of the kind of power in his body.

"Let me go," I whispered, stopping my movements because I knew they were to no avail and praying he'd listen to me.

He didn't listen to me.

"Why?" he repeated, his voice now openly annoyed and leaning toward harsh.

"I...that was...I didn't..." I swallowed. "Today, I'm moving."

"Carissa, just fucked you for the first time after a scene where we both spouted a lotta shit we gotta go over. I think the move can wait right now."

"Please, let me go so we can—"

I stopped talking when he gave me a gentle shake. "Tell me why you're acting jacked."

Darn it!

"I was...that was..." I closed my eyes and admitted softly, "Embarrassing."

His hold loosened as he muttered, "What the fuck?"

I took advantage, pulling out of his arms and taking a quick step away, turning to him but not quite meeting his eyes. "I'm sorry. That was..." I shook my head. "I'm sorry. So, so sorry. I shouldn't have started that."

"You shouldn't have started that?"

"No."

His head tipped to the side and his tone turned nasty. "So golden girl Carissa Teodoro thought she wanted rough trade, got it, and now she's woken up and realized in gettin' it, she didn't want it and more, she's tainted."

I blinked and immediately found his eyes. "What?"

He didn't tell me what.

He bit out, "Fuck this." To demonstrate *this*, he threw his hand up between us, his face cold and hard and scary before he went on crudely and seriously offensively, "And fuck you. You wanna leave, fuckin' leave."

I stared at him as his words processed through me. *All* of his words.

When they processed fully, I did not like it one bit.

"Are you...do you think...?" I couldn't finish because I was struggling to get a lock on what I was feeling.

No, I was struggling to get a lock on the fact I was feeling angrier than I'd ever felt *in my life*.

"You wanna leave?" He turned to the side and swung an arm toward the door. "Fuckin' leave."

"I conked you on the jaw!" I shouted.

This time, Joker blinked.

I dropped my eyes to his side and saw the red welts my nails made. I fought back the wince and looked back to his face.

"I hurt you," I snapped.

"Caris—"

I leaned into him. "You had to instruct me," I hissed. "That was *embarrassing*," I kept hissing. I leaned back. "I mean, I've got a son. I'm hardly a virgin, but I couldn't cope with all I was feeling and I *messed it all up!*" I yelled.

He made to move to me but I lifted my hand and he stopped.

"That was supposed to be beautiful. It was supposed to be perfect. *You* were perfect. *You're* flawless. Look at you!" I cried. "You're like...top-to-toe beauty. Every inch. And I'm..." I slashed a hand down my front, "*not.*"

"Butterfly—"

"No. Butterfly doesn't work here, Joker. That was *awful. I* made it that way. Not for me. For me it was *amazing*. But for you...in the end, you didn't kiss me, barely touched me, just did what you had to do to get it over with."

Suddenly, with those words out of my mouth, making them real, I wanted to cry, and just as suddenly, I wanted more than I ever had in my whole life to have the strength not to do it.

But I knew I was going to do it so I had to get *out of there*.

And to do that, I needed my T-shirt, my shoes.

I looked to my feet.

I also needed my footies.

I didn't even notice him taking off my footies.

When did he take off my footies?

He did and I couldn't dwell.

I had to *go*.

In order to do that, I bent and snatched my top from the floor and then started tearing through the bedclothes to find my footies.

"Baby," he called gently.

I found one and balled it in my fist, looking for the other one.

His hand lighted on the skin of my spine just above my jeans.

"Carrie," he said softly.

"This is…this was…I can't believe I messed this up," I whispered, my voice breaking. "It was supposed to be special and I…I…c-conked you on the jaw."

I got that out (barely) and then I was on my back in the bed with Joker on top of me.

I looked to the side and begged shakily, "Please let me go."

"Tell you something," he replied and I pressed my lips together as I dropped my stuff and lifted my hands to the unyielding warmth of his shoulders and pushed (again to no avail, he didn't budge an inch). "The first time I had you mostly naked, wet and hot in my bed in a way that I was gonna get to bury my cock inside you, the only way that was gonna go down was with me watching the whole fucking thing."

I froze.

Then my head righted and I stared.

"It gets hot like that, Carrie, shit happens. I don't give a fuck you nearly bust my jaw with your head, especially when you do it after ripping my tee off and going for me with your mouth."

My lips parted.

"And, trust me, you can't scratch too hard. It took me by surprise but I liked it a fuckuva lot. The problem was, after you did it, you got skittish and didn't roll with it."

"Really?" I whispered.

"Fuck yeah," he replied firmly. "That's why I told you to relax. The rest, baby, you were closin' down on me, I knew why and I needed to get you past that. Not to fuck with your head, but I had my share of hard bodies. I liked 'em. I like women in a lot of different varieties. But if I have a choice, my preference would be yours. Soft, sweet, seriously wet, and definitely *hot*."

"I..." I breathed then finished, *"Really?"*

"Why would I lie when what I say has the goal of gettin' me more of you? If I didn't fuckin' love what I got, I wouldn't fuckin' lie. I'd let you leave."

That made sense.

"And Carrie, I know what I want in bed and I'm not a man who has a problem with communicatin' that. It isn't about instruction. It's about gettin' off the way I wanna get off and guidin' you there with me. You were in the moment, totally into what I was doin', and that was fuckin' *great*. But I intended to make it better. And, baby, you gotta know, that shit isn't gonna stop. I know what I want, you're gonna give it to me while I give it to you, and you'll learn to roll with that too."

That also made sense.

And was more than a little arousing.

"Fuck," he snarled and I tensed under him at the intensity. "It sucks you didn't get what I got outta that, Carrie. You hot and wet and squirming and panting and I got to watch the whole fuckin' thing. It was magnificent. Unbelievable. Better than I could imagine, and Butterfly, I did a lot of imagining from about the time you were fourteen."

Oh.

Wow.

"And it fucking sucks you didn't come away with the same fucking thing," he finished.

"I did, at first," I told him hesitantly. "You were...*are* amazing, but you were, during and right after..." I faltered then forged ahead. "Then you just said, 'be back' and didn't kiss me or anything."

"If I kissed you again I'd want it to last a while and lead direct into some post-fuck cuddling which I'd hope would lead to more fucking and I couldn't do any a' that with a used condom on my dick."

"Oh," I whispered, again feeling embarrassed and again it was different.

"Yeah. Oh," he replied, not looking embarrassed, and no longer looking frustrated. Instead, looking like he was fighting against laughing, which had the fortunate result of making me feel less embarrassed.

"I think I may have messed up again," I told him and he dipped his face closer to me.

"No, you feel it, you share it. Don't hold back with me, Butterfly."

That was good advice. Good advice for a relationship two people were building.

Which I hoped with all that had just happened we were still doing.

On this thought, I blurted, "Are you mad at me?"

His brows went up. "About what?"

If he had to ask then he wasn't mad so I didn't think I should remind him of all the reasons he could be.

But he'd just told me not to hold back so I figured I should go with that.

"Well, there's me not recognizing you," I reminded him carefully. "There's also me pitching a drama after you made love to me for the first time. Then there's me accusing you of treating me like a charity—"

He interrupted me by suggesting, "Maybe you should stop."

I shut my mouth.

He stared me in the eyes then suddenly asked, "Did you really crush on me back then?"

I nodded and answered quietly, "Yeah."

He closed his eyes, shook his head, and ended the shake looking away from me.

I lifted my hand and pressed it to his smooth cheek, forcing him back.

When he opened his eyes, I told him, "Your hair looks nice but I miss the beard."

I barely finished speaking before he made a noise that I felt rip through me. It was full of pain, which I didn't like, and something else I couldn't read.

He didn't hesitate to give me that something else. "Fucked up."

"How?" I asked.

"Shoulda taken you for a Blizzard."

He remembered. He remembered me asking him to go to Dairy Queen the day he disappeared.

My eyes started stinging.

"Take me tonight," I whispered.

He closed his eyes again but this time dropped his forehead so it rested on mine.

I slid my hand from his face to wrap my arm around his shoulders and did the same with my other arm around his back.

"I'm so sorry I didn't recognize you." He opened his eyes and lifted his head but he didn't go very far. I took that as him not pulling away so I kept speaking. "I even knew it when you showed me your drawings. I just couldn't put my finger on it." I forced a smile, my eyes still stinging. "I got your sketch of me. I still have it. I even had it framed and I used to keep it in my bedroom. But when we got married, Aaron wouldn't let me put it—"

"Stop talking."

I again shut up.

Joker didn't.

"It was always you. Only you. I was into you back then, Carissa, in a big fuckin' way."

I felt a tear slide out the side of my eye.

Joker watched it before he looked back to me.

"And that hasn't changed."

Oh *God*.

I could take no more.

I burst into tears.

Joker gave me his weight for a moment so he could roll us to our sides and gather me close in his arms.

I held him back and did it tight as I shoved my face in his perfect chest and bawled my eyes out.

"I . . . I . . . c-can't believe I didn't recognize you!" I cried into his skin.

He held me with one arm and stroked my hair with his other hand, ordering, "You didn't. The minute I looked like me you did. Get over it. I am."

I tipped my head back and declared loudly, "I hurt you!"

"Just fucked you, Butterfly, gonna do it again as soon as I can, so I think I'm over it."

I blinked through my tears.

Then I slapped his arm. "We don't *fuck*," I hissed, making it plain I did not like to be forced to use the f-word. "We *make love*."

My breath stopped when his face all of a sudden was close and his voice dipped low to say, "Yeah. That's what I just did to you. I'm glad you finally get that. And that's what I'll keep doin' to you. But prepare, Carrie, 'cause I'm also gonna fuck you and from what I just got outta you, I know you're gonna like it."

I started breathing, but erratically, and said nothing.

I apparently started breathing erratically *and* doing it visibly because he asked, "You want me to do that now?"

I totally did.

Unfortunately, I had to answer, "I'm moving today."

He looked perplexed for a second like he forgot our plans for the day, which was cute and sweet. I'd never seen Joker be the former, and I liked it, but I had experienced him being the latter, and I'd always liked that.

Then his face cleared and he muttered, "Fuck."

"Yes," I agreed.

"We better do that," he said.

I didn't want to do that. My exhaustion had been swept away in the drama and lovemaking but now, especially after the drama, and most especially after the lovemaking, all I wanted to do was curl into his heat and go to sleep.

I couldn't do that so I repeated, "Yeah, we better do that."

He gave me a squeeze but didn't let me go.

He looked deep into my eyes and said gently, "I should say I'm sorry I didn't give you that after givin' you a nice night out like you deserve. But I'm not sorry. Just in case shit twists for you, I wanna be sure it's clear. I like that it went down in a way that I'll never forget. I hope you're over the shit that warped it for you because it'd mean a lot to me you feel the same."

I closed my eyes, pressed closer, dipped my head, and pushed my face in his throat.

"I'm over that warped stuff," I whispered there. "And I feel the same."

"Good," he murmured into the top of my hair. "Now, sucks, but we gotta move you."

"Yes, it does suck." I tipped my head back. "But then I'll be moved. Travis and me will be safe and in a nice place. And that'll be that."

"Yeah," he replied on a grin.

"So maybe you'll kiss me so we can get on with that and get it over with," I suggested.

"Yeah," he repeated on a smile.

But he didn't kiss me.

So I called, "Joker?"

"Carissa Teodoro in my arms in my bed askin' me to kiss her," he said quietly like he wasn't talking to me and he couldn't quite believe his words were true.

I felt my body grow still.

Then I forced the stillness out and rolled Carson "Joker" Steele to his back, with me on top, murmuring, "He won't kiss me, I'll kiss him."

And I commenced in doing just that.

Lucky for me, Carson "Joker" Steele liked it.

So he kissed me back.

* * *

I stood in Tyra's house—*my* house—dead on my feet but still taking it all in as Joker closed the door on the last to leave, Tabby and Shy.

I was in.

Not in in the sense that tomorrow I had to unpack all I could before starting back to work the next day at the same time getting laundry done and also getting to the grocery store as well as back to my old place to do a deep clean.

In as in everything was unpacked, my pictures were even hung on the walls, the boxes were taken away, and I didn't have to go back to my old place except to take back my keys.

This was because the men had moved the stuff, put together the furniture, set up the TV and asked me where I wanted things so they could put them up on the walls. Snapper had even mounted my Dustbuster in the utility room.

This was done while the women unpacked, and it wasn't just Tyra, Tabby, and Lanie. Elvira had showed, bringing with her women named Gwen and Tess (who were gorgeous, nice, and had tons of energy). Not to mention other Chaos women came, including, to my disbelief but in the end deep gratitude, Stacy (Joker had understated it; she wasn't just a decent woman, she was really nice).

My dishes were in the cupboards. My bed was made. Travis's toys were in their baskets. My TV was good to go and the cable already worked. My clothes were in the closet. And with Stacy leading the crew at my old place before showing at the new, my apartment was spotless and I had a bunch of images on my phone that she took and texted to me to prove that fact should my landlord decide to mess with me.

"Carrie?" Joker called.

I looked to him and announced, "I'm gonna need to buy more pastries."

His lips twitched and I liked it.

But seriously, I really missed the beard.

He came to stand in front of me and put his hands to my hips.

"You gonna fall asleep on your feet or you gonna be able to make it to your bed?"

I had a strict rule, no matter what the day brought: clean sheets, clean body to put in those sheets.

I didn't eat bonbons while everyone was working.

I needed a shower.

"I have to shower," I told him.

His fingers dug into my hips as he muttered, "Do that. I'll leave you to it. Stop 'round tomorrow."

He was leaving?

Before I could think if it was right or wrong, I lifted my hands quickly and took hold of his T-shirt in both fists.

His eyes heated.

It was right.

Thank goodness.

"My bed is very comfy," I whispered.

It was kind of shy but I didn't care. I needed to say it so he wouldn't leave.

"You want me there with you?"

I nodded.

"You want me in the shower with you?"

Suddenly, I wasn't dead on my feet. Suddenly, I had a lot of energy.

And I *needed* a shower.

I nodded again.

He smiled. It was a new smile and it was amazing. So much so, I felt it all over my body.

But then he stated, "I'm starved."

It was seven thirty. I'd ordered a bunch of pizzas but we'd eaten them hours ago.

"Shower," Joker declared and I focused on him again. "Get you clean, order in, we eat. You fall asleep in your food, I'll get you to bed." He dipped his face closer. "I'll take you for a Blizzard tomorrow."

Something to look forward to.

In fact, *lots* of somethings.

I grinned at him. "That's a deal."

He bent his head and touched his mouth to mine.

It felt sweet.

He lifted his head. "Let's do this."

"Joker?"

"Right here."

I flattened my hands to his chest, loving those words, loving they were true, loving all that he made them mean.

"Thank you for everything."

"You don't have to—"

I pressed hard against his chest and lifted up on my toes to touch my mouth to his.

Once I did that and he quieted, I said softly, "I know I don't. And I love that I don't. But I need to. So," I slid my hands up to his shoulders and curled my fingers around, "*thank you*."

He made a noise I liked in the back of his throat, bent his head, and kissed me.

Continuing to do it, he shuffled me to the shower.

In the shower, I didn't conk him on the jaw with my head.

Though I did scratch him and hard.

He was right, since I'd let go and relaxed, I found out he liked it.

A lot.

After our shower, I didn't fall asleep in my shrimp fried rice.

But I did fall asleep the instant my head settled on Carson "Joker" Steele's chest in my bed.

And I did it with his arms around me.

After that, I slept deep.

And easy.

CHAPTER FOURTEEN

Let the Healing Begin

Joker

JOKER TRIED TO quiet the rustling of the plastic bags as he unpacked the groceries he went out to get while Carissa slept in.

She could finish up the generic ketchup, and then she was done with that shit.

He couldn't say this was generous. He didn't like generic ketchup and he intended to eat at her house and do it frequently.

So she was definitely done with that shit.

He also intended to sleep in her bed and do that frequently too.

It was partially about her mattress. It was firm but comfortable. His mattresses at the Compound weren't great. He'd inherited his room from Dog after the man left for Grand Junction, and his brothers had clearly not replaced them when he'd inherited the room years ago.

But this was mostly about having Carissa Teodoro, who'd crushed on him in high school and who'd whimpered, squirmed, and moaned for him, putting on a show he'd never fucking forget the first time he had her, cuddled up with him on that mattress.

He moved around Carissa's kitchen, putting groceries away liking that he was doing it. Not only because he was giving her brand-named ketchup, but that she had a big, nice kitchen she could cook in, put all her nice shit in, and take care of her boy in.

He shoved a bag of frozen corn in her freezer, closed the door, caught something at the side of his eye and stopped dead.

Carissa was standing at the entrance to the kitchen in a big, shapeless nightshirt she probably bought for her pregnancy. It hung low, almost to her knees. It was pink and had a scooped neck with a little rim of lace. That was the only hint at any femininity.

He instantly hated the thing. It didn't suit her. It looked like she was at her grandma's house, decided to stay over, and needed to borrow something to sleep in.

He did not hate the fact that her hair was a mess. Partially ratted out from sleep, it was two sizes bigger than it normally was, and his girl had a lot of hair.

Her face was kinda swollen and her eyes were sluggish. It was eleven thirty and it was written all over her she'd slept hard for the fourteen and a half hours she'd done it.

That, like her big bed head of hair, was cute.

Now she stood across the kitchen from him, unmoving, and Joker didn't know if she stood there because she was still mostly out of it or she was winding up to hand him shit for buying her groceries.

He could get how it was tough to accept kindness. He'd lived under that burden with Linus and Mrs. Heely for years. You knew you needed it, had to accept it, even go out and take it on occasion. But you worried you'd never be able to return it and that was not a good feeling.

Still, he had to get her to a place where she got over that. She'd be getting kindness for a long time to come from Joker, his brothers, and their families, so she had to learn not to fight it.

He opened his mouth to start that lesson when she whispered, "Carson Steele in my kitchen."

He shut his mouth and stared at her, feeling a lightness in his chest he'd never felt in his life.

She kept going, her drowsy face warming, telling him everything even as she put it in words.

"My biker, putting away groceries."

My biker.

He turned fully to her.

As was her way, she ran to him.

He had no choice but to catch her, and when he did, she took him back and he slammed into the counter, the pain of the hit spiraling up his spine.

But he didn't give a fuck seeing he had her ass in his hands, the insides of her thighs pressed to his hips and her hands at each side of his head.

She moved her thumbs along his cheeks, her eyes watching, doing this murmuring, "Stubble."

"Carrie," was all he could force out.

Her gaze caught his. "I want the beard back, sweetie. Will you grow it for me?"

He'd walk through hell for her so it went without saying he'd grow his beard back for her.

"Yeah," he replied.

Her eyes went soft as her lips curved up.

She gave him that look for a beat before she said softly, "Still taking care of me."

She meant the groceries.

"Don't fight it," he advised.

"Tell me you're gonna eat some of them and I won't."

With that she meant she wanted him around.

He smiled at her. "Generic ketchup sucks."

That was when she smiled at him.

So that was when he was done with their conversation and he communicated that by sliding a hand from her ass up her back and into her hair, putting pressure on.

He didn't need to. She tipped her face to him and gave him her mouth.

She might have been half asleep but she still had brushed her teeth.

She tasted fucking brilliant.

Though, she always did.

Still taking her mouth, he turned his back from the counter and planted her ass on it. She wound her legs around his hips as he dipped a hand up her nightshirt then down into her panties.

That got him a whimper as she pressed her heat against his crotch.

Fuck yes.

He broke the kiss but not the connection of their lips.

"You want coffee?" he asked.

"Yeah," she answered, all breathy, something that made his dick, already getting hard, get harder.

"Breakfast?"

"Yeah."

"Before or after I give you your fucking?"

With that, she pressed everything against him and tightened her arms around his shoulders.

"I think...after," she said shyly, but did it still holding his eyes.

"Like your bed," he muttered.

"Then let's do it there," she muttered back, sliding a hand into his hair to cup the back of his head.

"You got it, Butterfly," he replied, lifted her off the counter, took her mouth, and, kissing her, walked her out of the kitchen and to her new bedroom.

She liked him kissing her. She got off on it. He liked it too, because she tasted good, she made noise, she gave back; and she also lost it so he was able to get her nightshirt off her with her barely noticing.

After that, he gave her his mouth in other places, taking her in this time and doing it lazy, like he didn't do in his bed at the Compound or in her shower.

She had great tits, bigger than high school, with rosy nipples that tightened instantly against his tongue as he pulled them in his mouth. He heard her heavy breathing turn to panting and she slid both hands in his hair to hold him to her, showing him she liked what he was doing.

Jesus.

Carissa.

Going from one tit to the other, he had her pressing up, clutching his hair before he slid down, circling her navel with his tongue, and down, his body coming off her bed.

He curled his fingers around the side of her panties and yanked them off, her body jerking, her half-closed eyes widening in a way that made his stiff cock jump.

He clasped his hands on her hips, yanked her to the edge of the bed and dropped down to his knees.

"Joker," she breathed.

He said nothing.

Instead, he tossed her legs over his shoulders, seeing her honey curls between her legs glistening, his dick so hard and straining against his jeans, it hurt.

And he liked it.

He dipped in and ran his tongue through her moist.

She tasted good there too.

Perfection.

Her heels dug in and she pushed her pussy into his mouth as she arched on the bed and cried, "Joker!"

Fuck yeah.

He bent in and went down on her, grasping her hips and pulling her deeper into his mouth as he licked her, ate her, sucked her clit, and tongue-fucked her cunt. She loved it, showed it, her legs clamped around him, her sounds drifting down at him or piercing the room sharply. When she slid the fingers of one hand in his hair and those fingers fisted, her noises coming quick and desperate, her body moving frantically in his hold, he knew she was ready.

He lifted up.

"Oh!"

He heard her frustrated surprise as he shoved through her legs and bent to her, looming over her with his hand in the bed.

It was hot as fuck watching her struggle to focus on him even as she clenched a fist in his shirt and tugged it to her, her other hand wandering close to the honey curls between her legs.

"Ready to get fucked?" he asked.

"Yes," she answered instantly.

Christ. She was gone.

Perfection.

"Baby, gonna fuck you. Ready for that?" he pushed.

She tugged harder on his shirt. "*Yes*, Joker," she said impatiently.

He almost grinned.

Instead, he slid his free hand down her belly, knocking hers aside and toying with her curls.

When he did, he watched her lips part and felt her hips lift to deepen his touch.

"Joker," she begged.

"Say it, Butterfly," he ordered gently.

Her eyes widened briefly and flared.

Then she licked her lips and he almost lost it watching her do that before she said, "Hurry, sweetheart, and fuck me."

That's what he wanted.

That's what he gave.

Flipping her to her stomach, he yanked her up so her knees were to the edge of the mattress, her fucking phenomenal heart-shaped ass right there for him, the smooth skin of her back, the mass of her curls along her shoulders and all over the bed.

He pulled out his wallet, dealt with the condom one-handed while he slid his fingers through her wet to keep her ready.

But even as he did it fast, he took too much time.

He knew it when she begged, "Carson, sweetie, *please*."

He looked from her ass to see she had her neck twisted, her face filled with need.

Carissa Teodoro.

A hot little piece.

Fuck, *his* hot little piece, naked, ass in the air, lips begging.

Holding her eyes, he positioned the tip and didn't hesitate before he drove inside.

Her ass jerked up as her back arched toward the bed and her head shot back, her ringlets flying.

Jesus.

Fuck.

Perfection.

"Move," she panted.

He moved, pulling out, thrusting in, and giving it to her fast.

"Harder," she begged, rearing back, lifting up on her forearms to give her leverage.

Totally fucking perfect.

He took her harder.

"Faster, more, Carson, *please,*" she whimpered, dropping her head and driving back to meet his thrusts.

He slid a hand around her hip and in, found her, and she started bucking.

"Goddamn perfection," he grunted, slamming into her pussy, manipulating her clit, watching her take it, watching her love getting it and fucking loving giving it to her.

"Don't stop," she pleaded.

Was she insane?

He wasn't going to stop. Christ, he wished he never had to stop.

"Oh, *God*, Joker, *don't stop!*" she cried, losing it, her neck arched, her ass tipped, her whimpers coming constant but catching every time she took his cock. "Sweetheart," she panted. "Sweetie," she moaned. "Joker! Yes!" she cried and he felt the drenched heat of her clutch him and he knew she was there.

He took his finger from her clit, grasped her hips and pulled her back into his thrusts, listening to her come, feeling it, fucking loving it. Letting her sleek wet clench him and pull it out of him, he drove deep and kept doing it, pounding her back on his dick, listening to her sweet, sharp mews as she took it.

Then he got it. His head jerking back, he fucked her as he came inside her, doing both *hard.*

As it started to leave him, he dropped his head and after a few beats the smooth cheeks of her ass came in focus.

His fingers still clamped around her hips, he took her gentle as he slid his palms to her cheeks, watching her pussy take his cock, his thumbs move over the swells of her ass. An ass he'd seen in cheerleader panties. An ass he'd watch move in her khakis. An ass he'd wanted like this for so long, it wasn't fucking funny. A dream he'd made up, his hand on his cock, pumping until he came, the dream so good, even jacking off, the orgasm was always amazing.

But not like the real thing.

Nothing like it.

Not even close.

"Sweetie," she called, her tone tentative, and Joker stopped watching his thumbs move over her flesh and looked to her.

He saw her body was tense and her neck was twisted, her eyes on him unsure.

He pulled out, flipped her over, lifted her up into his arms and put a knee to the bed. He moved them from the edge and dropped her to her back, his weight hitting soft body, pressing it into the bed, feeling it against him, her thighs holding him tight at his hips.

He lifted a hand and pulled a tangle of ringlets out of her face.

Then he bent and kissed her, soft, deep, so fucking sweet, and he kept doing it until she was holding on tight with all of her limbs.

Only then did he break it and ask, "You good?"

"Yeah," she whispered but she didn't need to. The uncertainty was gone. She was gazing up at him, dazed, her body warm and loose under his even if her limbs were still wound tight.

Suddenly, she looked to his nose.

"I liked the part where you . . . um, flipped me around. Or, I should say the, uh . . . *parts*."

He grinned even though he wasn't the kind of man who settled in for a blow by blow processing of a great fuck.

But if she wanted that, he'd give it to her.

"And when you had your, well . . ." her eyes dropped to his mouth, "mouth between my legs."

He grinned bigger.

Her eyes skittered to his then to his hair and finally over to his ear.

"And the..." she bit her lip, let it go and brought her gaze to his, "edge of the bed thing. It felt..." her hand slid up into his hair and her voice dipped quiet, "kinda naughty."

That was cute but if she thought that was naughty, and she liked it that way, he had a lot to teach her.

Even as he got off on that idea, something bothered him about it.

Her words came to him.

Don't stop.

She'd said that in his bed in the Compound.

Fuck, she'd even said it when he was fingering her in the shower.

And he knew why she did.

Her ex stopped. Her ex didn't go the distance with her before taking himself there. Her ex didn't fuck her on her knees at the side of the bed.

Jesus, with a hot little number like Carissa, what was that asshole's problem?

"Joker?" she called, and he focused on her.

Part of him wanted to ask. Part of him wanted to know if she'd ever been taken care of in any way, in bed or out of it, by Aaron Jackhole Neiland.

The rest of him didn't give a fuck. He'd give her that every way he could.

"Right here, Carrie," he muttered.

Her lips curved into a soft smile and she slid a hand up and around to cup his jaw and again run her thumb over his stubble.

"So, you got the groceries, that leaves only laundry." Her smile grew. "In other words, a lazy day." She moved her hand down, gliding her thumb over his jaw before it went down again to the side of his neck and she stroked his throat, telling him, "I haven't had one of those in a long time."

"Then we'll be lazy," he whispered.

She kept smiling even as she lifted her head and brushed her mouth against his.

She rested back on the bed and kept stroking, trailing her thumb up his throat and back to his jaw.

"You sleep good?" he asked.

"Awesome," she answered.

That time, he smiled.

Then he said, "Gotta take care a' this condom and get my girl some coffee."

"That'd be good," she replied.

He bent in and returned the lip brush before deciding it wasn't enough. Tangling his fingers into the side of her hair, he slanted his head and took her mouth in a slow, wet kiss.

She gave back what she got.

He broke the kiss, knifed out of bed, his arm wrapped around her to take her with him. She went straight for her nightshirt as he bent to nab her panties, holding up his jeans. Her shirt was falling over her hips when he handed her the panties, bent in to take another taste of her mouth then whispered, "Meet you in the kitchen."

"Okay, sweetheart."

He grinned.

She grinned back.

He walked to the bathroom, took care of business, and joined his girl in the kitchen.

*   *   *

That night, Joker sat across from Carissa in a booth at Dairy Queen.

They'd gone there for more than just Blizzards. He'd

bought her chicken strips and fries, himself a burger and onion rings. They'd eaten them, shooting the shit, the mood mellow and easy.

Then he'd gone back to the counter to get them their Blizzards.

For both of them, it was Reece's Pieces and Cups, and she'd been right all those years ago. It was the best.

He swallowed a spoonful and looked to her to see her eyes to the side, the Blizzard cup held up, her spoon empty and forgotten in her fingers, her thoughts a mile away.

"Butterfly."

Her head jolted and she looked to him.

"Hey," she said softly.

Fuck, he felt that in his dick.

"Hey," he replied and tilted his head. "You're a million miles away."

"No, just eight years."

"What?" he asked.

That was when she landed the blow, giving him more pain he didn't mind feeling.

"Waited eight years to sit and have a Blizzard with you, Carson."

He felt his throat start burning.

"I'm glad you cut your hair," she said, her voice quiet, her eyes on him steady, her intent was to say something with them and more than just her words. "I liked it before but it looks really good now."

"That's good, Butterfly," he murmured.

She swallowed and when she did, something washed through her face he didn't like. "I wish I'd remembered you on I-25. I wish I'd done it so I could have had my Blizzard—"

He dropped his spoon in his cup and reached out, grabbing the hand she held her spoon in and holding it tight.

"Stop it."

"I don't want you to look back on it and be mad at me."

"I'm over it."

"You say that but—"

He gently tugged her hand. "I'm over it, Carrie. You're takin' this all on yourself, but don't forget I had it to give to you, let you off the hook, and I didn't. I let it go on too long. That's on me. Don't take it all on, 'cause it ain't yours. You fucked up. I fucked up. Even."

She stared in his eyes. She did this a long time.

Hers started to get bright, but when he was about to say something to stop that shit, she pulled in breath through her nose and said, "I'm glad you cut your hair."

He knew what that meant. He knew it meant she was glad they were past that. That they had what they had yesterday. That morning. That day. She was glad they were here, eating Blizzards. It meant a lot to her. A fuckuva lot.

And that meant a lot to him.

He let her go, ordering, "Eat your Blizzard."

"Okay," she said shakily, turning her attention back to her cup.

But he wasn't finished.

"Want you done so I can get your ass home and get it naked."

Her eyes shot to his.

"So hurry," he said.

The melancholy moved from her face as excitement moved into it which shifted straight to sassy.

"I am not rushing my first Blizzard with Carson Steele."

"You'll get other ones from me."

She straightened her shoulders and got even sassier.

"This is the first one. I'm savoring it."

"Baby, you'll savor more, you down that, get your ass in

my truck and I get you home. Got a hankerin' to make my girl feel naughty."

Another eye flare before she turned her attention direct to her ice cream.

Joker sat back and turned his attention to his.

He did this smiling.

In the end, it was Joker who didn't feel like making his girl feel naughty.

After their first Blizzard together, as ridiculous as it was, high school crap, a lost fantasy resurrected in a bed with a phenomenal mattress, he took his time. He painstakingly built it for her, for both of them.

But he didn't fuck Carissa.

He made love to her.

Slowly.

Gently.

So when he made her come, she whispered, "Carson," into his mouth.

It was the best moment of his life.

And it was that in a way he was determined it wouldn't remain that way making that moment the first time in his life he wanted more.

And he was going to get it.

Further, even if he had to bust his balls, eat shit, walk through hell . . .

He was going to give it to her.

*   *   *

Late the next afternoon, Joker had his ass resting on his bike that was parked next to a five-year-old SUV, his arms crossed on his chest, his eyes to the door of the high school.

The last fifteen minutes he was there, he'd gotten looks. He'd gotten questions. He'd given vague answers.

And he'd waited.

The wait was over when he saw Mr. Robinson walk out the door.

Through his shades, Joker took him in. He'd aged, but it was a testament to the man that he didn't look beaten. He'd been through it to get a kid, but he was also a high school teacher. They got paid dick, put up with a lot of shit, had one of the most important jobs anyone could have, and got little respect, and all he looked like was a man who was leaving work, ready to go home to his wife and dinner.

Joker watched him walk to the SUV, and he wasn't surprised when Mr. Robinson clocked him almost the minute he walked out the door. He kept Joker in his sights as he walked the ten parking spots to his SUV.

Joker also wasn't surprised he didn't let a biker hanging in a teacher's parking lot slide like the others did.

He stopped and asked, "Can I help you?"

"Good to see you again, Mr. Robinson," Joker replied.

His head tilted. His eyes narrowed. "I'm sorry, do I...?" he started before his face cleared. "Carson?" he asked quietly.

Joker nodded, pushed up from his bike, and walked to the sidewalk.

He extended his hand.

Mr. Robinson took it, his face cracking into a smile.

"Carson," he repeated, clasping Joker's hand and pumping it. "Yes. Definitely. Good to see you too."

They ended on a squeeze before they broke off and Joker asked, "How're things?"

"Things are things," Mr. Robinson replied, still smiling, saying they were normal but he didn't mind. "You?"

"Things are good."

Mr. Robinson's gaze grew intent as he studied Joker and said, "Good to hear."

"Yeah," Joker muttered, cleared his throat and told him, "Been back a while. Thought about you. Wanted to connect. Wasn't in that place. Now I am."

"That's good to hear, too." He seemed to struggle with what he wanted to say next, won it and asked, "You took off—"

Joker gave it to him easy. "Got my diploma. Took night classes. Now I'm a licensed mechanic. I'm a brother of Chaos and design and build cars at Ride."

"What you wanted to do," Mr. Robinson muttered.

He remembered. All the kids he saw year to year, the man remembered.

"Yeah," Joker agreed.

"Are you married? Settled? Seeing a girl?"

"Yup. You remember Carissa Teodoro?"

At that, Mr. Robinson smiled huge and remarked, "I see she finally got you to notice her."

Fuck. The man didn't miss anything, even shit Joker, who wanted that to be true and paid attention, didn't see.

"Yeah," was all he said. Then he went for it. "Are things really good with you?"

If he remembered Carissa's crush, Joker wanting to be a mechanic, he sure as fuck wouldn't forget where they were the last time they saw each other . . . and why they were there.

Even if it wasn't his business, Mr. Robinson gave it to him, also easy. "They're fine. We haven't been able to . . ." he trailed off, cleared his throat and kept going. "We've settled into the we we need to be. We wanted more. But you've got to learn when to let go and focus on what you have." He grinned, it was part sad, part defiant. "Prettiest girl I ever saw, best wife a man can have. It could be worse."

It sure fucking could.

Joker just hoped he could find a way to give him better.

He didn't say that.

He said, "You always had it goin' on."

The grin stayed in place when Mr. Robinson replied, "Glad you agree."

That day, while Carissa was on shift, Joker had worked at Ride. She'd be off shift soon and Robinson had worked all day.

He needed to let him get home to his wife and dinner.

So he reached into his back pocket, took out his wallet, pulled out a card, and shoved his wallet back in while extending the card to his old history teacher.

"Card for Ride. You can call in, ask for me. But my cell's on the back. Just in case you're interested in what I'm building, you can stop around. Anytime. You tell me when, I'll be there and I'll show you."

Mr. Robinson didn't hesitate. "Couldn't keep me away."

That hit him in the throat, and Joker forced a swallow to wash it away before he said gruffly, "Right. Let you go. Call when you want." He jerked up his chin and finished on, "Good to see you again, Mr. Robinson."

"Man to man now, Carson. I'm Keith."

Joker nodded to him. "Keith."

They shook hands again and Keith Robinson lifted up the card. "I'll give you a call."

"Look forward to it."

Robinson gave him a smile and headed to his SUV.

Joker went to his bike.

Mounted on it, he looked left into the cab of the truck.

Robinson was shifting into gear, doing it looking down and also doing it smiling.

He'd worried.

Joker had given him closure. He'd also given him relief.

But back in high school Keith Robinson had given Joker a whole lot more.

And on that thought, the impact of all Carissa was forced

to accept due to circumstances struck him so hard it felt like a power punch to the gut.

He'd run away, worked his ass off, ate shit, walked through hell, got his diploma, worked to get his mechanic's license, and come out the other side.

So he'd forgotten how it felt. How deep it ran. How intense the desire was, how extreme the hope was that you'd one day be in a position to give back to those who put brightness in a dark life, cutting through the black.

Unconsciously, even if years had passed, once he'd opened his eyes, he'd set himself on a course of giving back.

And taking in the smile he gave a man he respected, he determined he'd stay true to that course.

No matter what it took.

*　　*　　*

When she walked in the back door, Joker was at Carissa's stove, stirring the thickening sauce, dinner around the corner because she'd texted him half an hour ago with *I'm off in thirty. Then I'm on my way home. You better be there, sweetie, because I'm STARVED.*

He'd been there.

He turned to see her walk in and toss her purse on the counter.

"Yo," he greeted.

She grinned at him.

Then she blinked.

After that she asked, "What on earth is *that*?"

He looked down into the pot then to her. "Étouffée sauce."

Her eyes got big.

Fucking cute.

"Like, *shrimp* étouffée?"

"No. Got crawfish. So, like, crawfish étouffée."

She wandered to him, her eyes on the pot. "Where'd you get crawfish?"

"Got it at the LeLane's close to Ride. Also got the étouffée mix at the LeLane's close to Ride."

Her head tipped back and her eyes caught his.

Now she was pouting.

Totally fucking cute.

"You didn't come to my store?"

"Carrie, you gave me half an hour to pull this shit together. Ride is close to your pad, but your LeLane's overshoots this house by ten minutes. The LeLane's by Ride is only a few minutes outta the way."

"I see," she muttered, her eyes drifting back down to the pot.

"You done chattin'?" he asked, and she looked up at him.

"I'm not sure."

Absolutely fucking cute.

"How about you be done for a minute and kiss me?"

"I can do that," she said.

"So do it," he ordered when she didn't kiss him.

She smiled.

That was the cutest of all.

Then she lifted up on her toes with her hand to his abs.

After that, she kissed him.

He kissed her back.

When he was done, he let her change out of her LeLane's outfit.

And finally, both of them sitting at her dining room table, he fed his hungry girl.

* * *

Jesus, but she was a hot little piece.

After dinner and camping out in front of the TV, he'd

started it with her. He'd done it intending to make out on her enormous couch and then take it to her fantastic mattress.

But now he found himself sitting on his ass, his girl straddling him, rubbing her hot crotch against his hard one with her hands up his shirt roaming all over him, and if she didn't quit that shit with her pussy, her hands, and her tongue in his mouth, he was going to come in his jeans.

He needed to get his cock in her cunt or things would get messy.

He didn't have that chance when her hands suddenly shoved up, forcing his arms up with them, so she could tear off his tee.

Letting her do that, Joker was intent on getting to his fly, wondering how he could manage that, and getting her out of her jeans, and getting a condom on, all in the span of three seconds.

Carissa was intent on getting her mouth on him.

But he felt her abruptly still and he found his line to his fly diverted when she caught his wrist in her fingers and shoved his arm up.

What the fuck?

"Carrie..." he started, focusing on her, but when he did, he too went still.

And at the look on her face, the lightness in his chest that he was getting used to feeling, grew heavy and dark.

"What...?" she whispered, her fingers releasing his wrist only to trail down the inside of his biceps.

He pulled his arm away.

Her eyes sliced to his.

"Joker—"

He put his hands to her ass and muttered, "Let's take this to the bedroom."

She went solid and held him where he was by landing her hands on his shoulders and pressing down.

"Lift your arm, let me see," she demanded.

"Baby," he ground up against her, a message she couldn't misinterpret, "in a certain mood."

"Lift your arm," she said gentle but firm. "Sweetie, let me see."

"It's nothing."

"Let me see."

"Carissa, it's—"

He shut up when he saw tears all of a sudden fill her eyes.

"Do you . . . did you smoke?" she asked.

Fuck.

"Baby—"

She cut him off, saying quickly, "Boys do that. They get drunk and they challenge themselves or each other. Is that how you got those?"

He clenched his teeth and through them said, "No."

Her chin wobbled and she whispered, "He gave those to you."

She knew it. She knew his old man had burned him.

Joker wrapped his arms around her and pulled her close. "Long time ago. Now, Carrie,—"

"He gave those to you."

"Carissa, it's—"

"*He gave those to you!*"

At her enraged shriek, his arms went slack and she tore out of them, finding her feet.

"He gave those to you," she snapped, tears still in her eyes but not falling, her face growing pink.

He pushed out of the couch and she scuttled back.

"I got away from him, remember?" he pointed out, going for a calming tone.

And failing.

"Not soon enough," she bit out.

Shit.

"Come here, Carrie."

"*She* left you to that and *he* gave those to you," she hissed.

They had to get off this.

"It was a long time ago," he repeated. "They've healed. It's over. Just let it be over."

She stared at him, her chest rising and falling fast, breathing hard to hold back what she was feeling, all of it, and it was visibly massive.

And it was for him.

For him.

Jesus.

Then she let fly and when she did, the path Carson "Joker" Steele found himself on the second he saw a woman holding a baby on the side of I-25 and decided to pull off and help came to its conclusion. Just like *that*, Carson Steele was exactly where he'd always needed to be, with the woman he needed at his side, doing it as the man he never dreamed of becoming.

But somehow was.

And all this came about when she stated, "You don't heal from that, Carson. Not from that. My *God*," she threw out both hands, "how magnificent of a man do you have to be to go through what you went through, doing it alone, nobody to ease the way, the pain, no mother, no brother, no sister, all by yourself enduring that and fight your way to becoming *all that you are*. It isn't amazing. It's a darned miracle."

His body stone, only his mouth moved, "Come here, Carrie."

She ignored him, shook her hair and declared, "I'm going to help you heal."

"Come *here,* Carrie."

Her head jerked, her eyes got wide, and fucking finally she moved her ass to him.

The second she got close, he took her down to the couch.

He did not make love to her.

He kissed her hard, bruising her mouth.

And she didn't give a shit.

He touched her, tearing at her clothes, ripping her underwear.

And she whimpered through it.

Then he fucked her and she took it, her mouth taking his tongue at the same time, her body lurching violently with each thrust.

And she got off on it, moaning her orgasm down his throat, her cunt tightening around his dick, doing that even before he got his thumb to her clit.

Once she found it, Joker came rough and hard, his hand fisted in her hair to hold her stationary so she could take him through it.

And she went back to whimpering, clutching him tight, swallowing his groan.

When he was done, not even recovered, he had two thoughts.

One was that he was glad she was his hot little piece so the three seconds he took to roll on a condom didn't cool her in any way.

The other was that he'd lost control and she was definitely hot for it.

But she was Carissa. His girl.

And that shit shouldn't happen.

So, still recovering from his orgasm, he lifted both hands to cup either side of her head and looked into her eyes.

"I hurt you?"

"No way," she gasped, also still feeling hers, "No how," she finished on a breath.

"Don't lie to me," he warned.

"That was..." she shook her head in his hands. "I don't

know what it was but it was so much of what it was, I'm thinking about starting a diary."

He held her eyes.

"I've never had a diary," she went on.

He kept looking at her, trying to get a read on if she was lying.

"But that needs to be recorded for posterity."

It was that that made him drop his forehead to hers in relief.

"Then again, I should have started that diary two days ago. I was just tired from the move and all," she carried on. "But right after shift tomorrow, I'm going out and getting one."

He lifted up and watched her smile at him as he felt her hand sift into his hair.

"Just to finish our earlier discussion," she whispered, he tensed, but she gave it to him. "I *am* going to heal you, Carson Steele. It's gonna happen. That's it. No response necessary."

It was on the tip of his tongue to tell her he didn't need that. Not anymore. She'd already done it. And not by taking him hard.

By making him see what everyone but his father saw.

By making him see past what his father made him see.

But he didn't say it.

He wanted to see how she'd do it. He also wanted to let her do it because he intended to take care of her, give her everything she needed, and he knew she needed that.

And he'd finally realized he was a man who deserved a good woman who'd go out of her way to do just that.

That meant in the end, he'd just kissed her and she'd kissed him back, holding on, giving him everything in a way that when he broke the kiss, he was smiling.

Let the healing begin.

CHAPTER FIFTEEN

Already Winnin' the One You're In

Carissa

KNOWING JOKER WAS at my house after my shift the next day and Travis was still at his dad's, I didn't go out and get a diary.

But I didn't go home either.

I went to Ride.

I was becoming accustomed to the cars and bikes, so I knew Tack's bike was out front, as well as Tyra's vintage Mustang. Therefore, I went to the office first.

I walked up the steps, through the door, and hit pay dirt.

Because in it was Tyra, seated in her desk chair. Sitting on her desk was Tack. Lazing on the couch by the front window was Hound. And standing by the side door to the garage was Hop, holding some papers and going over them with High.

"Yo, Carrie," Hound greeted.

"Hey, Hound," I greeted back on a smile. I turned that smile Tack's way. "Hey."

"Hey, darlin'," he replied, his expression welcoming, but he was also watching me closely.

"All good at the house?" Tyra asked.

I looked to her. "Perfect."

She grinned. I grinned back and then gave my grin to Hop and High as a greeting before I looked right back to Tack.

"Can we talk?" I asked.

He straightened slightly as Tyra's gaze moved to her husband.

"Need privacy?" Hop asked and I turned his way.

"Not really." I gave my attention back to Tack and because Joker was at my house and I wanted to be there with him, but also because I was nervous doing this, I launched right in, "Does Joker have anything to do with his father?"

The feel of the room turned funny, which I thought was telling, but I ignored it as well as the fact that Tack's expression blanked completely.

"Gotta ask him, girl," he said gently.

I nodded briskly. "That means no. So question two, do you know his dad?"

"Never met the man," Tack told me.

"Do you know where he lives?" I pushed.

"Babe," I heard High call and I looked his way. "Not bein' a dick, but you need to take this up with your man."

"You said don't give up," I returned, my voice a whisper, and I watched his mouth clamp shut. When it did, I shared, "He said he's over it."

"Maybe he is," Hound put in.

I twisted to him, thinking that said a lot.

And what that said was that in his time as a brother, Joker hadn't given it to them either.

But I sensed High knew. I sensed Tack did too.

I looked from Hound to Hop.

He knew as well.

They'd been around him and they weren't stupid. They'd probably even seen the scars.

So I knew they knew.

"Carrie, babe, listen to me," Tack said, and I turned to see he'd straightened from the desk and was facing me. "Man's gotta face his own shit in his own time."

I heard him, loud and clear.

I just didn't like what he had to say.

That being, they knew, and they hadn't done a thing about it.

I straightened my shoulders and kept his gaze. "Okay, I understand. So this is mine."

"Babe—" Tack started.

"No," I said softly and watched him shut his mouth. "They hurt him. Now they need to hurt."

Tack's brows went up. "They?"

"His mother," I told him. "I'm going to find her too."

Tack drew in breath before he said quietly, "He's gettin' there. You in his life, he's movin' in a direction he wasn't close to takin' before he found you."

That felt nice.

But not nice enough.

"Maybe, but he's not there," I returned. "And you knew. You couldn't do anything because you have a manly man biker code you have to follow. But I don't."

Tack swung his head toward his wife. "Red, you wanna help me here?"

Tyra shrugged. "I don't follow the manly man biker code either."

After she delivered that, she grinned at me.

I grinned back.

"Trust me, this is not a good idea," Tack growled to his woman and shifted his gaze to me. "Seriously, Carissa."

"You knew," I stated and softened my tone. "You know."

"I did and I do," Tack confirmed. "And I'll tell you somethin' you gotta learn, darlin'. You took up this life, you entered our world, you got one a' my brothers in your bed, and if you want him to stay there, this has gotta sink in. My woman fought my battles for me, that would make me far from happy. And Joker is a brother for a reason, that reason bein', like every man here, we share blood of a different variety."

I understood what he was saying, and what he was saying didn't sound good.

I swallowed.

"Think on this and don't do anything hasty," Tack advised.

Maybe I should take his advice.

I looked to Tyra.

She scrunched her nose and tipped her head to the side.

I didn't understand that, and in the company of four Chaos brothers, I couldn't ask.

I gave my gaze to Tack. "Okay. I won't be hasty."

He appeared visibly relieved, which kind of scared me that I might be doing the wrong thing.

"I . . . Joker's at my house. I need to get home," I said.

"Tell him we said hey," Hound ordered good-naturedly.

I gave him a shaky grin and nodded.

Then I gave my farewells and got out of there.

I got in my car and backed out of my spot by the stairs to Ride's office.

Okay, that didn't go as planned. Perhaps I should have thought it through more fully.

But I hadn't been able to get it out of my head. Even after what happened the night before (the good part on the couch, before and after the drama), falling asleep with Joker again, getting up with Joker (again), getting ready and heading out to work (with Joker...again), I could force myself to let it go.

But all day I'd be scanning groceries, doing it seeing the insides of his biceps. The random pattern of white rings surrounded by puckered skin.

Dozens of them.

All over.

When had he endured that?

I couldn't imagine the boy I knew in high school would allow that to happen. I'd seen him with split lips and black eyes, holding himself funny. But although he was larger now, had filled out, he was no scrawny kid. He'd have fought back if his father tried to do that to him.

Wouldn't he?

I shook my head as I drove.

He would.

Anyone would.

Burning.

This all could only mean one of two things. His father did it to him when he was younger and couldn't fight back, which was utterly unthinkable. Or his father did it to him when he was older, but did it after he made it so he couldn't fight back, which was also utterly unthinkable.

But even so, I couldn't quit thinking about it.

So I had to do something about it.

I was halfway home when my phone binged with a text. Being a mother, and now a girlfriend (I hoped, we hadn't made it official, but that was the only thought that made me smile all day), I didn't ignore it. I grabbed my phone and looked at it when I was stopped at a red light.

It was a text from Tyra that read *Don't worry. I'm on it.*

Oh no.

I wasn't sure that was a good thing.

I didn't text back but got another bing when I was idling, waiting for Tyra's garage door to open (the house even had a garage with a remote opener—I mean, could it *get* better?).

I drove in and parked, but before I got out of the car, I looked at the text and saw it was from Elvira.

It read *Tyra called. We're sorting shit. Give me a few days.*

This meant giving her boss, who from what I could tell was a private eye or something, a few days. Elvira, I knew because she threatened it repeatedly on any occasion that warranted it (or didn't), would drag him in.

What had I done?

I got out of my car feeling funny. Not feeling like I should feel knowing I was walking into a clean, safe, lovely house to a tall, handsome biker boyfriend (or at least I thought he was my boyfriend, it was early but we *did* spend a lot of time together) who was growing back his beard for me.

I walked in the back door expecting Joker to be at the stove (this being how accustomed I'd become to him taking care of me) only to find the kitchen empty.

I dumped my purse, started to move toward the living room/dining room area that ran along the front of the house, my mouth opening to call, just as Joker turned the corner and walked into the kitchen.

He was grinning at me.

I stopped and took him in.

Navy tee, faded jeans, heavy black boots, lengthy stubble, messy hair, so, so handsome.

"Hey, Butterfly."

"I think I messed up again."

He stopped dead because I blurted that out but also because he must have read something on my face since he was right then examining it closely.

"What'd you mess up?" he asked slowly.

I took in a deep breath and shared, "I'll preface this by saying that I was upset."

I stopped talking.

Joker didn't say anything.

I kept going, "And I'll also say that I'm very aware that you're a man."

His face got a little scary.

But he still remained silent.

"A manly man," I went on.

His face got scarier.

"A manly man biker," I kept at it.

"Jesus," he bit off. "What'd you do?"

Oh well.

The faster the better, like pulling off a Band-Aid.

"I kinda went to Tack, and Hop, High, Hound, and Tyra were there, and I, well..." I paused then finished hurriedly, "Asked them where your dad lives."

He looked to the ceiling.

"I was upset," I reminded him.

He looked to me.

"He needs to pay," I whispered.

"Yeah, Carrie, and how you gonna make him do that?"

That was a good question.

"I hadn't gotten to that part of the plan yet," I admitted.

"Right," he stated, crossing his arms on his chest. "You do know that Tabby went behind Shy's back and hired a private investigator to find the guy who murdered his parents."

No. I didn't know that. I didn't even know Shy's parents had been murdered.

How awful.

"That didn't go down too good," Joker continued to inform me.

Wonderful.

"Um...did the investigator find him?" I asked, curious for more than one reason, wondering if Tabby used Elvira's boss.

"Yeah. And shit came to a head. They worked it out. But it was ugly."

I pressed my lips together and felt my eyes go round.

Joker shook his head.

"Butterfly, you're cute all the time, cuter some times more than others, and it's fucked up because right now you're bein' a pain in the ass and this is one of those times that you're cuter. But you gotta get this so you can get over it. My old man doesn't exist for me. I left him and that life behind, and I don't want it back in any way it can come back."

"He burned you," I whispered.

"Yeah, Carrie, he burned *me*. I took it. I survived it. I got outta that shit. And he's there. I know where he is. The same house. The same broads he's bangin' on the couch. The same beer he's guzzling, vodka he's shootin'. An empty life full of bitterness and anger at absolutely nothing. Every day I walk into that Compound knowin' I got my patch, which means I got my brothers. Every day I walk into the garage knowin' I got nothing on for my day but usin' my hands and brain to create things I like. And now, with you a part of my life, every day I got somethin' more. Somethin' he'd never get. Somethin' he couldn't hold on to. Somethin' he doesn't have it in him to earn. I don't know if my ma was a good woman. I do know she left his ass and left him empty. That is not me. I got brothers. I got work I dig. And now, I got you and your boy. He lives a life of pain. I don't. I don't need to expend effort to get revenge, to give him pain. All I got that he doesn't *is* my revenge, baby."

That was so huge, so profound, so smart, so amazing, coming from a man who I was beginning to think really, truly had no flaws (at all), and he was mine, I couldn't hold it back.

"I think I might be falling in love with you," I blurted and watched his face change to an expression I would have rushed to my phone to capture if I wasn't captivated by it, not wanting to miss an instant.

"Then quit thinkin', Carrie, because I know I'm fallin' for you."

I stared at him a moment, feeling all that made me feel, before lifting my hand and waving it in front of my face, announcing, "I'm gonna cry."

"Then for fuck's sake, get over here so you can be in my arms while you do it."

At that, I burst into tears.

When I did, not moving an inch because he came to me, I was in his arms.

I wrapped him in mine.

In the middle of it, I reared back and looked at his face through watery eyes, crying loudly, "I wish I had that flat tire. I'd bronze it!"

"Shut up, you fuckin' goofball," Joker returned, his body shaking, his voice vibrating with his humor, his arms tightening around me.

"Don't call me a goofball," I sniffled, pushing closer.

"Don't act like one."

"I'm not acting like a goofball," I snapped. "I'm sharing with you I like you..." I got up on my toes to get in his face, "*a lot.*"

"You haven't made that a secret."

"Maybe I should start doing that," I retorted, taking one arm from around him so I could swipe at my face.

"Butterfly, advice. Don't start playin' new games when you're already winnin' the one you're in."

That made me shut my mouth.

I know I'm fallin' for you.

His words filled my head so full I couldn't hold it up and therefore pressed my face in his chest.

"I don't feel like cookin'," he announced matter-of-factly, like we weren't having a hugely important conversation, the kind that changed lives, the kind that changed *the world*. "You've been on your feet behind a register all day so you're not cookin', either. We're goin' to Beau Jo's."

Everything left my mind as my entire body filled with glee and I pulled my face out of his chest.

"Mountain pies?" I asked excitedly.

"Not goin' there for their salad bar."

I smiled at him and did it brightly.

Then I quit smiling and said quietly, "I, uh...have to change and get gussied up."

"It's pizza at Beau Jo's, Carrie. Not a fancy steak joint like The Broker."

"I also have to call Tyra and Elvira to get them off the case," I admitted. "Tyra was there when Tack shut me down in my quest to claim vengeance against your dad. She didn't agree with Tack and she wasted no time rallying the troops."

He frowned. "This means Elvira's ropin' in Hawk."

I bit my lip.

Just then his phone rang.

He held me even as he pulled it out of his pocket, looked at it, looked at me in a way I couldn't decipher but it seemed kind of like he wanted to laugh.

Then he touched the screen and put it to his ear. "Yo, Hawk."

My eyes went wide.

Joker glanced back to me but said into the phone, "Yeah, she got home, confessed to bein' a goof, we talked it out. You're off duty."

There it was. The manly man's code.

Elvira roped him in and Hawk wasted no time telling on me.

Joker paused, muttered, "Uh-huh." Another pause before he said, "I'll tell her." One final pause before, "Yeah, later." Then he shoved his phone back in his pocket and declared, "Gwen likes you. Had a good time helpin' you move. We're invited over for dinner with our only requirement being bringing Travis. Gwen will sort that shit direct with you."

"That'll be nice," I said carefully. Then went on just as carefully, "Though, before we move on, I just wanted to point out I didn't actually confess to being a goof."

He just lifted his brows.

I let that go.

"And I'll add that was uncanny in an eerie way, Hawk calling you right when we started talking about him."

"Lee Nightingale is a supreme badass. Hawk's a bona fide superhero who doesn't wear a ridiculous suit. This is no joke. He probably sensed our discussion through powers he got when his mom was pushin' him out and got struck by lightning or something. I don't ask. He's an ally. He's also a brother of Tack's. I'm just happy he isn't an enemy."

"I kinda wanna meet him now," I shared.

"That's good, seein' as we're goin' to dinner at his pad."

"Right," I murmured.

"Speakin' a' dinner, as sweet as it is havin' you in my arms, your man needs to get fed."

My man.

I grinned.

He was *so totally* my boyfriend.

Carson Steele and Carissa Teodoro, boyfriend/girlfriend.

This made me happy.

We even had names that matched!

Joker watched me smile, watched me continue doing it without moving, so he shook me and said, "Dinner, Carrie."

It was then it occurred to me I was the one who had to let him go and get my behind in gear.

And it occurred to me I had to do that because he didn't want to let me go.

So that was when it occurred to me I hadn't kissed *my man* since I got home from work.

Therefore, I rolled up on my toes in my Converse and did that.

He took over, as he was wont to do.

But I didn't mind.

Then I got ready and *my man* took me out for a mountain pie.

*　　*　　*

In the dark, in my bed, I lay on top, straddling Joker's naked body.

It wasn't late. It wasn't early. I had a belly full of mountain pie and a body that just sustained two remarkable orgasms. And I'd managed to get the last without causing Joker bodily injury.

I was feeling a strange feeling that was ecstatically happy in a peaceful way I didn't quite understand. I'd never felt it.

But I had a feeling it was content.

Never having felt that feeling, I wouldn't have said it was one of the more profound feelings in the myriad you could experience.

But it really, *really* was.

Slowly gliding my hands over his warm skin, my nose along his bristly jaw, my lips along his throat, Joker held me with one arm draped across my back, hand cupping my behind, his other hand was up in my hair, fiddling with it.

"Are you my man?" I whispered against the skin of his neck.

His hand at my bottom squeezed.

"Yep," he replied easily.

Yes.

Ecstatically happy, but peaceful.

I slid my lips up to his ear. "Am I your woman?"

"Goes hand in hand, Butterfly."

That settled in me, and instead of making me want to jump around and do back hand springs, it made me melt deeper into him, where I was supposed to be. "You make me happy," I declared.

Like he wasn't telling it to do so, his hand at my head yanked me closer to his face.

"Look at my life, Carson. Outside Travis, happy is hard. But honestly, I could be in my old apartment, paying through the nose for daycare for Travis, squirting generic ketchup on generic tater tots, but if I also had you, I'd be happy."

"You need to shut up or you're gonna get fucked, Carrie."

"I..." I shook my head in confusion. "What?"

He took his hand from my hair, caught mine with it, shoved them between us and I pulled in a sharp breath when he wrapped my fingers around his hard cock.

"Keep bein' sweet you're gonna get fucked, not slow and gentle, *hard*. You're tired, you wanna go to sleep, you gotta shut up."

I wasn't listening to him.

I was feeling him hard in my hand.

He was ready again.

Already!

Automatically (honestly, it felt so good, I couldn't help myself), I stroked.

"Right, baby, you called it," Joker growled before he moved.

Fast.

He was up, I was in his arms, then I was back to the bed.

"Gotta get my girl ready," he muttered to himself, his fingers wrapping around my ankles and tugging them apart.

"Carson," I breathed.

That's all I got out.

He bent deep and his mouth was on me between my legs.

My entire body shuddered and he wasted no time getting me ready.

When I was so ready I thought it would run away with me, he pulled away, lifted me up, twisted me, planted me in the bed, and I was on my knees in the pillows, facing the headboard.

Joker was there but not with me for a few seconds before I felt his knee pushing mine further apart, and he went in from the front and back.

Finger to my clit, cock ramming deep.

My head fell back, slammed into his shoulder, and his hand wrapped around my jaw, twisting it toward him.

He took my mouth, worked me, and yes, *fucked* me.

I liked it like that. I couldn't deny it. It was crazy good. Astounding.

So I came fast and got to glory in the feel, moving with him, pushing my hands back to grasp his hips and feel the power of them flexing as he kept ramming into me, mewing then gasping at each stroke until he came too.

He buried himself deep and dropped his forehead to my shoulder.

"Okay," I panted, still not in control of my breathing. "If that's the official going steady ceremony, tomorrow I'm expecting a promise ring. But warning, I'm breaking up with you tomorrow night so we can make up and decide to go steady again."

Joker wrapped his arms around me, shoved his face in my neck, and still connected to me, burst out laughing, his amusement rocking through me in a way it became part of me and that was in a way I'd never forget.

Aaron had never done that. Aaron and I had never, *ever* had a moment like that. That simple. That remarkable. That memorable. That *beautiful*.

Joker's laughter reduced to chuckles and he kissed my neck.

"To do list tomorrow, promise ring and stock up on condoms," he muttered.

"I approve of this list," I told him.

I could feel, *actually feel*, him smile against my skin.

I slid my hands along his arms and held him to me.

We stayed like that, naked, intimate, connected, and I wanted to shout my joy that he wanted that at the same time giving it to me.

So only when the time was right did he slide out gently, turn me in his arms, settle me back in bed, and kiss my temple before he pulled the covers up and said, "Be right back."

"Okay, sweetie."

That bought me a brief kiss on the lips before he did just what he said.

He was in bed beside me, gathering me close when he asked, "You want your panties?"

"Mm-hmm."

Pure Joker, he twisted, reached to the floor and got them for me.

I pulled them on under the covers.

"Nightshirt?" he asked.

"It's under the pillow."

"Butterfly, just sayin', you got a great body and that thing does nothin' for it."

"Well, it wouldn't, it's my preggers nightie."

"It's gotta go."

I blinked through the dark as he again folded me in his arms.

"Travis isn't in your belly, Carrie. You're a mom, but you're also a beautiful woman with a beautiful body and a man in her bed who appreciates both. Lose it."

"I, well..." I mentally inventoried my drawers and wondered if my pre-baby nighties would look good. I hadn't tried them. Not one. They were cute and some were cute/sexy so I had no reason to try them.

Until now.

"Okay," I finished.

"Now, you good with just panties?"

I felt his hard body tight against mine, his arms pulling me mostly on him, and I rested against his chest as I pressed my arms to his sides and my cheek to his shoulder.

"Yeah," I murmured. "I'm good with just panties."

To show his approval, he dipped his hand inside said panties and again cupped my bottom.

I sighed.

My body was loosening, my eyes drooping, when Joker called, "Carrie?"

"Yeah, sweetheart?"

"Means everything, fuckin' everything, you'd want to pull out all the stops to take on my dad for me. Got men who wear a cut who'd do that for me. Some people from back in the day. And you. That's it. And you gotta know, it means everything."

I closed my eyes tight, turned my head, pressed my lips against the base of his throat and said there, "Good."

"Still don't want you doin' dick."

I grinned and settled back, cheek to shoulder. "I won't."

"Good," he muttered, giving my behind a squeeze.

"Though, if I ever see your dad, even though I have no idea what he looks like, I won't be responsible for sending him a killing look."

There was a smile in his voice when he returned, "That you can do."

"And if he should later turn up with his car keyed, I'll say now, it wasn't me."

His body shook, I gloried in it, though his humor had no noise.

But the smile was deep in his voice when he ordered, "Shut up and go to sleep."

"Just to say, I'm going to do that but only because I was going to do that anyway."

"If you were, why aren't you shuttin' up?"

"I was just saying it just to say."

"You're still not shuttin' up."

"Whatever," I muttered.

"And still," he pointed out.

I lifted my head and snapped, "Joker!"

He caught me at the back of my head, pulled me in, lifted up, and gave me a hard, sweet, short kiss.

Then he tucked my cheek back to his shoulder, my forehead in the side of his neck, and said, "*Now* shut up and go to sleep."

I grinned at his throat.

Then I shut up, closed my eyes, and went to sleep.

CHAPTER SIXTEEN

End of Story

Carissa

WITH AN INSTINCT born in me the second Aaron's swimmers fertilized my egg, that next Monday, I knew my son was on his way to the front door without me even seeing him through the window.

Thus, after a week that included me getting myself and my boy into a great new house, only one double shift since LeLane's flu epidemic was settling down, and a whole lot of time spent with my awesome new boyfriend, I was lounging (more like fidgeting with anticipation) while Joker hung out with me on my couch.

So, with excitement at what would herald an even better week—that being having my son back—I pushed up, planted a knee, and threw myself over Joker *and* the back of the couch.

Unfortunately, when I did this I heard Joker grunt. This gave me the uncomfortable feeling I'd planted said knee somewhere *in* Joker. Therefore, when my bare feet hit the floor at the back of the couch, I stopped my mad dash and looked at him.

"Jesus, Carrie," he muttered, pushing up while looking at me, lips quirking, one hand to his stomach.

"Sorry," I whispered, then grinned, "Travis is home."

I got a return grin that said more than his lips quirking that he wasn't angry with me, so I bent in, grabbed his head on either side, gave him a quick kiss, let him go, and ran to the door.

The bell rang right when I got to it.

I unlocked it and pulled it open.

And there was Aaron, not Tory, holding Travis in his arm, his diaper bag looped on Aaron's shoulder.

Aaron stood tall, as usual, but he'd taken off his suit and was in jeans and a nice shirt that was pink and worked well with his coloring.

I saw this but mostly I saw my baby.

Lifting up my hands, I clapped them quietly in front of me, smiling at my son.

Then I held my hands out to him. "Hey, Googly. Welcome to your new home."

Travis smiled a wet, open-mouthed smile back to his mommy, twisted in his father's arms, and lurched toward me.

Catching him and pulling him to me, I hoped I'd never forget moments like these. Seeing my baby's eyes light up when he saw his mommy. Seeing him reach to me. Catching his little warm body in my arms. Little moments that could be easy to forget, but they were so precious they should always be remembered.

I cuddled him to me, kissing his neck, giving him squeezes, listening to his baby giggles as he latched on to my hair and tugged.

It felt *wonderful*.

I turned away from the door, muttering, "You can drop the bag by the door. Thanks, Aaron."

"Jesus, I knew I knew you," Aaron said, and I turned back to see him looking at Joker. "Fuck, you're Carson Steele."

I looked Joker's way to see he was on his feet.

His eyes were on Aaron.

"Yep," he answered.

Okay, I hadn't expected that moment to come, since I hadn't expected Aaron to return Travis. Though I knew it would eventually happen, but I didn't know that eventuality would come so quickly.

But now it was done and it was family time, Travis, Joker, and me, so it was also time to move on.

"Thanks for bringing him," I said to Aaron firmly and repeated, "You can drop the bag by the door."

Aaron looked to me and his brows went up. "You're dating Carson Steele?"

I looked to Joker then back to Aaron, answering, "Well... yeah." When he looked at a loss for words, and considering I didn't really care what he had to say whatever it might be, I again repeated, "Just throw the bag by the door. I'll sort it out later."

"You told me I didn't know who he was," Aaron pointed out, not taking my not-very-veiled hint that he should go.

I wasn't going to explain my mess-up to my ex-husband.

So instead, I asked, "Did you know him back in high school?"

"You know I didn't, not really," Aaron returned. "But I still knew him, Carissa."

"Is it necessary to go over this before you take off?" Joker joined in and I turned my gaze back to him to see him staring steadily at Aaron, but doing it looking impatient.

I swung my gaze to Aaron to see he was also studying Joker. Then he drew in breath and turned his attention back to me.

"I need to have a word," he announced.

Fabulous.

"Shit," Joker muttered, obviously feeling the same as me.

Aaron's eyes sliced to him. "You don't need to be here."

"Actually," I said quickly. "This is my house so I get to make that call. And my call is, Joker's not going anywhere. Now, I have bonding to do with my son. If you need a word, have it, Aaron, so we can get on with our night."

My heart sank as, when I said this, Aaron took a step in, closed the door behind him, and dropped the diaper bag to the floor.

At this move, I felt tension hit the room, and not just my own, as I cuddled my boy, who still had a fistful of my hair, which he was shoving in his mouth. I carefully extricated it from his grip, and he immediately grabbed on to my top and bent forward, shoving that in his mouth.

All this happened while Aaron looked around.

I knew what he saw. I liked that he saw it because I liked that I was living it and able to give it to Travis. It wasn't a huge house like the four-bedroom one I'd left that Aaron now lived in with Tory. It was just two bedrooms, one bath, a living room that shared its space with the dining room.

But regardless, it was a very nice one, and that was plain to see.

And the "ex-our" furniture looked fantastic in it.

Aaron gave me his gaze. "This is a great house, Riss."

Riss.

Ulk.

"Thanks, I know," I replied.

"Is that the word you wanted to have?" Joker prompted.

Aaron shot him a killing look then turned his attention back to me and promptly rearranged his features.

Ulk again.

"I'm pleased you landed in a nice place," he told me.

"I am too," I stated the obvious.

"If you're goin' for a tour, not sure I'm big on Carrie obliging," Joker put in.

Aaron cut his gaze to Joker. "It would help this go faster if you didn't participate."

"It would help this go faster if you got to the point," Joker noted rationally.

I fought back my giggle as I saw Aaron's jaw grow hard.

"Okay," I cut in and when I got my ex-husband's attention, I asked. "Aaron, what do you need?"

He stopped looking annoyed and started looking something I knew very well from him.

Contrite.

I cuddled Travis closer and braced.

"Listen," he began. "My attorney is going to call your attorney tomorrow, but I thought, since I had you, I'd tell you now. I'm going to have to postpone our meeting."

I felt more tension in the room, this was mostly mine but definitely some of Joker's, and I stared at Aaron, knowing exactly what he was up to.

He could attempt to postpone until the cows came home and he would. There were a variety of reasons for this. He could be doing it just to mess with me. He could be doing it because he didn't want to spend his precious time going to court to battle me. He could be doing it because he knew Angie was the bomb and he'd lose so he wanted to drag out the preliminaries for as long as he could. Or he could be doing it because he thought doing it would wear me down to the point I'd give up.

Whatever he was doing, he was doing for himself with little thought for me.

Or his son.

The same old story.

"Before you jump to conclusions, Riss," he went on quickly, "I had a big case get pushed up. We're not ready. We're in court this week and I'm going from here right back to the office. I'll be up to my neck in it, and I'll need to be in court when we're supposed to have our meeting. The case is going to go for a while, at least a few weeks. Now I'm telling you that I'd appreciate it if you'd have patience with that process."

"You've gotta be kidding," Joker growled, and Aaron turned angry eyes his way.

"Man, you are not in this," he clipped.

"Excuse me," I said when Joker opened his mouth, and in doing so, I got both of their attention. But I was looking at Aaron. "Again, I'll say this is *my house*. Joker and I aren't dating. We're seeing each other. He's part of my life and therefore part of my home. He's welcome here. This is my home, and I get to say what he's in, and since he's in my life, he's in everything that has anything to do with me. The person who isn't and who doesn't get to say that is *you*."

I felt some of the strain in the air leave (all this was Joker, I was still angry) but I kept my focus on Aaron because I wasn't finished talking.

"If you postpone, I'm afraid that I'll have to speak to Angie about deviating from this meeting and returning to our preliminary strategy of filing our motions."

Aaron took a step toward me and when the air again grew heavy (this entirely from Joker) and my body visibly stiffened, he stopped.

He lowered his voice to conciliatory when he carried on, "Riss, I understand I haven't given you a lot of reason to trust me, but I'm telling the truth. This case is huge for my firm and I'm first chair. It's my first big case taking that chair and I need to have my head in the game."

That was big for him. Huge. He'd take that seriously. He'd want to give it his all.

But it had nothing to do with me.

"This is not my problem," I returned.

He nodded as if he understood, and while I was dealing with the surprise of that, he kept speaking.

"I know things are tough, they're probably tougher with this move because the rent on this place can't come cheap. I appreciate whatever sacrifice you're making for our son to get him into a nice home. So in the meantime, until we can set up another meeting to discuss the changes we're making, in Travis's bag, there's five hundred dollars in cash."

I blinked.

Aaron kept going.

"If this case takes as long as I think it will, I'll give you the same when I return Travis to you after his next time with me."

"I—" I started.

"Take it, Butterfly," Joker said quietly.

I saw Aaron shoot him another acid glance as I, too, looked Joker's way.

"Maybe I should talk to Angie," I suggested.

"You wanna talk to Angie, do it. But for now, take the cash," Joker replied. "You can give it back if she says it's a bad idea."

"I know it's none of my business," Aaron said carefully, and I looked back to see he was addressing me. "But this is a really nice place, Carissa. I..." He shook his head and the next came out like he was forcing it to, "I've seen your clothes. Your car. I know you were unhappy having Travis in your old place and I expect you're cutting even further back to give him this one. I'm asking you to let me help."

At his words, something started building in me. A pressure I didn't understand, but I knew it had to do with the fact that my ex-husband, who killed my dream and destroyed my life, forcing me to rebuild it and do it the hard way, felt sorry for me.

I shook my hair, straightened my shoulders and locked eyes with him. "I'm fine."

"Let me help," Aaron repeated.

"I'm not sure what you're doing but if this is an actual wake-up for you, okay. We can sort that out through our attorneys. Until then, Aaron, I don't need your pity."

He flinched and I drew my son closer, his smell, his warmth, his little baby body giving me strength as he luckily seemed a-okay with twisting my top in his hand and alternately wetting it with baby saliva while all this happened.

"I don't pity you, Riss," Aaron said gently.

And again with the *Riss*.

Plus talking to me gently.

What was his game?

No, really, I didn't care. I wanted him out of my house so I could have Travis (and Joker) time.

"You're right," I told him to get things moving. "It's more expensive here. But my life has changed so it isn't the sacrifice you think it is."

"Carrie," Joker murmured, and it sounded like a warning.

I didn't heed that warning.

"And you're also right," I kept speaking. "It's time I quit sacrificing. There are things Travis needs since he's growing, like new clothes. And there are things that I need to take care of to make things a little less tight for me. But I'll be seeing to those myself. If Angie says it's okay, I'll take your cash for Travis. But just so you know, I'll be selling our guest room furniture, the bracelet your parents gave me, the bangles you used to give me, and our wedding rings. That should help me sort out some things financially, therefore you can stop feeling sorry for me."

When I finished speaking, I stared at my ex-husband because he looked like he'd been struck, his face was pale, his eyes pained.

"You're going to sell my bangles?" he whispered.

I couldn't understand his reaction, but I had to admit, whatever it was, it troubled me.

So my reply was soft when I said, "Yes, Aaron. They're mine, you gave them to me, but I don't live the life they represent. Not the part where you gave them to me but also not the part where they fit the life I lead. I work in a grocery store. I'm not a lady who lunches who needs expensive jewelry. I need other things. So I'm going to make them useful."

It was like I said not a word.

Aaron's tone was nearly tortured when he asked, "Our *wedding rings*?"

My head shook automatically in startled confusion as I felt Travis fidget in my arms. I looked down at him to see he'd sensed his daddy's strange dismay and was no longer focused on my top, but on his father.

That was when Joker was in my space, his hands on Travis.

I looked up at him.

"Deal with him," he whispered, jerking his head Aaron's way. "I got Travis."

Then he did have Travis because my son was in his arms and he was walking away with Travis looking up at him.

I twisted to watch them head toward the hall, Joker muttering, "Wanna see your new room?"

Travis cried, "Dah, bah, buh!" and yanked on Joker's earlobe.

That almost made me smile, but I didn't when I looked back at Aaron, who was not watching Joker with Travis.

He was watching me.

"I don't really understand your response, Aaron," I told

him and did it carefully. "But I'll reiterate those things were given to me. They're mine. I have uses for them, and I'll be putting them to those uses."

"I gave you your engagement ring on the bricks of Boston Harbor," he returned. "I asked you to marry me with the lights on the water."

He did. He'd put a knee to those bricks. The clock had just struck midnight. He'd held my hand and looked up at me, asking me to be his wife, the night lights of Boston illuminating the moment, making it almost like a fantasy.

In any other circumstance, it would have been unbearably romantic. At the time, I'd even convinced myself it was.

But in truth, the months before, he'd been with another woman.

"You don't want to do this," I warned him quietly. "I don't need emotional manipulation with everything else. But just to say, I know what you were doing and who you were doing it with when you proposed. I've got ammunition. You want fire for fire, I'll give it to you. But I'd prefer we not go there."

He shook his head as if he suddenly realized where he was and what was happening.

Then he stated, "I'm not manipulating you emotionally, Riss. God."

"You have never, not once, shown any indication you cared about what you threw away," I replied. "Now I'm fighting back and have a man in my life and suddenly—"

"Speaking of that," he interrupted me, his eyes going to the hall and back to me. "Carson Steele? Honey, really?"

Oh no.

Absolutely *not*.

"Do not," I snapped, my back straight, my eyes I could actually feel shooting icicles.

Aaron's back straightened too.

"He's—"

I leaned toward him. "*Mine*," I bit out and leaned back. "He's great with Travis and wonderful to me. *Wonderful*, Aaron. Flawless. *Amazing*. The way he treats me, something I've never had *in my life*"—I threw out a hand to him, making a point I knew he didn't miss when his face got hard—"you don't get to judge. You don't get to say a thing. That's mine. I don't share my thoughts about who you spend your time with. I expect you to return that favor."

"I don't spend my time with the high school loser grown up to be whatever the fuck he is now, but just looking at him, I know it's no good," Aaron shot back.

Oh no.

Absolutely not!

"No, you spend your time with a woman who has no problem sleeping with a married man," I returned sharply. "A married man who had a pregnant wife. Then accepting that man's ring after he scraped off that pregnant wife *while she was still pregnant*. A woman who stands by watching her man make the mother of his son's life a misery. She's shown signs of humanity recently, Aaron. But don't you dare think you can compare when Joker *wipes the floor with her*."

He looked furious but he didn't volley.

Instead, he reached into his back pocket and pulled out his wallet. Walking to the coffee table we bought together for the home we were supposed to share for eternity, he opened his wallet, took out a bunch of bills and dropped them on the table.

He then turned to me, "I know you like your clothes. You need to look nice for your loser, use that." He pointed to the bills. "*Don't* sell my rings."

I couldn't imagine why he cared one little bit about those rings. He'd never cared before.

But I couldn't think on that. I had to think about the fact that my head was about to explode with the pressure of mounting fury the likes I'd never experienced.

"For your information," I hissed. "*When* I sell all that stuff, I'll be using it to pay off my old attorney's bills. It'd be lovely to have a few new tops and some shoes that are cute that aren't made of plastic. But Joker likes me as I am. He doesn't need me in two-hundred-dollar sandals. He takes me as I come."

"He wouldn't, seeing as *Joker*, whatever the fuck the deal is with *that* shit, the guy's name is fucking Carson, probably doesn't know shoes can cost two hundred dollars."

"I suspect that his motorcycle boots don't come cheap," I retorted.

Aaron's lip curled as he asked derisively, "Motorcycle boots? Seriously?"

I had my reply on the tip of my tongue but didn't get to say it because Joker said from the mouth of the hall. "You're done, friend. Leave."

I looked to him to see he still had Travis and now Travis had a toy he was shoving in his mouth.

Even as angry as I was, it wasn't lost on me that Joker looked fabulous with my son in his arms.

This made me wonder what he would look like if he held *our* child in his arms.

Probably the same. No more. No less.

Simply fabulous.

"I'm not your friend," Aaron ground out.

"No, you're not," Joker returned.

There was silence. This stretched. There was hostility in the air. It built.

When I was about to put a stop to it by walking to the door and opening it, Aaron asked a strange question.

And he asked it to Joker.

"Do you think you can beat me?"

I felt my breath catch, understanding the question and not liking it one...little...*bit*.

Joker also understood the question.

Completely.

This was why he answered, "You lost way before I entered the picture."

"Gentlemen—" I began.

"We'll see," Aaron spoke over me, his gaze intent, irate, and locked on Joker.

Joker shook his head, his lips curved up, and he muttered, "Whatever."

"We're done," I announced, walking to the door, opening it and looking to Aaron. "If you wouldn't mind..."

Aaron tore his gaze from Joker and looked at me. He then studied me for a moment that went on too long.

He did this taking in my hair, which was down and poofed out, I knew, because that was what happened when Joker played with it. And while we were lounging, Joker had been playing with it.

He also took in my cute top that was cream, mostly sheer, scoop necked, long sleeved, had little orange flowers on it with tiny green leaves and fit snugly over the tangerine cami I wore underneath. And he took in my beaten-up, faded green lowrider army pants that I got for a song at a thrift shop. They'd had a grease stain that I'd OxiCleaned, and now they were not beaten-up and stained gross but beaten-up and not-stained awesome.

It was not an outfit I would have worn in any of the years I was with him.

It was cute but it was edgy, not by choice, but because it was all I could afford.

I still liked it, and I liked it more now because it suited the *new* me.

Cute and edgy.

That was me.

Fortunately, before I had to prompt him to get his behind moving, he walked to me standing by the door.

It seemed he was going straight through the door but regrettably he stopped and looked down at me.

"We're not done, Riss," he said softly, his tone a tone I knew. It was the tone he used when he was trying to get something from me. Me to forgive him. Me to change into the dress he wanted me to wear to dinner with his parents and not the one I'd chosen. Me to come to bed so he could have sex with me.

The fact that he was using it now didn't give me a good feeling.

"You and I will never be done," he went on. "We both know that."

He gave me the look with his interesting blue eyes that used to undo me but right then made me fight rolling my eyes before his perfectly formed lips twitched.

"Take care of yourself, honey," he murmured, allowed his mouth to form a grin, then he walked through the door.

I shoved it closed behind him, locked it, turned to Joker and declared, "I would say it's an understatement that it doesn't excite me he's found a different way to be annoying."

Joker burst out laughing.

I watched him, liking it. I kept watching him, liking it more when Travis became mesmerized by Joker's laughter before he decided to join in in his baby way by smacking his toy against Joker's mouth.

Joker started chuckling and looked down at my son.

When he did, Travis went for the gusto by shoving the

toy in his mouth at the same time he lurched up and tried to latch on to Joker's mouth, thus slamming both his wet lips and the toy into Joker's face.

"Come get your kid before he chews my lips off," Joker said in a way garbled by toy and baby.

I did as not-quite-requested (but I decided to take it that way).

When I was again cuddling my son, I felt Joker's hand on my hip and I lifted my eyes to his.

"You okay?" he asked quietly.

"He intends to be more annoying," I replied.

"Got that," Joker stated. "So, you okay?"

I sighed.

Then I said, "I got through the other ways he's been annoying. I'll get through this."

Joker squeezed my hip. "Yeah, Carrie. You will."

I grinned at him as I leaned up and kissed his stubbly jaw.

Travis conked me in the head with his toy.

This made me laugh and give my attention back to my son. Which started me putting that scene with Aaron out of my head and doing what I should have been able to do ten minutes ago.

Welcome my son home. Give him a full tour of the house. And ended the tour with spending time with both my boys—my baby one and my biker one—in my new safe, clean, pretty house.

*　　*　　*

"He's gonna try to win you back."

It was that night. Travis was asleep. It was late. It was after the news. After making love with Joker in my bed. The baby monitor I had in storage but hadn't had to use in months since Travis had slept in the same room in the apartment with me was on, its red light lit, and it was on the nightstand on Joker's side, where my biker put it.

"Sweetie," I whispered but said no more.

When it happened with Aaron, I didn't want to think of it.

But I knew it immediately.

Aaron was intensely competitive. I'd noticed it all the way back in high school. I'd always disliked it, and that was the only thing I didn't bury but let show. We'd even fought about it more than once.

I first started noticing it when the team lost a football game and Aaron would react to it in a way that was a little scary.

And not only me but his mother, who pretty much let her husband do whatever he wanted, would get agitated when father or son would challenge each other to anything. It could be a board game or a tennis match. They'd go at it, and each other, with a viciousness that was frightening.

Aaron's father would taunt him anytime Aaron made a mistake, and I hated that.

But not as much as Aaron's behavior. Aaron would rub it in whenever he got one over on his dad. I hated that too. It was relentless, he kept at it to the point it was cruel, and I always thought it said ugly things about him.

Heck, about the both of them.

I had no idea if Aaron's behavior changed a few weeks ago because he knew I had a good attorney or because he saw me walking to my apartment with Joker.

Or if one led into the other.

I just knew that the landscape of my life was changing in a variety of ways, including whatever changes Aaron saw fit to force on it by any means available.

And seeing his ex-wife with another man had an effect I wouldn't have guessed, considering the way he'd treated me. But I probably should have.

And as usual, I didn't like it.

"Gonna do whatever he can to get you, and he's gonna run his current bitch through the wringer to do it," Joker informed me.

I sighed, lifted my cheek from where I was resting it on Joker's chest, and found his eyes through the shadows.

"He and I are done," I declared.

"Heard a lot of what you said when Travis and me weren't in the room, Butterfly, so I know you're into me." I grinned through the dark but Joker kept going. "That's not what bothers me. That jackhole is gonna run his bitch through the wringer, and he's gonna do the same with you and your boy. Man like him doesn't give a fuck about anything . . . but winning."

"I know," I said quietly.

"You gotta call Angie, tell her all that shit," Joker advised.

"I will, tomorrow," I promised.

"And you and her gotta come up with some way that's gonna make it clear to him that whatever deal you strike about how you take care of your kid is it. Whatever he's got in his head to do to try to best me, he's gotta let it go."

"I'll mention that to Angie."

I had hoped that would end it, but Joker kept at me.

"I know he was yours, you cared about him, you gave him years of your life, your hand, a kid, and I know he fucked you and you're over it. But you gotta know, your ex was a massive dick in high school, and I'm thinkin' maturity didn't wean that outta him."

"He was just—" I started, not in defense of Aaron, more in defense of why I'd put up with the way Aaron was.

"You weren't around," Joker interrupted me. "Lookin' back, the real shit he pulled, the foul shit that was beyond the pale, Carrie, he pulled it only when you weren't there to witness it. If you knew what that motherfucker was up to, you'd have gotten quit of him before you hit your sophomore year, and my guess is, he knew it."

I didn't like the sound of that.

"Like what?" I asked.

"Doesn't matter," Joker didn't answer. "Hope the kids he pulled that crap on got over it. It was so brutal, they probably didn't. But that's not on you. Everyone knew you were cool. Everyone also knew he was not."

"Did he... do anything to you?" I asked hesitantly.

"Tried," Joker answered and I felt my body string tight. "Cornered me, but with bad timing. Had a neighbor, man's still a friend, he drove up when they were settin' up for their beatdown, your ex-motherfucker and five of his crew. Linus got outta his truck and shared some wisdom with them. He was an adult. He's a big man. One look at him you know he can handle himself. And he's got a way with words. The words he used made it clear, they fuck with me ever, they fuck with him, and the way he'd fuck back would be surprising."

I was struggling with contradictory feelings of relief that Joker's old neighbor had good timing and upset that Aaron and his friends had targeted Joker, so I didn't get a reply in before Joker carried on.

"Wouldn't have mattered if Linus hadn't shown. I can take care of myself, and by that time had learned to take a beating."

That didn't make me feel any better.

Joker wasn't quite finished.

"But other kids who didn't have that, Neiland put the screws to 'em. There are bullies, and there are people like Neiland. He broke the mold of a bully. He was a tyrant. He was king of the school, liked his ass on that throne, and actively sought out ways to make sure no one would forget that was his place. He got off on admiration. He also got off on humiliation. Those he considered weak, he wanted them cowed. And he got that however he needed to get it with his crew of buddies who were nothing short of high school enforcers."

"This is making me feel a little sick, Carson," I told him the truth, my stomach beginning to roil with nausea.

He slid his hand up my back, to the side of my neck, the calluses catching on my skin, making it tingle in a way that was oddly soothing, probably because it was a part of him. Then he glided his fingers into my hair, and when he spoke again, his tone had gentled.

"Done now, baby, and I know I'm scarin' you. It sucks I gotta do that. I can see you're ready to fight, able to do it, got sass in you and fire, and you're done with him. You make that clear. But I'm doin' what I'm doin' now 'cause I'm worried shit that's been ugly is gonna get uglier. And you gotta toughen up, Carrie. 'Cause he doesn't get what he wants and he doesn't get the message this is a battle he should let go, he's gonna come at you with all he's got."

"No," I said softly. "He's gonna come at you."

That was the truth, and it made me feel *worse.*

"That, you don't worry about," Joker said.

"But," my voice was pitched higher, "he's got a lot of money and knows people in high—"

"You think anyone dicks with Chaos?"

I shut up because I had a feeling they didn't. Or if they were stupid enough to try, they didn't get very far.

I mean, all the guys were really nice to me because they were just plain really nice.

But still, each one of them was a little scary.

Including Joker.

"I'm Chaos. And, Butterfly, I claimed you, and you might not get this because we haven't discussed it so I'll make it clear now. Claimin' you makes you Chaos too. The fight might get ugly, and you gotta be prepared for that. But the way you got your head sorted and the firepower you got at your back, you will never lose."

"Ugh," I muttered before shoving my face in the side of his neck, doing this because I had no reply. I knew he was right about the good but also about the bad.

I was glad I had him and his *firepower*, but I still wasn't looking forward to whatever Aaron had up his sleeve.

Joker used his fingers in my hair to massage my scalp soothingly. Strangely, it did the trick. Even with all that we were discussing, just his fingers digging in firm but gentle were comforting.

So I relaxed against him.

"I might want to bronze that tire, but if I keep being a pain in your behind, you may wish it never existed," I muttered against his skin.

"Look at me."

My relaxed body instantly stiffened at the severity of his command.

It was not firm. It was beyond that. It was something I not only had never heard from him but I'd never heard *at all*.

It was meant to be obeyed.

Without question.

And I obeyed it.

Without question.

When he had my gaze through the shadows, his hand slid down, fingertips in my hair, palm to my ear, thumb digging into my cheekbone. It didn't hurt, but it did convey a message.

The touch was an assertion. Another command. He said he'd claimed me, and that was a physical demonstration I knew in that instant I had to understand, do it completely and also without question.

I suddenly found it hard to breathe.

"I don't know where this will lead," he stated. "You and me and your boy. I know what we got. I know I like what we got. I know I wanna keep that strong and make it stronger. Shit happens. I hope like fuck it happens to us, we'll fight through to the other side. But I know this and you gotta know it too. No matter what happens, I will never, not ever, not fuckin' *ever*, Carissa, regret ridin' down that shoulder to help you and your boy. It's the best decision I ever made in my life, and I know that in a way I know I'll feel that until the day I fuckin' die."

His thumb was still on my cheek so he felt the silent tear that fell from my eye and collided with it.

"You scared a' that?" he asked harshly.

"It's the most beautiful thing I've ever heard," I whispered huskily.

And it was. Excepting the first time I heard Travis cry, it absolutely was.

"Then you get me." His voice was no longer harsh, but it was rough.

"I get you, sweetie."

He pulled me down to kiss me.

That too was an assertion. Like his hand on me, his words to me, that moment in the dark in my bed, even with all we'd shared before, was the beginning and it was also an ending.

I was his, for certain, for sure, no matter what had gone before, it started right then.

I was Carson "Joker" Steele's.

End of story.

He was mine too, but with a manly man biker, that was secondary. It went with the territory, hand in hand with him staking his claim.

This did not bother me. It didn't trouble me. It didn't annoy me.

It utterly *thrilled* me.

That might be wrong, but in that instant, for the first time in my life, I didn't care if it was wrong. If it was wrong, I didn't want to be right.

Joker shared all this with his mouth. He then broke the kiss, leaving me breathless, and tucked my face back into his neck.

"Now, baby, sleep," he ordered thickly. "Even if you got the day off tomorrow, Travis'll be up early and we got a day together with your boy in your new house. I don't want you draggin'."

I wanted to cry again. Cry with relief that life had brought this man to me. Cry with happiness that I'd made it through the thorny path that led away from him in high school but then led me right back.

I didn't.

I snuggled closer, with my arm wrapped around him pulling him to me as I did, and I tipped my eyes over his throat to the red light lit on *his* nightstand. Where *he'd* put it. So, even though we slept cuddled, the baby monitor was still closer to him so he'd be sure to hear if Travis needed us.

Us.

Us.

That thought almost made me cry too.

But I didn't.

Because it was done.

In that moment I knew it was finally over.

I'd lost Althea. I'd lost Mom. To deal with the pain and

make sure I lost nothing else, I'd put blinders on, made my mistakes, and then my dream had died.

But now the loss was over.

The blinders were off.

And I had Travis.

Then I got Joker.

And he gave me Chaos.

So it was done.

I was done losing.

And in being done, eyes open, facing ahead, back straight, head in the game, I was ready to win.

CHAPTER SEVENTEEN

A Biker Named Joker

Carissa

EARLY THE NEXT afternoon, I was wandering the living room/dining room area, bouncing my son, who was bawling.

Joker walked in from the kitchen with a fresh soda in his hand and I stopped, looked to him, still bouncing, and declared, "I don't get it. He's had his nap, it was shorter than normal, but that's never a big thing with him. Still, he woke up fussy. He ate his food then was cranky. But he's had his food, his diaper is clean, he's been bathed. He can get grouchy his first day back from his dad's, but not like this." I looked down at Travis and finished on a mutter, "Maybe he's not feeling well. He's got another tooth coming in. Maybe that's it."

Travis had no answer, except to keep crying loudly.

My head came up when I felt Joker get close.

"New place, Butterfly," he said over Travis's blubbering. "This time, he's got more to get used to. New room. New space. Away from his dad's."

This made sense, and I wondered why I hadn't thought of that.

Joker set his can on the dining room table, pulled my boy out of my arms, and walked away, also bouncing him.

I watched as he bent to Travis's toy basket and picked it up. Then I watched as he came back and dumped the entire thing across the floor behind the couch.

At that, Travis jumped slightly in his arms, shoved his fist in his mouth, stopped bawling, started sniveling, and gave Joker's actions his complete attention seeing as Travis was always up for making a mess of pretty much anything.

Joker crouched down and planted Travis's baby booty on the floor next to the toys. When he had my son down, on the other side of the toys he dropped to his hip and stretched out on his side, long jeans-covered legs out, feet bare, faded black tee drawn tight across his chest, his upper body rested on a forearm.

I kept watching as Joker picked up a blue giraffe and poked Travis in the belly with it.

Travis took his hand from his mouth and pumped both his fists in the air at his sides before he went after the giraffe.

Joker pulled it away then poked Travis in the belly with it again.

Travis went for it again but almost immediately lost interest in it, what with all the toys scattered across the floor. He bent forward and grasped a red donut ring.

"Giraffe'll get lonely, kid," Joker told him, poking him in the belly with it again.

On his hip, leaning into his hand on the ring, Travis's head came up to look at Joker. He then pushed fully forward and crawled across the toys, dragging the ring with him, heading toward Joker. He pounded his hands, including the one with the ring, into Joker's chest, and Joker fell on his back.

Travis emitted a little giggle before he carried the now forgotten donut with him to the best toy ever.

The living, breathing, biker jungle gym.

He crawled on top of Joker, banging him with his donut, as Joker put his hands to Travis's sides, where he was most ticklish.

Then he tickled.

No little giggles at that, Travis let loose and that was when I watched biker and baby fake wrestle on the floor among a bunch of toys, Joker letting Travis win while getting clocked repeatedly in the face, head, neck, shoulders, and chest by a plastic red donut.

Joker took it smiling, sometimes chuckling, and giving his full attention to my son, who was no longer crying but having the time of his life.

I watched it smiling and knowing without any doubts that I'd have more moments like that. Moments when Joker would do something where I'd know straightaway I was falling in love with him. And I watched it loving that I knew Joker would give that to me at the same time loving that he was giving what he was giving to my son.

Then I kept watching as Joker grabbed Travis and lifted him up in the air, sent him flying a few inches, Travis's laughter pealed through the room, and Joker caught him, bringing him down to his face.

"Now, boy, this place ain't so bad, is it?" he asked.

Travis's reply was to conk Joker on the cheekbone with the donut he hadn't let go and shout, "Bah la dah!"

"That's what I thought," Joker muttered.

I drew in breath through my nose and did it deeply to control the emotion swelling inside me.

Then I went to the kitchen and got myself a soda.

A brand name one.

One a biker named Joker put in my fridge.

Joker

The next day, safety glasses and gloves on, welding gun in his hand, sparks flying, Joker heard, "Joke! Cherry wants to talk to you in the office!"

He turned from the metal he was working on to see Roscoe at the top of the stairs that led to the office through the garage of Ride. When Roscoe got his gaze, he jerked his head to the closed door then turned and jogged down the stairs.

Joker dealt with the equipment, pulled off his gloves and glasses, and moved to the office.

He was through and the door was closing on his back when he went solid at the look on Cherry's face.

He took a quick step forward. "Babe, you need me to get Tack?"

"I...uh..." she shook her head, her long, thick, dark red hair brushing her shoulders, and seeing it, it wasn't the first time she gave him proof why she was worth her man literally walking through a hail of bullets for her. "This is about you."

His gut froze as he pushed out, "Carrie?"

"No, honey," she said softly. "*You.*"

"Me what?" he asked curtly.

"Twenty minutes ago, I got a call from *Wilde and Hay*," she told him.

"Say again?" he asked.

"*Wilde and Hay*," she repeated.

"What the fuck is that?"

Her brows drew together. "You don't know *Wilde and Hay*?"

Joker began to get impatient. "Respect, Cherry, but got shit I wanna get done today on my car and Carrie's got the day shift. Means I wanna be at her house when she's there, which means I gotta get shit done."

"*Wilde and Hay* is a magazine, Joker," she informed him.

"Right, and . . . ?" he prompted.

"A very good magazine," she kept on. "Glossy. Respected. They do serious stuff, big-time exposés. They also do in-depth interviews with celebrities. Not the ass-kissing kind. The no-bullshit kind. They get into politics. They do travel spreads. They do reviews of movies, music, TV. They dig into social issues. They use the *best* photographers—"

Joker cut her off, "Babe, not sure why you're tellin' me this."

"They want to do an article on Ride."

Joker stared.

Then he grinned. "Fuckin' awesome."

"Yes, Joke," she said softly, watching him intently. "They said they want to interview the brothers who do the builds but with a focus on the brothers who do the designs. They sent me pictures of the builds they want to feature and asked for the brothers who designed those builds specifically. I just got their email." She reached a hand to her computer. "And these are the builds they want to feature."

She pushed her monitor around and he looked down at it. There was an email open with pictures on it. She put her hand to her mouse and scrolled down.

There were six builds. They were all his.

"In other words, Joke," she said as he watched the images scroll, "they want *you*."

He looked back to her.

"They're sending Henry Gagnon," she kept going. "And before you ask, he's *the freaking best* photographer out there. He does celebrities. He does models. He goes to war-torn nations and he does that. He does *everything*. He had an exhibit at the Denver Art Museum, and I dragged Tack to it and even Tack said the guy was the shit. Because he just is.

And they want him taking pictures of your builds, you building them, and *you*."

"If you're askin', tell 'em yes. It'll be good for Ride," Joker said to her. "But there's more than just me to any build, Cherry. They come, they focus on all we do here."

Her head tipped to the side, "I don't think you—"

She didn't finish because the door to the front opened and they both looked that way to watch Tack walk through.

He smiled at his old lady but then he looked to Joker and came direct to him.

Joker knew by the expression on Tack's face and what came next that Cherry had called her husband with this news.

And what came next was that Tack walked right to him, lifted his hand, gripped Joker at the back of the neck, and yanked him forward.

At this, Joker went still.

He'd seen Tack do that to Rush, back in the day when Rush was a kid and Joker had stood at the fence watching, and he did it still.

He'd also seen Tack give to Rush what he did next.

Tack yanked him forward further and their chests collided, Tack's hand tightened rough on Joker's neck as he wound his arm around and pounded Joker on his back, doing it hard.

But it felt good.

Then Tack fisted his hand in the back of his shirt and held him there as he said low and gravelly in his ear, "I knew it, brothers knew it. We wanted you with us because we wanted *you* with us. But Hop and Boz said straight out, you had the talent to take Ride to the next level. You did, and you didn't fuck around doin' that." He pulled back but didn't let go as he looked Joker in the eyes. "This is good seein' as my woman's baby crazy, and I reckon by the time we're done I'll be forkin' out about twelve college tuitions." He grinned big. "And you're gonna make it so I can afford that."

Joker could say nothing. Taking in the look on Tack's face, gratification, pride, respect, feeling all Tack just gave him, his mind couldn't bring up words.

Luckily, at this juncture, Cherry butted in.

"After Cut turned up the oven when I was cooking brownies and incinerated them *and* the pan they were in, I've decided I don't want another child, because I may not cook often but my husband's good at it and I like shoes, not to have to buy new kitchen items every other week. In other words, since we have our hands full, I'm pushing Shy to get his shit together so he and Tab can essentially give me a baby by having their own. That way, their kid can incinerate brownies and I get to laugh but my pans are safe."

Tack let Joker go to turn to his wife and the look he'd been giving Joker was gone.

Completely.

Now he looked sick.

"Do not say that shit to me again," he ordered.

"What shit?" Cherry asked, looking confused.

"Talkin' to me about my baby girl pushin' out a kid."

"Tack, she's gonna do it," Cherry pointed out.

"Yeah, she is, and I'll have to deal with it when she does. But I do not fuckin' gotta talk about it before it happens," Tack growled.

Cherry smiled huge at him.

Tack turned his pissed off mug Joker's way and said tersely, "Proud a' you, brother. This is gonna be huge for Ride. We had attention, not on this scale. You got us that with your talent. We knew it the minute we saw your drawings that you had it in you to make them real. Your builds are outstanding, Joke, and I'm fuckin' thrilled they're gonna get the attention they deserve."

After that, with a scowl at his woman, he turned and stormed out of the office.

Joker stood unmoving, staring at the door.

"They are," Cherry said quietly, and Joker forced his eyes to her. "They are and you are." She went on. "I've seen a lot of cars and bikes come out of this garage, Joker, and they've always been spectacular. But your stuff is beyond the beyond."

He didn't know what to do with that or all it made him feel on top of all Tack made him feel, so he just said, "Thanks."

"You giving Ride this, you're doing a lot for your brothers," she went on. "Tack does the books, and since you started your builds, income from the garage has risen twenty-seven percent. We always had a waiting list for clients but that was usually six months out. Now it's over a year, so that goodness isn't going to stop, and I suspect that Tack's going to bring garage expansion to the Club table to be discussed soon before that gets out of hand. And that expansion is all about you."

Joker's throat suddenly felt scratchy.

"We do well, all the shops, the garage," she continued quietly. "But everyone likes doing better, especially when that comes with getting more. You give your brothers more, Joker, and their families. You should know that's lost on no one and it's appreciated."

Still not able to come up with anything to say, he just jerked up his chin and muttered, "Thanks again, Cherry. And set it up with that magazine. Whenever they're ready, I'll be here."

"Okay, honey," she replied softly.

Joker nodded to her and took off.

He went back to work liking a fuckuva lot what he was feeling.

He also got it.

It was about what he did, what he loved doing getting recognized. It felt good, that shit coming from out there, outside this garage, outside their world.

It felt better coming from his brothers.

But it was more.

As he worked, he came to the understanding that he would never pay back the people in his life who put him right there. Who gave all they could give to keep him sane and show him there was goodness in this world, which kept him from being buried under the dark.

But they didn't need payback. If you're a good person, you do good things. Simple as that.

But they knew, like Joker now knew, that good built good. So what they gave Joker meant that he'd not lost hold. Didn't give up and become a junkie, a felon, a jackhole banging women on his couch, drinking himself sloppy, or making babies only to fill their lives full of black.

Instead, he was in the position to give back. To his brothers. To Carissa. To Travis.

The good he got from the people who cared about him set him up to return it, maybe not to them, but to people who deserved it.

And that was what it was all about. The meaning of life. Why every person on the planet was there.

They got what they gave and then they gave what they got, and it was the measure of you if you could endure the shit that came with life and still find it in you to focus on the good and put that out there.

He was that man.

And he was glad to be that man.

So he kept working, giving goodness to his brothers until it was time to call it quits and go home to his woman and her boy, where they'd also give him goodness they didn't know they gave just by breathing.

And he would take it.

And give it back.

Carissa

It was late when I got home. I'd had an unusual afternoon shift that Sharon tried not to give me when I had Travis, but she couldn't play favorites, so it happened.

I heard the TV on but saw no Joker in the kitchen so I plopped my purse on the counter, walked through the kitchen, and into the living room.

I stopped dead when I saw Big Petey, Roscoe, and Boz lounged all over my couch, along with Joker.

"Yo, girl," Big Petey said to the TV but lifted the beer bottle in his hand as a greeting to me.

"Carrie," Roscoe also said to the TV with no beer bottle lift.

"Babe, lookin' good," Boz stated, his head turned my way, his grin devilish.

I grinned back at Boz then gave my attention to Joker as his eyes came over the back of the couch.

"Boys are over," he told me unnecessarily. "Travis is down."

"Okay, sweetie," I said, knowing it was past his bedtime, glad he was getting his sleep, but disappointed all the same that I didn't get a cuddle in before he got that way.

Boz turned his head to Joker.

"Sweetie," he muttered.

"Fuck off," Joker replied.

I ignored that since I had a priority task at hand and went about doing it. This meant I walked to Travis's room. The door was closed against the sound of the TV. I was okay with this considering I'd also noted the baby monitor was sitting on the coffee table by Joker's feet.

I checked my son, putting my hand to his chest, feeling his warmth, his steady breathing. Then I lifted my hand to my mouth, touched the tips of my fingers to my lips, then put them to his soft, chubby cheek.

He didn't move. He was out.

Quietly, I left the room and carefully closed the door behind me.

When I got out to the living room/dining area, Joker's eyes were again to me.

"He okay?" he asked.

Gosh, he was so amazing.

"Yeah," I answered. "Can I...um, talk to you?"

His brows drew together, then he looked to the men before he pushed up to his feet.

I took in the guys lounged on my couch, unmoving, eyes glued to the screen, bottles of beers in their hands and scattered over surfaces. There was a burly guy with a pointy beard and a bald head wearing strange glasses on the TV talking while sparks flew in a cement room behind him.

I had no idea what that program was, just that it probably wouldn't interest me. I wasn't into sparks flying.

Then again, who knew? I thought I wasn't into bikers and I was *really* wrong about that.

I also had a feeling I liked, seeing my big couch covered in men drinking beer. I'd picked it hoping one day it would get crawled all over by babies and then lounged all over by babies grown big.

But I'd take bikers.

For now.

I felt Joker get close and I looked to him right before I turned away and walked down the hall.

I went right to my room and Joker followed me.

I took four steps in and turned to see Joker closing the door behind him.

He stayed right in front of the door.

I thought this was strange but I didn't comment on it.

I asked, "Something you should have told me?"

He looked toward the wall on the other side of which was the living room then back to me.

"Shoulda said somethin', Butterfly," he said quietly. "You don't want the boys around, that's cool. I'll go out and—"

I threw out a hand and spoke, interrupting him. "They're welcome here whenever you want them here. Or whenever they want to show up. That's not it."

His head jerked and he asked, "If that's not it then what is it?"

"Something you should have shared yesterday," I pressed.

"Carrie, just spit it out."

"*Wilde and Hay?*"

Joker's expression turned funny.

"Tyra called me," I told him. "She said she got the call yesterday and she told you yesterday."

I waited, he didn't reply, so I kept going.

"She told you yesterday but you didn't mention it to me."

Joker just kept looking funny and doing it not saying anything.

"Sweetheart, that's huge."

He shrugged.

I stared.

"Carson, that's amazing," I kept at him.

"Build cars for a livin', Carrie. Ride's got press before. This isn't out of the ordinary."

"It is," I said softly. "Because this isn't about Ride. According to Ty-Ty, it's about you."

"It's about both."

"It's about you."

We stared at each other. This lasted a while.

To get past it, which would bring me to maybe getting a hello kiss (belatedly), I stated, "You're magnificent, Carson Steele. And if you wanna pass this off as nothing, okay. You're a manly man biker. I have to give that to you. But everyone knows it's incredible. *You're* incredible. So we can know that and you can go about your business. I'll do cartwheels later and then maybe share a bottle of champagne with the old ladies. You don't have to be involved. Now, that's done and I want a hello kiss."

"That, I'll oblige," he muttered, his lips curved up, all this while coming to me and promptly obliging.

When he finished obliging, I had my arms around his shoulders, one hand in his hair, and was pressing myself close.

"Go, commune with your brothers," I ordered a little breathlessly. "I need a snack and then I need to go to bed. I have a day shift tomorrow."

"Get rid of them soon's the show's over," he told me.

"Get rid of them whenever," I murmured, rolling up on my toes to kiss his jaw. I rolled back and caught his eyes. "But kiss me when you come to bed."

He smiled at me with his eyes. "I'll be happy to oblige that too."

I smiled back. "And I'll be happy that you do."

He bent in to touch his mouth to mine before he broke from my hold. Then he claimed me right back with an arm draped around my shoulders which he used to guide me to the door.

I slid my arm along his waist and we walked that way, having to shift sideways to get through the door while connected, but we stayed connected down the hall.

We broke off at the mouth of the hall after he gave my temple a light kiss.

Joker went to the couch.

I went to the kitchen, calling out to ask if anyone needed a fresh brew.

I got four yays. I took four bottles out to the boys and got a soft look from my biker when I did.

After that, I ate some crackers and cheese, washed them down with some flavored fizzy water, and shut down the kitchen. I gave verbal goodnights to the boys.

Joker's was given physically as I bent over the couch and he tipped his head way back so I could give him a brief kiss.

He added running his fingers along my jaw with a finale of a warm look. I memorized that to give it back one day.

I checked on Travis one last time, and when I hit my room, I was suddenly exhausted in a way I knew I was crashing after a long day.

But it was the first time since the time we had the chat about my pregnancy nightshirt that I'd gone to bed without Joker. So it was the first time I went to bed needing a nightgown, seeing as Joker was always in the mood when we hit the bed and he went about disrobing me. After that, I usually had enough in me to pull on panties and pass out.

So I went to my drawers and tiredly fretted as I pawed through my pre-pregnancy nighties.

I picked a stretchy one (for obvious reasons) that had a fullish bottom (also chosen for obvious reasons) and a ruched bodice, empire waist, a tiny row of white lace across the top and hem and it was periwinkle blue.

I put it on and it fit snug at my breasts (not surprising) but otherwise, looking down at myself, it wasn't that bad. Still, I inspected myself in the master bathroom mirror while I brushed my teeth and washed my face.

It would do. And anyway, I would be sleeping so I didn't have to deal with whatever Joker's reaction would be until morning.

I went to bed not thinking about my nightie but thinking about how I liked knowing my boyfriend's buds (who were also my friends) were hanging on my couch watching TV. It felt nice. It felt normal. It felt like something that might fit in my revised dream, which was turning out better than the one I thought I wanted.

I fell asleep thinking that.

I was woken up by Joker's kiss, which included his hand on my hip, feeling my nightie.

Thus I was woken up learning early how Joker felt about the nightie he could feel but not so much see.

And what I learned was that he liked it.

And how I learned that was, when Joker was done showing me how he felt, I fell back into a sated sleep snuggled up with my biker with the nightie on the floor, wearing nothing but panties.

Joker

The next day, Joker was walking through the Compound after taking a shower and changing clothes. Even though Carissa was off, he'd worked that day at the garage because his build was on a deadline. Now, he was done with what he needed to do, showered, and on his way to her.

He had his hand to the front door when his phone rang.

He pulled it out as he pulled open the door and stepped into the Denver sunlight, which meant he had to squint at his phone.

He grinned, took the call, and put the phone to his ear as he pulled his shades out of his hair and put them over his eyes.

"Yo, Lie," he greeted.

"Okay, bud, you can't strut your Carson goodness back into our lives then disappear," Linus said as reply. "Mrs. Heely is pissed. Which means command performance at her place for dinner. Tuesday. And Car, prepare 'cause my brood and you at her place for dinner is a tight fit. But she's not takin' no for an answer. She called Kam and gave her what for about you, which meant my woman gave me what for about you. And even though Kam offered her our kitchen, Mrs. Heely is standin' firm. Her place. I figure this means we're all in for it because she intends to trot the lot of us out to her cronies. She's big on doin' that. Old folk jockey for position, and the best ammo they got is to brag about how many people give a shit about them. So best be on your game 'cause you're gonna get picked over by a bunch of biddies and none a' them are gonna like your hairstyle."

Joker had stopped at his bike and was grinning when he said, "Sorry, Lie. Shit's gone down that I had to focus on. But I'll give you and Mrs. Heely a call if I can make it."

"You didn't hear me, Car," Linus returned. "This is a command performance. There's no *if* about it."

"Gotta talk to my girl and see if she's free."

This bought him several beats of silence before, "Your girl?"

"The shit's that gone down I had to focus on," Joker explained.

"Right," Linus said slowly. "Few weeks ago you rolled your bike to my garage tellin' me you been around awhile and just got your shit sorted to make an approach, but no woman involved in that shit. Now you got one and she's one you'd bring to Kam *and* Mrs. Heely?"

"Yeah," Joker answered easily.

"Uh, son, maybe you don't get this. You don't bring just

any woman to Kam and especially not Mrs. Heely. Those women are gonna pick her over like vultures. Nothin' but the best for the kid they let into their hearts but lost then got back only very recently."

That felt good, but still Joker shared, "Wouldn't bring anything but the best to either of them, brother."

Linus was again quiet before, "You sayin' this is serious?"

"I'm sayin' you meet her, you know I'd be a fool not to make it that way. And, Lie, I'm no fool. So I didn't fuck around makin' it that way."

"Shee-it," Linus pushed out. "You can say that again. It's only been a coupla weeks."

"Not like you, I know I got it good, I don't wait a year to tag it as mine," Joke gave him shit.

"Below the belt, bud," Linus replied, a smile in his voice. "Now I gotta hope like fuck she's off work. This I gotta see."

"Goin' to her now. I'll ask. Text you if I can confirm and I'll get in touch with Mrs. Heely," Joker said.

"Right. Either way, 'spect I'll see you soon."

"You will, Lie. Tell Kam I said hey, and same to your kids."

"You got it. Later, Car."

"Later, Lie."

They disconnected and Joker shoved his phone in his pocket before mounting his bike. He was riding to Carissa when he felt it ring. Riding, he didn't grab it.

He was still riding when he felt it vibrate with a text.

At a red light, he took it out.

The missed call was Carissa.

The text was her too.

I need you home, sweetie.

He didn't like that, the call and then a text and what that might say with all the shit she was swimming through.

But he liked the way she used the word *home*.

He sent a quick text back, *Almost there.*

Then he got his ass there.

He parked in the back and came through the back door to see her in the kitchen, Travis to her hip, her eyes on him, and her expression openly freaked.

He didn't like that either. Not at all.

"Talk to me," he ordered and it came out almost like a bark.

"Okay, I went to that place that Stacy told you to tell me gives good money and doesn't mess you around on used jewelry."

"Knew you were doin' that today, Carrie," he told her, and he did know. He just hoped Stacy was right and they didn't fuck his girl over because he was in the mood to have dinner and relax with his woman and her boy, not go out and teach some jeweler asshole a lesson with his fists.

"Well, before I went, I looked it up on the Internet. Checked to see what I should get, you know, on online auctions and other places, just in case he still tried to undercut me."

"Right," he bit out when she stopped talking.

"And they didn't. They actually gave me better. It's quality stuff and my engagement ring was three and a half carats. The tennis bracelet brought almost as much as the engagement ring. It was a lot, Carson. Far more than I expected. And they don't do commission. He bought them right there." She shook her head. "It's enough to pay off my attorney bill *and* my credit card *and* get Travis some new clothes *and* have some left over to actually start a savings for when I might be able to go to school to be a stylist. I mean, I should have thought of doing this months ago."

"None a' this explains why you look freaked," he pointed out.

"Well, I was excited," she stated, bouncing Travis further up on her hip, which brought Joker's attention to the kid and he saw belatedly that Travis had a ring with a duck head in his hand. The minute he got Joker's attention, though, the ring was on the floor and he reached out to Joker with both arms, twisting to do so.

Carissa contained him but Joker didn't make her do it for long. He strode forward and pulled the boy out of her arms and into his.

Travis reached up and latched onto his lip.

Joker ignored it and lifted his brows to Carissa.

She gave a start, her eyes on her son, and looked to Joker. "I was excited," she repeated.

"Said that," he told her, and when he did, Travis made a noise, clearly enjoying the feel of Joker's lip moving while he was latched on to it.

"So," she went on immediately. "I went to the bank. I made a deposit. Started a savings account. Then I went to my old attorney to settle the bill."

When she stopped and didn't go on, he prompted, "And?"

"And . . . it was paid."

Joker's hold on Travis tightened just as Travis lost interest in his lip, let it go, and started to bang his hand against the base of Joker's throat.

He looked down at him and muttered, "Be with you in a sec, kid."

"Bah, lah, gah," Travis replied.

"Gotta talk to your ma," Joker told him.

"Bah, bah, *dah*!" Travis cried.

"Patience, son," Joker advised.

"Gah!" Travis yelled on a throat slap.

Joker looked back at Carissa.

"Neiland," he guessed quietly.

She nodded her head. "I asked. They confirmed. It wasn't anonymous. He wanted me to know."

Joker put his teeth to the back of his bottom lip, about to clip *fuck* but stopped himself just as Carissa kept talking.

"As you know, Angie said to keep the money he gave me Monday, use it, but keep track of it, what I used it for, and don't go crazy. But this…"

She trailed off and he asked, "You call her about this?"

"Yes, right before I called you. She said it's not my problem if he makes a decision to pay those fees. We didn't request it. It was done by his own choice, so he can't come after us or use it against us. And she thought it was a bit fishy that my old attorney accepted it without informing me, but payment is payment and everyone likes to get paid. Once paid, if he doesn't get what he wants out of that gesture, Aaron can't go after them to get it back. Since the request didn't come from us and we didn't do anything else to lean on him to do it, she also can't see any way he can use it to get to me. But she's wary."

She had a right to be wary.

This was the beginning.

"He's starting his game by tryin' to buy his way back. It's a faulty strategy," he stated. "Straight up, he gave you that debt, Carrie. It's his. Always been his. It's never been yours. He's not finally mannin' up and accepting his responsibility for that fuck-up. He's makin' another play. But that's not on you. He did what he did. Only thing you can do is move on without that liability that wasn't yours in the first place. If it means you breathe easier financially, then good, 'cause you shouldn't have had to take that hit in the first place." He hefted Travis up a couple of inches and finished, "Done."

"You think it's that easy?" she asked.

"Why would it not be?" he asked back.

"Because nothing with him is ever that easy."

Joker finally moved to her, and when he got there, he curled his hand around the side of her neck and bent close.

"You got two choices," he began. "You can worry about this or you can let it be done. He's got more to throw at you, we both know that. But no point in you makin' something easy into somethin' hard just by frettin' about it bein' easy."

"That makes sense," she muttered, her eyes drifting to her boy as her hand did the same to come up and rest on Travis's back.

"Butterfly," Joker called and got her attention. "He wants in. He's startin' that by tryin' to make you think he's sorry. I can see that play. That gets in there, he can build on that."

"He won't build on that," she returned sharply.

Joker grinned.

She was his girl, straight up, no bullshit, and she wanted to make sure he knew it, even with her ex knocking on her door.

He liked it, but he was surprised as fuck he didn't need it.

He knew he was in there. He knew why. He knew that was his place to be. Because he knew he deserved to be there.

And this was why he figured he didn't lose it with her ex-jackhole. From the beginning, the way she was with her ex and the way she was with Joker, it wasn't a struggle. It was actually *easy* to check it.

Tack had been right.

Knowing he'd end the day with his cock buried inside her, go to sleep with her weight resting against him, knowing she'd given him that just as he'd earned it, he could keep his cool, mainly because he didn't want to jack it up by doing something stupid and lose any of that.

Not to mention, Carissa had demonstrated she had sass

and not only didn't take his shit but was capable of shoving it right back.

That didn't mean the guy wasn't irritating as fuck and Joker wasn't concerned about what that asshole intended to put his Carrie through. It just meant Joker didn't make matters worse for his girl by losing his shit.

He didn't get into any of that with her.

He said, "Just statin' his play."

"I paid the attorneys one hundred and fifty dollars a month. I couldn't afford it, but that's the payment plan they would accept. That's gonna mean a lot to me," she declared. "And what stinks is, I'll think of him when I'm paying my bills every month and don't have to pay that."

"You'll think of him for a month, then you'll quit doin' it."

"He'll make me think of him other ways," she said.

"Only in ways that irritate the crap outta you."

"This is true," she murmured, her eyes again sliding to her boy.

"Baby," he called and she looked back to him. "It's done. You got the power to believe that. So make it done."

"Okay, I'll make that done because I'm hungry and I've cooked tonight and it's good stuff. But one more thing."

"What?" he asked.

"Big Petey won't accept money."

Joker dropped his hand and leaned back. "Carrie, I told you—"

"I know what you said but that's unacceptable. He's refused now *three times*. So when he put his wallet on the counter yesterday, I put three hundred dollars in it. Today, when I went into the cupboard for some food for Travis, those bills were shoved between the jars."

Joker started laughing.

"It's not funny," she snapped.

"It is," he replied, still laughing.

"It is *not*," she returned.

He quit laughing (slowly) and gave it to her.

"Thirty years or less, Butterfly, you'll be at a time in your life when your house is empty and you got time on your hands you wanna fill with what you like doin'. This boy," he hefted up Travis again, "might be married, have kids, maybe need his ma. You step in, regular or just so he can take his woman out for a Blizzard, you gonna make him pay?"

Her face told him his point was made but she still retorted, "Big Petey isn't my father."

"Big Petey is everyone's father," Joker shot back. "He likes it like that. He's lived a long time to build that respect. He's earned it and he should get it. Give it to him."

She again told him without words he got in there but that didn't mean she didn't push it.

"He barely knows me."

"Love and care don't come with time. They just come. My old neighbor I told you about, Linus, took one look at me and knew I needed a good man in my life. He didn't step in after he spent years gettin' to know me. The minute he had my attention, he asked me over to watch a game. I needed that so much, I didn't make him wait years before I went over and watched that game. Growin' up, I had two safe places. His house and any time I was with another neighbor a' mine, Mrs. Heely. And she didn't give what she had to give to me after takin' years to get to know me either."

He bent in again, holding her son, touching her only with his forehead to hers, and he finished.

"I know you give good. And I know you like how it feels when you give it. You were in his position to do good, you'd jump at it. Put your feet in his shoes. Feel what he feels when he gives to you. Then let Pete have this."

She held his eyes from up close and he saw hers get bright.

Travis slapped his cheek.

He watched her eyes smile.

"Okay, sweetie," she whispered.

He bent in to kiss her and got another smack from Travis, so he made it unfortunately brief.

When he pulled away, he asked, "What're you gonna feed me?"

She grinned. "Carnitas."

With the drama over, he realized he could smell it. He also realized she hadn't cooked anything for him but that pie. But from his experience of the pie, and what he could smell, he knew she was about to give him something else that was going to make him fall more in love with her.

"You do Travis, I'll sort our dinner," she ordered.

"Gotcha," he muttered, moving to the cupboard with the baby food, fighting back a grin just thinking of Pete putting the money there.

"Gah, duh, buh, buh, buh, muh!" Travis placed his order when Joker opened the cupboard.

"Carson?" she called.

He twisted her way.

Then he stilled.

She said nothing. Just looked at him.

But the softness of her features. The warmth in her eyes. The way she held her body. She didn't need to say anything.

That said it all.

Then her face got softer, her eyes warmer, and she pursed her lips slightly, making no noise, but blowing him a kiss.

After that she turned away.

Joker turned back to the cupboard and his voice was rougher than normal when he asked Travis, "What do you think, boy? Carrots?"

"Buh nuh," Travis declined, and Joker looked at him to see him staring into the cupboard with serious baby face.

Joker smiled.

Then, his chest light, precious held in his arm, his boots on the floor of a kitchen in a house owned by good people and occupied by his dream, he picked sweet potato and beef.

Carissa

That Sunday, I stood in Joker's room at the Compound in my boyfriend jeans, Converse, and the Ride tee I'd splurged on as a no-more-attorney's-fee celebration (Speck, at the cash register in the store, tried to give it to me for free, I refused, we made a deal at forty percent off so it was a very *small* splurge).

I was staring around at the mess that had accumulated in what I'd thought was a short period of time since I last cleaned.

Travis was crawling through the debris, which was mostly dirty clothes, and thankfully no choking hazards like coins, having the time of his life.

We'd been headed to lunch, but on the way Joker had to stop to have a quick meeting with his brothers.

So there I was, facing what might not have been as colossal as the first challenge, but it was still a mess.

My body jerked when Joker surprisingly rounded the door much earlier than I expected, announcing, "Meet's done, Butterfly."

"That didn't take long," I noted.

"It was important, but there wasn't much to say," he replied, not coming to me, going straight to Travis, whereupon I watched him bend deep and gently pull the sock Travis was about to shove in his mouth out of his baby fist. "We don't suck on socks, kid, dirty or otherwise."

Travis, sitting on his booty, slammed his fists into his thighs and yelled, "Bah, jah, kah, lah!"

"Whatever," Joker returned, grabbed him and lifted him up.

Travis squealed in protest, preferring the wonders of Joker's floor to what I thought was far more wondrous, being in his arms.

"You wanna go?" he asked me.

"Do you ever do laundry?" I asked him.

"Not until I have to," he told me.

"Has it occurred to you that you can dump your clothes on my floor and the miracle of Tyra's washing machine will get them clean when *I* do laundry, something that happens regularly?"

The air in the room went electric, but I didn't understand it.

"Joker?" I called when he stood there, holding a struggling Travis, who wanted to be back on the floor. "Carson," I said when he still didn't reply.

Joker shook his head shortly, shaking himself out of his strange stupor.

Then he said, "Carrie, told you you don't have to do payback like that."

"I do laundry, Joker. I'm a woman. I like clean clothes," I returned. "I'm also a mother who likes her son to be in clean clothes. In other words, it's no skin off my nose my biker's jeans and tees are in a load with the rest of our stuff."

His voice was oddly gentle when he stated, "Baby, I see you're not gettin' this is a leap in where we're headin', and as much as I like that leap, I'm not takin' it without you gettin' it."

"Getting what?"

"Me droppin' my clothes on your floor."

"I would prefer the hamper," I replied. "But I'll take the floor if I don't have to haul your stuff from here to home or make a special trip and do it in the machines here."

"Carrie, you're still not getting it," he pushed carefully.

"What?" I asked impatiently.

"A man and woman are in a certain place, he drops his clothes on her floor."

I threw my hands in the air. "Well, obviously. But I'm seeing *you* don't get it. A woman has to be in a certain place with a man to let him feed her baby and claim him every time he's even close. So I'm there. A handsome biker is the only being that stops to help me with my tire in rush hour, congested traffic on I-25, that biker being all that's *you*, I got there quickly. It's you lagging behind, leaving your dirty clothes in the wrong building."

The air started zapping when he whispered, "Are you seriously asking me to move in with you?"

My head jerked to the side in surprise.

He was usually so quick.

"Do I have to ask? I mean," I tossed a hand to the bed, "when's the last time you slept here?"

He didn't answer.

I kept at him. "Am I yours?"

"Fu..." He clenched his teeth and forced out, "Yes."

"So what am I not getting?" I asked.

"It's fast," he pointed out.

"Okay, it is," I agreed. "But is it wrong?"

He stared at me.

Then he said, "No."

"If it freaks you out, we won't make it official," I offered. "We can make it official when you take me on a date where

I can wear my fabulous new top I haven't been able to wear since Elvira bought it for me. But we can start by you leaving your laundry where it's convenient *for me*."

Joker kept staring at me.

"So should we get a trash bag or do you have a duffel or something?" I prompted.

He didn't move.

"Joker," I called.

That's when he did it.

It.

It being putting his hand up to cover the side of Travis's head and pressing the other side into his chest, before saying, "Shits me how bad I wanna fuck you right now, seein' as I can't do it."

It was my turn to say nothing.

Because part of *it* was the fact that I just then noticed, since the meeting with Angie, he'd cursed, but only in front of me.

Never in front of Travis.

Except right then, when Travis would have no idea what he said, but because I didn't want it, Joker made it so he couldn't hear it anyway.

Then more of *it* happened right there in front of me.

Travis shrieked, pushed away, grabbed Joker's thumb, shoved it in his mouth, and bit down. He was a baby so everything went into his mouth. But he'd been teething for a while and had one coming in, so that bite and his current stubbornness was about that. And I knew from experience it didn't feel all that great.

Joker didn't even wince.

And taking that in, I knew more of *it* was knowing Joker was going to be an excellent father, and I knew this because he already was one. He might not share blood with my boy and Travis already had a dad.

But now he had two.

Another part of *it* was what he said giving me a shiver, making me want what he wanted in a way I wanted it too, right there, right then. And I loved that he wanted it. I loved that my handsome, manly man biker wanted me, just as I was, making me feel wantable.

And the last part of that *it* was that leaving his laundry for me, which meant leaving his clothes at my house, meant a great deal to him. He wanted that. And he showed me he did.

Finally I pulled it together.

"Is there anyone out there to watch Travis for half an hour?" I asked and it came out breathy.

"Sunday plans. All a' them. They scattered," Joker answered and it came out rough.

"Darn," I whispered.

"Later," he said and it was a promise. I could tell by the look on his face that made me shiver again.

"Okay." I was still whispering.

"Naughty," he said softly.

Another shiver. A bigger one. And my legs started shaking.

"Okay," I repeated breathily.

"Now, lunch."

I nodded.

"After I feed you, we'll come back and get my laundry."

Another nod, but this time I did it with the curious feeling of being utterly delighted at the thought of having more laundry.

He lifted his hand my way. "Come here, Butterfly."

I went there.

I took his hand.

He gripped mine tight.

Then he walked us out of his room to his truck, where he put my son in his car seat in the back.

He took us to lunch.

And later, after we went back and collected his laundry in a duffel (as well as a plastic bag), while Travis had his afternoon nap, Joker made good on his promise.

We had a quiet, necessarily muffled but spectacular laundry celebration on my couch.

And it was naughty.

CHAPTER EIGHTEEN

Waver

Joker

THE NEXT EVENING, Joker sat in his truck, idling at the curb in front of a huge-ass house that screamed *I'm fucking loaded*.

He did this watching Carissa walk up the path to the home she once shared with her ex-jackhole, carrying her kid and his diaper bag.

He'd parked visible and he'd done it so he could watch and be seen.

Not surprisingly, the jackhole opened the door.

Also not surprisingly, even after Carissa gave her boy kisses and cuddles and handed him and the bag over, her jackhole kept her engaged in conversation.

Further not surprisingly, he saw the jackhole clock him the minute the man had opened the door.

As this went on, Joker didn't honk. He didn't get out of the truck, round it, and make his presence known more aggressively by leaning against it and watching. Or more aggressive than that, walking up to the house.

He waited.

It cost him.

But Carissa was who she was, where she was, with that jackhole, and where she was with Joker.

So as he knew she'd do, when she'd had enough, she shut it down and turned her back, walking away while the guy was still talking.

Joker looked to the steering wheel and fought back a grin.

He heard the door open and turned his head to watch her get in.

The second her door was closed and she reached for the belt, he didn't fuck around getting them on the road.

He heard the click and stopped crawling, putting on the gas as he asked, "You okay?"

"Every time, hate that." She paused and it was lower when she repeated, "*Hate* it."

He could see that, he didn't like it much either.

"What can I give you, Butterfly?" he asked quietly.

She didn't answer.

He glanced at her. "Want dinner?"

"Not hungry," she mumbled.

"Wanna talk?" he offered.

"Nothing to talk about," she said.

"He give you shit?" Joker asked.

"Just asked a bunch of stuff about Travis. How our week went. He's never asked before, so it isn't hard to read he doesn't really care now. It's just the game he's playing."

"He talk about paying the attorney?"

"No, though he did look like he expected me to say something. But I'm not gonna say thanks for him taking care of a debt he gave me."

Oh yeah, the guy expected her to say something. And it was a good play she didn't give him what he wanted.

"You want, next time you stay in the truck, I'll take Trav up to the door," Joker offered.

"I might want," she said quietly, and he glanced at her again to see she was looking out the side window.

"You up for tomorrow night?" he asked, looking back at the road and hoping a subject change might help.

But even as he hoped, he knew this sucked. He had her while her kid wasn't around and she was Carissa. She was his girl. It was good to the point it was awesome.

But having her when her kid was around was something else. She was Carissa, his girl, his girl with both her boys with her, and that made her so happy it wasn't good. It was spectacular.

He could tell she'd turned to face him when she asked, "Dinner with the people who made your life bearable when you were with your dad?"

"Yeah," he answered.

"Absolutely," she declared resolutely.

He glanced at her again then back to the road before he asked carefully, "Nervous?"

"No. I give good girlfriend. Aaron's folks always loved me. Until he kicked me out, that is."

He bit back laughter, not questioning the fact she gave good girlfriend since he was well acquainted with that, but he still warned, "Mrs. Heely lost her boy. He was in the military. Died servin'. Then she unofficially adopted me. I've never tested it, but thinkin' she might be protective."

"Good," she stated.

"And picky," he went on.

"She should be. You deserve the best."

He grinned at the road, muttering, "Lucky I got that."

That was when he felt her fingers curl around his thigh.

He switched hands on the steering wheel and pulled her fingers from his thigh by wrapping his around hers. Then he rested them there, giving them a squeeze.

"A week, we'll have him back," he said softly.

"A week, we will," she replied the same way.

They fell silent as he drove them home.

They remained mostly silent when they got home, reheated leftover carnitas, and ate them camped out on the couch.

Joker did this, giving Carissa time to deal with losing her boy. He didn't give her space, because she made it clear she didn't want that, sticking close, being her usual touchy with him, but he gave her space in her head.

He took that time to be in his own head.

He'd shifted his patrol every time he was up since she gave herself to him. Two weeks, he was with her every night all night.

This wasn't a problem. Without a woman or kids in his life, he'd taken patrol for his brothers so often, he had enough markers to be with her a month and still have some to spare.

But he needed to get back on the street.

Tack wanted the Club to claim more territory and the Club had agreed. They'd pushed and they got the same action, just more of it, warning dealers and hookers off their expanded patch.

It had gone easy, too easy. The boys were suspicious. No one was saying anything, and Benito Valenzuela hadn't struck back, but Joker needed to get on the street. He needed to get the feel of it. Talk to his sources. Get his presence out there. Be one with his brothers and show that to those who should see it.

Carissa didn't know he did patrol, and he'd have to get into that with her soon. He'd give her that night because she needed it. He'd give himself the next night because it was a big night for him, Carissa, Linus, Mrs. Heely.

But Wednesday, his ass had to be on the street.

So they had to have that conversation.

Not then.

Just soon.

On this thought, he decided he needed another beer. Their plates were on the coffee table, so he also decided they should be in the sink.

He was about to see to that when Carissa moved, suddenly swinging over to straddle him.

He tipped his head back, putting his hands to her hips as he looked to her eyes to see them on his tee.

"Baby?" he whispered.

She lifted her gaze to his. "Need you."

There was something in her tone. Something he didn't like. It was the same thing she gave him with her words and the look on her face.

It was need.

But what she needed...no, *why* she needed it, right then, suddenly swinging astride him, that tone in her voice, the look on her face troubled him.

Regardless, she needed it, so he was going to give it to her.

He slid his hands up her sides and whispered, "Take what you need."

She took him up on his offer.

But she didn't kiss him.

She latched on to his tee and pulled it up. He lifted his arms for her and she tugged it free, tossing it behind the couch.

Then she went in.

Not to his mouth.

To his neck.

She spent time there then curved her back to give the same to his chest.

His nipples.

Down, he opened his legs as she slid off his lap onto her knees on the floor.

Fuck.

Fuck.

She was going to suck him off.

She hadn't done that yet, and just the thought of watching her honey curls spread around his crotch as she worked him with her mouth made his cock, already stiff with what she'd been giving him, throb.

He wanted that.

But she hadn't gone there. Not yet. He got her loose and gave her good but he did all the work.

This didn't bother him. He liked it. Got off on it. Got off on her getting off on it.

But even as he wanted it, her giving this to him now didn't sit right.

She slid her lips across the waistband of his jeans and his voice was thick when he asked, "You takin' what you need, Butterfly, or givin' me what you think I need?"

She tilted her head back, fingers to his fly, and he bit his lip as the pulse in his cock pulled up his balls with just one look at her face.

She was in the zone.

Totally.

"I need to give you what you need," she whispered.

"Baby, let me give that to you," he whispered back as she released button two.

She shook her head. "Not this time, sweetheart."

She couldn't miss he gave it all but still, it felt good knowing she didn't.

"Carrie—"

Another button then, "You wanna give that to me, let me."

She wanted it, he'd be insane not to let her have it.

"Okay, baby, not gonna stop you."

She smiled. It was soft and barely there but it did something to her eyes that made his entire body clench.

Then she dropped her head, finished with his fly and dug her fingers in at the sides of his jeans to yank them down.

His dick flew free and he heard her swift, hot intake of breath before she went for it.

Not leading into it, like she'd been starved of it, she grabbed hold, positioned him, and took him deep into her wet, hot mouth.

Jesus.

Fuck.

Joker slid down the couch as his head automatically dropped back and he tightened his body against rearing up, taking over, fucking her mouth, which felt so goddamned sweet.

Then she blew him, and Jesus, no holding back, she sucked hard, she pumped with her hand harder, she took him deep. If she needed a break, she gave it licking, rolling, stroking with her fist.

She could be klutzy. She could get so excited she bumped, slammed, scratched, bit, moved one way when he wanted her to go the other. It was cute. It was a turn on. It was her.

But she fucking *rocked* at giving head.

"Fuck, *Carrie,*" he groaned, so far gone he almost didn't have it in him to warn her she was about to swallow, when he lost her.

That was when she went from giving him good to giving him phenomenal.

"Condom, sweetie," she whispered, her face flushed, her eyes gone, her movements hurried.

He did as she asked, reaching to his pocket for his wallet, not tearing his eyes from her as she took her feet and ripped her clothes off. Right in front of him. Standing between his legs.

Her eyes were hot and hungry on his cock as he rolled

the condom on and he barely got it to the root before she climbed on.

"Need it," she begged, rolling her hips, and he gave her what she wanted, holding his dick for her to take.

She found the tip and drove down.

Joker clasped her at the waist as she arched powerfully, her head dropping back, giving him hair, jaw, tits, belly, pussy.

Fuck.

Gorgeous.

"Ride me, baby," he groaned.

She righted her head and instantly wrapped her arms tight around his shoulders, holding on as she moved, taking him fast and deep, and as usual, vocal. Giving him the whimpers. The mews. The moans. The soft cries. Driving him to the edge.

Her temple pressed to his, she gave him her noises right in his ear as he roamed her skin with his hands. Cupping one breast, he tweaked the nipple, and just with that, she bit his earlobe and her cunt seized his dick.

Fuck, he was done.

His control snapped. He pulled her off his cock and planted her on her knees beside him in the seat, facing the back of the couch.

"No! Joker, don't stop."

He didn't. He rolled to his knees behind her. His hand wrapped around his dick, he slid the tip through her wet, found her, and drove up.

She held on to the back of the couch and angled her ass higher.

His hot little piece.

Christ.

"There you go, Butterfly," he grunted, taking her, all of her, his hands moving on her, tweaking her tits, pulling on her nipples, rolling them, moving over her belly, down, one went in and he circled her clit.

"Don't stop," she pleaded, moving with him, hair bouncing and brushing his face as he kept his chin to her neck and watched her tits bounce too as he pounded her.

Fuck.

"Won't stop," he groaned.

"Don't stop, baby, please," she whimpered, taking a hand from the couch, twisting her arm and cupping the back of his head with it, holding strong.

He touched his tongue to her neck before he whispered, "Won't stop, Carrie. Give you what you need. Take it, Butterfly."

She took it, taking his fucking as she rode his dick through it, giving it to herself.

She twisted her head and he had her eyes, knowing she was nearly there with one look.

"Sweetie," she breathed.

He took her mouth.

When he thrust his tongue inside and tasted her, her frame went still as she came, her fingers fisting in his hair, her moan driving down his throat, her body moving only because he didn't stop fucking her because he couldn't.

And he didn't. He kissed her. He fucked her. He pulled at her tit and rolled her clit until her whimpers again filled his mouth, became cries and she lost it again, jolting in his arms violently as she broke the kiss, latched hard on his lower lip with her teeth before she let it go and moaned, "*Carson.*"

That was when he drove deep and let go, and Christ, it was so goddamned magnificent, he sank his teeth into her shoulder and instead of groaning, he sucked in and did it hard before he sank his teeth in harder.

"*Yes*," she whispered, and through his orgasm he vaguely sensed she was still coming as she took his mark and her body shuddered in his hold.

He held her until it left them both and he kept hold of her after it was gone.

Then he slid out, pulling her off the couch with him so they were both on their feet. He held her steady even as he turned her to face him and hitched up his jeans with one hand as he took her into his other arm.

He bent his head to kiss her parted lips, his eyes open and staring into her hazy ones. Seeing that haze, his lips were smiling when they brushed hers.

"Stay here, be back," he muttered, waited for her dreamy nod and he smiled again when he let her go and quickly walked around the couch.

He bent to nab his shirt, lifted up, and it sucked when he saw her standing there, still fuzzy, her face soft and unfocused from her double orgasm, her beautiful body on show, and he was all the way around the back of the couch and had to do what he had to do.

But it was what she needed so he called, "Butterfly."

She focused on him and he tossed her his shirt.

Just like Carrie, she bobbled it and it dropped to the couch but she caught it up and looked to him.

"Thanks, sweetie."

He grinned then when she started to bunch up his tee to put it on, he went to the bathroom to take care of business.

He came back out and didn't delay in claiming her and getting her where he wanted her for what he decided between fucking and bathroom needed to happen next.

Which meant he got her in his tee on her back on the couch with him on top. Then he reached out to the remote and switched off the TV.

After that, he planted his forearms in the cushions and framed her head in his hands.

"First up, you on the Pill?" he began.

She blinked then shook her head. "No."

"Why?"

"Well, uh...I didn't need it."

"Got dick in your bed that likes your pussy so that's past tense," he pointed out the very obvious then suggested what was really a demand, "Let's get on that."

"It's a co-pay," she said quietly.

"Say again?" he asked.

"I have insurance. Aaron insures Travis so it's not that bad but I picked the plan that costs me the least and any prescription has a pretty hefty co-pay so—"

"Carrie, I'd offer to pay but that would mess with you so just sayin', no attorney's fees means you can probably take on a co-pay. Then your man can get tested. I come up clean then I can take you with nothin' in between."

Her eyes grew wide and she whispered, "Oh."

She wanted that.

"So let's get on that, yeah?" he demanded on a request.

She nodded.

"Right, how about you do that without delay," he said.

Her mouth quirked and she nodded again.

That was done.

Next.

"Okay, second," he started. "I hesitate to bring him up after the hot, sweet piece of ass you just offered up to me, how much I liked it, and that ass being bare right now and all you're wearin' is my tee, and I like that too, but did your ex ever take you there?"

"Take me..." she hesitated, her head tilting on the cushion, "where?"

"There, Carrie, *there*," Joker replied. "He go the distance? Make you come?"

He watched her expression go guarded even as pink slid into her cheeks, but pure Carissa, she still gave it to him.

"Sometimes, after, he'd give me the time."

Fucking shit.

"Not during?"

"I didn't...I wasn't..." she swallowed. "You're better."

"No shit," he returned. "But not once?"

She slid her hand up his back to between his shoulder blades. "What I mean is, you're better with me. You, well... bring it out in me."

He shook his head. "No, Carissa, you got it and you let it loose and give it to me. You had it with him. He just didn't take care of that. Some guys are selfish and they're all about their dicks. Trust me, you are a seriously hot fuck. It takes almost no effort at all to read that and roll with it. The fact that motherfucker didn't even try to make that effort pisses me off."

She looked confused.

Adorably confused.

But he was pissed at her fucking ex, so seeing it, he found there was one time when her being adorable didn't cut through his anger.

"I would...well, sweetheart, wouldn't you actually *like* that you give me something he didn't?" she asked.

"No, because it means you didn't have it, for fuckin' years, which sucks for you, and I don't like anything that sucks for you. Not to mention you keep beggin' me not to stop, when no way I would until I got you there."

Her face closed down and her voice was whipped when she said, "I'll quit doing that."

She took that wrong, so he pressed into the side of her head with one hand.

"No, Carrie. You do what comes natural. Not complainin' that you beg 'cause you want me to keep at you. That's hot too. Any man would want you naked, wet, panting, and begging for more. They'd be insane not to. That's my point. Any man would be insane not to, and if they're any man at all, they got that, they give it and not get off and *sometimes* give it back after. That shit's fucked. But in the now, I gotta know what I got on my hands. I thought I understood where that came from but now it's certain. And it pisses me off."

She started stroking his spine as she noted cautiously, "I think we both understand that Aaron wasn't quite all that in a lot of ways."

"Well, that one's important," he returned. "Then again, all of the ways you can take care of your woman are. He just didn't do dick about any of them."

He felt her body tighten then loosen almost immediately under him but he didn't really register it.

He was focused.

And they had one more thing to go over.

"Now, Butterfly, get it right now I'm good anytime you want me to fuck your cares away. But after I give you my dick, you gotta give me whatever it is you wanted me to fuck away. An orgasm is a very good thing. Two of them are better. But they'll never clear what's fuckin' up your head."

She stared into his eyes with easy-to-read shock that he'd cottoned on to that before her gaze slid to the side, then to his chin, and finally back to his when she said, "I want this to last."

What the fuck?

"I ain't goin' anywhere," he growled.

She wrapped both arms around him and held tight.

"I know, sweetie. That's not what I mean."

"What do you mean?"

"I mean he's being nice to me. Giving me money. Showing at the door to take Travis. And you were only around to see the results of the last time he messed with me. I just started to get to the other side of that and now he's changing tactics and I...I don't..." She shook her head. "I don't want to go through it again."

There it was.

"And I don't want to drag you through it with me," she finished.

And there it all was.

"I'll repeat, Carissa, I'm not goin' anywhere."

"We're new," she told him.

"We're solid," he told her.

"I...you're awesome." Her voice suddenly was pitched louder. "Me? My messes? My baggage? My son? You took it all on. Men don't do that. When will it be enough?"

He instantly realized his mistake.

No more head space for Carissa.

"Jesus, baby, where did this shit come from?" he asked.

"I didn't used to have any baggage, and still the man I turned my son over to a couple of hours ago had enough and got rid of me."

"That's where it comes from," he muttered.

"Seeing him," she kept going, "it reminds me that he got rid of me. Didn't think about it. Threw me away. And that was devastating. I honestly didn't know if I'd survive it. At the time. But I'd been with him a long time and the blinders were pulled off. I had a baby in my belly, which made it worse. And I had nothing but a lot of furniture and a settlement that was such a joke, it's not funny. I was just too young and stupid and scared not to know it was just that. So that was that. But what I have with you, if the same happened, what would I do? What would Travis do? I lost a bad husband that I'd eventually figure out was bad and maybe down the road would have wanted to lose. But that's never going to happen with you."

"No, it fucking isn't."

Her chin jerked back at his words.

Or maybe it was his tone.

He didn't give a fuck what it was. He wasn't done talking.

"I get you see him, and with him fuckin' with your head, this all surfaces, and I get that'll fuck with you. But, Carissa, I am not him."

"Of course," she whispered.

"I want your pussy free and open to me. I wanna come inside you so you actually got my cum inside you and I want that in a way I know I'm gonna keep wantin' that. No way in fuck I'd want that, take it, and fuck someone else too. That shit isn't happening. You're it for me. I thought I made that clear."

"Well . . . you did."

She gave him that.

He still wasn't done talking.

"Man like me is not gonna live without pussy, Carrie. So I want yours exclusive, and long term that means I want you both those ways and I don't want you just because I wanna fuck you. *I want you.* Thought I made that clear too."

"Uh . . . well, you did."

"Then let that other shit go."

"I . . . okay." She held his eyes and asked hesitantly, "Are you, um . . . angry with me?"

"No, I'm pissed at him for fuckin' with your head so you're not lyin' under me in my tee at peace with the knowledge that you're the whole package. Hot piece of ass. Totally fuckin' cute. An absolute goofball. Sweet. Kind. Funny. Stubborn. Sassy. The best mom there could be. The kind of package guys would give their dicks to keep right," he pressed into her, "*here*."

"Oh," she whispered.

"And I'd prefer to have easy with you as often as I can get it, but I'm thinkin' I got work to do to get you to that place and he gave me that but most of all he gave *you* that and like I said, that pisses me off."

"Um...well, just to say, your colorful way of sharing all this has been quite educational in that arena."

"So by that you mean I got through?"

Her head again tipped to the side just as her eyes lit.

"Well, you *are* Carson Steele, the boy every girl crushed on in high school. And you *are* Joker, the Chaos member who *Wilde and Hay* think is an automotive design genius. And you *are* lying on me, declaring your devotion to my... um, special parts after making me climax *twice*. So I think I'm pretty happy lying beneath you in your tee because if you like my whole package, just to say, I like your whole package a whole lot more."

Finally, Joker relaxed and started chuckling.

She kept going.

"So yes, I'd say with all that, you got through."

"Good," he muttered, still laughing.

She took a hand from his back to put it on his cheek and she slid her thumb across his heavy stubble but did it holding his eyes.

"I'll survive whatever he has in store," she said quietly. "But you may have to bear with me."

That made Joker stop laughing.

"I'll bear with you, Carrie, but while I do it, you're gonna have to accept the honesty."

And finally for her, with that, she smiled. "I like your honesty."

"Good," he muttered again.

"I also like couch sex," she declared.

"Got that yesterday when I rode you here and you got off for me."

She kept smiling.

It started to die as she lifted her head and touched her mouth to his before she dropped it back to the cushion. Her face was dead serious.

"I'm still falling in love with you, Carson."

Fucking brilliant.

"Same here, Butterfly."

She gave him what he needed with her eyes.

So he gave her what she needed by taking her mouth.

They made out. They cuddled. They felt each other up. They whispered about important things, like Linus and Mrs. Heely and her dad and gramma. They did it a long time and through all that, he got her to peace.

And putting their plates in the sink to soak was the last thing he did before joining her in bed, where Carissa fell asleep against him wearing his tee.

*   *   *

His phone on the nightstand rang and Joker opened his eyes.

Carissa was pressing against him, stretching and lifting her head as he reached out and nabbed it.

He looked at the display, saw who was calling as well as the time, and he tensed and took the call. "Yeah?"

"Sorry, brother, know you're in Carrie's bed so fucks me to say this, Nightingale found Heidi," Tack told him. "But not the Nightingale you put on it. Hank."

Lee's brother.

A cop.

Shit.

He had a feeling this was not good.

"Joke, hate sayin' this more, but what was found was ugly. I gotta call all the brothers in."

"Where?" he grunted.

Tack gave him the address and finished with, "Mount up."

"You got it," Joker replied, disconnected, and turned to his girl.

"Is everything okay?" she asked immediately.

"Club business, Carrie, gotta go," he told her.

Through the shadows she looked beyond him to the alarm clock.

"Club business at two thirty in the morning?" she asked.

"I gotta go," he repeated. "I find out what's happening, when I get back, I'll explain."

She pushed up to her forearm. "Is someone hurt?"

"No," he lied. "Not in the Club," he gave her the truth. "But I don't think it's good, and I gotta go."

"I...um...okay, sweetie."

It was hesitant but he had to take it, so he took it by leaning in to give her a quick kiss.

Then he rolled out of bed.

He was on his bike and at the address Tack gave him in thirty-five minutes. But Tack could have given him the vicinity and he'd have been able to find it. There were cop cars all around, lights flashing, crime scene tape cordoning off the alley, and bystanders even though it was the dead of night. That much police activity, they crawled out of bed or stopped on the road to find out what was happening.

Joker rode to the line of bikes, parked his, and saw his brothers huddling on the sidewalk beyond the thin line of bystanders and police tape. Tack was there and had already been joined by Hop, Shy, Boz, High, Roscoe, and Snapper.

Lee Nightingale and his right-hand man, Luke Stark, were with them.

And last, Hawk Delgado, Mitch Lawson, and Brock "Slim" Lucas were there too.

In other words, essentially every badass in Denver, outside the rest of Lee's team, the rest of Hawk's team, the rest of the Chaos brothers, and Knight Sebring and his crew. Joker wasn't surprised to see Knight wasn't there, since Knight was not on the right side of the law or even straddling the line like Chaos, Nightingale, and Delgado.

But with what Knight did as a side business and what Joker suspected he was about to learn, Knight Sebring would get interested.

And if he did, this shit that Joker knew in his gut just got messy would blow sky high.

Joker approached the large group of men watching Tack.

But when they adjusted to allow him in the circle, it was Lee who spoke.

"Sorry, Joke, Hank caught the case. He knew I was on it for you so he could give me a heads-up if he heard anything. He heard something and called me."

"Heidi bought it," Joker guessed.

"Yeah," Lee confirmed.

"Joke, brother," Tack called him, and Joker looked to him. "There's a reason the brothers are here. You need to see. But before you go behind the tape, you need to get your shit tight."

"You said it's ugly," Joker said.

"This kinda thing is never pretty," Tack replied quietly. "But this is worse."

"Valenzuela?" Joker asked.

"Absolutely," High growled, and it was a pissed-off growl that was beyond Valenzuela making a move and doing it using a woman.

So Joker knew he wasn't going to see ugly.

He was going to see *ugly*.

He looked to Tack. "Show me."

Tack nodded and turned to Lee, but Luke Stark had already peeled off and was standing at the tape with Lee's brother, Hank.

Tack and Joker moved that way, and after chin lifts, Hank pulled up the tape. Joker and Tack ducked under. Hank dropped the tape and started walking. Joker and Tack followed.

"Anonymous nine-one-one called her in," Hank muttered. "Probably a junkie usin' this alley for his fix or to hook up to buy." He stopped and looked to Joker. "You good?"

No. He wasn't. He couldn't say he liked Heidi, but he could say he didn't want whatever happened to her to happen to her.

"I'm good," he answered.

Hank nodded and kept walking.

Cops were milling around, taking pictures, putting markers on the asphalt, writing crap down, huddling, and conversing.

They finally got to her.

She'd been covered.

"Do me a favor, yeah?" Hank called, and a uniform looked his way, got his message, and crouched by the body.

When he did, Joker noted the uniform was a good cop. He knew this with the way the man carefully peeled back the cover over Heidi. She was a dead woman in an alley who deserved respect. She wasn't just a body on display, and he treated her that way.

Joker looked at her and froze solid.

This was not because he saw a lifeless Heidi.

It was because the word *Chaos* had been carved into her forehead.

"Ugly," Tack said quietly beside him. "But, Joke, there's more and it ain't good either."

"Show me," Joker grunted.

The uniform looked to Hank and must have gotten the go-ahead because he pulled the cover further.

Her shirt was up.

And in her stomach, the word *Joker* was carved.

"Fuck me, fuck me, *fuck me*," Joker clipped out.

The uniform dropped the cover.

"Tack says you boys knew her," Hank noted, and Joker looked to him.

"Valenzuela's stable, sent to work our patch," Joker told him what he knew Tack would have already told him.

"She special to you?" Hank asked.

"We had a relationship," Joker shared.

"You wanna share that with me?" Hank pushed.

"She got cash for info on Valenzuela," Tack told him. "Gave you that already, Nightingale."

"Tryin' to understand why Valenzuela, if he did that shit, would carve one of your boy's names in her stomach," Hank returned.

"Like I told you already, she snitched and her handler was Joker," Tack replied.

"And she was pregnant," Joker put in, and Hank looked to him.

"It yours?"

"Nope," Joker said. "Never touched her."

"Valenzuela think differently?" Hank went on.

"Obviously," Joker bit out.

"Could be a different message, brother. Just sayin' he knew she was yours," Tack told him.

"Could be, but it doesn't fuckin' matter what that asshole's message is, except the fact a woman and her baby are dead to give it," Joker returned.

"Calm, Joke," Tack warned, reading him easily.

"I'm calm," he clipped, but he was *not*.

He still expended the effort to find it. He couldn't grab hold, but he got enough of the edge not to lose his mind, turn on his boot, and find someone to hurt.

"Tack says she left Valenzuela's stable 'cause she was pregnant, that right?" Hank asked.

Joker nodded and added, "She was gone, Hank. Be surprised she was still in town. Valenzuela did this, no doubt, but he tracked her down to do it."

"Before this happened, Lee told me you were lookin' for her because she shared she was up for findin' a home for her baby," Hank continued.

That was a nice way to put it.

"Yeah," Joker confirmed.

Hank got close so Tack got close.

But Joker didn't take his eyes from Hank.

"Pretty clear this isn't Chaos, but it's also clear shit that's sticky just got stickier. I am not in the know with what you're doin' with Mitch and Slim. I don't wanna be in the know. What I do know is you got two of *my brothers* in the know. They got blue blood. And they gotta keep their team clean. So I'll need alibis for all of Chaos, and I don't give a fuck that gets your backs up. You do what you gotta do to keep that team clean."

"You'll have them," Tack said.

Hank turned to Joker. "Please God, tell me you got an alibi."

"With my woman all night."

Hank sighed as he nodded.

"Why you prayin' to God?" Tack asked, and Hank looked to him.

"Because Joke is a focus, and Valenzuela's focus is not good to have. Might just be that woman," he tipped his head to the street where Heidi was. "Might be a specific vendetta.

Valenzuela plays any angle, and Chaos is known for a weapon of choice. Those bein' knives."

"Not gonna carve my own name and my Club in a dead woman's body," Joker ground out.

"No, you wouldn't," Hank said. "But past history, when Chaos was a different club, members had a way with knives and were so up their own asses, they didn't mind markin' their territory."

This was history not shared while he was a recruit, and Joker looked to Tack.

Tack looked pissed.

"That isn't past history, Hank, it's ancient history," Tack stated. "Only one fuck did that, and his back is blacked for puttin' Chaos out there with shit like that, not to mention seein' as he's doin' time until he dies for havin' his head up his ass. He carved Chaos, but when the Club was fucked, he was *more* fucked, and even the brothers who wanted to walk that dark path we were on before I pulled the Club out were all over strippin' his patch."

"Regardless if you wanna claim it, it's still Chaos. Shit like that makes legend, and legend never dies," Hank returned.

"So you think Valenzuela is settin' up the Club?" Tack asked.

"I think it's lost on nobody you're cleaning a new patch, and that nobody includes Valenzuela," Hank said by way of answer. "Now, you already know to watch your back, so I won't repeat it." He looked to Joker. "Don't know if you were tight with her, but sorry for your loss."

He wasn't tight with her, but he didn't want her and her kid dead.

"Thanks," he muttered.

There was hand shaking, and Tack and Joker walked back to the tape. When they did, Joker saw Lee had broken off and was standing with Luke and another member of his team, Hector Chavez.

They got looks and nods and ducked under the tape to go to their own crew, which had grown to include every member of Chaos, excluding those on patrol, but including Big Petey.

They barely stopped before Hawk declared, "Know you're not gonna like it, but I think you need to pull back from claimin' more territory."

"That's not gonna happen," Tack replied.

"A woman's dead," Hawk returned.

"Chaos didn't kill her," Tack bit back.

"Your advance was too aggressive," Hawk retorted.

"It's done and it's not gonna get undone," Tack stated. "We took our turf, we hold steady."

"Then what?" Hawk asked. "His return play was that," and he pointed to the tape, indicating Heidi.

"Right," Brock Lucas put in, eyes to Hawk. "You and Tack could argue about the color of the sky."

No matter how tight Hawk and Tack were, that was the damned truth. Then again, well before Cherry, Tack had made a play for Hawk's now wife and the mother of his three kids. A play that was almost successful. Shit went down to make them brothers, but even brothers fought. Especially when women were involved. Both men were good with what they got. But no man ever let that kind of shit go.

"Someone talked, gave up Heidi," Hop put in.

"The one you tried to turn," Hawk replied to Hop.

"Could be any a' them. They all knew she gave it up to Joker," Snapper told Hawk.

"Right, and he was lookin' for a way to send a message and, I'll repeat, his return play was *that*," Hawk growled.

"Chaos made their play. They can't back down, Hawk, and you know it," Brock cut in. "And somethin' had to give, we all knew it," he said this looking at his partner and fellow cop, Mitch Lawson. "Valenzuela is greedy but he's careful, and we've all been lying in wait with nothing happening. He's gotta be tripped to make a mistake. Chaos pushed and we gotta hope he'll fall. For now, bottom line, no one is responsible for that woman in the alley except Valenzuela. Any of us could take that on, because all of us were a go with Chaos pushing. We just didn't know how Valenzuela would push back. It sucks, but this is war, and these fuckers don't fight fair. Not even close. So we gotta suck it up and keep on our path. Vigilance. Information. Message. Now can I go home to my wife?"

"I know I'm goin' home to mine," Tack said.

Lawson looked to the heavens.

He wasn't on board, Joker knew. Then again, he was a straight shooter. Or as straight as he could be, possed up to a commando, an ex-DEA deep-cover agent, and a biker with a mission.

But as much of a straight shooter as he was, he was a better man. A man who took his brothers' backs no matter what that meant.

So he might not be on board, but he was along for the ride.

The men broke up, but Joker caught the glances between the brothers, these emanating from Tack and his lieutenants, Hop and Shy.

No words were exchanged, but Joker knew.

Heidi might have been what Heidi was for reasons she had to be that.

But she'd backed Chaos, she was theirs.

Now she was dead in an alley, her baby dead inside her, with words carved in her skin.

So the expanded team had the goal of vigilance, information, and message.

But Chaos just added vengeance.

Several of his brothers stuck close to Joker as they walked to their bikes.

As he stood at his pulling on his gloves, he felt a hand on his shoulder and turned to see Shy.

"You good?" Shy asked.

"I'm good," Joker answered.

"Fucked up way to go, brother, sorry," Shy said.

Joker had no response to that because what Shy said was true.

"Listen to Lucas," Snapper, whose bike was next to Joker's said. "That's not on you."

He knew it wasn't. Time had passed. She was gone. Safe. Nightingale would find her, but he'd find her nowhere near Denver.

Valenzuela found her too. Dragged her back and laid her out for his message.

"Say it one last time," Joker said to Snapper but did it quiet, not pissed. "I'm good."

"Mount up," Hop called, already astride his bike.

Those around him moved away and Joker swung his leg over his bike.

They started up, backed out…

Then as one, Chaos rolled.

* * *

Carissa sat in the bed, legs crossed in front of her under the covers, wearing his tee, lights on, and she stared at him.

Not surprisingly, she'd waited up for him.

Not surprisingly, when he got back, she asked if everything was okay.

Not surprisingly, she looked way fucking worried.

So sooner than he wanted to share at a time so deep in the morning he just wanted to go to sleep, he shared.

Everything.

Or everything he knew his brothers gave to their old ladies. There were no lies, but that didn't mean old ladies weren't kept safe from some truths.

Some brothers shared more than others.

Needless to say, Joker didn't include the fact he'd just been to a crime scene where there was a murdered woman with his and his Club's names carved into her skin.

But she knew about Chaos history and their mission, their turf and patrol.

She also knew some history about Valenzuela.

Now it was after five in the morning, and she had all she was going to get.

"Butterfly, it's late. You got a shift in a couple of hours and I got a deadline. I just laid out a lot for you, and I don't wanna push, but I need you to talk to me so I know where you're at."

"So…" she started, stopped, started again, "You're…" again with the stop and then the start, "Essentially…" Her head tipped to the side. "Vigilantes?"

There really wasn't anything *essentially* about it.

"Essentially," he stated.

"And there's a bad guy who's mad at you because you saved Tabby's friend, who's a junkie, from being in a porno movie?"

He never in his life wanted to be discussing porn flicks with his good girl, Carissa, unless she got a wild hair and had a hankering to be seriously naughty and watch one with him.

He didn't get into that.

He just said, "Yeah."

"Are you in danger?"

"Cops are involved, so the hope is it won't come to that."

"But you're in danger," she whispered.

"Potentially," he hedged.

She fell silent.

"You're not. This guy knows his beef is with the brothers," he assured her.

"I hadn't thought of that," she muttered.

Fuck.

"Baby—" he began.

"I don't want to offend you by making the comparison," she said over him and kept going. "But Aaron defends criminals. You . . . don't."

That was good.

He thought.

So he gave her more in hopes of making her understand.

"Like I said, Club was tied to some nasty shit," he told her. "Tack took over the Club, it was hostile, and he got them out. This was before me. But I hope it goes without sayin', I would not be a brother if that's where they were still at. That said, not sayin' if I knew where Tack was leadin' them, I wouldn't be all in to get the Club where it is now. We got two missions. Keep the store and garage thriving, keep our patch clean so that shit can't ever touch the Club again. I came on board knowin' both and givin' allegiance knowin' it. Chaos is not a club I'm a member of, Carrie. It's a part of me. That work is a part of me. And I need you to understand that."

"Well, of course."

It was then he was staring at her.

"That's it?" he asked.

"What's it?"

"You're down with that?"

She shrugged. "If you changed my tire and took me to coffee, sharing all this, probably not. But now I know you. I know them. I know who you are. I know what you all stand for. And it isn't the garage and the store and vigilantism. It's family. So am I happy my new, handsome, manly man biker boyfriend and his brothers are in a power struggle with a bad guy? No. Am I okay with the fact that you take me as I am, all my baggage, the way my life was messed up, the unknown ways Aaron hopes to keep messing it up, and you don't waver? Yes. A thousand times yes. So it wouldn't say much for me at my first opportunity, I waver against you."

Fuck, he loved her.

Straight up, down to his gut, for the rest of his life, *loved her.*

He didn't tell her that.

He told her, "The manly man biker shit you spout is cute, Butterfly, but it's also goofy."

She grinned, pushed forward on her knees, then crawled to him where he sat on the edge of her bed, twisted to her. She got close, landed on her hip pressed to his, and put a hand on his chest.

"I'm not goofy," she whispered.

She totally was.

"Whatever," he whispered back.

"Not sure I can get back to sleep for the whole hour I could do that," she shared.

"What are you sure you can do?" he asked.

She leaned in and ran her nose along his jaw.

That was what he was hoping would be her answer.

And it was an answer to a lot of things, all of what they'd just talked about.

An answer he liked.

Luckily, he was sure he could do that too.

So he pulled her into his arms, took her to her back, and they did it.

CHAPTER NINETEEN

Give Good Girlfriend

Carissa

WHILE MY BIKER was in the kitchen making coffee, droopy-eyed, I stood at the bathroom sink brushing my teeth, thinking about all that had happened the night before and early that morning.

I gave Joker what I needed to give him when we had our talk.

That didn't mean what he said didn't alarm me.

It did.

And in the light of the coming day, tired and facing work and an important meet-the-friends dinner that night, that alarm grew.

Still brushing, I saw Joker walk in wearing nothing but his jeans (and by that, I meant *nothing*—he'd pulled them on commando to go make coffee), his miraculous chest (and shoulders, and head, and face, etc.) on display.

And I saw his tattoos.

He had a variety of them he'd explained were Chaos tattoos. A big one on his back, one on his inside biceps, one on his outside forearm.

He also had a tattoo over his left pectoral that was a playing card of a joker.

To be honest, I'd never liked tattoos. I thought they were common, not in the sense they were low-class, but when everyone started getting them, the coolness factor went out of them.

But Joker had told me the story of his Chaos tattoos, and the joker card was obvious.

So I'd changed my mind.

First of all, they were amazing to look at. I was no art expert, but it was clear they were that. Art on skin.

But it was more. They told the story of the person who had them. Inked forever in their skin was their history, or what was important to them, or lessons they'd learned they didn't want to forget.

This made me look at all Chaos brothers' tattoos more closely, and I'd stopped being judgmental as I read their lives, their thoughts, their life lessons on their skin.

For Joker, I liked most the fact that his tattoos showed his life started when he found the brotherhood. He didn't have tattoos from before, angry ones he got after he left his father and struck out to make his own life with a car full of stuff and not much else.

I liked it that instead, he'd inked his skin when he'd found his place, knowing it with such certainty, he vowed allegiance to it and put it in a forever way right on his body.

From a man like Carson "Joker" Steele, that said a lot about the place he found.

My eyes lifted from his chest to his eyes as he walked up behind me. I kept brushing but did it automatically when he put a hand to my hip and slid it over my nightie (another stretchy, blousy one that still fit and looked okay, this one in green) to my belly.

Then I watched as he bent his dark head and kissed my shoulder.

That was when my eyes went to my shoulder and I saw the love bite he'd given me there. It was more than a hickey. There were indistinct purple teeth marks all around it.

And that was where Joker's lips right then touched.

My stomach dropped and I locked my legs as his hand slid up to my ribs and he moved his lips to kiss my neck.

He let me go, moved away, and reached for his own toothbrush.

But I was brushing and staring at that mark.

My physical reaction was only partially due to Joker's touch, liking it, the intimacy of it, the familiarity of it, and the beauty of watching him give it to me in the mirror.

Mostly, it was about that mark. About him kissing it. About him *making* it.

About me wearing it.

And having it, how I got it, what was said after, and later, the honest way Joker gave me what he had to give me early that morning, the apprehension I was feeling slid away.

Chaos were bikers. And being around them I'd learned that bikers were just like any people.

I was sure there were scarier clubs, more dangerous ones, ones that attracted that kind of guy. There were probably more casual ones, ones about riding on the weekends and having guys to hang out with, a different kind of brotherhood that wasn't as important as family.

And then there was Chaos.

It had not been lost on me the men were tough, rough, and edgy. Even before Joker shared what he shared with me, I would not expect they sang in the choir at church on Sundays.

But Tack had picked Tyra.

And Hop had picked Lanie.

And Tabby had picked Shy.

They'd gotten married. They were making babies.

And they were devoted.

Not like Aaron was "devoted" to me.

They were *devoted*.

Truly.

Not to mention, Stacy was really nice and she was no one's old lady, but the boys liked her hanging around and I knew why.

Because the guys were tough, rough, edgy, about family, and good to their souls. It might be a different definition of good that included vigilantism, which was arguably not the right thing.

But it was their thing.

So who was anyone to judge?

I couldn't say I was happy that my biker and his friends who were now my friends were possibly in danger.

I could say that I knew down to my gut they not only could take care of themselves, they wouldn't do anything stupid to put themselves in jeopardy. What was happening with this bad guy wasn't about that. They weren't about that. And they wouldn't put their loved ones through that.

So I had to trust, and I'd spent a decade trusting the wrong man so I'd learned.

This time, I had it right. I knew that down to my gut too.

Feeling content in this, having sorted it out in my head, I quit brushing, spit, rinsed, and moved to my man. I shoved close, forcing him away from the counter, and went in.

He kissed the mark he gave me.

I kissed the mark he gave himself, touching my lips to the joker card.

Then I tipped my head back and whispered, "I'll go pour the coffee."

He kept brushing but his eyes, already warm at my touch, got soft.

I allowed myself time to take that in before I moved away to get my man and me some coffee.

*   *   *

At my first coffee break at work, I was no longer feeling content.

This was because we'd had a slow morning and Sharon, me, and the other cashiers had a chance to gab.

I'd shared I was seeing someone and was meeting his friends that night.

They were ecstatic for me (they all didn't know everything about Aaron, but they all knew he was a jerk).

Then Sharon asked me what I was wearing.

And I instantly started to panic, because meeting your man's friends did not say tube top or clingy T-shirt dress or tank with cool sequins.

Especially when one of them lived in assisted living!

And I had nothing postpregnancy weight that would do.

Not one thing.

So I had to form a plan, which I did.

And now I was in the break room with phone in hand and it was ringing in my ear.

"Yo, girlie, what's shakin'?" Elvira asked in my ear as greeting.

"Panic stations!" I cried.

"Uh...what?"

"I'm meeting Joker's friends tonight," I told her on a rush. "Not, like, biker friends. Like, the woman who looked after him when he was a kid and his dad was off carousing and left him home alone without dinner. And when I say kid, I mean, he was eight."

"Yikes," she muttered.

"Also the guy who gave him a good man in his life, seeing as he didn't have one, is going to be there too. *And* his family!"

"Lordy, Carissa, this shit's big." Elvira told me something I already knew.

"I know, and I have nothing to wear."

"Uh-oh," she mumbled, totally understanding me, as I knew she would since she was a girl.

"I'm at work but Tyra says you can get time off to shop," I said leadingly (and hopefully).

"Right. Got it. I'm on it," she replied immediately.

I blinked at my locker.

That was easy.

"Really?" I asked.

She didn't answer. She just said, "Budget."

"Um . . . well, I need shoes too."

"Budget, girl," she demanded.

Gosh, this hurt. It really hurt. Surprisingly, after months of money being so tight it was a wonder I could breathe, I had thousands of dollars in a savings account *and* my monthly expenses had decreased dramatically.

But it *had* been tight and anything could happen (like your car needing four new tires). I had a buffer now when it felt like I'd never have a buffer in my life. It was good to have. And I was terrified of drawing it down, definitely not doing it for new clothes.

Further, I hadn't spent money on me for so long, focusing on Travis and his needs (as it should be), it felt strange to consider doing it.

Strange as in *guilty*.

"Carissa," Elvira prompted impatiently.

"Okay, maybe two hundred, *at most*, all of it together."

Eek!

"You need undies?" she asked.

I actually kinda did but I didn't know how to ask Elvira to take care of that. Anyway, only Joker would see those, and unlike my nighties, he'd never mentioned my undies (which were, admittedly, not all that much to write home about) so I didn't think they were a priority.

"You need undies," she decided for me. "When you gotta be at their table?"

"Six thirty."

"Your house. Five."

"I get home at ten after five."

"Your house, ten after five."

"Okay," I whispered.

"On it. Later," she said then I heard her disconnect.

"Did I just make a mistake?" I asked the locker.

There was no reply, and I needed to throw back some coffee and get to my register, so I couldn't wait for what was never going to come to me from a bunch of steel.

I could also fret no longer.

And anyway, I'd set Elvira on her course. She was Elvira. I hadn't known her a long time but one thing I did know.

Unless I was a man named Hawk who put the kibosh on it (and I wasn't), there was no turning back now.

*   *   *

At my lunch break, I went to my locker to get my phone to see if Joker had texted me (because he always texted me when I was at work, another way he was sweet).

I pulled it open like I'd pulled it open repeatedly for months.

But this time, I did it and froze because, staring unseeing into the locker, a memory hit me, and on its heels came another one.

These being that all my stuff, excepting the guest room

furniture, was out of the storage locker. Everything was unpacked. Everything was put away.

But the sketch Carson Steele gave me before he left town then came back as Joker was not at my house.

"Oh no," I whispered, because I had also suddenly remembered something in all the turmoil of the last year that I'd completely forgotten.

I had stuff in the attic of Aaron's house. A couple of boxes filled with yearbooks, some photo albums, commemorative coins my mom's uncle used to give me for reasons I didn't understand but I'd always kept them.

And that was where Joker's sketch was, framed and tucked away because Aaron didn't like it, no matter that it was of me and it was beautiful. When we moved in together after the wedding, I'd put it out and he'd told me (not asked me) to put it away.

I'd put it away.

And then, in a dither that my life was a mess, I left it behind.

"No," I whispered again.

I needed to get it back.

Darn it!

I grabbed my phone, turned it to me, and slid my thumb on the screen.

As usual, Joker had texted me, and as usual, it was sweet. This time, it was, *You're on my mind.*

I liked that.

What I didn't like was the notification above it that said I had a missed call and voicemail from Aaron.

Ulk.

Well, he had my son and it could be about Travis, not to mention I needed to talk to him about the boxes, so I quickly texted Joker back with, *Me too, sweetie. See you tonight.*

Then I listened to Aaron's voicemail, which only said,

"Riss, hey. When you have a second, call me. Okay? Later, honey." All of this like we left voicemails for each other every day due to the fact we were in love, married, had a baby, and all was hunky dory.

This was not a surprise. This was the way he behaved when he went about getting back into my good graces the other times he'd jerked me around.

But this time, I didn't feel hope from his behavior.

I only felt exasperation.

I drew in breath and hit the Call Back button, hoping all was okay with Travis, further hoping that Aaron wouldn't give me any guff about me getting the boxes in the attic, and last hoping that I got voicemail (of course, only if Travis was okay).

It rang twice before he greeted, "Hey, Riss."

I fought a gag and asked, "Is Travis okay?"

"He's fine, babe."

Babe?

He'd never called me *babe*.

"Listen," he carried on. "I'll be working into the night. Can you come to the office? We need to talk. I'll get food in and we can talk over Chinese or something."

Was he crazy?

"I have plans tonight, Aaron," I told him. "So perhaps you can tell me what you'd like to discuss while you have me now."

"I'd like to do it in person."

"Is this about Travis?" I pushed.

"In a way," he hedged.

I didn't have time for this.

"Okay, Aaron, I'm at work on lunch break and I need to eat so I don't have a lot of time. It'd help if you could be more forthcoming."

He hesitated for a moment before he said, "It's about Travis, you, and me."

You and me?

"You may have missed this, but there is no you and me," I pointed out.

"Riss—"

"Stop," I whispered.

He stopped.

Then he started again.

"That was wrong to ask."

He was so right.

Then, as he was wont to do, he went wrong.

"The wrong way to go about it. This is important. I'll ask Mom to look after Travis and I'll take you to dinner so we can talk. It may be a while before I can get away but I'll take you somewhere nice."

He *was* crazy.

"Aaron, please don't do this," I said quietly.

"Do what?" he asked. "Sit down with my wife to talk about our family?"

His wife?

Our *family*?

I wanted to kick him. Since I couldn't, I lost patience with him.

"I can't do this now," I snapped.

"I messed up," he said gently. "I've been thinking a lot, can't get it out of my head. I messed up, Riss, and I want to fix it. I'm trying to fix it. And I have to talk to you about what I've been thinking."

"I just said I can't do this now," I reminded him. "I'm at work. I have to get my lunch and get back to my register."

Before I could continue in order to finish our conversation, he muttered, "I hate you work a cash register at a fuck-ing grocery store."

I let that go, since in reality *he* put me at that register but

I didn't think it would end our conversation any quicker if I reminded him of that.

Instead, I kept on with what I wanted to say.

"Since I have you, I've discovered after the move that I left some things in your attic. A couple of boxes. I'd like them back."

"I'll bring them over to your place tonight," he offered instantly.

That was easy, which was good, just not what I needed.

"Like I said, I have plans," I told him. "But maybe I can come over after work some night this week and get them?"

"Whenever you want, Riss. I'll cut out of the office and be there. And maybe you can have dinner with Travis and me or something."

What about Tory?

I didn't ask.

I said, "I'll text you, let you know."

"Great. I'll go up and get them down."

I studied my memory banks and couldn't remember so I could only hope that the boxes were closed and taped.

I also could only hope he didn't go through them. I'd told him about that sketch and who'd done it. If he saw it again, who knew what he'd do with it.

And I wanted it back.

No, I *needed* it back.

"Right, um . . . talk to you later, Aaron."

"All right, honey, have a good day."

He was making me queasy.

Still, to keep him from turning into a jerk (or exposing he still was one), I said, "You have a good one too. Good luck with the case."

"Thanks, sweetheart."

I swallowed back another gag and said goodbye.

I didn't wait for him to return my farewell before I rang off, ran out, got myself a sandwich from the deli, went back to the break room, and ate it while calling Joker and telling him my latest tales of ridiculousness from Aaron (though I left out the part where Aaron still had Joker's sketch).

When I was done telling him and had precisely six minutes before I had to be back at my register, he remarked, "Gotta admit, this shit is kinda funny."

"I'm glad you think so," I mumbled.

"Ride it out, Butterfly," he advised. "And the best way to do it is twist it from what it seems to you, a pain in your ass, to what it just is. Desperate acts from an asshole who fucked up his life by lettin' go the best thing he had in it. You win by just bein' you. He's rubbin' his own nose in his loss."

That was a much better way to look at it.

"Thanks, sweetheart," I said softly.

"No probs, Carrie. You gotta get back?" he asked.

"Yes," I answered unhappily.

"Okay, baby, see you tonight."

"Tonight."

"Later, Butterfly."

"'Bye, sweetie."

I shut down my phone, put it in my locker, sucked the rest of my soda up its straw, cleaned up, and went back to my register.

*   *   *

I dashed in the back door, tossing my purse to the side, where I heard it skid across the counter and fall to the floor.

I didn't even pause to look at it.

I just shuddered to a halt at the side counter and dumped the huge bouquet of LeLane's flowers I'd bought as well as the box of cupcakes I got from the bakery and then resumed my dash.

When I did, Joker rounded into the kitchen, saying, "Carissa, Elvira and—"

"No time, no time, no time!" I cried, waving my hand at him and not looking at him either as I sprinted right by him.

I rounded the corner from the kitchen into the living room and skidded to a dead stop on my Converse.

All my insides seized at what befell my eyes.

This being Elvira standing (in a fabulous wraparound dress and even more fabulous platform pumps) by my coffee table with my couch covered in so many bags, it was terrifying.

Except one wing of the sectional was occupied by a large black man (large as in tall and built) with a bald head and a perfectly formed goatee. He was lounging with his legs crossed casually.

I paid no heed to the black man.

"*We had a budget!*" I screeched.

"I know, I know, I know," Elvira replied, lifting her hands up, palms toward me, pressing them my way repeatedly. "But, girlie, I don't do cute. I got flummoxed. I lost it, ended up in Forever 21 and had a breakdown. It got so extreme, I had to call in Malik."

On the word *Malik* she threw a hand toward the man on my couch and I looked to him.

"I'm Malik," he said in a voice that slid over me like warm syrup. "Elvira's man."

I was in a panic, but still, regardless of Elvira's exceptional style, her beautiful face, her fabulous skin, and her hairdo that I knew even without the stylist education I intended to get one day suited her absolutely perfectly, I took the precious time to be shocked at her man.

Not that she could land him.

Just that he was Hollywood handsome in the sense that

I was pretty sure he was famous, because if there was anything right in this world, he simply had to be.

"Uh...hi," I greeted shyly.

His full lips curled up, exposing white teeth.

My scalp started tingling.

"Malik can shop," Elvira stated and I tore my eyes off her man. "He's so good at it, I could retire. Example," she swept her hand down her fabulous dress to flick out, indicating her more fabulous shoes, telling me Malik picked them, which said it all. "I won't retire, because if I can't shop, I might stop breathing, but just sayin', he's good at it."

"I can see that, Elvira," I snapped, walking to the back of the couch. "Since there are *seven thousand bags in my living room*!" I ended this on a yell.

"We can take back what you don't want," Elvira returned. "But now we got a lot to go through and you don't got a lotta time. So, girl," she rolled her hand at me, "get your ass over here."

I got my behind over there, and I did it by putting a hand to the back of the couch and leaping over it, which knocked five bags to the floor.

Elvira's eyebrows shot up. I heard deep laughter that was like vocal silk, along with a rough biker chuckle that was almost the best sound in the world (second only to Travis's giggle).

I ignored all that and started dumping stuff out of bags.

Elvira joined me and we were laying out outfits (embarrassingly with matching undies but I couldn't give in to the embarrassment of doing this in front of Malik, or the possibility he'd picked some of them for me, I had to focus) when I heard Joker say, "Mrs. Heely, gotta let you know that we're probably gonna be a little late."

At that, my head snapped to the side, my vision blurred

with livid horror and I screeched, *"Don't tell her that! She's gonna think I'm rude! You're never late to a dinner party, even if it's family! We'll be on time if it kills me!"*

Joker grinned at me and kept on, "Carrie just got off work and she's pickin' an outfit."

I felt my eyes go huge as my heart stopped.

I thought I might black out as Elvira muttered, "Men. No clue." Then I felt her hand on my arm and her lips at my ear. "Focus."

I nodded repeatedly. "Right, yes, focus. Right."

In no time (since half the stuff only Elvira could pull off, some of it only Lanie could pull off, a few things only Tyra could pull off, and only three outfits I could pull off) we'd narrowed it down.

They were draped on my couch and I was bouncing foot to foot.

"What do you think?" I asked.

"I like them all. They're perfect for you. I can't make a decision. Shit!" Elvira answered, my panic clearly settling in on her.

"What happened to, 'I'm not nervous. I give good girlfriend?'" Joker asked and my head (and Elvira's) again snapped his way. "Let's go back to that," he finished.

"You are *not* helping," Elvira informed him.

"Darlin'," smooth came at me as a hand hit my back and I jumped, tipped my head back and caught Malik's warm espresso eyes. "Pink," he said softly.

I looked down and suddenly it was like a beacon.

It was absolutely the pink.

I bent, snatched it up (filmy pink dress with v-neck, frilly ruffles adorning it, the same for the short sleeves, with a modest but becoming hem that would hit several inches above my knees, plus undies, and cream platform wedge espadrilles that had a glittery gold threaded through the fabric and ribbons that wound around and tied at the ankles).

I pushed through Elvira and Malik, dashing around the couch, shouting, "Thank you!" and I kept running down the hall, yelling, "I owe you!"

Then I ran into my room and slammed the door.

*   *   *

I sat in Joker's truck, pulling at the hem of my skirt, thinking it was modest when I was standing, not so much when I was sitting down, thus fretting about it.

"Butterfly, relax. They aren't gonna eat you."

I looked to the side to see Joker, who I had not noted during my earlier crisis had shaved.

"You look sweet," he went on.

"Thanks," I mumbled, pulling at my hem.

He glanced at me and back to the road before he asked, "What changed from yesterday's calm to today's mega-freak?"

"Sharon asked me what I was gonna wear," I answered.

"That's all it takes?"

"That and the realization that what I wear is not only a reflection on me, but on you. And that I gave good girlfriend to Aaron's parents likely because deep down inside, I would hope, I'm not a total imbecile and I knew somewhere buried there that Aaron was a total jerk. So I probably really didn't care what they thought of me because, deep down inside, I had some notion they would not be in my life for long. Alas, I didn't figure this out before I wasted years on him and gave him a child. Fortunately for me, I get that child too. But now, with you, these people, what they mean to you and what they gave you, they matter. What they think of me and what they think of you choosing me is important. Hence... mega-freak."

We were driving through a residential area but still, Joker swung immediately to the curb behind a parked car. I gasped as he shoved the truck into park, undid my seatbelt, hooked me with an arm, and yanked me to him.

Then he kissed me, hard and thoroughly, with tongue.

I was breathing heavily when he broke the kiss, and as surprising as it was, I didn't ask after it.

I knew what it was about.

His people mattered, *he* mattered, and he liked that I knew it.

So instead, I moved the hand I'd had in his hair to his smooth cheek.

"You got rid of your stubble," I whispered.

"Yeah," he whispered back. "Cut my hair and shaved for Mrs. Heely. She didn't like where they were before." He paused before he finished, "And she matters."

I felt my eyes get wet.

"I'll explain it to her, Carrie," he continued. "Start growin' it back again for you. She'll get it and put up with it."

"Your face, sweetheart, your call."

I watched him smile before he moved even closer (and he wasn't that far), dipped, and slid his nose along my jaw, ending that bit of fabulousness by landing a light kiss on my neck.

Then he put me back in my seat and turned to the wheel.

I drew in a steadying breath and buckled up.

Joker pulled out.

In a few minutes, we turned into a development that was clearly assisted living.

I instantly hated it.

It was tidy. It was attractive. There were flowers and window boxes.

But each unit was tiny.

Joker had told me Mrs. Heely lost her son not in a war but during some military operation. He'd been Special Forces and things had gone awry. His team had achieved their aim, but they'd sadly lost two men doing it, one of them Mrs. Heely's son.

I had no idea how old she was but I didn't care.

I was my father's daughter. My gramma was not in good shape, and she still lived at home because my dad made that so.

Thus I believed no one should live in a place like that.

And if Mrs. Heely's son had been Special Forces, I was absolutely certain he'd agree with me.

"There's the flag," Joker muttered and I looked right, to what was clearly the clubhouse, and saw the tattered flag hanging there.

He'd told me about that too.

And staring at it, I felt it should be hanging a lot closer to the woman who only had that tattered piece of fabric left of her son.

Joker parked behind a black GMC Acadia and I looked to the diminutive row of houses. One with a window box had the lights on inside, curtains open, people visible through the window, and the door was opening.

"Oh geez," I whispered.

"They'll love you," Joker muttered, and I heard his door open.

I had my door open and Joker was at it helping me down when I saw an elderly woman in a pretty dress with perfectly coiffed silver-white hair coming down the walk, smiling.

"He shaved!" she cried in glee.

"Told you," Joker said under his breath to me.

I smiled.

He got me clear of the door, slammed it, and we took one

step before the woman who had to be Mrs. Heely latched on to Joker's face.

She tugged it down and moved it side to side.

"There it is. The handsome," she declared.

I loved her instantly.

"Don't get used to it. Carrie likes the beard," Joker replied.

My heart lurched and my hand lifted so I could slap his arm.

"Do you *want* her to dislike me?" I snapped.

Joker pulled away from the grip Mrs. Heely had on him and grinned at me as he slung his arm around her shoulders.

"Mrs. Heely, this is Carrie," he introduced.

"What a pretty dress," she remarked, looking me over in a kind rather than sharp way, which was a relief.

"Thanks," I replied, lifting a hand.

"Oh no," she said, grabbing it and tugging on it, her look changing entirely. It was still kind but also welcoming and very warm. "We do hugs in this *family*."

This family.

Gosh, I was glad Joker had that.

Though, it was strange how she emphasized it.

As Joker dropped his arm from around her, I bent in and hugged her. She hugged me back.

So far so good.

I heard the back door to the truck open and close as we let each other go.

"From Carrie. She works at LeLane's. She got you the good stuff," Joker said, holding the bakery box by the string and the bouquet in his other arm her way.

Mrs. Heely threw her hands up. "Too much!" she cried but didn't hesitate reaching out and snatching both from Joker. She shoved her face in the flowers and said after pulling it out, "I haven't had flowers in the house in *years*."

Okay, that was also good.

I again smiled.

"Come inside. Candy has to see your new look, Carson," Mrs. Heely stated, then ordered in a bossy mom's voice, "Let's go."

We went (she *was* giving us the bossy mom), but following her to the house, Joker didn't grab my hand. He slid his arm around my shoulders and guided us in.

When we got in, I found I was right. The place was tiny. And made more so by a bunch of furniture that used to be in a much bigger living room stuffed in, not to mention the large, good-looking man, his beautiful wife, and their three kids who were occupying it.

We barely were through the door with Joker closing it behind us before the man took one look at me and strangely burst into gales of laughter.

I went stiff.

Joker felt it.

"Something funny, brother?" he asked with low warning.

The man, who had to be Linus, kept laughing (though not roaring with it) and shook his head, saying through it, "Car, buddy, you're the only badass biker on the planet who'd pick the prom queen as his woman."

"I was homecoming queen. I only made the court at prom," I told him, my voice as stiff as my body.

He burst into more laughter.

The beautiful woman with him, who I knew was his wife Kamryn, slapped his arm (a lot harder than I had earlier slapped Joker's).

"Cut it out, Linus!" she hissed.

He quit laughing so quickly, I jumped.

He also did it focused on me.

"You're beautiful," he whispered, his voice rough. "Perfect."

The force of his words and the emotion behind them made me push into Joker's side and his arm tightened reflexively around my shoulders when I did.

Linus looked to Joker and his voice was still rough with meaning. "I know you're done with him, Car, but swear to Christ, I'd pay to see his face, you walked in as all you are with this girl on your arm. *Pay* to see that shit."

"Stop cursing in front of the kids," Kamryn snapped.

Linus curved an arm around her waist and pulled her tight to his side.

I looked up at Joker. "I think I like him."

"I'd like him more if he'd watch his mouth," Mrs. Heely declared.

Kamryn grinned at her then turned her grin to me.

I grinned back.

"Candy, Miss Carissa gave me flowers. Do you want to help your Momma Heely put them in water?" Mrs. Heely asked a pretty little girl who was sitting on an armchair wearing a pretty little dress and swinging her legs.

She didn't hesitate to hop right off the chair and push her way through bodies to Mrs. Heely.

When she got close, she grabbed the woman's hand.

Apparently, that was her answer.

They got to the doorway of the kitchen before, shyly, little Candy turned back and called, "Like your hair, Mister Carson."

"Thanks, doll," Joker called back.

Kamryn came forward, hand up to me. "Hey there, Carissa, so nice to meet you. I'm Kam."

Thus it began, the introductions, hand clasps, hugs, smiles, but this finished with Mrs. Heely yelling through the opening that had a view from the kitchen, "I've made Carson's favorite, my pot roast. But I've also made brussels sprouts, and I'm saying right now, *all* my boys are eating them." She pointed a tangerine rose at Joker through the opening before swinging it to Linus. "Including my *big* boys. Am I understood?"

"Yes, ma'am," Linus answered on a grin.

"Shit," Joker said under his breath.

"What did I just hear?" Mrs. Heely called on a snap.

"Just don't put too much of that…stuff on my plate," Joker called back.

"Six," she returned.

"Two," Joker fired back.

"Four," she haggled.

"Two," Joker repeated.

"Three," she snapped.

"Deal," Joker said.

I started giggling.

Kam giggled with me.

All my panic slid away, and I was finally good to go to give good girlfriend.

*　　*　　*

"Next, I want a Candy," I declared somewhat tiredly, belly full of pot roast, potatoes, rolls, and brussels sprouts (which I detested but forced down five), apple crumble pie and ice cream, and with this, several glasses of wine.

After all that food and not much sleep the night before, I was ready for snuggle time with Joker and then bed (with Joker).

We were in his truck and almost home and I was in love with a little girl named Candy.

Well, I was in love with them all, but Candy was just *so sweet*. She said practically nothing and was shy as could be. But she also loved her daddy loads, whispered with her mother and "Momma Heely" with her hands on their necks, put up with her rambunctious brothers with a great deal of patience, and studied Joker timidly like she had a crush on him.

All of which (particularly the last) was exactly why she was so stinking *sweet*.

"Say again?" he asked, his hand in mine holding them at his thigh.

"A little girl," I explained.

His hand convulsed in mine and the good company, good food, and wine-induced mood melted instantly as I realized what I'd just said.

I turned my head to him. "Not immediately, of course."

By the dashboard lights, I saw him grin at the road as he murmured, "Of course."

I shut up and looked at the street.

We drove in silence for a while before Joker asked, "How many you want?"

"How many what?" I asked, purposefully obtusely, scared, what with him already taking on one child (who, incidentally, was not his own) that this was *way too soon* for us to be talking about future children.

But more scared it would scare him.

Joker didn't play my game.

He gave it to me straight.

"Me. Four. That includes Travis. And I don't give a shit what they come out to be."

I wasn't breathing right when I turned again to look at him.

Therefore, it sounded funny when I asked, "You want four kids?"

"Including Travis."

My heart skipped a beat.

"This goes the distance, you good to push out three more?" he asked.

I was good to push out seven more (okay, perhaps that was slightly overstating it).

"Yes," I croaked.

He squeezed my hand. "Good."

I stared at him.

Then I blurted, "All I ever wanted was to be a wife and mom."

I watched him grin at the road again before he teased, "Shocker. No burning desire to be a grocery store clerk?"

"I lost my sister when I was six," I whispered, and his hand tightened again in mine but this time didn't loosen. "My mom when I was seventeen. Losing half my family, I know it can slip through your fingers so easily. So all I ever wanted was to spend every waking minute of my day taking care of my husband and my kids."

Joker said nothing but the air in the cab was far from light.

I swallowed, thinking I read his thoughts, and looked back to the windshield. "It's lame. I know. I should want to be a graphic designer or bank president or something."

"Most important job in the world."

I looked back at him.

"Not one fuckin' thing lame about that," he stated firmly, his hand still holding mine tight. I watched as he lifted it to his lips and brushed them against my knuckles. I was breathing strange again when he dropped our hands back to his thigh. "Not one fuckin' thing."

"Well, now, I kinda wanna be a stylist," I shared.

"Then do it," he said. "We'll get you there. You want part-time and the rest of the time family, that'll happen. You want full-time, whatever. Days where you didn't get what you want are done, Carrie."

"I can't take night classes with my work schedule," I told him.

He glanced at me again then back to the road before replying, "Day at a time. Week at a time. We'll deal with your ex. We'll be together and make the solid we got unshakable. Then we'll sort it out."

"It's easy with you," I said straight out, got another glance and kept going. "I didn't realize how hard it was with him until you gave the easy of you."

"Butterfly, I think we've both had enough hard. We could use some easy."

I wished I was driving. If I was driving, right that second, I'd pull over and kiss him.

Since I couldn't do that, I again faced forward, muttering, "Totally wish I could bronze that tire."

Joker started chuckling.

Then he turned into the alley that ran behind Tyra's house and let my hand go to lift his to the garage door opener I'd given him.

He parked beside the red wreck and shut down.

We walked to the back of the house with our arms around each other.

He let me go to unlock the door (obviously, I'd also given him keys to the house).

Joker waited for me to precede him, which I did. I tossed my purse aside and didn't turn on the light since the switch was right by the door and I didn't want to make him wait even a moment to make his way in. He'd turn on the light.

Except he didn't.

I heard the door close, then with a quiet cry, I was tugged back and found myself pressed to it, face first, my hands up in front of me.

Then my skirt was yanked up and I felt Joker's chest pressed to my back.

My breath caught.

His hand slid over my bottom.

"Saw these panties on the couch. Knowin' they were on you, fucked with me all night."

Okay, maybe he'd noticed my usual underwear, but since it came in a five pack and wasn't exciting by any stretch of the imagination, like the pink, lacy, semi-thong I was currently wearing, he just hadn't said anything.

He slid his finger along the edge of the lace that ran over the top of my cheek, and he didn't stop even as it disappeared in my cleft.

I started panting.

"Dress off, Butterfly," he growled.

Immediately, the area between my legs saturated with wet as I trembled against the door.

"Here?" I asked breathlessly.

"Now," he answered.

In the minimal space provided, I pulled my dress off.

"Spread," he grunted.

I shifted my legs apart and felt heat drench my private parts.

He slid his finger down, around, and through.

Oh yes.

My head fell back to his shoulder.

His other hand slid from my hip to my belly and up to cup my breast.

I turned my head and pressed my lips against his neck.

"Tonight, you gave good girlfriend to my friends, baby," he whispered.

"Thanks," I gasped as his fingers continued to glide between my legs.

"Now you're gonna give it to me."

"O-okay," I stammered.

He rubbed my nipple through the lacy bra with his thumb and I whimpered.

Then he pulled away.

But only for a half a second before I was turned, lifted up, thrown over his shoulder, and he prowled through the dark kitchen, the dark house, to the bedroom, where he tossed me on the bed.

He turned the light on before he commenced fucking me.

But it was proved irrevocably true through those highly pleasant proceedings that he liked nice, cute, sexy underwear.

I was going to take back the outfits I didn't wear. I loved them but one splurge was all I could handle.

But I was keeping the underwear.

All of it.

Definitely.

CHAPTER TWENTY

Start and Finish

Joker

THE NEXT MORNING, Joker was in Cherry's office pouring a cup of coffee and about to nab a donut when his cell went.

He put the coffee down, pulled out his phone, and looked at the display.

Tack had texted.

Slade. ASAP. No weapons.

Joker clenched his teeth and left the coffee where it was. Cherry was there but in the garage talking to someone.

Which meant he didn't have to delay getting on his bike by saying goodbye.

So he didn't.

He headed off of Chaos and onto Broadway, knowing what Tack's text meant.

Slade was the nightclub Knight Sebring owned.

Sebring had heard about Heidi.

And he was pissed.

Knight Sebring was loaded. On the surface of it, and Joker suspected some of that leaked into his skin, he was also total class.

But if you hurt a woman, he'd slit your throat, do it personally, and walk away forgetting you existed.

Contradictory to this, he had a stable of call girls.

He was not a pimp.

He was a protector.

Joker was no financial genius, but he knew Sebring made his money off that club. A lot of money. The man sold more drinks in a night than any other bar or restaurant in downtown Denver. And even if his cover charge was insane, night after night, the place was heaving.

He took a percentage off his girls, but Joker knew the men in his crew. They were skilled. They were cold. They believed in Sebring's mission. And they were not available to Sebring 24/7 for them to provide crowd control and keep drugs out of his club (something else Sebring had zero tolerance for). They were available 24/7 to protect his girls.

His team was large, and paying them and providing what he did for his girls, client vetting and a serious smackdown if a guy didn't treat one right, would be a hit. The man had to take a loss on his side business because Joker knew his percentage was dick.

Rumor had it Sebring did this because his mom had been a prostitute, and she'd been that because she'd been an addict. He'd lived that life with her from birth, and it had scarred him.

Joker got that. He'd entered the underground fight circuit because he'd taken so much physical abuse he had to let it out, and the way he did that had to be as violent as the way he took it.

As jacked as what Sebring did was, when he was a kid, he'd been unable to protect his mom. So now, he did what he had to do to work out the powerlessness that had to have carved itself into his soul.

Yeah, Joker definitely got that.

He parked outside Slade next to Tack, Hop, and Shy's bikes. He then went to the door that would have a fifty foot long velvet rope leading up to it that night. He put his hand on the handle and opened it.

Slade was where men who put shit in their hair and women who spent eight hundred dollars on shoes went to hook up. So the only times Joker had been there were times like this. When it was empty, silent, cavernous, a huge shell of opulence that was creepy by daylight.

As he walked across the massive space, he saw Tack, Hop, and Shy heading his way.

They stopped in the middle.

"Knight heard about Heidi," Joker started it.

Tack jerked up his chin. "Needless to say, this didn't make him happy."

"Do we want him in this?" Joker asked. "When it comes to shit like this, he has no off button and he doesn't mind mess."

"Considering Valenzuela's involvement and the fact Knight keeps his ear to the ground, when he heard about Heidi, he didn't go gonzo and tip Armageddon," Tack told him. "Which would be why we're here now. And why Mitch and Slim are up in Knight's office with Hank Nightingale and Valenzuela's on his way."

That was a surprise.

"You're shittin' me," Joker said.

"No," Tack replied. "He's got somethin' to say and he wants a sit-down to say it. Whatever it is, Knight agreed not to cave his head in and instead act as mediator."

"What he did to Heidi, we're here, we sayin' we're not gonna cave his head in?" Joker asked and went on before any of them could answer. "And if that's true, why?"

"Knight says he makes a convincing case he didn't do it," Tack said.

"Bullshit," Joker bit out.

"You know Sebring's no idiot," Shy said quietly.

He did know that.

Fuck.

But if Valenzuela didn't do it, who did?

Joker looked to Hop and Shy before turning his gaze back to Tack. "This is the sit-down I think it is, not sure why I'm here, brother. I'm not a lieutenant."

"'Cause a woman had your name carved in her stomach," Hop stated, and Joker looked back to him.

That was good enough reason.

Joker nodded.

"Let's go, but Joke," Tack started and Joker gave him his eyes. "Knight wouldn't lead us into an ambush, either verbal or otherwise. There's a reason we're here. But Valenzuela is a wildcard. He wouldn't blink at fuckin' Knight's good intentions to do something to bare the beast in any of us. So whatever that motherfucker has to say, do not give the beast to him. Keep your shit tight."

Joker nodded again.

They moved the rest of the way across the space and into a hall to a door that had one of Sebring's boys, a man called Live, standing outside it. They made nonverbal greetings as the guy opened the door, and they headed up a set of stairs that led to Sebring's sound-proofed office.

Like Tack said, Knight was there, as were Mitch, Slim, and Hank, as well as Knight's right-hand man, Rhashan Banks.

Greetings were extended, and they just got done with that when Rhash's phone buzzed. He looked at it and then to Knight.

"Valenzuela's here," he announced.

The minute Valenzuela entered the room with his soldier,

the air turned stagnant. Not a single man there wanted to be in the presence of the two who walked in, and as copasetic as this was supposed to be, that was communicated.

Men took seats at Sebring's conference table by the window that overlooked the club and Joker watched how this happened so he could be where Tack needed him to be.

Knight sat, as did Tack, Mitch, Brock, Hank, and Valenzuela, at the table. Shy lounged on Sebring's couch. Hop sat on the arm of the couch. Valenzuela's soldier stood close to his back. Rhashan leaned against the door.

So Joker took his seat on the arm of one of the chairs in front of Sebring's desk.

Valenzuela started it.

And he did it with a surprise opener.

"I come to barter."

"Barter what?" Knight asked, looking displeased because whatever he thought this was, that was not it.

"I know who killed Heidi. I give that up, you…" Valenzuela's eyes went to Tack, "retreat to Chaos."

"And how would you know that?" Mitch asked.

Valenzuela looked to Joker. "I got birds who sing too."

Joker's back snapped straight, but he kept his seat when Hop's eyes sliced to him.

"We'll consider our territory eight miles around Chaos, you give us the name," Tack said.

Tack was giving up two miles for Heidi.

Said a lot about him but it fucked their cause.

It would be worth it.

Valenzuela looked to him. "Retreat *to Chaos*," he stated. "By that I mean *Ride*."

Shy shifted from ass in the couch to ass on the edge of it and Hop took his feet but hung back.

They did this because that was an insult. Heidi's life was

worth a lot, but Chaos giving up what they'd given blood for, which meant giving in, giving up, and letting filth infest their turf was asking too fucking much.

Brock, who had more experience in a very real way, living among scum like Valenzuela when he was undercover for the DEA, stood. "This is a waste of time."

"Don't be hasty, detective," Valenzuela urged.

"Then make an offer that isn't bullshit," Brock shot back.

Valenzuela smiled. "I give you the name, you give me Monk's fights." He looked to Tack. "And a marker."

Shit.

Fuck.

Owing Valenzuela.

Joker hoped like fuck Tack did not give that.

And they didn't have the fights. The boys had voted it down. They'd let Monk swing.

Weirdly, Valenzuela didn't know that.

Brock sat back down.

"You been talkin' to Monk?" Tack asked.

He shook his head. "He says that goes through your fighter," then he tipped his head to Joker.

Goddamned shit.

They'd let Monk swing and he still was using Joker's name to keep his shit free of Valenzuela.

"You got the fights," Tack gave him something they didn't have, which meant it didn't cost to give it. "No marker."

Valenzuela shook his head again but said, "No marker, then I'll take the two miles."

"That's off the table, seein' as you showed disrespect by startin' the way you did."

"Then no name unless there's a marker," Valenzuela volleyed.

"Right," Tack shot back. "Marker with conditions. No

bitches. No drugs. No felonies. Nothin' fuckin' illegal. Which means no enforcement. No transportation. No muscle."

"This leaves selling cookies, Tack, and I don't sell cookies," Valenzuela returned, his voice turning impatient.

"It leaves you havin' a month of Chaos turnin' the other way. And you wanna jump on that, Benito, and I know you get me," Tack retorted.

Joker knew Valenzuela got Tack. Brock and Mitch were there for that reason.

Chaos was keeping their patch clean.

They were also keeping tabs. Anything they heard was fed to the cops.

Valenzuela just couldn't know what they were—or weren't—hearing.

The truth was, the majority of lowlifes on the street were scared shitless of Valenzuela, which meant Chaos usually got dick.

But Valenzuela didn't know that.

"You do know," Hank butted in, "that I'm listenin' to this bullshit as a courtesy to men I respect. But I'm also the investigating officer on the homicide in question. So if you know a name, make your deal real fuckin' quick and say it or you'll be in handcuffs for obstruction of justice."

Valenzuela's mouth tightened and Joker dropped his head as he fought back a smile.

Hank being there would not have been his call. As much as Lee straddled the line of the law, doing what he had to do to get done whatever job he had to get done, Hank was like Mitch. A straight shooter. He could easily give up his badge and make wads of cash with his brother.

Instead he protected and served.

Valenzuela had assumed incorrectly that Hank was one with their crew.

Tack had brought in a ringer.

So that shit that just went down was funny.

"At those fights, Chaos recently sent a message."

At these words from Valenzuela, Joker's head came back up.

He felt a chill slide down his spine when he saw Valenzuela's eyes on him.

"I knew about Heidi," he said in a creepy, low voice. "Thought you were the man who'd get her out of the life. She'd do anything for you."

Joker's throat closed.

He didn't know that. He did. But he still didn't.

Valenzuela wasn't done.

"I let her do what she had to do. It made her happy, and Heidi did better work when she was happy. But everyone knew what she was up to. *Everyone*."

"Jesus, give it to us," Tack growled.

"Vendetta. Against Chaos," Valenzuela declared. "And who's left in Denver who has enough history to know about the calling card a former Chaos brother used to leave who also has that kind of vendetta and who is not me?"

"Monk," Joker whispered.

Hank stood ready to roll before Chaos did.

"This your word or you got more?" he asked.

"Tine handled the transaction," Valenzuela told Hank. "If you can find him, he might help you."

Tine was Monk's money man.

And Valenzuela had forced it out of him. So if he left him breathing, he was vapor.

Hank wasted no more time. He strode to the door.

"Hank," Tack called. Hank looked back, still moving. "Find him before we do."

Hank said nothing.

He walked out the door.

"I hear you've hung up your gloves, as it were," Valenzuela said, and Joker looked back to him to see the asshole had eyes on him. "If you ever want to fight for me, I don't mind having Chaos blood on my cement."

Joker just stared at him.

But he allowed his lip to curl.

Valenzuela smiled and pushed away from the table, saying, "I think we're done here."

He was two steps from the table before Knight spoke. "Benito."

Valenzuela turned back.

"You ever think of usin' me to negotiate your bullshit again without you sharin' with me you wanna negotiate your bullshit, rethink," Knight warned.

"Sebring, you're aware I don't act out of the kindness of my heart," Valenzuela returned.

"Seein' as you don't have one, yeah. That isn't lost on me," Knight stated. "But you told me you wanted peace and a safe place to share you weren't involved with what happened to that woman so Chaos wouldn't act on assumptions. You want a sit-down and me to keep that peaceful, you do not feed me a line of bullshit, or a player in this town who's keepin' himself to himself is gonna have to reconsider his position."

Convinced he was made of steel, Valenzuela just smiled.

Since he wasn't, Knight knew it, and he liked disrespect about as much as Tack did, he added, "And stop sendin' your girls to work Chaos."

Valenzuela stopped smiling. "Is this keeping yourself to yourself?"

"You know about the girls," Knight said low, and Joker looked to Shy.

Shy's lips hitched up and his eyes lit.

Fucking shit.

Knight was throwing down.

"You do business your way, I'll do it mine," Valenzuela retorted.

"I get word your way is a way I don't like, we'll be having another meeting and it won't be as comfortable," Knight fired back.

"You don't wanna get involved in this," Valenzuela warned.

"Take care of your girls," Knight ordered.

Hop moved and Joker looked to him to see he'd again sat on the arm of the couch. He'd also dropped his head.

He did this to hide his smile.

In that moment, Joker knew.

Sebring was clearly using this meeting, and the way Valenzuela played it, as an excuse to wade in.

There were not a lot of pimps who went head to head with Knight. He might have been considering throwing his hat in the ring for a while.

But the time had come.

Joker wondered if Tack, Shy, and Hop knew before the meet, but it didn't really matter.

Whether they wanted him or not, Sebring was on the team.

Valenzuela didn't say another word. He and his soldier walked out.

When the door closed behind them, Joker announced, "I want Monk."

"Joke," Mitch said on a sigh.

"Hank'll take care of it," Brock put in.

Tack stood, eyes to Brock. "He's got a day."

Mitch looked to the ceiling.

Brock leaned forward to reach for his phone, muttering,

"Best call Lee to get his ass with his brother before half our team is incarcerated, awaiting trial for homicide."

"I take it you just etched your name on the invitation list for our little coffee klatch," Mitch noted, now looking at Sebring.

Knight grinned. "I'll bring the pastries."

"Fuck me," Mitch muttered.

Hop smiled at Shy, who smiled back.

Joker did not smile.

Handshakes, gratitude, chin lifts, and nods were given and Chaos strolled out.

Joker waited until they were standing at their bikes before he repeated, "I want Monk."

Tack, head bent as he pulled on his gloves, sliced his eyes to Joker.

"Monk no longer exists."

Another chill slid down Joker's spine as he stared into Tack's eyes, seeing a look in them he'd never seen before on any man in his life.

Tack finished yanking on his gloves and swung his leg over his bike. Joker didn't do the same because Hop reached out a hand and wrapped his fingers around Joker's forearm for a beat before he let him go, this telling him to hold.

He held.

Tack roared off.

Joker looked to Hop.

"Hank'll get Monk," Hop said.

Joker opened his mouth to speak, but Hop kept going.

"And Monk will go down inside."

Joker shut his mouth.

"You'll be clean. Chaos will be clean. But we'll be one marker lighter," Hop finished.

"That gonna work for you?" Shy asked.

Joker's head filled with Heidi dead in an alley. She'd been

pretty. Marred by a little man with a small dick who'd been shamed by bikers and used her to make them pay.

She'd had a thing for Joker. He had no idea how she'd hung her hopes on him, but he knew she'd had a thing for him.

She had never made him laugh. She annoyed him more than anything, and it had never been cute.

Mostly, when he was with her, he felt nothing.

But she was someone's daughter. She was going to give someone a child. And there was no telling who she could have been if she'd been allowed to keep breathing.

Now she was dead.

No, it didn't work for him.

But he had a woman, a kid, a brotherhood, family.

So it had to.

He jerked up his chin.

Hop nodded.

Shy clapped him on the shoulder.

Then they got on their bikes and rode.

*   *   *

That night after dinner, Carissa, sitting next to him on the couch, started poking hard at the laptop on her lap with her finger, grunting "Unh! Unh! Unh!" with each poke.

She then tossed it on the coffee table, where it skidded, taking the little basket she put the remotes in with it.

The basket went down.

The laptop was still up but half of it was hanging off the table.

"It's broken!" she cried.

"I hope so, or you poundin' on it and tossin' it around wouldn't be all that smart," Joker muttered, his eyes still on the TV.

He felt her turn to him.

She ignored his comment and asked, "Do you have a laptop I can use to put the furniture in storage on Craigslist?"

"I don't have a storage unit,' and you cleaned my room. Did you find a laptop?" he asked back.

"No," she bit out, damned cute.

"So...no," he answered.

"Ugh!" she grunted, also cute, so he looked her way and saw her drop her head to the back of the couch, which was again cute.

He twisted to her, wrapping an arm around her and leaning up to get in her face.

"I'll buy you a laptop for your birthday."

She lifted her head off the couch an inch. "That's not going to help me sell the furniture *now*. Dad's paying for that unit. He has two boxes in there. We can put the boxes in the garage and he can save that money."

"An early birthday present."

She rolled her eyes and dropped her head back.

He knew that wouldn't go over.

Still.

"Butterfly, you made a date with Elvira to return eight thousand dollars' worth of clothes and shoes and two of the outfits in that mix would look spectacular on you and cost nowhere near eight thousand dollars. You got money in the bank but you won't splurge. Thank Christ you didn't feel the same about the panties and bras. But none of that costs as much as a laptop and you still didn't keep it. So with that, I gotta ask, when're you gonna lay out the cake to buy a laptop that in this day and age you need?"

She lifted her head up another inch. "After I put the bedroom furniture in the front yard, tape signs up around the neighborhood, and sit out there all day waiting for someone who'll happen by and pay me what I'm asking, making it so

I don't have to take a hit to the savings I like having to buy a laptop."

"That's one way to go. But how much do you want outta that shit?"

"It all cost nearly six thousand dollars, it's seen nearly no use, and is less than three years old, so I was hoping maybe five hundred dollars."

He sat back, still turned to her and she came up.

"Six thousand dollars?" he asked.

"His mother picked it," she mumbled. "It includes mattresses, which are expensive, and the furniture wasn't exactly Ikea." Her eyes slid away. "She might break into hives if she went to Ikea. Though the maze bit scares me, I love the bottom floor where all the gadgets are."

"How 'bout this," he ignored her rambling on Ikea and the fact she spent six times more on a guest bedroom set than he did on rent his first year away from his dad. "I take the laptop in and see if Cherry's got a fix on someone who looks at computers. She's got one in the office, it can't work all the time, and the woman is a lot of things, but an IT geek isn't one of them. We also pass it around you got that shit available. But you don't take anything less than three K for it, Carrie. If it's near-new and quality, you do not take that hit. You sell for as much as you can, get a laptop that's dependable, and bank the rest."

"That sounds like a plan," she said.

That was easy.

Now for the last.

"You're worried about your dad payin' for that unit, we'll shift crap around at the Compound or the stockroom at the store. We put it there."

She grinned. "My manly man biker. He has an answer for everything."

"My goofball Butterfly. She's got a knack for makin' me hard even when she's bein' a total goof," he shot back.

Her eyes fired and her hand came up to hit his chest.

"Little high, baby," he muttered.

Her gaze heated further, but as she slid her hand down, she asked, "Is this much sex natural?"

That said her ex not only didn't have talent, but it would seem he also didn't have stamina.

"Natural to what?" he asked back, going in, aiming for her jaw.

"Natural to a body's health. I mean, I wouldn't want you to have a heart attack in your twenties with all the effort you put in to pleasuring me."

Pleasuring me.

And the woman didn't think she was a goofball.

He grinned, finished running his lips down her jaw, lifted up, and pressed closer.

"I think my body can hack it," he told her.

"Well that's good," she mumbled, eyes on his mouth, which he felt on his mouth and also in his dick.

"What you want, Carrie?" he whispered.

She lifted her gaze to his and whispered back, "You can start by kissing me, sweetie."

He started there.

Some time later, he finished a fuckuva lot differently.

Tack

Tack stood on the deck of his house, his eyes to the silent dark of the woods on his mountain.

He had his phone to his ear and it was ringing.

"Tack," Knight greeted.

"Yo, you hear?" Tack asked.

"Not yet," Knight answered.

"Lee found Tine. He sang for Hank. They're booking Monk right now for conspiracy to commit murder," Tack told him.

Knight was silent.

Tack gave him that for a few beats before he said low, "We need to deal."

"He stands trial," Knight returned quickly. "He goes down. I want him to squirm."

"Agreed," Tack replied.

"He'll be taken care of after he goes down."

Tack drew breath in through his nose.

Then he stated, "You got a Chaos marker."

"No," Knight said quietly. "No marker from Chaos. I do this for a woman I didn't know named Heidi."

Tack heard the disconnect.

He didn't smile at his phone.

He dropped his hand and stared at the quiet peace of his mountain.

Then he turned and went inside to his woman and their boys.

CHAPTER TWENTY-ONE

My Place

Carissa

THE NEXT EVENING, I was at the stove making dinner. Joker was still at Ride. There was a meeting of the brothers. Therefore, for the first time when we'd both worked during the day, he was going to be home later than me.

This meant I got my house all to myself, another first.

I didn't mind solitude. I liked it.

But I wasn't a woman who wanted a big family just because. I preferred company.

So I was looking forward to him being home.

On that thought, my phone rang.

I turned down the water that would eventually be boiling the broccoli and went to the counter where my phone was.

I saw the name on the screen and sighed.

Then I took the call and put it to my ear.

"Hello, Aaron. Is Travis okay?" I greeted.

"Hey, Riss. He's fine," he replied. "Listen, I have some interns working on things for me at the office and that means I have a break. I thought I could bring Travis over and we could all go out to dinner."

I wouldn't mind him bringing Travis over but only if Aaron left him and he could have dinner with Joker and me.

I didn't say this to Aaron because I didn't think he'd be big on that idea.

"I'm not sure that's a good idea," I mumbled.

"I'll bring your boxes."

Darn.

I wanted those boxes.

"Did you get them out of the attic?" I asked cautiously.

"Yes, Riss. I can just load them up, grab Travis, and we could be over there in fifteen minutes."

He had the boxes down and he was bringing them.

Maybe he hadn't looked inside.

"How about if you bring them when you return Travis to me on Monday?" I suggested.

"Would like to see you sooner, honey," he said softly.

"Aaron—" I started.

"We shouldn't be apart," he declared, a declaration that seriously concerned me. "This isn't good for us. For Travis. For you, having to stand on your feet behind a cash register at a fucking grocery store all day. Travis being with people who aren't his parents while we both work."

He was *such* a jerk.

He knew that'd get to me. He knew I wanted to be a stay-at-home mom.

But things had changed. Big Petey was awesome. And as much as I hated to admit it, Tory loved Travis. She watched him during the day for Aaron, and as far as I knew, she liked doing it. It wasn't optimal, but any child should have as many people love him (or her) as they could get.

Further, I liked my job. LeLane's was great. They took me on when I was pregnant, knowing I'd have to take a maternity leave imminently, but they'd still done it. Sharon managed everyone's schedules as best she could to fit their lives. They employed nice people. They were family owned, and as such, they treated their employees as if they were family.

Scanning groceries might not be very challenging, but I liked people. I liked gabbing with the folks who came through my line. I liked making the ones I'd become familiar with feel a part of the LeLane family.

It didn't pay a lot but it was good work.

I didn't like the way he'd started knocking it.

I also didn't think I should tell him that.

"I'm thinking we should start to talk only through our attorneys," I told him instead.

"Don't do that, Riss. Not to Travis."

Emotional blackmail.

Another something not new from Aaron.

But I was in a pickle.

I needed those boxes. I needed to stay in his good graces so he didn't get angry and do something ugly, not only with those boxes but to me and through me to our son.

But I also needed him to stop doing this.

Treading carefully, I said, "Aaron, if you've been thinking on things, I'd like to ask you to think more. Think about all the water that's under the bridge. Think about what's happened and where we are now and the fact that leads to us moving on but doing it in a way where we can take care of our son, just separately."

"It's always been you," he whispered.

I closed my eyes, feeling the heat of anger hit my cheeks.

He did this too, telling me these things, trying to make me feel special after he tore me apart.

And anyway, what about Tory?

I didn't get the chance to ask that.

"You know that, Riss," he continued. "No matter what

we've been through, you know it's always been you. It'll always *be* you."

"No matter what *you* put me through," I hissed, unable to stop it from coming out of my mouth.

"I know," he agreed immediately. "I know I fucked up. I know I did it repeatedly. And I know this is the biggest fuck-up of them all."

I could take no more, but more importantly, I didn't want to.

"I can't do this," I told him. "I don't want to do it ever, but if you feel you must, I can't do it now. I also don't want to do it over the phone."

"Then let me bring our son over."

"I don't think that's a good idea," I told him firmly. "It goes without saying I want to see Travis, but Joker will be here soon. If you're fine with him being here then okay. Joker can look after Travis while we talk. He'd like that. But if you come, I want you to bring the boxes, and before you come, I need to talk to Joker to ask if he's okay with that."

"Why would you need to ask him?" he asked. "It's your house."

"Because we have plans," I answered. "I'm making him dinner right now, and it's rude to change plans at the last second or force someone to spend time with someone they might not wish to spend time with after they've had a long day at work."

"You do know he belongs to a motorcycle gang," Aaron suddenly informed me, and my head jerked as frost formed all over my skin.

"I do," I said slowly. "However, it's a club, not a gang," I corrected. "Though, what I'd like to know is how you know."

"Were you meaning to keep that from me?" he asked.

"I wasn't. It's just that Joker really isn't your business," I shared.

"He spends time with my wife and son."

"Your ex-wife, Aaron," I corrected again. "And yes, he spends time with your son. So does Tory. Shall we go over Tory versus Joker, or did I make my point the last time?"

"That might factor if Tory was going to be in my life for very much longer."

I drew in a hissed breath.

There was the answer about Tory.

"This isn't you, Carissa, spending time with some guy in a biker gang," he told me.

"You don't know me," I whispered. "We spent a decade together, and in that time you didn't make the effort to know me."

"I certainly didn't, if you're the kind of woman who thinks it's okay to expose her child to a biker gang."

"*Club*," I snapped.

"*Whatever*," he snapped back.

All right.

I was done treading cautiously.

"It's not *whatever*. It's important," I educated him. "And further, in not taking the time to get to know me, you failed to learn that I'm not stupid. I may have done stupid things because I loved you, but I'm not stupid. And not being stupid, I know this is a threat."

"Riss—"

I cut him off.

"You're looking into me. I don't like that, Aaron. It's invasive and insulting and ultimately will be destructive. I'll tell you now, I'd like very much if we can move beyond what's happened between us to build a relationship that's considerate of each other in order to provide a healthy upbringing for our son. That's what I'd like."

I took in a quick breath and before he could say anything—because I had a lot to say he needed to hear—I continued.

"Until I can get on my feet in order to take care of Travis financially, I'd also like your financial assistance. It won't be decades. It'll be until I can get an education to build a career where I can make more money. And further, while he's still so very young, I'd like for him to have a more stable home life rather than being passed back and forth every week. And as his mother, I believe that time should be spent with me. In order to give him time to do something crucial in his life, bond with his father, I'm willing to give you days, evenings, et cetera, with your son so you can continue to do that. That's what I want from you. *All* I want from you."

I drew in another swift breath and launched right back in.

"What I *don't* want is to fight with you. I don't want Travis to grow up with two parents who hate each other, who are always battling and bickering. That would *not* be good for our son. As he grows, as I get on my feet, I'll be less dependent on your financial assistance and he'll need more time with his father. If we can get to a place where we can make these decisions and instigate these changes when they're needed without tearing into each other, Travis will benefit. But I'll say, if you fight me, I'll fight back. And if you fight me, Aaron, it will tell me *precisely* how you feel, not only about me, but about your duties as father to our son."

I pulled in more breath and finished, giving it to him completely in the hopes that for once in his life he'd care what I had to say and *listen* to me.

"The idea of us getting back together, Aaron, honestly, I don't want to hurt you. I know you might not believe that but it's true. However, we're *over*. You didn't hurt me. You destroyed me. I picked myself up, put myself back together, and came out of that stronger, seeing the mistakes I made in the past. I'm delighted that from the love we once had we made a son we both adore. But there is no longer anything there. I have a man in my life I'm coming to care about enormously. He treats me well, and he's falling in love with our boy. Truthfully, if you care about me at all, you not only will allow me to have that but *want* it for me. And with that, this conversation is over. I just ask that you please think on all I've said. And I ask you, when you bring Travis back to me on Monday, that you also bring my things. Now, have a good evening."

With that, not knowing if it was the right thing to do not to let him get a word in, and concerned it wasn't, I disconnected the call.

I put the phone down not only uneasy about essentially hanging up on Aaron and how he'd react to that, but downright worried about that entire conversation.

He might or might not be breaking up with Tory (but it seemed he was).

He might or might not after I'd said my piece wish to get back with me.

But he also might be saying these things to buy time to look into me in order to come to our meeting, or to court, with whatever ammunition he felt he needed, dragging in anyone he felt would aid his cause, and at his sole discretion dragging *down* everyone that he felt he could use to get what he wanted.

I looked around my lovely kitchen, which I'd yet to really take in.

It was at least three times the size of the kitchen at my old apartment, and in that moment I realized it wasn't a lot smaller than the kitchen I had in the house I'd lived in with Aaron.

A house his parents bought us for our wedding. A house I hadn't even viewed before it was given to me as a big surprise present with all the fanfare his father made of it as we stood on the dance floor at our reception with him and his wife making the grand announcement. And after we returned from Massachusetts, I was moved into it.

I wandered out of the kitchen, into the dining room/living room and gazed around.

My furniture fit here. The furniture I'd picked that was attractive and welcoming and comfortable, it fit in this house.

Perfectly.

Like I'd bought it for right here.

This was my place.

This was me.

I moved to the big picture window by the dining room table and looked out.

Big lawn. Room for kids to play. Same in the back with a nice deck. A place to grill out. A place to relax.

Quiet neighborhood.

I waited and watched and I did this for a while.

Only two cars drove down the street. They didn't race down it. They didn't have blaring music. They drove sedately through a safe, quiet, family neighborhood.

"This is my place. This is me," I whispered.

I was where I needed to be for my son.

But also for me.

I had the man I needed to have who loved my son.

But also he was falling in love with me.

Aaron was going to pull out all the stops.

And he was going to ruin *everything*.

I heard the back door open just as I focused on a sign in the yard at a house across the street.

"Carrie, water's boiling," Joker called.

"Can you turn it off?" I called back, my eyes glued to that sign.

Seconds passed.

"Hey," I heard.

"Hey," I replied, eyes to that sign.

I felt him get close. I felt his hand light on the small of my back. I felt his heat. I felt his strength.

"Hey," he said softly, one syllable, one word repeated, but the change in tone said everything.

"The house across the street is for rent," I told him, staring at that sign.

"Yeah?" he asked gently.

"We should talk to Mrs. Heely. See if she wants to move. Get her out of that place," I told him.

"Carrie."

"Yes?"

"Look at me, Butterfly."

I tore my gaze from the sign and looked up at him.

He also looked at me.

"Fuck, baby, what happened?"

"Aaron is investigating me."

His jaw clenched.

"He knows you belong to Chaos," I told him.

"I'm not hidin' that, nor would I ever hide that," he told me.

"I know," I whispered.

He stared at me. He did this for a while, his hand on my back, light, not claiming like he usually touched me.

Just there.

Suddenly he announced, "Fought the underground fight circuit."

I blinked.

Then I asked, "What?"

"Illegal fights, illegal betting. Did it for years. Never got caught. Made a shit ton of money. All cash. Didn't pay taxes on it and won't if I don't have to."

I stared.

Joker kept talking.

"Didn't live a quiet life, but never did anything really stupid and never got caught doin' the semi-stupid stuff I did do. In other words, I don't have a rap sheet, Carissa."

"I...okay," I replied.

"I've done drugs," he went on, and my head jerked. "Smoked pot. Snorted coke. Nothin' else. Don't mind the mellow of a joint but didn't like the high of blow. But as a fighter, neither did good things for me, so I stopped doin' that shit a long time ago."

I was faintly shaking my head as I repeated, "Okay."

"Chaos has been a clean club for over a decade," he kept going. "Not a single member has been taken in for anything more than misdemeanors. Drunk and disorderly, that kinda shit. There are boys who got sheets, but nothin' serious. Not for a long fuckin' time."

With that, it started dawning on me, and what was dawning on me also started warming me.

"Okay, Joker," I whispered.

"And what I didn't give you a coupla nights ago," he carried on, "was somethin' I knew would freak you and somethin' I knew the Club would have in hand. That bein' an informant for Chaos, a woman, a former prostitute, was murdered. She was not killed by the guy who has an issue with the Club. She was killed by a weasel with a grudge. It shits me to have to tell you this because I wanted to protect you from it, but you gotta have it all just in case that jackhole gets it. She had words carved in her skin, one was Chaos and the other was my name because she was my snitch."

"Oh my gosh," I breathed, feeling my eyes grow round.

"She wasn't a good woman but she tried to do good by the Club, even if in doin' it, she got paid for it. That was her world and that's the way it needed to be. But she's dead and she'll be avenged. The Club will see to that, but they won't see to it directly. The way it's done will never color the Club."

I turned to him, putting a hand to his stomach, feeling all he was giving me, *why* he was giving it to me, warm me with a heat that sunk straight into my bones.

"Joker—"

"That's it," he stated. "That's all of me. Or all of me that could hurt you and Travis. Now, straight up, if you needed me to leave the Club 'cause you think that would make your case stronger, I'll tell you, I'd consider it. But that'd say somethin' about you. Somethin' about what you think of my brothers, who are me. And in the end, I know it would fuck with me, which would fuck with us. So I can't give that to you, Carrie."

"I—"

"But I will walk away."

My body locked.

He kept talking.

"It'll kill me. I want you in my life. I want your son in my life. I like what we got, and I like the idea of where we're going, what we're building. Never dreamed in my life. But now I dream of that. Givin' it to you. Givin' you your Candy. And more. Havin' that for me. But for you and your boy, you need me to, I'll walk away."

No.

No, no, no!

"You were a fighter?" I asked hoarsely, emotion clogging my throat, needing to ask that because I couldn't even think of how he finished all he had to give me.

"Had a father beat on me," he answered and I fought my flinch. "Had to let that go. Had to get it out. So I did."

"A woman was murdered?" I went on.

"Yeah. And I won't know who or how or when, but if the man responsible bites it, I'll know why."

I fell silent.

His hand left me.

I felt bereft.

"Carissa, if this has to happen, it's gotta happen now," he declared. "You need this done, I gotta walk out the door. You give me more of you, more of Trav, make that decision later, you'll strip somethin' off of me that'll never heal."

"If you walk away from me, you'd kill me."

His head jerked.

But I wasn't done.

"And if you ever turn your back on the Club, I'd never forgive you, Carson Steele."

Joker stood there, completely still, and stared at me.

"Aaron is going to do everything he can to ruin everything," I told him. "And he might succeed. That frightens me. No, it *terrifies* me, because I don't want to go through it again. But this time, I don't want to put you or anyone else I care about through it. That said, whatever he takes, wherever I land the next time, and the next, and maybe even the next, I'll survive, just as long as I still have Travis and just as long as I still have you."

I got my last word out and then I had my back to the floor and Joker was on me.

He was tugging at my clothes.

I returned the gesture.

Desperate, breathing heavily, clothes flying, lips dragging, mouths connecting, tongues tasting, hands roaming, nails scratching, fingers tangling, we went at each other, Joker on top, me on top, and back, and again, until I could take no more.

"Condom, baby," I breathed my plea.

He reached out and dragged his jeans our way.

"Back, spread, hold for me, Carrie," he ordered.

I rolled off him to my back and did as he asked.

He rolled on the condom and wasted no time covering me.

But as frantic as it was getting to that point, right then, his body on mine, my legs circling his hips, my arms curved up his back, hands splayed on his shoulder blades, his eyes locked to mine, his weight in one forearm, the other arm under me, wrapped around my waist, I felt the tip and then he slid in slowly.

My lips parted as I took him inch by inch until he was buried completely.

"So fuckin' pretty," he murmured, gaze still on me.

I closed my eyes.

I was in love.

I opened them and whispered, "Please, *please*, don't ever mention leaving me again."

His response was to dip his head and slide his nose along mine as he groaned, "I won't, Butterfly."

"Ever, Carson. Promise me."

"Promise, baby."

I touched my lips to his. "Thank you, sweetie."

He slanted his head and kissed me.

Then as slowly as he entered me, he made love to me, on the floor by the dining room set.

Necessarily, of course, it ended up faster, harder, breathtaking, overwhelming.

Astounding.

And after, lying on my back on the floor under Joker feeling my climax leave me as his weight and warmth pressed into me, his breaths feathering against my neck, it came to me again.

This was my place.

This was me.

This was precisely where I was meant to be.

"Did you turn off the water?" I asked.

Joker's body moved sharply with his short, startled laugh.

Then he lifted his head, looked me in the eyes, and answered, "Yeah, Carrie."

"Good," I mumbled.

His hand came up and he brushed some curls away from my forehead before he said, "We're gonna be okay."

I nodded.

"It's all gonna be okay, baby," he whispered.

I stared into his eyes and I knew it would.

I knew it.

Because I knew, lying there on the floor with Joker still inside me, his weight bearing into me, this was *his* place.

And like me, he liked his place.

So he'd never leave.

Joker

The next day, Joker waited a long time, leaning against his bike next to the black Lexus SUV.

Eventually he showed.

Walking to his car from the courthouse, the fucker clocked him, stopped, took out his phone, and shot a picture of Joker.

Joker didn't move.

He knew what the jackhole would do next.

Aaron Neiland was not a man to let the opportunity for a confrontation slide.

So he did what Joker knew he'd do.

He walked right up to Joker and declared, "You can't intimidate me."

"She's happy."

The man went stock-still.

"Unless you're on the phone fuckin' with her head, or after, when you get in there and I got work to do to sort her out, she's happy. She's the mother of your kid, man, you should want that for her. She hasn't had a lot of it in her life, but now she's got steady. She's got peace. Leave her be and give her that."

"She deserves better," Neiland retorted.

"You're right," Joker agreed. "You had your shot and you tore her up. Now she's found better."

Neiland's upper lip lifted in a sneer. "Are you saying you're better than me?"

"I'm sayin' for Carissa I am."

He shook his head. "Unbelievable that you've convinced yourself of that."

"No," Joker returned. "What's unbelievable is that you two made a kid. You made a fuckin' *miracle*, man, and doin' it, you assumed a responsibility. And the mother of that kid has lost her little sister. Her mother. The man she loved cheated on her, kicked her out of his bed, his house, put another woman in it, forced her to live in a shit place that wasn't safe for her or their baby, and he can stand there thinkin' he's better for her than me. *That* is unbelievable."

Unable to counter that point, he turned away, "I'm not talking to you about my family."

It was too important so Joker didn't let it go. "All I'm askin' is for you to let her be happy."

He turned back. "*I* can make her happy."

"Good job you've done of it."

He leaned toward Joker. "She needs you now, *friend*. What happens when she doesn't?"

"She'll still be with me."

He leaned back, smiling a nasty smile. "You're sure?"

"Absolutely."

"Dream world, Steele," he scoffed.

Joker pushed away from his bike and turned fully toward him, watching the man go alert but keep his position. Though his eyes darting side to side said it all.

He didn't want to lose face but he needed an escape plan, because he knew if it came down to fists, he'd take a beating.

But Joker didn't move an inch toward him.

"Didn't wanna get into this, and you don't get it all. It's mine and Carrie's. But she gets from me what she didn't get from you in a variety of ways, Neiland. She loves it. Some, she begs for it."

"Crass, but not surprising," he hissed.

"You mistake me," Joker said quietly. "Part of it I see you get, but you don't get it all. You're so up your own ass you think *she's* gotta work for it to make her deserve *you*. You go your own way, do your own thing, get off with who you want when you want. Test after test, and she passes, accepts you as however you wanna be, or she's out. With me, she told me, straight up, it's easy. I give her easy. *We're* easy. And that's because she knows where she stands with me and that ground I put her on, man, is not shaky. Now, I ask you, you want her back so bad, you want your *family*, then I gotta think you got some feeling for her. Some small amount a' feeling. If you don't, then this is not about her but about you havin' a need to best her, or me, or both of us. But if you feel something, what I'd wanna know is, why wouldn't you want her to have easy?"

Again, unable to counter, Neiland announced, "We're done," and turned away.

"Of course we are," Joker muttered, looking to his boots.

"Man to man, as you obviously want this to be," Neiland said and Joker looked back at him. "Once I'm done with *you*, Carissa won't want herself or our son anywhere near you."

"Good luck with that, friend," Joker replied.

Another sneer. "You've no idea."

Without hesitation, Joker gave him his ideas.

"She knows I was a fighter. She knows I smoked pot. She knows and likes every member of my Club."

"She know a hooker had your name carved into her belly?" he retorted.

"I didn't share the location, but yeah, she knows that too."

Neiland blinked.

"Got more?" Joker asked, but he knew he didn't, so as Neiland stood there staring at him, Joker shook his head. "Then I guess we're done."

"We're far from done."

Joker kept shaking his head and started to turn to his bike.

"She has a man with a criminal record looking after our son," he bit out, and Joker grinned but he did it so he wouldn't laugh.

He looked back to him. "Good call, go after Pete. That'll work."

Neiland exposed uncertainty for only a beat before he hid it and said, "That doesn't say Carissa's able to make appropriate decisions about our child's upbringing."

"You sure you wanna share your whole strategy with me? If you do, I'm cool, but give me a second to get some paper so I can take notes."

"You're an asshole," he sneered.

"I'm in love with your ex-wife," Joker returned, no amusement in his voice, his eyes locked to Neiland's. "I've loved her since high school, man. She means everything to me. You gotta drag her down, that'll suck, but I'll pick her back up. You gotta rip her apart, I'll fuckin' hate watchin' it, but I'll put her back together. Do what you gotta do to make you feel like you got the bigger dick. But know this, in the end, it's gonna be her and me. So take your shot. Spend your money. Score those marks on your soul. Scar your son. Push her to the point she can't stand the sight of you. But do it knowin' that's all on you. Just like everything that went before, it's all on you."

With that, Joker dismissed him. Turning to his bike, mounting it, switching the ignition, backing out, he didn't even look at the man.

He rode away knowing that wouldn't be the end. He also rode away knowing he had to have a chat with his brothers.

But he rode away hoping that whatever end that man pushed for, it didn't scar his son.

The rest, Joker had in hand.

* * *

He wasn't surprised Carissa was tense that Monday while waiting for Neiland to return Travis.

He just didn't know all the reasons why she was tense.

When the man showed, like he'd been making a habit of doing, Joker stood back, making sure she knew he had her back and Neiland registered his presence.

This time, fortunately, the drop off lasted a much shorter time.

But it curled nauseatingly in his gut, watching as Neiland tried to crawl right up her ass, deciding to ignore Joker and focus solely on her, giving so much saccharine, it was a wonder the room didn't explode with it.

But she was all about her kid, forcing the courtesy, and the two boxes that Neiland made a big show about going back to his car and getting for her.

She was only slightly pushy in closing the door on his ass.

But once he was gone, cuddling Travis to her, she moved right to the window and watched him go.

So Joker did too.

The second the Lexus pulled from the curb, Carissa was in his space.

"Say hi to Joker, sweetie pie. Mommy's gotta do something real quickly," she said, giving Travis a kiss, a cuddle and handing him off to Joker.

Then she dropped right down to the boxes, tearing off the tape.

Joker gave his own cuddles to the kid, glad to have him back, his weight in his arms, hearing the noises he made.

But his eyes were on Carissa.

She dug through the first box in a frenzy, and watching it, Joker felt his frame string tight.

"Carrie, what the—?"

He cut himself off when she made a weird, panicky noise, turned desperately to the next box and tore off the tape.

Travis started fretting in his arm.

"Carrie," he whispered as she pulled back the flaps and dug through.

Then suddenly, she yanked a frame to her chest and fell to her ass, knees up, curling her upper body over it, rocking.

He crouched beside her. "Baby."

"Now I have everything I need from him. Now I don't need anything from him. Now I have everything I need," she said like a chant, her voice husky.

Travis made an unhappy sound as Joker lifted his hand and pulled her hair away from her shoulder.

He saw the tears wetting her cheek.

"Carrie," his voice, too, was thick, "talk to me."

Her damp eyes came to him as she uncurled, dropping her arms and the back of the frame hit her thighs, exposing what was in it.

Joker looked at it and his throat closed.

"Now I have everything I need," she whispered, her words trembling.

Joker dropped to a knee, tightened his arm on her boy, holding him close as he slid the fingers of his other hand into her hair, pulling her head back gently.

He went in for the kiss.

Travis gave them what they needed, allowing time for Joker's mouth to move on hers, drinking at the same time giving her all he had to give in order to say all he had to say.

Then the kid was done and they both knew it when he shrieked, latched on and yanked on both their hair.

Which meant when they quit kissing, they were smiling.

*   *   *

That night in a big bed with expensive sheets and a fantastic mattress, while a little boy snoozed in his crib a room away, Carson Steele and Carissa Teodoro slept a deep sleep, tangled together with a sketch in a frame resting on Carissa's nightstand.

In its proper place.

Where it should be.

As was everything and every being in that home.

In its proper place.

Precisely where it should be.

CHAPTER TWENTY-TWO

Being Right

Joker

JOKER WAS STANDING in the garage, hands to hips, staring at the car he was building, its hood up, new engine shining, scratch guards draped over the sides, interior empty because the seats they'd ordered wouldn't be in for a couple of days.

But if they stayed on schedule, they'd be turning the key at the end of the next day.

He just hoped she'd turn over and catch. As many builds as he'd done, that was always a crapshoot, and if it didn't happen, finding out why could tack on anywhere from half an hour to half a week.

"Joker! Honey! You have a visitor!"

He turned to the door to the office at Cherry's call.

Then he smiled when he saw the man walk out behind her. Mr. Robinson. Keith.

The man had his hand out before they met, and they were shaking when they did.

"You told me to call," Keith said. "But I was close so I thought I'd just stop by."

"Glad you did," Joker replied, breaking contact.

Keith's eyes went to the car. "Is she yours?"

Joker looked to the car too. "The one I'm workin' on now, yeah."

Joker felt the man's eyes on him when he stated, "She's a beauty."

He looked to Keith and grinned. "Wanna see?"

Keith nodded and Joker led him to the car.

"So what's your responsibility with this?" Keith asked as they walked.

"All a' it," Joker told him.

They stopped by the car and Keith looked to him. "Sorry?"

"Design, chassis, body, exhaust, suspension, transmission, engine, wheels, interior, paint." He looked to the car. "Bumper to bumper, roof to wheels, she's mine."

"That's, uh...I...Carson..." Joker looked back to him as he stammered. "That's incredibly impressive."

That felt good, but even so, Joker shrugged.

"My job," he muttered and went on, "Don't stitch leather or anything. Most of the interior we subcontract the build or restore, utilizing kickass shit we find in vehicles that are beyond restoration. We refurbish and manipulate it to fit. And I don't paint. We got a paint guy who does that, another one who does pinstriping. I envision airbrushing, I do some a' that, but if it's time-consuming, we're on deadline and I don't got that time, we got a guy who helps out—"

"You airbrush?" Keith asked and again Joker shrugged.

"Yeah."

Slowly, Keith smiled before he said, "I'd like to see some of that."

Joker nodded. "Cherry's got a book in the office of old builds. I can—"

He stopped talking when he heard, "Sweetie!"

He turned and didn't even try to stop his big smile when he saw Carissa hurrying toward him wearing a cute dress that swung around her thighs, exposing her legs from the knees down, high-heeled, girlie sandals, her hair loose and big, light makeup, Travis on her hip.

And with her was Mrs. Heely.

"Look who I have!" she cried, turning slightly to indicate Mrs. Heely.

"Yo, Butterfly," he called and looked to the woman with her. "Momma Heely."

Mrs. Heely rolled her eyes.

Carissa came right to him, deep into his space, hand to his stomach, and rolled up to kiss his stubbled jaw.

Travis latched on in a way that when she pulled back, he was still claiming Joker. Joker took the hint and pulled the kid into his arms.

"Yo, boy," he said to him.

"Goo, dah, bah," Travis replied.

"That good a day?" Joker asked.

"Bah!" Travis agreed, lifting his hands and smacking Joker in the jaw with one, the mouth with the other, where he curled in and tugged.

Joker let him and did it grinning.

Then he turned and bent to Mrs. Heely so she could touch her hand to his cheek.

Her eyes were smiling but her lips were muttering, "And again, he doesn't shave."

He kept grinning at her as he straightened away.

"Oh my gosh! Look at this! It's all coming together from your sketch and it's *amazing*!" Carissa cried and Joker turned to her to see her hands clasped in front of her.

Then she leaned into the cover over the fender and watching her do it, he decided after the ignition caught, the test runs were done, it was late, and the garage was deserted, he was dropping the hood and fucking her right there.

In those shoes.

She turned to him and exclaimed again, "Amazing!" She twisted to look at Mrs. Heely. "Isn't this amazing?"

"Did you build this, Carson?" the woman asked, and Carson looked to her to see she looked her brand of what Carissa looked.

Amazed.

"Yeah," he muttered.

Mrs. Heely moved eyes shining with pride to him. "Obviously, I don't see myself behind the wheel, but that makes it no less magnificent."

"I see it's unanimous," Keith put in, and Joker caught Carissa straightening from the car and turning to him.

"I'm so sorry. We interrupted. I . . ." Her eyes got huge, Carson took in how cute that was, and she clapped her hands in front of her three times and yelled, "Mr. Robinson!"

"You caught me," Keith said on a smile.

Carissa rushed him and gave him a quick hug. She leaned back, hands still on his biceps, smiling like a lunatic up in his face.

"This is *so* wonderful!" she exclaimed. "Are you here because you heard about *Wilde and Hay*?"

She let him go and stepped away as Keith shook his head, looking mildly confused, and asked, "Sorry, no. *Wilde and Hay*?"

"They're doing a big spread on Joker," she told him then added, "Carson," when Keith continued to look confused.

The man stopped looking confused as his eyes slowly turned to Joker.

"No," he answered Carissa quietly. "Just came to see

Carson's work. I had no idea." His voice dropped quieter.
"But I'm not surprised."

Joker hefted up Travis, who'd let go of his lip but latched
on to his shirt, and Keith's eyes went to the kid.

Joker stopped feeling the good that was heating his chest,
and he braced when Keith took in Travis.

His eyes came back. "You didn't mention you and Carissa
had a son."

Before Joker could say anything, Carissa pushed under
his arm, forcing him to drape it around her shoulders (not
that he wouldn't do that anyway), and curling hers around
his waist as she pressed into his side and said, "Travis is
Aaron Neiland's, Mr. Robinson. We were married. Now
we're not and I'm with Jo...Carson."

"Ah," Keith murmured.

Carissa reached across and gently pulled Travis's hand
from Joker's shirt. Waving it at Keith, she ordered, "Say
hello to Mr. Robinson, Googly."

"Gah doo," Travis said, yanked his hand from his ma's
and shoved his fist in his mouth.

Mr. Robinson smiled.

"That's why we're here, sweetie, kind of," she said and
Joker looked down at her to see her looking up at him. "Mrs.
Heely wanted to meet Travis so I took him around. We got
to chatting. Then we spoke to Kam. We're having everyone
over for dinner tonight. Is that okay?"

She had an ulterior motive, he knew. She'd been on about
getting Mrs. Heely in the house across the street since she'd
noticed it was for rent.

It was Tuesday. They hadn't even had Travis back for
twenty-four hours. And now she was using Mrs. Heely
asking to meet her boy as her excuse to wrangle what she
wanted.

Having Mrs. Heely across the street would absolutely not suck, so he told her, "It's good with me."

"Great!" she cried, bouncing a little at his side with her excitement, something that was cute and hot. Then she pulled away. "Oh my gosh! So rude. Mr. Robinson, this is Mrs. Heely. She used to be Carson's neighbor but she's really Carson's family," she announced.

Mrs. Heely visibly swelled with pride as she offered her hand.

"Mr. Robinson was our history teacher in high school," Joker told her.

Mrs. Heely's eyes lit. "Lovely to meet you, and so nice to see a teacher taking a continuing interest in his students."

They were holding hands in greeting as Keith replied, "There's always been lots to be interested in with Carson, as is evidenced right there."

They broke off with Mrs. Heely smiling. "I wholeheartedly agree."

"Me too," Carissa mumbled under her breath.

Fuck, this crew didn't shut the fuck up about how awesome he was, he'd actually have to acknowledge it. It felt great, but it was still awkward as shit.

Like she knew what he was feeling, Carissa bulldozed right in there.

"Now, I hate to say it, but it's already late and we have to get to the grocery store." She looked to Keith. "We're suddenly feeding nine people. I need to get food in." She tipped her head to the side. "Would you like to join us?"

"Some other time, Carissa. My wife and I have plans tonight," Keith answered.

"Bummer, but I understand. Short notice. We'll set it up for another night." She turned to Mrs. Heely. "You ready to hit the store?"

"Whenever you are," Mrs. Heely answered.

She came back to Joker, lifting her hands to her son. "Come on, baby boy, Mommy and Mrs. Heely need to get to the grocery store pronto."

Travis lurched in Joker's arms, tried to find purchase on his jaw, and shouted, "Bah, moo mah!"

She shot her eyes to Joker like she did anytime Travis said "moo mah," convinced it was "mommy."

Joker didn't know if she was right. But he liked to see her face when it happened.

She tore her eyes from Joker's and put her hands to her son, who started climbing on Joker, shouting, "Bah! Dah! Kah! Duh! Buh!" then he pounded on Joker's shoulder and gave her angry baby face.

"He's good with me," he told her.

"He sure is," Mrs. Heely said, a smile in her voice.

"You don't have your truck," Carissa told him.

"Swing back around when you're done, you can take him home and I'll ride behind you," he said.

"Okay, sweetheart," she murmured, leaned in and this time he turned his head so she didn't get his jaw with her kiss but his lips. "See you later," she whispered when she pulled away. She bent in to Travis, who turned his face into Joker's neck and pressed, thinking she was going to try to separate them.

She blew a raspberry on his neck and he giggled but kept shoving into Joker.

She moved away.

"So cool to see you again, Mr. Robinson," she said.

"Keith, Carissa," he invited.

"Keith," she said warmly.

They shook. Mrs. Heely said her goodbyes to Keith. Carissa came in for another lip touch for Joker and a raspberry for Travis. After that, Keith and Joker watched Carissa and Mrs. Heely walk to his woman's wreck.

With his mother walking away, Travis exposed his plan and started struggling to get down, showing that he may like Joker, but what he really wanted was to crawl all over the dirt and grime of a garage.

Joker held him steady, eyes locked on Travis's mother's sweet ass.

"How old is he?"

At this question from Keith, Joker tore his eyes from Carissa's ass and looked to the man beside him.

"Nine months."

Something moved over Keith's face that was easy to read. Unhappiness and anger.

"Please tell me Mr. Neiland is a better father than he obviously was a husband," he requested.

Yep.

Nothing got by Keith Robinson. He knew exactly how big a jackass Aaron Neiland was back in the day, which was why he was a bigger one now.

"Far's I can tell, he digs his son."

"And Carissa has you," Keith said quietly.

"And I got them both," Joker replied.

"Would you like to know one of the best feelings in the world, Carson?" Keith asked.

Joker wasn't sure he did. With all that had just gone down, anything could come of that. All that just happened but also, Joker was holding in his arms what Keith and his wife could not have.

Still, he said, "Sure."

Keith looked him deep in the eye, Joker tensed at the force of his gaze, and the man whispered, "Being right."

Joker drew in breath.

Travis shouted, "Bah goo dee fah luh dah koo!"

Keith grinned, looked to Joker's car and said, "Now, if you have time, show me everything."

Holding an annoyed Travis close, Joker did that.

*   *   *

Sitting at Carissa's dining room table with the dirty dishes holding the remnants of the cherry pie Mrs. Heely made in Carissa's kitchen, Joker felt something.

He looked to his right.

He was at the head of the table.

Carissa, being Carissa, had given Mrs. Heely the foot.

So she was sitting to his right.

And when he looked at her, he saw she had eyes to the couches and a look on her face he felt in his gut.

He turned his head that way and saw Linus and Kam's boys crawling all over the couch, mostly wrestling with a lot of grunting.

Candy was sitting to the side, her little dress pristine, her eyes on her brothers like she didn't know what to make of them but what she was coming up with wasn't much.

As he looked, he saw Travis crawl around the corner of the couch, roll to his diapered ass, pound his fists in his knees, and screech, "*Kee lah*!"

He wanted in on the boy action.

Joker looked back to Carissa.

She just wanted that. All of it.

Kids and babies all over her couch and living room.

And watching the mix of peaceful, happy, and eager on her face, Joker determined not to freak her shit out by moving them forward at the speed he wanted, that being taking her ring shopping next week, hitching her ass to his the week after when they had Travis back, and planting a kid in her belly the second one of his boys conquered an egg.

But he still wasn't going to delay.

Maybe a month.

If he could hack it, two.

"I got two boys who better cool it or they're gonna get their booties tanned by Poppa's hand!" Linus boomed the second after they heard a thud, which meant the wrestling fell off the couch.

Joker looked that way and saw Candy had her head turned to the dining table and she was clearly a five-year-old little girl who worried at the state of boys today.

His eyes went back to Carissa when he felt her kick him under the table.

She was staring at him.

He lifted his brows.

She jerked her head to the foot of the table.

He shook his head.

She kicked him again and jutted her chin to him almost imperceptibly.

He sighed.

She'd found her time in the whirlwind that was throwing together this dinner to take him aside and tell him it was Joker who had to broach the subject with Mrs. Heely. Even though it was Carissa's idea, she said she didn't know Mrs. Heely all that well and it might seem weird coming from her, the fact she wanted the woman to move in across the street.

Joker figured Mrs. Heely didn't give a fuck. She obviously liked Carissa. She'd like the idea that Joker's woman, like Joker, wanted her close.

Carissa reiterated it would seem strange.

He didn't agree.

She was called away before they could come to an agreement, but obviously she felt that somewhere between their hurried, whispered conversation in the hall, he'd come around to her way of thinking.

She jerked her head to the foot of the table again and this time it was a lot more perceptible.

"Butterfly, just talk to her," he said out loud.

Her eyes got huge and then narrowed.

"Talk to who?" Kam asked.

Joker turned his attention to Kam. "Carissa's got somethin' she wants to mention to Mrs. Heely."

"Yes?" Mrs. Heely asked. "What's that, dear?"

"Actually, Joker has something to mention," Carissa said.

"Wasn't my idea, Carrie," he reminded her.

She kicked him under the table again.

He dropped his head and grinned at his cherry pie–smeared plate.

"Well, someone spit it out," Linus put in.

Joker turned eyes to his woman and again lifted his brows.

She made an irritated noise that was fucking cute before she cast her eyes down the table.

"There's a house for rent across the street," she announced.

Linus looked to Kam.

Mrs. Heely's brows drew together in confusion. "There is?"

"It's two bedrooms," Carissa declared. "Not small, not huge, a lot like this house. I went over and chatted with the current renter. She's really nice and she loves that house, but she got a job in Boulder so she's moving there."

"Is that so?" Mrs. Heely said, still looking confused.

"It has a big yard but that should be okay. There aren't a lot of plants and shrubs to maintain," Carissa went on.

Mrs. Heely didn't look any less confused.

Jesus.

"Carrie wants you to move into it, Mrs. Heely," Joker stated.

Linus grinned at Kam.

Joker's attention was diverted by Travis hightailing his ass across the floor toward the dining room table.

"I…um, I…well, I don't know what to say," Mrs. Heely said as Joker pushed back his chair and got up to go get Travis.

"The for rent sign has a number. I can call. We can have a look," Carissa told her.

"I'm in a place, sweetheart," Mrs. Heely replied.

"I know," Carissa said and Joker could hear the caution.

He bent and lifted up Travis.

Travis immediately shoved an arm out toward the couch.

Joker took him there.

"But this place is bigger," Carissa went on. "And it's closer to Carson. He doesn't officially live here, but he's here a lot. And he'd mow your lawn."

Joker sat on the back of the couch and looked to Linus, and he didn't try to hide how he felt about how he was now going to mow Mrs. Heely's lawn, something he didn't know was part of the deal.

Linus was shaking and doing it hard, trying not to laugh out loud.

"Carissa, you're being very sweet, but I'm happy where I am," Mrs. Heely told her.

Joker took in the look on his girl's face, knowing she didn't believe that.

"I have company," Mrs. Heely said gently. "Anytime I want, there are folks around. We have things to do. They plan activities away and we all get on buses and go. It's fun. And I still have my car, so it isn't like I don't have my freedom. I just have to let someone know I'm going."

"Okay," Carissa mumbled.

"And I'm halfway between you, Carson and Travis and Linus, Kam and the kids. Perfect spot," Mrs. Heely kept at her.

"Right," Carissa said, adjusting her plate in front of her.

"I love you want me close," Mrs. Heely said on a loud whisper, and Joker looked at the back of her head. "That's very sweet. But I've got friends where I am, and I like that I can still take care of my own place. Anything bigger, even a little bit bigger, that would be a lot on me."

"I could help," Carissa offered immediately.

"You want Carson to have his family," Mrs. Heely replied quietly and Joker's back shot straight.

He didn't know that was it. He just thought it was Carrie being Carrie, taking care of people, taking care of a woman who meant something to him like her father took care of the woman who raised him.

Carissa didn't answer, but it wasn't lost on Joker that she avoided looking at him.

And there it was, that was it.

"I'm not far away," Mrs. Heely said.

"You're right. It was a stupid idea. I'm sorry. I shouldn't have brought it up," Carissa returned and Joker could see the pink in her cheeks. She made a move to get up and start collecting dishes.

"Carrie," Mrs. Heely called.

Carissa stopped moving, planted her ass back in her chair, and looked to Mrs. Heely.

Mrs. Heely said nothing.

But then again, Joker didn't see her face.

What he saw was that Mrs. Heely actually did say something. Just not with words. He knew it when Carissa's face went soft, her eyes especially. He knew it when Linus cleared his throat. And he knew it when Kam fidgeted, pulling her napkin from her lap and suddenly pushing back, grabbing some plates, averting her eyes, and moving directly to the kitchen.

"Okay," Carrie whispered.

"Okay," Mrs. Heely whispered back.

Whatever she said was huge.

That being, he figured, Mrs. Heely officially passing the buck of looking after Joker to his girl.

Joker didn't make a big deal of it. It was over and the women started to clear the table.

So he joined the boys on the couch, or actually he let Travis do it, but he allowed this when he could pay attention as they rough-housed with their toddler friend to make sure Jackson and Tyler didn't do any damage.

Linus joined him and he shot the shit with his friend as the women shot the shit over dishes in the kitchen. Then they all shot the shit lounging on Carissa's couch, the men with fresh beers, Kam and Carrie with their wine, Mrs. Heely with her decaf.

They did this until it was time for Linus and Kam to get their brood home and Carson to get his ass in his truck to take Mrs. Heely to hers.

It all went well until he was walking Mrs. Heely to her door and she suddenly shouted, "Yes, Bertie! This is the Carson I told you about!" while tugging at his arm.

He looked through the fading light to see the shadow of a woman in her doorway in the place next to Mrs. Heely's.

She was waving like a lunatic.

He lifted a hand then dropped it.

"She has six sons," Mrs. Heely hissed. "*Six.* They're always coming around then she's on about telling us how they're fixing her light switches. Bringing her her favorite LaMar's. Taking her out for fancy steak dinners." Her voice switched to cocky when she said, "But not one of them has found a woman, and some of them are in their *forties*. Six men, no wives. And not one *single* grandchild."

Joker stopped them at her door and looked down to see a look on her face that said, clearly, she'd won.

"Good you got four," he muttered.

She screwed her eyes up at him. "I better get more."

He felt his lips twitch. "You tellin' me to knock up Carrie?"

"I'm telling you that if you don't, she's going to expire from longing."

She didn't miss it then.

"Doubtful," he muttered on a tease.

"She wants to be tied to you," Mrs. Heely replied. She was not teasing, so he felt that hit his chest, and it was also warm. "She wants you to have all the things you didn't. She wants to give them to you personally. She wants it herself, but she wants it more for you."

Joker stood still and said nothing.

But he thought that what Mrs. Heely didn't say was what Carissa really wanted.

She wanted to heal him.

And to do that, she was using family.

Maybe he needed to let her off the hook on that and let her know that was already done.

"You like her?" he asked quietly.

"There's nothing not to like. I will say that I was uncertain when you shared at her age she'd had a child and had already been divorced. But seeing her with you, her son, she hasn't told me her story, but I can well imagine. Before we learn what's right, we put our trust in the wrong people, and it's never good to start life's adventures, especially important ones like marriage, when we're too young even to know ourselves. But she's bounced back from that very well, I think."

"She has," Joker agreed.

"Smart enough not to give up...on a variety of things... as well as find help."

Joker got what she was saying so he grinned.

Mrs. Heely put a hand light to his chest. "I like her for you. I like the way you are with her. You seem happy."

"I am, Mrs. Heely," he confirmed.

He could swear he saw her eyes twinkle as she said, "Who would have thought my Carson Steele would catch butterflies."

That was when Joker threw his head back and laughed.

Mrs. Heely laughed with him.

When they quit doing that, he got her safe inside and walked to his truck, knowing that Bertie was watching because he could see her at her window.

When he got back to Carissa's house he found her in Travis's room, her son in her arms, his PJs on. She was cooing and swaying as she paced the room. Travis had his hands around his bottle with her spotting him, his eyes drooping.

Joker rested against the jamb and watched, thinking she needed a rocking chair in that room and deciding to get her one.

When Carissa turned his way, she saw him, and that was when she gave it to him again.

Soft face. Warm eyes. Lips pursed. Blowing him a kiss.

He took it with a chin lift then walked out and left her to have some time with her boy.

When she had Travis down, she came out and spent some time stretched on the couch with her other boy.

He fiddled with her hair, his eyes on the TV, feeling her weight, her soft tits pressed to his side.

He gave it time.

Then he muttered, "You know I'm good."

"I know you're good," she muttered back.

"No, baby, I'm *good*," he said, emphasizing it but keeping it light, eyes still to the TV. "You don't gotta make me better."

"Okay," she whispered.

"Mrs. Heely likes where she is," he told her.

"Those places aren't the greatest," she told him.

"You don't think so, and I get that. But she's happy there."

"Right," she murmured.

"Don't mean she won't like company," he noted.

"Of course," she replied.

"A lot of it."

There was a beat before she said, "That we can do."

We.

He grinned at the TV, fiddled with her hair, and let it go.

Carissa fell silent and let it go too.

They finished the program, and that was when Joker decided it was time for bed.

He put in some effort, but in the end it didn't take a lot for Carrie to agree.

CHAPTER TWENTY-THREE

We Were Free

Carissa

THAT NEXT TUESDAY, with my son sadly back with his father, who was thankfully being nice but mostly leaving me alone, it was after work and Joker and I were grocery shopping.

I stopped suddenly in the aisle next to the shelves of beans (we were not at LeLane's; they were great and gave an employee discount on some things, but they were way too expensive for everyday shopping needs).

Joker, trailing me, slouched over and pushing the cart with his forearms, halted just shy of slamming into me and muttered, "Jesus, baby."

I looked his way. "Do you like chili?"

"Yeah."

"Chili," I declared and started to grab cans of beans.

"You know, a list helps," he remarked.

"I have a mental list," I told him, tossing kidney beans in the cart and going back for black.

"Was chili on it?" he asked.

I looked to him. "Don't you want chili?"

"What I want is not to wander every aisle so we're here

for an hour rather than bein' here for twenty minutes gettin' shit from a list."

"If I stick to a list, inspiration can't strike, like the fact I suddenly have a craving for chili," I told him.

He shook his head, grinning and muttering, "Whatever."

He wasn't annoyed.

He was easy.

So I turned back and grabbed black beans. Then I got some chili beans. I finished up with pinto.

Four-bean chili. The best.

I tossed the last in and said, "That should do it."

I was about to start walking but glanced his way first.

I halted completely because Joker was frozen, leaning into our cart, his eyes aimed down the aisle, a look on his face that could be described no other way than haunted.

I turned my head the other way and that was when I froze.

I did this because there was a man at the other end of the aisle. Tall. Broad shoulders. Silvered black hair that was messy and ill-kempt. Exceptionally handsome profile. Terrible clothes that were wrinkled and well-worn and not in a good way. Serious beer belly. He was glowering at the shelves, his side turned to us.

But Carson Steele was written all over him.

Joker's father.

Oh my God.

Joker's father.

I forced my head Joker's way and saw he was on the move.

This move being he had straightened. Hands on the bar of the cart, he was flipping it around.

"We done in this aisle?" he asked tersely.

We weren't.

But now we very much were.

"Yeah, sweetie," I said softly.

He didn't even look at me.

He exited the aisle immediately.

I looked back the other way and watched Joker's father's profile as he scowled at an elderly woman who was turning her cart into the aisle as he was walking out of it. His scowl was so ferocious the lady stared at him in blank shock.

I waited and saw him move opposite to the way we were heading.

I let out a relieved breath and quickly followed Joker.

Had a father beat on me. Had to let that go. Had to get it out. So I did.

But he didn't.

He didn't get it out. He might have tried, illegally fighting (whatever that meant but it conjured images of *Fight Club*, images that were daunting, images that made me sick for him that he'd turn to that to let out his rage, rage given to him by his dad, so I hadn't yet asked).

But if he'd gotten it out, he wouldn't have left the aisle.

He would have walked down it, which was where we were heading, and ignored his father. Or, if his father saw him and didn't ignore him, he would have faced him secure in the knowledge that he was past it.

He hadn't done that.

I knew from what I'd just witnessed that he also hadn't seen him since he'd been back.

Of course, he wouldn't search him out. He was *past that*.

Or telling himself he was.

They undoubtedly didn't run in the same circles.

Further, Joker lived in a room in a motorcycle club compound. He didn't have a kitchen to keep stocked. Happening onto his father in a grocery store wasn't going to happen.

But now he was with me so he had a kitchen and it did.

And Joker didn't let it roll off his back.

He retreated.

My Joker didn't retreat.

He moved forward. He built fabulous cars. He took on a single mom and her kid. He patrolled the streets with his brothers to keep them safe.

But from his father, a still-handsome but aging, beer-bellied man who'd scowl at an old lady for getting in his way in a grocery store, Joker retreated.

This troubled me for obvious reasons.

But mostly because what just happened proved my biker was not good, as he said he was.

He was not good at all.

And that was very, *very* troubling.

*   *   *

"Yeah?"

"Linus, it's Carrie."

"Carrie, darlin', what's up?" Linus asked through the phone at my ear.

I was hiding in the bathroom.

This was immature and possibly hazardous, considering why I was doing it and the fact that Joker might get angry about it.

But I was doing it.

I'd also filched Joker's phone to get Linus's number. I had Kam's and Mrs. Heely's.

But this had to be Linus.

"Can you talk for a second, Linus?" I asked back.

"Sure," he said, but that one word was cautious.

I drew in breath.

Then I did what I had to do.

This being whispering, "How bad was it?"

"Sorry, darlin'?" he asked.

"Carson's father," I kept whispering. "How bad was it?"

There was a pause before he asked, "Is Car okay?"

"Tonight, we saw his dad."

"Fuck," Linus muttered.

"He, well...Linus, he...ran away," I shared, guilt plaguing me that I gave Joker's friend that weakness, but something stronger was driving me onward. "My Carson...my *Joker* isn't about that."

"No," Linus bit off.

"I saw the cigarette burns," I confided.

"Yeah, Mrs. Heely told me about that," he replied immediately. "She saw 'em too when Car was eight."

Oh no.

Eight?

"Before my time," Linus carried on. "But she told me about 'em. She also told Social Services about 'em. No clue how that motherfucker got off on that one. Just know he did and the burns stopped."

Eight.

He got those burns when he was *eight.*

I didn't want to ask what I had to ask.

But I asked because it had to be asked.

"What else?"

"He talk to you about this at all?" Linus queried in return.

"He doesn't hide it," I told him. "He speaks freely of it. You'd think he was what he wants me to believe, over it. But when I saw the burns, he tried to hide it, pull away, pass it off. I...well, I don't know how to broach it or even if I should, since he's convinced himself he's beyond it." I paused and shared softly, "He's not beyond it, Linus."

"Lotsa ways to fuck up a kid, and Jefferson Steele did 'em all," Linus declared.

My chest depressed.

Linus kept speaking.

"Had women over, didn't hide it, sight or sound, what he did with 'em even at an age way too young for a kid to see that shit. But also when Carson was gettin' older and all that would be on his mind *was* that shit. Car, do not know what he's made of, have no idea how he didn't get twisted by that, but I'd see him with his girls. I knew there were a lot of 'em, I figured he got some from 'em, but from what little I saw when he was with 'em, he respected 'em."

I saw that too. And every girl who had him loved being with him (which was torture for me at the time, luckily, fates changed).

Those girls just never had him for long.

"On top a' that, beat the shit outta him," Linus said. "Left him standin' but didn't mind doin' it visible. Shouted at 'im. Not sure more than a couple days went by before the whole block heard him lay into Car. Call him a piece of shit. Tear him up. Never heard Car say a word back, Carrie, not once."

I was pretty certain I could feel my heart bleeding, and as much as I hated the feeling, I had to concentrate on containing it so I was unable to respond.

Regardless, there really was nothing to say.

"Got no good from the man," Linus continued into my silence. "If he wasn't yellin' at him or beatin' on him, Carson didn't exist. That is, except to serve him. Anything got done in that house, vacuum goin', trash out, food cooked, Carson did it because his old man ordered it. No way he'd court gettin' what he'd get if he told the guy to go fuck himself, so he did it. He was a slave, Carrie, whipped and broken. He was a strong kid, built, no clue why he didn't fight back. But he didn't. Then he took too much and fought back. That was the end."

"It wasn't the end," I whispered.

At that, Linus didn't reply.

"What do I do?" I asked.

"Be with him, give him what you're givin' him. He appreciates it, darlin'."

I knew he did.

It just wasn't enough.

I didn't say that.

"Listen to me, sweetheart," Linus said gently. "Car has already won. He's on the other side. Good job. Good people around him. Pretty girl. Nice house. A boy he gets to love on and right the wrongs done to him. Just be patient. Carson is not dumb. He'll come to terms and do it through and through. Just be with him while he goes through that process."

Linus probably wasn't wrong.

But that also wasn't enough.

"Okay," I lied, more guilt hitting me because I wasn't a big fan of lying.

"*You* okay?" Linus asked.

Joker's friends were so wonderful.

"I'll be fine," I told him, hoping that wasn't a lie.

"All right, Carrie. Hang tight, stay tough, the hard part is done, gettin' to this spot and findin' each other. Now you get the easy."

He was only half right.

Joker gave me easy.

I just wanted him to have his.

"Thanks, Linus," I said.

"Not a problem, Carrie. See you later, darlin'."

"Yes. Say hi to Kam and the kids for me."

"Will do." He didn't bid me to do the same considering he probably knew Joker would never be privy to this conversation. "Later."

"Bye."

I disconnected but continued to hold my phone and poke the screen. I did it quickly and I did it before I could think about it.

And once it was done, I put my phone to my ear.

"Hey, girlie, it's late. Everything okay?" Elvira asked.

"I...no," I answered.

"Travis?" she asked quickly.

"No," I answered just as quickly, then launched in, "Okay, listen, I'm sorry. I'm sorry to drag you into this again but Joker saw his dad at the grocery store tonight. His response was..." I shook my head, not about to give to her what I gave to Joker's friend, and carried on, "Promise me you will *not* go to your boss and I promise you I'll do something to pay back this favor, but I want his dad's address, and I'm hoping you can get it for me."

"What you gonna do?"

"I don't know. Maybe nothing. I just...I'd just feel better having it."

Elvira didn't respond and through her silence I thought about her question.

What was I going to do?

Nothing.

I was going to do nothing.

"You're right," I said, my shoulders slumping. "This is stupid. The last time I started this, Joker told me—"

"I'll get you the address on one condition. You don't go in without backup."

My head jerked. "Go in where?"

"Anywhere, girl," she returned.

"I probably won't do anything. It's just—"

"You're gonna do somethin'. It's gonna be crazy. And a crazy bitch with a vendetta who wears butterfly shoes is gonna get her shit fucked up. I'll get you the address. You get your courage up to make a move, before you make it, you make a call."

I didn't lie. I probably wasn't going to do anything. What was there to do? Go to Joker's dad's house and browbeat him into apologizing for being an abusive, lowlife, child-burning, slave-driving...*asshole*?

Still, I told myself, I wanted that address just in case, God forbid, something happened like Joker needed a kidney.

I wouldn't ask for said kidney. I'd use my savings to hire someone to knock Joker's dad out and leave him in a bathtub filled with ice after harvesting his kidney and calling 911 so Joker's dad could survive, just with one kidney.

It was extreme and it was a little scary I could even think like that.

But there it was.

"Okay, I promise," I told Elvira.

"I'll have it to you tomorrow."

"Thanks."

"Always got your back, girl. Now I got a man to get in the mood 'cause I'm in the mood. Lucky for me, he goes from baseball mood to a little somethin'-somethin' mood in half a second, and he reads eyes so all I gotta do is walk out and look at him. So I'm gonna get on that."

I grinned. "Have fun."

"Hope you get your fun too. Later, Carrie."

"'Bye, Elvira."

I drew in a breath, disconnected, and looked in the mirror.

I was just getting the address. That was it. I wasn't going to do anything with it. I would just feel better having it.

Had a father beat on me.

Car was eight.

Yes, I would just feel better having it.

On that thought, I left the bathroom.

*   *   *

The next day I stood in the break room staring at the text on my phone.

It was an address.

My first thought was *alibi*.

My second thought was I had to do this when Travis was still at his dad's and I had to do it before I chickened out.

I didn't know what *it* was.

I just knew I had to do it.

And soon.

So that was why my finger moved on the screen and I put the phone to my ear.

"Hey, honey," Tyra answered. "How're things?"

"They're great!" I chirped with fake enthusiasm. "Listen, Joker's on patrol tonight and I haven't had a girls' night out in ages and I've got a tube top I haven't worn."

She didn't say anything for long moments that kind of scared me before she said hesitantly, "Not sure that tube top is for a night Joker isn't there to see you wear it."

This was a point to ponder but I didn't have the time to ponder it.

I could feel myself chickening out.

"I'll wear a jacket over it," I promised.

"I . . . well—"

"Are you free?" I spoke over her.

"Well, sure," she said.

"Good!" It came out as another chirp. "I'll, uh . . . call Tabby. And maybe Lanie. And Elvira. We'll decide where to go and then we'll go."

"Okay, honey, I'll look forward to it."

"Fantastic!" I said with forced enthusiasm. "I'll text you with the plans."

"Great."

"Okay, see you later," I said.

"Right, Carrie, see you."

We hung up. I did a lot of texting. I was nearly hyperventilating when I called Joker to let him know I was going out with the girls that night.

Not surprisingly, he thought that was a great idea since he liked me having a life and friends and fun (I left out mention of my tube top) and then he promised me he'd be good hanging with his brothers at the Compound before patrol.

With all this, I was three minutes late getting back to my register.

That had never happened before.

Sharon said nothing.

And I prayed I wouldn't mess up my drawer because for the rest of my shift, my mind was whirling.

I was off a dollar and seventy-two cents.

That had only happened twice before.

Again, Sharon didn't say anything.

Then I went home.

*   *   *

I sat in my car in my good jeans (the only pair I had, post-pregnancy), tube top, spike-heeled black leather booties (pre-divorce and pre-pregnancy, they were designer, cost a fortune, and luckily, my feet had not changed sizes with Travis), and black leather jacket (also pre-divorce and I was happy it still fit me and looked great) and I poked at my phone.

I group texted the girls, *Running a little late! Sorry! Hair emergency! Be there soon!*

I looked up from the phone and stared at the house.

Okay, I was going to do this.

Time to do this.

Right, just open the door and do this.

My phone rang in my hand and I jumped.

I looked down at it and my heart skipped a beat when I saw it was Tory.

I took the call and put the phone to my ear.

"Tory, is Travis okay?"

"I get it," she whispered on a sniffle.

Oh no.

This was *not* happening.

I didn't ever want to do this, I couldn't imagine why she was calling me to do this, but right then, I simply *couldn't* do it.

"Tory, I'm in the mid—"

"I stole him from you, of course you'd steal him back from me."

Darn it!

"Really, listen, right now I can't—"

"And if it wasn't you, it'd be someone," she spoke over me. "If he'd leave his wife who's pretty and sweet and freaking *pregnant*, what was up for me? This. He told me he wanted *space* two weeks ago. So since it's his house, I had to move in with a girlfriend. Tonight, he officially kicked me out."

Ugh.

But, if Tory was gone, who was looking after Travis while Aaron was at work? And why hadn't he told his attorney to tell my attorney there was this change in circumstance?

I wasn't going to get into that with Tory. Unfortunately, I'd have to get into it with Aaron through Angie.

"Okay, I can hear you're upset," I told her. "But—"

"Don't take him back," she hissed, hiccupped, and kept going, "He's just going to do it again."

"I'm not taking him back, Tory. I'm with another man."

"He said you were getting back together," she told me,

now sounding perplexed. "He said we were through because you were putting your family back together."

"He lied," I shared. "But this is between you and him. There is no him and me. When I say I'm with someone else, I'm *with* him. We're unofficially living together. And Aaron knows it."

"That *asshole*!" she yelled.

I shook my head. "I know you're upset and angry, and I'm sorry about that for you. We have an odd relationship, and I can't say you've been my favorite person. You made some choices that affected me in not-so-good ways. But in the end, I got where I wanted to be partially because of them. So I can't really hold ill will. And because of that, I'll say right now, it doesn't feel like it, but you're better off too. Now you can find someone who'll be good to you. And Aaron isn't very good at that."

"You're right about that!" she snapped just as my phone buzzed in my hand in the way it did when I had another call.

"Anyway, I'm in the middle of something and have another call coming through. I have to go. But take care of yourself."

"I'll start doing that," she told me sharply. "And he can go fuck himself."

"Okay, well … good attitude," I forced out encouragingly. "Now, I gotta go."

"Right. Sorry. I don't even know why I called. It's uncool. I was just—"

My phone kept notifying me of another call so I interrupted her. "Tory, I *have to go*."

"Right. Well … uh … later."

"'Bye. Good luck," I replied, took the phone from my ear, dragged down the screen without really looking at it, and put it back to my ear. "Hello?"

"Hey, Riss."

Aaron.

Why me?

Why?

"Aaron, I—"

"I want you to know I heard you. What you said during our last phone conversation. I know you want me to think on things. I promise I'm doing that. But I'd like you to think on things too. And while you're thinking, you should know, I've finished it with Tory. Until I can get him into daycare at work, Mom's been looking after Travis while I'm at work. Tory officially moved out tonight."

It was on the tip of my tongue to tell him she shared that with me already but I needed him off the phone. I'd texted my *I'm late* alibi to the girls and time was running out for me to get done what I had to get done and get to them so *they* could be my alibi.

"Thanks for the information, Aaron, but I'm in the middle of something."

"With *Joker*?" he asked, derision sliding into his tone.

"No, he's with his brothers tonight. I'm heading to the girls and I'm driving and you know how I don't like to talk on the phone while I'm driving," I lied.

"Yes, I do," he stated immediately. "And you're right not to do so. It's unsafe."

I rolled my eyes.

He always talked on the phone in his car and not just in his Bluetooth ear thingie.

"So I'll let you go," he finished.

"Great. Thanks. That'd be nice."

"We'll talk more later."

I hoped not.

"Goodbye, Aaron."

"'Bye, honey.'"

Ulk.

I hung up, tossed the phone on the seat next to me, grabbed my keys, and before anything else could happen or I could talk myself out of doing what I was going to do, I opened the door, threw my leg out, and hauled myself out of my car.

Quickly, I dashed across the street and up the drive.

Thankfully, Joker's dad parked his truck outside. I didn't know why, he had a garage, but he did.

Which was good for me.

So I did what I needed to do.

I went to the passenger's side (the driver's side could be seen from the house and the curtains were open), got my key firm in position in my hand, then I dragged the tip hard against the steel from the back gate along the bed across the passenger door and up the entire fender, the paint curling away as I did.

I stopped, took my key away and stared at the mark.

There.

Done.

Did I feel better?

It was immature and a little crazy, but I absolutely did.

I grinned to myself, turned to dash back to my car, and stopped dead.

"Right on," Tabby muttered, staring at the mark.

"What now?" Tyra asked, looking at me.

"Girl, broad daylight, you crazy?" Elvira asked, also looking at me.

"Love the booties," Lanie noted, looking at my boots.

"Wh-what are you guys doing here?" I asked, staring at them standing three feet from me in Joker's dad's driveway.

"Followed your ass," Elvira said, "Girls' night out when

you're all cozied up with your biker, playin' house, haven't pulled that tube top out *for weeks*?" She shook her head. "We ain't stupid. That tube top is insurance just in case you get hauled in, Joker has to bail you out, he sees you in that top, he doesn't spank your ass for bein' stupid except in a way you like it."

I hadn't really thought it out that fully.

Though I wished I had. Joker hadn't taken naughty to that level, but I found the thought intriguing.

"So... what now?" Tyra asked.

"Did you bring a bag of poo?" Lanie asked.

"Of... what?" I asked.

"Poo," Lanie said, "To light it on fire and knock on his door."

"Poo?" Tabby queried derisively then looked to me. "I got a lighter and we can light something on fire, but we'll call the fire department before we do it."

"And, say, do that shit when it's not evening, it's *night*, so we don't still have sunlight and every eye in the 'hood isn't on us," Elvira put in.

"I'm not lighting Joker's father's house on fire," I whispered, aghast.

"We'll call the fire department before so there won't be much damage," Tabby reiterated.

"You are *so* your father's daughter," Tyra mumbled, but she sounded almost proud.

"That's arson, that would be a felony," I told them.

"This is vandalism," Elvira shared, tossing a hand out to the truck.

"I know, but I'm pretty sure that's not a felony," I replied.

"There *is* felony vandalism," Elvira returned.

Oh no.

Was there?

Was keying a car felony vandalism?

Maybe it was. It was a nice truck. Newish. Clean. He obviously took care of it, which meant he cared about it.

To get that fixed, it would probably cost a lot of money.

"Uh-oh," Elvira muttered as I considered the alarming possibility that I hadn't committed a misdemeanor, I'd actually committed a felony.

"Let's go," Lanie whispered.

"What the *fuck*!" a man yelled.

I jumped, whirled around and tipped my head back to stare at Joker's very angry-looking father.

Uh-oh.

"We're gone, let's *go*," Tyra said urgently.

That sounded like a good idea.

I started to do that when Joker's dad asked, "You key my truck?" I kept trying to go but didn't get very far when he grabbed my upper arm tight and thundered, "*Bitch! You key my truck?*"

His hand hurt.

And *he* was touching me.

Therefore, without thought, I wrenched my arm free, reared back with my other one, keys still in position, and I swung at him with all I was worth, putting my full body into it.

"*Ow!*" I yelped as the impact cracked through my hand and sliced through my palm, where I held the keys.

"Jesus, *fuck*!" he yelled, not having anticipated my actions, so the likely puny blow I landed took him by surprise, which took him back two paces, his upper body jerking to the side, his hands coming up to his face.

"Let's go, let's go, let's *go*!" Tabby yelled, grabbing my hand and pulling me.

I watched in horror, keys dangling from where I was

pressing them at the junction between thumb and forefinger as I shook the sting out of my hand, while he righted himself.

I saw the mark.

I'd torn through the flesh of his cheek with my key and he was bleeding.

Profusely.

And he looked mad.

Seriously.

I turned on my stiletto heeled booties and ran.

"Follow the leader!" Tyra yelled.

"Got it!" Tabby yelled back. "I'm with Curly."

Curly?

We made it to the red wreck and she pulled my keys out of my hand.

"I drive," she declared.

I was shaking top to toe so I was okay with that.

I dashed to the passenger side just as Joker's dad made it to the car.

Luckily, Tabby was already in.

Blood pouring down his cheek, he tore open her door, and I squealed as he went for her but she went for the ignition.

I barely had my bottom to the seat before she roared out, her door open, my door open and *everything*.

He staggered back.

She raced to the tail of Tyra's Mustang in front of us, her car door slamming with the movement of the vehicle.

Unfortunately, I had to reach out and grab mine.

I did, taking my life in my hands to slam it shut.

Then I buckled up.

Only then did I realize I was hyperventilating.

"That was rad," she muttered.

She was crazy.

I looked at her to see she was grinning like the crazy I thought she was at the windshield.

"Keyed his truck, keyed his face. Abuser fuckwad, bested by a girl with curly hair. Totally…fucking…*rad*," Tabby decreed.

Her words hit me.

They soaked in.

And I began grinning.

She was right.

It was.

It absolutely was.

Totally…fucking…*rad*.

*   *   *

Following Lanie, Tyra, and Elvira into a very posh establishment that I'd never been to, Elvira instantly bellied up to the bar, hand up, fingers snapping, and a bartender came right to her.

"Five cosmos, one bag of ice, immediately, but not in that order."

"I'm driving, Elvira," I told her and her head snapped around to face me.

"We'll get you home."

I took one look at her and shut up.

The bartender put a towel filled with ice on the bar.

"Hand," Elvira ordered.

I got close and gave her my hand.

She grabbed it by the wrist, placed it on the bar and set the bag on it, holding it there.

That felt good.

"Now, girl, what the fuck?" she asked.

"Um…" I answered.

"What'd I say about backup?" she pushed.

"Well, uh...just to say, if you guys hadn't showed, I'm pretty sure I would have gotten away with the keying."

"Right, let's talk about that," she stated, then repeated, "What the fuck?"

"What the eff what?" I asked.

Her brows shot up. "Keying his car? What's that gonna do?"

I straightened my shoulders and answered, "Make me feel better."

"I hear you," she replied instantly. "What I mean is, what's it gonna do for your man?"

"Nothing," I stated. "I wasn't gonna tell him. My job with him is to be at his side and let him deal with it in his own time. What I did tonight was for me."

"Totally rad," I heard Tabby mutter.

Elvira stared at me.

"He has a nice truck," I told Elvira. "His house is run down. His body is run down. He scowls at old ladies in the grocery store, so clearly he's in a perpetually bad mood, not to mention he's rude. But his truck is nice, newish, and clean. He likes it. Now it's messed up. He's messed up a lot of things far more important and got away with it. He should have something of his that's messed up. Now he does."

"Yeah, like his face," Tyra mumbled.

I looked at her, now that the rush of it was over, feeling kind of sick about that. "That wasn't the plan."

She grinned at me. "It was a good addition."

I bit my lip.

"You done with that shit?" Elvira asked and I turned back to her.

"I think so."

"You're done with it," she declared. "But if you get another wild hair up your ass and decide to roll with it, you," she leaned into me, "*call your girls.*"

"All right," I whispered.

"Shit," she muttered, looking to the side. "Where's my cosmo?"

"Here," the bartender said, setting up five martini glasses and starting to fill them from a cocktail shaker. "Just so you know, these are on the guy down there." He jerked his head down the bar but his eyes came to me. "He wanted you in particular to know he hopes your hand is okay."

I looked down the bar at a man in a suit, no tie, dark blond hair, very nice looking, eyes on me, smiling.

"She's Chaos!" Tabby shouted. "Don't you see the tube top?"

The guy blinked.

I started shaking, but not from fear, from something else entirely.

Then I started giggling.

Lanie started giggling with me.

Tyra burst out with it.

Elvira muttered, "Biker bitches. Someone kill me."

That was when Tabby burst out with it.

And I did too.

* * *

I sat on the couch in my living room, boots on, jacket off, one light lit at my side, waiting.

And fretting.

It was nearly three o'clock in the morning and the mellow of the cosmos (I'd had two, which was one too many, but they were tasty) and girl time had worn off.

Several hours ago, Elvira had driven me home in my car with Tyra trailing. She'd joined them and they'd taken off on waves and smiles.

Girl time was good.

Cosmos were yummy (I'd never had one).

But now it was hitting me what I'd done.

I'd vandalized Joker's dad's car and I didn't get away with it.

He caught me. He saw me. He saw all the girls. He could pick me out of a lineup. He could probably pick all of us out of a lineup.

Then I'd hit him, causing him damage.

He'd call the police.

Then they'd find me.

They'd find *us*.

And we'd be in trouble, and Joker would find out I'd done something stupid. He'd have no choice but to deal with his father as his father pressed charges against me. It could all blow sky high as I'd have to explain my actions were due to my biker boyfriend enduring abuse.

And with all that, Joker might never forgive me.

And I didn't like to think of what Hop and Shy would do.

Or—I swallowed at the thought—Tack.

Eek!

I jumped a foot when I heard the back door open.

Joker was home.

Time to face the music.

I turned my head to the side and saw him round the corner, shrugging off his cut.

He threw it over the back of a dining chair, turned, caught sight of me, and stopped.

"Baby . . ." he whispered, his face taking on an expression I never wanted to see again. "Is it Travis?"

Slowly, I stood, saying, "No, sweetie. Travis is fine."

"Then what—?"

"I did something stupid," I blurted. "And the police could be here any minute. Or they could arrest me at LeLane's tomorrow once they've tracked me down. Or they could—"

"What the fuck?" he cut me off to ask.

"You're gonna be mad," I told him.

"Then I'll be mad, but tell me what the fuck is happening," he shot back.

"I saw your dad in the grocery store," I said hurriedly, and I didn't think it was good that his entire torso swung back almost like he was evading a blow. "I saw your reaction," I pushed onward. "It upset me. I found out his address. Then I went to his house and keyed his truck."

No torso swing on that.

Joker blinked.

"Unfortunately," I went on, "I had to ask Elvira for her help. I was using girls' night out as an alibi, and since we'd never had one of those and I asked for one out of the blue, they knew something was up. They followed me. And after I keyed his truck, they joined me at his house. As we were discussing whether or not to set his house on fire...that was Tabby's idea, incidentally, not mine," I added swiftly so he wouldn't think I was totally unhinged, "your dad came out."

"*Fuck*," he hissed.

I closed my eyes tight, opened them quickly, and kept speaking.

"He saw his truck and he got a little angry. To get away, I was..." I didn't think it would be good to tell Joker his dad put his hand on me so I skimmed past that part, "well, *forced* to get physical. I forgot I had my keys in my hand when I punched him. He fell back and when we were running away, I saw that I'd broken skin and he was bleeding."

Joker stared at me.

"So, he has me on vandalism and assault," I boiled it down. "And he was pretty mad, so I've been waiting up to tell you and/or face the police when they got to our door."

Joker kept staring at me.

I kept talking.

"You have my permission to use my savings as bail money. And if Aaron successfully uses this lunacy to get full custody of my son, all I request is that you hide the sharp knives and razorblades."

"Come here."

"I . . ." I shook my head. "What?"

"Get your ass over here."

His expression and tone weren't giving me anything.

I debated the merits of going to him.

I debated the merits of not going to him.

I did this in seconds then went to him.

He turned as I did, so when I stopped two feet away, he was facing me full on.

"First, my dad's a dick," he stated.

"I, well, I know that, Carson," I whispered.

"He's just a dick, but he also thinks he has a big one. No way in fuck he'd report it to the police that a woman marked him. He wouldn't take that hit to the cred he thinks he's got at all, but especially gettin' that mark from a curly-haired ex-cheerleader."

"Really?" I asked, hope blooming.

He nodded. "Really. It's not gonna happen. Even if you didn't mark him, just got a punch in, he wouldn't share that with anyone."

Well, that was good.

"Good," I whispered.

"Second," he began and the minute amount I'd relaxed raced away. "He saw you. He saw me. At the grocery store while you were dumpin' beans in the cart, he looked right at me . . . and you. He knew in a glance who you were to me, what we have, what I've got. He looked away, Carissa. I coulda made an approach and rubbed it in, but why the fuck would I waste my time with that shit? It isn't worth it. Bein' in a grocery store with a beautiful girl who likes bein' with me who's babbling about chili hit him harder than I could ever do it even if I wanted to put in that effort. I took off to get outta his space. He doesn't deserve that, but I had my pretty girl with me babblin' about chili. We were settin' up for a good night 'cause that's what we always have. I introduce him into it, it means she might not have a good night. So I got us the fuck outta there."

"Oh," I said softly, thinking perhaps I should have discussed things with him before I went out and committed felonies.

He went on like I didn't make the sound.

"Not to mention, wandering a grocery store isn't big with me. You're in one, you act like you're in a mall. So I'm seein' if I gotta go to the store, I go alone. You gotta go, you go alone, but while you're out, I contact my brothers just in case we gotta convene a search party. The way you are in a grocery store, you *ever* gotta go to the mall, you go without me. Deal?"

How did we get to talking about how we shopped?

I didn't think it was a good idea to request that information.

I just said, "Deal." Then I asked, "So he scowled at that old lady because he saw you and you with me?"

"He did what?"

"He gave a dirty look to an old lady," I told him, then added, "It was very rude."

"Who knows why he does the shit he does?" Joker asked. "But yeah, probably. I kicked his ass and left him out cold on his living room floor last time I saw him. Years later I'm with a cute, sweet, honey-haired, ex-cheerleader, once homecoming queen piece of ass. And before you say it," he said when I opened my mouth, "all that is written all over you. He's an asshole and an asshole to women, but he wouldn't miss any a' that."

"Okay," I whispered.

"My ma was fuckin' gorgeous, but even in his glory days, he couldn't nail a piece like you, and I'm leanin' on a cart while you toss in enough beans to feed chili to my entire Club."

"You never know when the chili craving will come over you," I said quietly. "Most of those were for the pantry, just in case."

He stared at me.

Then he muttered (like it was a bad thing), "Jesus, you do it for me."

"I do . . ." I paused uncertainly, "*what* for you?"

"Everything."

I started breathing funny.

"You keyed him?" he asked.

I nodded.

"Vehicle and face?"

"The last was a mistake, kind of gross, and I don't feel proud—"

"Butterfly, I need you to get this," he interrupted me firmly. "I've been in love with you since high school. I'll be in love with you when you walk down the aisle to me, push out our first kid, our second, our third, cry when they go off to college, nag at them to give you grandbabies, and sit next to me on our couch in our pad in assisted living. I got that. I got my family. I got my brothers. *I'm healed.* You do not have to go off keyin' my dad's car. I'm *good*. Stop tryin' to make me that way. You already got me there."

I loved all he said.

All of it.

But I was focused on one thing.

"You've been in love with me since high school?" I breathed.

"Did you actually look at that sketch I gave you?"

Tears wet my eyes.

He'd been in love with me since high school.

"Yeah, Carrie," he answered. "It's you. It's always been you. It'll always be you. Fuckin' *always*."

Aaron had said that more than once, and each time until the last I'd convinced myself to believe it.

Now Joker said it and I knew the difference immediately.

I didn't have to convince myself of anything.

"Can I...can I...?" I started talking at the same time blubbering, "Are you angry with me?"

"Outside of wishin' you'd told me what you were up to so if you needed that, I coulda watched, no."

I kept blubbering but also started giggling.

"Now, Butterfly, tell me something," he demanded.

"Wh-what?" I asked through laughter and tears.

"You go out with the girls anyway?"

I nodded, pulling in breath to control my contradictory emotions.

"We had cosmos." I lifted my hand. "And I got ice for my hand."

His jaw went hard and I thought I knew why.

"It's okay," I assured him. "Elvira got me ice really quickly. It feels a little tight but it's fine."

His eyes came to mine and my heart stopped.

"You're tellin' me you went out with your girls to get drinks wearin' that top?"

"Um..." I mumbled.

"Um?" he pushed, tipping his head to the side.

"Only one guy bought me a drink," I shared.

His face changed.

Wrong thing to say!

"Tabby told him I was Chaos immediately," I went on quickly.

"Come here," he growled.

I was two feet away.

"I *am* here, Carson."

"Come . . . *here*."

I stared at him debating the merits of walking those two feet.

Then I did it debating the merits of not walking those two feet.

I walked those two feet.

Joker lifted his hand instantly, hooked a finger in the top of my tube top and slid it across.

My legs started shaking.

"There's clothes for when you go out with your girls," he said softly. "And there's clothes for when you go out with your man. Do I have to explain that fully, or do you get me?"

"I get you," I whispered.

He ran his finger back but stopped midway and dipped it in the space between my breasts.

My lips parted.

"Your hand really okay?" he asked.

I nodded, focusing on standing and breathing rather than speaking.

"Good, baby," he tipped his head toward me, "'cause you're gonna need to use it."

Oh yes.

I ran my teeth over my lower lip.

Joker watched.

I shivered while he watched.

And when I was done with my teeth and the shiver, he tugged on my tube top until I was pressed against him.

Then finally, he slanted his head and kissed me.

* * *

Dawn was kissing the sky.

The wind was in my hair.

My arms were around Joker's stomach.

My cheek was pressed to his leather.

The sun was rising on a day after a night when I'd had zero sleep.

Neither did my biker.

But after he told me he'd loved me since high school, we got through my tales of lunacy, he'd divested me of my tube top in a way I knew I was dipping into my savings, going back to that store, and buying every color, then he made love to me on the couch, he'd asked me if I wanted to ride.

It would be our first time together on his bike.

So I'd obviously said yes.

My ride with Snapper was amazing.

My ride with Joker was everything.

Suddenly, the wind quit whipping my hair as he slowed then pulled over, throwing out a boot to idle at the curb.

I stopped being lost in all Joker and his bike were giving me and lifted up to look around.

I did this just as Joker let out a long, low whistle.

Then I saw where we were and my arms convulsed around him.

"Fuck, Butterfly, bumper to bumper," Joker muttered as we both stared at his father's truck. "Nice."

I smiled.

Then I pressed close and lifted up so my lips were to his ear.

"You know, I love you too."

He kept his eyes to the truck and asked, "No shit?"

I squeezed his stomach so hard he grunted.

Then he twisted his head, looked at me, and when he

did, he was smiling, his teeth brilliant white and beautiful against the black stubble he was growing for me.

"I know you love me, Carrie," he said softly.

"Good," I whispered.

"Kiss me, baby."

I pushed forward and kissed Joker on his bike at the curb by his father's house. I kissed him hard. I kissed him deep. I gave him my tongue and kissed him wet.

He took it and kissed me back harder, deeper, and wetter.

When we broke it, I kept his gaze and said, "I'm feeling ill. I may have to take the day off."

His eyes smiled as his lips muttered, "My good girl, playin' hooky."

"Just this once," I whispered.

"Best get you home so we can get you to bed."

I wanted that but even so, I gave him another squeeze. "We can do that, but before, can we ride a little longer?" I tipped my head to the side. "Please?"

"Whatever you want, Carrie."

I smiled.

Joker touched his mouth to mine.

He turned to face forward.

I put my chin to his shoulder.

He pulled out.

The wind started whipping my hair.

And there it was, it came immediately.

As the sun rose in the Denver sky, both of us got it at the same time, together on the back of Joker's bike.

We were free.

CHAPTER TWENTY-FOUR

Do Better with That

Carissa

I GOT OFF Joker's bike first.

When I did, I pulled down the skirt of my T-shirt dress.

If you told me a year ago I'd go out to a fancy dinner in a clingy dress and high-heeled strappy sandals, doing this with a biker *on his bike*, I would have asked to check your temperature.

But the meal was delicious. The company *way* better. Joker and I had finally gotten our fancy dinner date at The Broker. Fat shrimp. Juicy steak. Delicious wine (for me; Joker drank beer).

Just me and Joker.

Travis was coming home tomorrow.

So life was good.

And now, for some reason, instead of taking us home after dinner, we were at Ride.

Not at the Chaos Compound; he'd parked outside the steps to the office of the garage.

There were tall overhead lights illuminating the space, and I watched Joker as he got off his bike.

"What are we doing here, sweetie?" I asked when he turned to me.

"Build's done," he stated, reaching out to grab my hand. "The guy who commissioned it is comin' tomorrow to pick it up. Want you to see it before he does."

I smiled up at him big and bright because I wanted that too.

He walked me up the steps and let my hand go to unlock the door. He went in, flipping on the light as he did, and I followed.

He closed the door behind me, and I thought it was strange that he locked it but I didn't ask after it as he grabbed my hand again and moved me to the other door that led to the garage.

We went through and I stood at the landing on top of the stairs. Joker hit switches and the overhead lights blinked on, filling the space with brightness.

The car, canary yellow with a plethora of sleek, fantastic swirling, curving, spiking red stripes leading from the wheel wells all the way down the sides, was shining on the floor.

"Oh my *gosh*!" I cried, hurrying to the stairs and down them, my eyes to the car. "It's *unbelievable*."

It was. Low to the ground. Amazing curves. A narrow slit for a windshield.

Road cool but so hot!

I rushed to it on my heels and took it in from a closer perspective.

It was even better.

"I'm scared to touch it," I breathed.

"Not even my best and she acts like I painted the *Mona Lisa*," Joker muttered from close behind me.

I whirled and looked up at him. "You can be humble because you *should* be humble. That doesn't mean it isn't *unbelievable*."

He grinned down at me.

I loved that grin.

I loved that man.

"Thank you for showing me," I said.

His hands came to my hips and he immediately started walking, shuffling me backward, murmuring, "You're welcome, Butterfly."

Since we were moving, I was going backward and doing it in heels, I lifted my hands to steady myself by curling my fingers on his shoulders.

He shifted slightly but kept moving me back.

"Uh…" I started, trailed off and was about to begin again when the backs of my legs hit car.

That was when I knew what he was up to.

And liked what he was up to.

"Joker," I whispered.

He moved his hands from my hips, back to cup my behind.

Automatically, my fingers dug into the leather at his shoulders as I arched into him.

"You gonna wanna see all my builds when they're done?" he asked quietly.

"Please," I answered breathily.

"Then, baby, you gotta know, I show 'em to you, you give back by taking my fucking on the hood."

"Oh," I whispered, answering that demand by gliding my hands to hold tight at the side of his neck.

"We got a deal?"

"I've never…I…*oh!*" I ended on a cry as his hands slid down, fingers curling into the hem of my skirt and yanking it up.

"We got a deal?" he repeated and glided his hands in my panties to cup my bottom, skin against skin.

"Deal," I panted.

He grinned, slanted his head and kissed me.

I slid my hands up into his hair and kissed him back.

He pushed my panties down until they fell to the floor of the garage. Then he grasped me where my thighs met my booty and lifted me up.

I felt the cold steel of the car on my behind.

I whimpered into his mouth as he bent over me, pushing me back, and I could feel the rough fabric of his jeans as I spread my legs to accommodate his hips.

"Like this dress," he murmured against my lips, trailing his hand inside my dress up my side, up and *up*.

"I'm glad," I whispered, moving my hands to his cut and shoving it over his shoulders.

His mouth went to my neck as his hands left me so I could shove his jacket down his arms.

I heard it slide to the ground as I went for his neck.

"We won't scratch it?" I asked, dipping my hands down and pulling his shirt (not a tee, a nice one for our fancy date, though he still wore his cut because he always wore his cut) from his jeans.

"We scratch it, I'll buff it," he answered then slid his tongue up my neck to my ear as he glided his hand over my ribs to my breast.

"Okay," I murmured as I reached inside his shirt, trailing up the hot skin of his back then changed directions and dug my fingertips into the waistband of his jeans.

He pressed his hips between my legs.

I nipped his jaw.

His mouth went from my ear to my lips and he kissed me.

I kissed him back and pressed up slightly as I trailed my fingers along the inside of his waistband, pulled them out and glided them down over his crotch.

He groaned and pressed his hardness into my hand.

I palmed him.

He growled and ground against me.

I panted against his lips and tightened my thighs against his hips, palming him harder, pressing and rubbing.

"Fuck, my hot little piece," he grunted against my mouth, his thumb dragging hard against my nipple over my bra.

"Yes," I forced out. "Hot," I panted. "Joker," I whimpered with need.

He slid his hand around my hip, down and through my wet.

That was my biker.

Always giving me what I needed.

I pressed into his hand and mewed.

He drove two fingers inside.

I arched, my head hit steel, my knees jerked up, and I moaned.

I felt Joker stay close but still move away, and I knew he was watching as his thumb rolled hard at my nipple, his other hand between my legs worked, fingers thrusting, thumb at my clit circling.

I grasped his hips with my thighs, rubbed his crotch with my hand as he ground into it, my other hand clutching at the flesh of his side, nails digging in.

At the same time, I rode his hand and whispered, "Baby, don't stop."

"Won't, Butterfly, give me your show," he growled.

I gave him what he wanted, writhing and squirming, arching and rocking, whimpering and mewing on top of his car as he worked me and watched.

Suddenly, my head jerked up and my eyes opened.

"Carson!" I cried, cupping his crotch hard, then my head fell back as the orgasm powered through me and I writhed and squirmed, arched and whimpered.

In the middle of it, I lost his hand but took his cock.

He was not gentle. He wasn't slow. We weren't making love. We were fucking on his car.

I loved it.

Coming down, I worked with him as he pounded inside to build it back up, legs and hands, fingers and lips, mouth and tongue—his and mine.

Eventually, he demanded on a grunt and an inward drive, "Get there, Carrie."

My hand in his hair fisted and I breathed, "I'm there, sweetheart."

Then I was.

And he was.

On his fabulous car.

In a garage called Ride.

It was naughty.

It was *amazing*.

It was Joker.

And it was me.

*   *   *

The next evening, feeling Joker close, standing alert at my back as he was always even when he wasn't in the same room with me (like he was then), I opened my front door.

I smiled bright and clapped my hands softly in front of me before I reached for my son in Aaron's arms and said, "Hey there, Googly-Foogly."

Travis twisted toward me, arms out, and I caught him, pulling him close, breathing in his scent, kissing the top of his head.

"Carissa, can we talk?" Aaron asked, and I looked up at him.

"Well—"

His eyes went beyond me. "Alone."

I really wished he'd stop this.

I drew in breath and said, "Aaron, I don't—"

"No," Joker answered for me.

Aaron looked back at me. "Riss, I'm asking for ten minutes alone."

"There's really nothing you can say that Joker can't hear," I replied.

"As a courtesy," he bit out. "Just ten minutes. You can't give that to the father of your son?"

I studied him.

Someone was losing patience.

Darn.

I wasn't feeling in a courteous mood. I had my son back. I had a biker who loved me. There was bonding to be done, TV to watch, and normal, easy, family stuff to be had.

Before I could get into it with Aaron, I felt Joker close.

I turned to him, and he had hands on Travis.

I looked into his eyes as he pulled my boy from my arms.

"Ten minutes, Carrie," he muttered.

Then he turned to Aaron and lifted a hand.

Aaron glared at him as he shrugged Travis's diaper bag off his shoulder before latching it onto Joker's hand.

Joker took it, hooked it on his shoulder, and walked away, muttering to Travis, "Right, you got ten minutes to tell me all about your trip to your dad's."

"Jew jah kah."

I blinked because that sounded kind of somewhat like *Joker.*

"Carissa," Aaron called, and I started before I looked to him to see he was inside, the door closed behind him.

I sighed.

"What would you like to talk about?" I asked.

His eyes went to the hall, and his voice was quiet when he stated, "There's another five hundred dollars in Travis's bag."

I tried to force gratitude into my "Thank you."

"I'm assuming," he continued, "since Steele's still here that you haven't thought on things."

I really needed to get this through to him.

So I clasped my hands in front of me in a physical effort to demonstrate my sincerity and held his eyes. "I'm sorry. I really am. But, Aaron, please believe me when I tell you there was nothing to think about."

His mouth got tight.

I took a small step toward him, wanting him to believe I was being genuine (because I was) but not wanting to get too close.

"This is...it's..." I struggled to find words before I found them. "It's very nice. It means a lot that you're thinking of Travis and want to give him a family. But families come in a lot of different ways, and now he's got a big one. You and your parents. Me and Joker and our friends."

"Yes, I want to give our son *his* family, but you're missing the fact that I also want my wife back," he returned.

"I think I've responded to that, Aaron," I told him.

"I got rid of Tory for you," he snapped.

Got rid of?

I pressed my lips together, chanting in my head, *do not get mad, do not get mad, do not get mad.*

I got a hold on it and said carefully, "I'm sorry you've broken up. That must be hard."

He threw up his hands and hissed, "What do you want? She's gone. She was a mistake. I don't even know what I was thinking. But it's done. I'm giving you money. I'm being cool about that *fucking* guy. Do you want me on my knees? Do you want me to beg? Do you want an apology in skywriting? What the fuck do you want?"

"I told you what I want, Aaron," I reminded him, trying to do it calmly.

He leaned toward me. "This is the best thing for our son. For us. *For you*."

I held my ground and his gaze when I replied, "I think I know better what's best for me."

"Yes?" He leaned back, throwing a hand toward the hall. "And he's it? Carson fucking Steele. High school loner. High school *loser*. Biker gang member. What kind of life is he going to give you, Carissa?"

He was going too far, saying those things about Joker.

I knew I shouldn't engage. I knew it.

But I did anyway.

"He won't cheat on me, for one," I replied, and Aaron's eyes narrowed. "He loves me, for another, really, truly, in the sense that it's genuine. In the sense that I believe in it... totally. In the sense that I believe in it in a way I know in my heart of hearts it's forever. Then there's the fact he doesn't ask me to change my dress for one he thinks is more appropriate. There's also the fact he doesn't look down on my job. He loves my son just like he's his own. He has fantastic friends who are loyal and care a lot about him, something he earned. He's talented. He has a great job that he's so good at, even *Wilde and Hay* know it, which is why they want to do an article about his work."

Aaron stared at me.

"But in the end," I carried on, "I really shouldn't be asked to explain this because it's really none of your business."

"I can give you a better life," Aaron told me.

"I already know that's not true," I retorted, and Aaron's face turned to stone.

"I love you too, Riss," he bit out.

I now knew what love was.

And I knew I gave that to Aaron.

He just didn't give it back.

"I hope you listen to this, Aaron," I replied. "Because it's important for you and your future and the woman you may someday have in it, but if you think that's love, the way you've treated me, you need to rethink it. I have love now, so I know by the way you treated me that you don't understand the right way to do it."

His eyes flashed with hurt, and I knew that was not a good thing. Aaron lashed out when he hurt.

I was right.

The hurt vanished and his lip curled as he said low, "Never thought that was you. If I'd known how you like it, I wouldn't have had to find Tory."

I was confused, so much so, I stupidly asked, "What are you talking about?"

His sneer turned to a leer, he inched closer, tipping his head down to me, and even though he was really close, I thought it best to stand my ground.

That time, I was wrong.

"You like it nasty, baby?" he whispered. "You like it rough? You like to get *fucked*?"

I felt steel coat my spine, didn't look away, and replied, "Actually, yes."

His head jerked with surprise.

"I like taking my fucking, getting it hard and rough on that couch," I told him casually, throwing a hand out to the couch. "In bed. On the floor." I threw my hand behind me. "On the hood of one of Joker's builds." I rolled up on my toes and changed my tone to suggestive. "Anywhere he wants it, any way he wants to give it, and he gives it *good*,

Aaron. I know because I get it good, *every time*, and I've had it the other way around, where I didn't know if my man would put in the effort. So yeah, *oh yeah*, I like it *just like that*."

He lifted his head so he could look down his nose at me. "You're disgusting."

I tipped my head to the side. "I don't understand. You just told me you found Tory to give you the nasty. You don't like it like that?"

He clamped his mouth shut.

"You are very, *very* done, friend."

I jumped and stepped back, my head turning to see Joker standing with his shoulder leaning against the wall of the doorway to the hall.

Travis was in his arms, crawling and burrowing, pulling hair and babbling.

The stance was calm and relaxed.

But Joker was absolutely not.

His eyes were locked to Aaron, and it was a wonder a trail of fire didn't go from them to my ex.

"You leave, or Carrie's got Travis and I put you out," Joker went on. "You don't got time to think about it. Use the door," he growled. "*Now.*"

Aaron glared at him.

"What'd I say?" Joker asked, and I felt a chill cover my skin at his tone and the look on his face.

"We're done," Aaron clipped, and my eyes went to him to see he was looking at me. "And you're fucked in ways you won't like to be, *baby.*"

With that, he turned to the door, threw it open, and slammed it behind him.

"Not again."

This was from Joker, and it was still in that chilling tone.

I turned to him.

"Attorneys only from now on, Carissa, are you hearing me?"

He'd heard.

I had a feeling he'd heard *everything*.

I nodded.

"We don't get this shit sorted and soon, the hand off, you do not see that fuck, when Travis comes or when he goes," he stated. "I do it."

I nodded but said gently, "I'm sorry. That was my fault. I lost my temper—"

"It was not your fault," he bit out, interrupting me. "But it's done and I mean *done*, you with me?"

I nodded again.

Travis, feeling the atmosphere, started fretting.

Joker, feeling Travis fretting, turned to him, took him in, then bent in and kissed his forehead.

After he did that, he ordered in a soft voice, "Your Joke is done, kid, you can cool it."

Travis studied him.

Then his head wobbled a bit before he dropped it to Joker's shoulder, cheek first, and grasped on to the neckline of Joker's tee like he knew Joker was upset and he was giving him a baby hug.

Gosh, but I loved my boy.

And I loved my biker.

I took in a breath.

"It's done," I whispered.

Joker nodded.

Then he said, "Come get your kid. He needs ma time."

I grinned. It was shaky but I pulled it off and walked across the room to get to my boy.

And my biker.

*   *   *

The next morning I was changing Travis's diaper on the floor in the living room. I had an afternoon shift, which stunk. But Joker was at work, and he was coming home to look after Travis while I was at work. Then I would be home and sleeping with Joker with Travis home so it would all be good.

My cell phone rang in the kitchen as I pressed down the last diaper strip.

Travis, very much done with the changing routine, instantly rolled and started crawling toward a scattering of toys on the floor.

I nabbed the balled-up dirty diaper, got up swiftly, and dashed into the kitchen to grab my phone.

Not surprisingly, but a little scarily, it was Angie.

"Hello," I greeted, heading to the Diaper Genie in the laundry room.

"Hey there, Carissa. It's Leanne. Can you hold for Angie?"

"Of course," I replied.

I held as I dealt with the diaper.

I was back in the kitchen when Angie came on.

"Hi, Carissa. How are you?"

"I'm good, Angie. Let me guess," I said, moving to the sink to wash my hands. "Aaron's attorneys have been in touch."

"Was there an incident?" she asked.

"It happened during the handover yesterday," I told her. "I haven't had a chance to call."

"Tell me about it now," she ordered.

I washed my hands and did so.

"Well then, this makes their demand that we set a meeting as soon as possible not as surprising as it seemed," she remarked when I was done. "I need you to give Leanne your work schedule for this week so we can schedule the meeting."

"I'll do that, but, Angie, I need to say that confrontation was unpleasant, so I feel from now on that we should talk through our attorneys only. And if this drags on, I'm not comfortable in Aaron's presence, so there will be someone else dropping Travis off at Aaron's and I'll not be opening the door when he brings him to my place."

"Will this be Mr. Steele?" she asked.

"Likely," I told her. "However, it could be another friend. It just won't be me."

"Noted. And if this drags on, I'll make that point. But I'll call them immediately to share that any further communications go through me. If you hear from Mr. Neiland, it should only be if there's an emergency about your son. If it isn't, you tell me as soon as you can."

"Thanks, Angie."

"Not a problem, Carissa. Now I'm handing you off to Leanne."

"All right. Speak to you later."

"You will. Take care."

She did the handoff. I gave Leanne my schedule as I walked into the living room and watched Travis rearranging the scattered toys.

We rang off and I called Joker immediately.

I gave him the news.

"Not a surprise," he said when I was done.

"He's angry, which means I'm scared," I told him.

"You're good, Carrie. But if he makes you not that way, then I'll be there to make you that way again."

"I know," I whispered, eyes to my boy as he played.

"Hang tight, this'll be done soon," he promised.

"Okay."

"Love you."

I closed my eyes.

Aaron had made me not good.

Then Joker was there to make me that way again.

When I opened my eyes, I was smiling. "Love you too."

I could hear the smile in his voice when he said, "Let you go. Later, Butterfly."

"Later, sweetie."

We disconnected.

Before I left for work a few hours later, Leanne called.

Aaron wasn't messing around.

The meeting was set for Thursday afternoon, the specter of which made me not good again.

So I called Joker.

And he made it all better.

Joker

Disconnecting with Carissa, Joker texted Tack.

It's happening.

Five minutes later, he got back, *Meet me at the table.*

Joker didn't waste time leaving the garage and walking across the forecourt to the Compound. He went directly to Chaos's table in the meeting room.

Tack was the only one there. He was standing by his seat at the head of the table, two piles of folders resting on the table in front of him.

One was very high. The other one wasn't near as high, but it was still tall.

Joker closed the door behind him, walked into the room, and stopped, his eyes on Tack.

"This," Tack said, his fingertips pressing into the high stack of folders, "is Chaos. Angie has it. She won't be blindsided."

Joker nodded. He didn't need to give gratitude. Tack

knew what he was giving was huge, and he knew Joker knew it.

They also both knew they had attorney/client confidentiality.

"This," Tack went on, touching his fingertips to the other stack, "Angie's also got. You need to study it, brother, then decide by how ugly it gets when or if you need to give the nod to Angie. Her ex isn't dirty. But he's a cheat, and I know Carrie knows it. I just don't think she knows he's had his dick in so much pussy, he makes Shy in his glory days look like a choirboy."

Fuck.

This meant he might have to have the conversation with her that she, too, should get tested.

Fuck.

"It's the father that's deep in dirt," Tack continued. "Shit in here gets loose, she's got destructive powers that if she gets queasy at markin' your old man, who she fuckin' hates, I'm not thinkin' our girl's got in her to use. But it's yours. It's hers. They force it, be smart how you use it. It gets to that point and you need a strategy session, you know where to find me."

Joker nodded again.

Tack held his eyes, and Joker saw in his what he saw after their meeting with Sebring and Valenzuela. It wasn't exactly the same, but only because it wasn't for the same reason.

Now, Joker knew the reason because he knew that he'd shared with Tack the trash talk Aaron Neiland had tried to shove down Carrie's throat.

And Tack had not liked that.

Therefore Tack's voice was granite when he stated, "They will not take her boy, and the time to fuck with Carissa Teodoro is now *over.*"

Joker's voice was a quiet growl when he stated, "You know you got my love, brother."

"I do," Tack returned. "And it's a privilege, Carson."

Joker felt that in his throat but only nodded again.

Tack tipped his head toward the end of the room, where there was a closet that held their massive safe. "Read. Lock it up when you're done."

"Yeah."

Tack moved, clapping Joker on the shoulder as he walked out.

Joker went to the folders.

He didn't touch the high stack.

But he read every page of the shorter one.

When he was done, he locked them away, and he didn't do it smiling.

But he did it relieved.

Chaos had them by the balls.

But Carrie would never know.

Not unless she needed to.

And all Joker could do was hope like fuck she never needed to.

Carissa

"Okay, this is not good," I whispered.

I was sitting in Angie's conference room. I was not in my tube top. I'd chickened out on the tube top.

Instead I was wearing my butterfly dress and shoes. It wasn't casual, exactly.

What it was, was me.

But also, it was my lucky dress. I deemed it so because I thought of it as Joker's.

A Joker who had been completely calm since all this

went down, thankfully, since (until that moment) his calm had been calming me.

He was there, but he was in Angie's office with Travis because Angie said we shouldn't goad Aaron with his presence or make the statement that I needed backup.

Both Joker and I agreed.

So he was close but too far.

But he was close, and that was all I needed.

"No, you're right. This is not good," Angie muttered.

I didn't need to look at her to know she was doing the same as me, looking through the windows of her conference room at Aaron approaching with his attorney.

And his father.

"Intimidation," Angie said quickly, and I tore my gaze from the approaching men to look at her just as she curled her hand around my forearm resting on the table. "To you, not me," she went on and squeezed my arm. "I got this, Carissa."

She seemed super confident, fortunately.

So I nodded.

The men came in.

Aaron glared ice at me.

His father glared daggers.

I sat and thought thoughts of my son sitting in the grass of my backyard with butterflies drifting around him while he giggled.

It worked for me.

Leanne got the men glasses of water then sat at the end of the table with her notebook while the men settled in across from Angie and me.

"Right, let's start," Angie said. "I believe you received our communication of where we'd like to begin negotiations."

Aaron glared ice at me.

His attorney opened his mouth to speak.

But it was his father who spoke.

"We'll see you in court. My son is going for full custody. We'll see Ms. Teodoro declared unfit. When we're done, if she manages to get any visitation, it will be supervised."

My insides shriveled, and slowly, I looked to my ex-husband.

He was looking at me and his look was glacial.

"It's a shame we've wasted this time, then," Angie said indifferently. "We'll see you in court."

"Your client should be aware that after this meeting, we'll be contacting Child Protection Services to instigate proceedings to have my grandson extricated from a home that's turned dangerous," Aaron's father stated.

My lips parted, and I slowly looked to him.

"Would you care to share the grounds you'll be using?" Angie asked courteously.

"She can hardly not know," Mr. Neiland replied. "However, if she's unaware, she should know. She has a man named Peter Waite looking after my grandson. He's a member of a motorcycle gang that's known to be felonious, and he himself has a history of criminal activities."

"Peter Waite," Angie said, sounding confused. "A man known as Big Petey?"

"I don't know what he's known as, Angie," Mr. Neiland said impatiently. "I just know it's a demonstration of a serious lack of conscience to allow an infant to be looked after by a known criminal."

"Well, Big Petey is also a man who won the Illinois lottery about nine years ago," Angie told Aaron's dad.

My head slowly turned to her.

She kept speaking.

"He won a good deal of money. He also gave most of it to

a hospice that was, at the time, providing his ailing daughter with care. So much money, he endowed it. Sadly, his daughter passed. But his generosity has made it so hundreds of patients and their families could avail themselves of the service from this hospice, which I do believe, since his hefty donation, has won awards."

I blinked.

She kept talking.

"He also volunteers at a hospice here in Denver. He's in charge of their small childcare facility. He supervises six other volunteers and he and his volunteers look after youngsters while the families of patients are visiting. Though, he mostly does the supervision as he offers the bulk of his time to my client to care for her son while she's working, as well as taking care of Kane and Tyra Allen's two boys, Mr. Allen being the operating manager of a well-known local business. Big Petey further sometimes looks after the young son of Hopper and Elaine Kincaid. Ms. Kincaid, you probably don't know, owns her own advertising agency. It's young, but regardless, it was recently declared by a glossy Denver magazine as Denver's top agency."

My eyes got big.

Wow.

Go Lanie!

"I would assume that Mr. and Mrs. Allen and Mr. and Mrs. Kincaid, not to mention the director of the hospice, would stand as character witness as to Mr. Waite's abilities to provide childcare," Angie stated.

I tried not to smile.

"And it's true," Angie went on. "Seventeen years ago, Big Petey was arrested for grand theft auto. However, he was released before trial due to lack of evidence. Although that would appear on his arrest record, it would be doubtful a judge would take that into account during a custody hearing considering the case was thrown out."

She lifted her hand but didn't quit talking.

"And, before you mention it, I understand he did some community service for a drunk and disorderly he pled guilty to. However, this occurred only weeks after his daughter's funeral service, so I do believe his behavior would be understood. Oh, and, of course, the judge allowed this service to be done at the hospice where, after, they took him on in a volunteer capacity."

"That does not negate the fact that my ex-daughter-in-law is consorting with a biker gang," Mr. Neiland retorted. "And I do believe you, *and she*, understand precisely what I mean by *consorting*."

"I would be very careful of any public disparagement of the Chaos Motorcycle Club, Judge Neiland," Angie said quietly.

"Is that a threat?" Aaron's dad asked snidely.

Angie looked to Aaron's attorney and offered, "Steven, perhaps you need a moment to confer with your client."

"He hardly does," Mr. Neiland sniped, and I looked at him to see him turning his attention to me. "We have a witness who will attest that they observed your *boyfriend* assaulting a man at an illegal underground fight, several of his gang members with him, and he did this brutally. The man was left bloodied, battered, unconscious, and barely breathing. And *you* are allowing this man to be around *my grandson*."

My body stopped functioning.

Luckily, Angie's didn't.

"Were charges filed?"

"What?" Aaron's dad snapped.

"Judge Neiland, were charges filed?" she repeated slowly.

"No, but—"

"No," she cut him off sharply. "And this man you speak of that Mr. Steele allegedly assaulted, is he not currently incarcerated without bail for ordering the murder of a young pregnant woman?" Angie asked.

My back went straight.

"That's beside the point," Mr. Neiland hissed.

"So he is," Angie stated.

"It's *beside the point*," Mr. Neiland bit out.

"You're right. It is," she conceded but didn't let it go. "Now, this witness you say you have, they were at an illegal underground fight?"

Aaron's father pressed his lips together.

Angie didn't let up.

"Did this witness, say, happen by this illegal underground fight while they were taking an evening stroll, then, perchance, they immediately phoned it in to the police, considering it was an illegal underground fight where an assault allegedly occurred?"

I watched Aaron's father glare at Angie.

I heard Angie address Aaron's attorney. "Steven, again, would you like a moment to confer with your client?"

I looked to Aaron.

He was staring at the table.

Sitting there, listening to this nastiness, not participating, and staring at the stupid table!

"I love him," I announced.

Aaron's head came up.

"Carissa," Angie said quietly, her hand back to my arm on the table.

Aaron's father made a disgusted noise.

But I was looking into Aaron's eyes.

"I loved you once, and you destroyed me."

"Carissa, please let me do the speaking," Angie urged beside me.

I didn't look away from Aaron.

"This is it," I told him. "I'm done. I won't allow you to hurt me anymore. Hurt me directly. Hurt me through Carson. Hurt me using my friends. Hurt me at all. Hurt *them* at all. I know what this means," I threw up a hand slightly, indicating our vile meeting. "You're set on destroying me. *Again*. Taking away the happiness I worked hard for. So congratulations, Aaron. You've finally done it. You've turned love to hate. I didn't want that. Not for me or you and especially not for Travis. I know it's not nice to hate someone, but I can say it's now official. Your willingness to be a party to this has made that so. What will be will be what you force it to be. I'll deal with it. If you force me to go down, I'll go down fighting. If you take everything from me, I'm okay with that as long as I keep hold of my baby. But there will be nothing that will make me stop hating you. I'll see you again only when I *have to* see you. Other than that, I hope I *never* see you."

I stood and Aaron's eyes followed me.

They were wounded and suffering.

Mine held his steady as they did because I didn't care even a little bit what he was feeling.

"I can't imagine it, what would make a man who has the love of a woman, a woman who wants nothing but to live a life loving him and the babies they make, strive to turn that to hate. If I could stand the sight of you, I'd be interested in you explaining that to me. But I can't stand the sight of you. So that will remain a mystery." I looked immediately to Angie and told her, "I'm sorry, Angie, but I have to go."

She nodded. "Go, Carissa."

I turned away, felt them and I hated them too.

But they came, the tears, as I walked blindly to the door, too overwhelmed by what I was feeling, the fear crawling inside me, to even worry that I might trip and make a fool of myself.

I didn't.

I got to the door, put my hand on the handle, and pulled it open.

I looked over my shoulder one last time at the man I once loved.

Then I walked away.

Aaron

"They hardly have a leg to stand on."

"Judge Neiland, we had a plan. You did not stick to the plan. That did *not* go well. Now, I urge you to listen to me…"

Aaron Neiland wasn't listening as he strode ahead of his father and his attorney.

It was his father's idea to come that day.

He hadn't seen Carissa recently. He didn't know how she'd changed.

And the pompous fuck wouldn't have listened anyway.

Aaron didn't give a shit if he came or not. The whole play was a grandstand so he could see Carissa's face when they told her they were taking her ass to court.

He did this because he wanted to watch her start to cave.

She was all about Travis. All about family. So he knew she would cave.

So he was shocked as shit that she didn't.

He walked right to the elevators but as he did, he saw it.

And when he saw it, he didn't stare. He looked away immediately.

But it was burned on his brain anyway.

He knew where Angie's office was in that suite.

Fuck, he should have taken the long way.

But he didn't.

So he saw it.

Carissa pressing her face into Carson Steele's chest, the man's head bent, lips to her hair, her shoulders shaking with her tears. He was holding Carissa close with one arm, hand buried in her ringlets, Aaron's fucking son held tight in his other arm.

That vision was obliterated by another one he also did not like—seeing that last look of hurt and hate thrown his way through her tears—as Aaron got in the elevator.

The doors closed on him, his father, and his friend and colleague, Steven.

"Son, we'll go back to the office and—" his dad began.

He turned his head and caught his father's eyes. "Please, shut up."

His chin jerked into his neck. "I beg your pardon?"

He heard her words.

I can't stand the sight of you.

His father had fucked up. Their investigator warned them strongly not to bring in Chaos. If they did, the investigator told them that Kane Allen would activate Nightingale or Delgado, "And unless you can open your closet doors wide and only celestial light shines out with no bones dangling, they'll eviscerate the both of you."

His words.

Precisely.

Neither his father nor Aaron could open those doors.

So Chaos was off-limits.

But his father was so fucking arrogant, his head so far up his fucking ass, he thought he could get away with anything.

The strategy was to shake Carissa up with their news about Peter Waite and to share that her boyfriend was capable of beating a man bloody. Shake her up and make her rethink. Shake her up and drive her back to Aaron.

Aaron had not foreseen Angie being *that* in the know about her Chaos clients. She'd made Steele sound like a crusader for justice, and Carissa hadn't even blinked.

She knew it all, or if she didn't know it all, she knew enough not to give a shit.

Then she'd walked out and right into Steele's arms.

Right into his arms.

"I said, shut up."

His father's face twisted.

"Don't let that little bitch get into your head," he hissed. "She's been fucking with it since she was fucking fourteen."

Carissa was a little bitch now. For over a decade, she'd been everything from an angel to a demon depending on his father's mood.

His mother had always loved her.

His mother detested Tory.

His father didn't mind staring at Tory's tits any time she was around, but he thought she was a low-class homewrecker, and he'd shared that straight to Aaron's face.

Repeatedly.

He'd never win with his dad.

But Carissa had always been a winner with his mother.

One out of two had not been bad.

Aaron advanced until he was nose to nose with his father, the man pressed to the side of the elevator.

"Aaron," Steven whispered.

"Do not *ever* call Carissa a bitch."

"I raised a weak son," his father sneered. "Mind filled with skirt."

I can't stand the sight of you.

The doors opened.

Aaron backed away from his dad and strode out.

*   *   *

Aaron Neiland didn't go to his office.

He went to his house.

The house his fucking father shoved down his throat.

He knew Carissa hated it. It was big and imposing, took forever to clean, it wasn't her. Not even a little bit.

It could have been her, if they'd worked up to it, they'd started smaller and he'd been able to give her bigger and do it gradually, but his parents planting them in it when he was just starting as a junior associate...

No.

He went to the kitchen, opened a cupboard, grabbed a glass, opened another cupboard, grabbed a bottle, but stopped himself before pouring.

The bottle held an expensive Scotch whisky.

His dad drank Scotch.

He stared at the bottle.

Fuck, why did he drink whisky? He hated it.

He poured it down the drain and made what he liked.

A gin and tonic.

Then he did what the asshole in a romantic movie would do.

He went to the box that Tory had filled and put in the closet of one of the guest rooms. He tugged it out. He grabbed the wedding album. He went to the bed and dropped it on it.

He slugged back some gin and tossed open the cover.

The first picture was of Carissa sitting on a green lawn, bouquet in her hand, massive dress spread all around, her eyes up and not looking at the camera, but shifted to the right.

She was laughing.

Carissa had asked their photographer to put a picture of the two of them together at the beginning of the album.

Carissa's dad had insisted on paying for the wedding, including the photographer, but still, even though she wasn't paying for it, his mother had vetoed Carissa's wishes and chosen that photo.

As usual, his mother got what she wanted.

Aaron stared at the picture, his gut twisting.

He looked at her face in the photo and remembered that moment. Remembered it exactly.

It had been half an hour after they'd been declared married. He'd spent half that time in the back of their limo making out with his beautiful new wife, enjoying himself immensely, and also enjoying pissing off his parents, who wanted his and his wife's asses in front of the photographer.

But as that photo was taken, he was standing to the photographer's left and it had been all about Carissa. All about how sure he was about her right there in that beautiful gown. All about how sure he'd always been that they would have that, him in a tux, her in a wedding dress.

He'd been happy, happy for himself, happy for her, and because of that he'd been teasing her. He'd made her laugh and the photographer had snapped the picture.

I can't stand the sight of you.

He swallowed, staring at the album.

That had been Aaron's favorite shot. He liked it up front. He'd never said anything, but whenever he opened that album, that was precisely the picture he wanted to see.

Carissa looking beautiful and happy, laughing because he gave her that.

He liked to tell himself that was what he intended to give

her for the rest of her life, even when he knew he was on the path to becoming his father, so he also knew it was a fucking lie.

He'd dicked her around. He knew that too. It was like he couldn't help himself.

His father told him it happened. "You just have to get it out of your system, son. You're young. You will. When you do, if she's worth having a Neiland and knows what's good for her, she'll be there. Trust me."

So he always knew, in the end, it would be her.

He was just so ridiculously arrogant, he didn't know, in the end, for her it shouldn't be him.

His mind filled with her weeping in Carson Steele's arm.

I've loved her since high school, man.

Aaron slugged back more gin and stared at the photo.

You gotta drag her down, that'll suck, but I'll pick her back up.

Carissa stared up at him.

Laughing.

You gotta rip her apart, I'll fuckin' hate watchin' it, but I'll put her back together.

He threw back the last of the gin.

Push her to the point she can't stand the sight of you. But do it knowin' that's all on you. Just like everything that went before, it's all on you.

Fuck, the asshole was right.

He never should have allowed his father to come that day. He had no clue what he was thinking. He wasn't seventeen and going to the principal's office.

He was fucking twenty-six and going to a meeting to negotiate his son's future.

As uncomfortable as it was, as hideous as it felt coming to the realization, Aaron had no choice. Too much was at stake with the most important parts of that being the happiness and well-being of the woman he loved and their child.

And that realization was the fact it was time he grew the fuck up.

I love him.

He drew in breath before he set the glass aside and reached into his inside suit jacket pocket.

He pulled out his phone and made the call to his investigator.

"Text me Steele's cell," he ordered.

The man texted.

Aaron made another call.

"Yo."

"Steele. Neiland."

Silence.

"If you don't make her happy, I'll destroy you, I don't give a fuck the weight you got behind you with that Club."

Steele still said nothing.

Aaron drew in another breath.

Quietly, he gave it to him.

"I actually do love her."

That got him something.

"Next one you get, do better with that."

Then Carson Steele hung up on him.

Aaron clenched his teeth.

Then he grabbed his glass, went down to the kitchen, poured another drink, and called his attorney.

CHAPTER TWENTY-FIVE

Start

Joker

"I WILL, ANGIE. And thank you." Pause then, "Right. I'll call when I decide. Thank you again for everything. 'Bye."

Carissa dropped her phone and looked to Joker.

"I don't get it," she declared.

Joker had been watching her lying on the couch, legs out, back up, talking on the phone while her son crawled all over her, alternately trying to eat her dress and the duck head toy he was dragging with him.

She might not get it.

But Joker got it.

Aaron Neiland had a soul.

Just barely, but he had one.

"Told you he phoned me, Carrie," he reminded her quietly.

"I know. But he offered a settlement of two hundred and fifty thousand dollars to see to Aaron's care and upbringing while I quit work and go to school," she announced.

Holy fuck.

Joker's body got tight.

That jackhole didn't get to take care of his girl.

If she wanted to quit and go to school, he could shove his money up his ass. Joker would take care of that for her.

He didn't get a chance to say that since she kept talking.

"She also said that Aaron's attorney told her that once I finish with school and start with my career, he'll continue child support until Travis is eighteen, if I so wish. Any adjustments to that due to cost of living or Travis's needs should be requested through my attorney and he'll consider it. And if Travis goes to college, a decision about continued support and who'll pay tuition and other expenses will be negotiated at the time."

"Visitation?" Joker forced out.

"He feels Travis is coping with the current schedule and encourages me to allow it to remain the same without further negotiations."

"And?" Joker asked.

"And what?" she asked back.

"What do you think of all this?" he prompted.

She threw up her phone hand then used it to catch her son before he rolled off her and the couch after he got too involved with banging her on the belly with his duck and lost balance.

"I don't know what to think, sweetie." It was a soft cry, probably so she wouldn't freak Travis. "That meeting was nasty. I told you how nasty it was. Now this?"

"He had a change of heart."

"Aaron doesn't get those," she muttered, putting both hands on Travis and setting him on the floor considering he was leaning that way and grunting.

Once on the floor, Travis boogied to where Joker was stretched out opposite her, pushed up to his knees and banged Joker on his hip with the duck.

Joker grabbed the kid and hauled him to his stomach.

He started crawling all over him.

"Then a miracle has happened," he told her. "Roll with it. What else would you do?"

"I don't want his money," she was still muttering, her eyes on her boy.

"Carrie," he called.

She looked to him. "I don't."

He hated the idea of her ex taking care of her.

But still, that was a shit-ton of money.

So it hurt, but for her, he had to ask, "Is that smart?"

"Maybe not, but, Joker, he was *nasty*. Or, his father was, and his father is an extension of *him*."

"I get you, but—"

"LeLane's hired me when I was pregnant," she cut him off to say. "They work with my schedule as best as they can. They deserve loyalty. I want to be a stylist, but *I* want to make it so I'm a stylist. Not be giving some woman fabulous hair and thinking that Aaron was the one who made it so I could do that."

Joker felt his lips twitch.

"So, I'll take support," she declared. "And he's right. Travis is okay with this schedule, and if Aaron stops being a jerk, then it'll settle even more for him because he'll feel it's settled for all of us. I'll work for a while at LeLane's, and with Travis's support money coming in, save up for my own education. Once I'm there and I can give it to myself, I'll go for it."

"You're turnin' down a quarter of a million that, bottom line, that guy owes you, baby," he said gently.

"I'm turning down guilt money that will make him feel better for being so mean to me," she returned. "I don't care if he feels better or not. I don't care about him at all. I'll take his support money for Travis because he's Travis's dad. Other than that, he doesn't exist for me."

He grinned at her.

"Your call," he said.

"It is. Now, it's time to feed my family. Are you doing the cooking and I'm doing Travis, or the other way around?"

"You ever gonna make that chili you promised me?"

She smiled at him. "Guess I'm doing the cooking."

Joker smiled back then grabbed hold of her boy.

He dragged him up his chest as the kid squealed.

When he got him face to face, he said, "That means I get you."

And for his troubles, he got clocked in the face with a duck.

* * *

Three weeks later, Joker was walking from Ride to the Compound when his phone rang.

He pulled it out, saw who was calling and put it to his ear.

"Yo, Lee."

"You busy right now?"

"Nope," he answered, seeing as he wasn't. Carissa's ex had Travis so she had an afternoon shift. He was done with what he wanted to get done on his new build that day, so he was headed to the Compound to have a few beers with his brothers.

"Need you at Children's Hospital," Lee told him.

Joker stopped dead.

"Why?"

"Callin' a marker, brother," Lee said quietly.

Fuck.

"I'm on my bike," Joker told him.

"Maternity," Lee replied.

Shit.

"Got it. I'll be there."

He shoved his phone in his pocket and went to his bike.

Then he rode to the hospital.

He hit maternity only to see Lee wasn't alone.

Hank was with him.

"I'm here, what?" he asked when he stopped close.

"Need you to suit up," Lee told him.

"What?"

Lee knocked on a door. It opened, a nurse peered out, looked at Joker, then raised her hand and crooked her finger.

Joker looked to Lee, to Hank, then to the woman.

He followed her.

Once inside the door, he suited up. Covers over his boots. Cut off and gown over his tee.

Once done, she led him to a room that had little domed cots.

She stopped beside one and he stopped with her, looked down, and stared at the tiniest baby he'd seen in his life. The kid couldn't be bigger than his hand. He had tubes in his mouth and in his thin arm, cotton taped over his eyes, yellowed mocha skin, tufts of soft black curly hair.

"Preemie," the nurse said softly. "Addict."

Those two words sliced through his stomach, and Joker cut his eyes to her.

"She'll be good," she said. "She got this far, no stopping her now."

Joker looked down at the baby, who was not a he but a she.

"Can she be held?" he asked.

"No, but she can be touched," the nurse answered. "Through those holes in the sides. Let me get you a glove."

She got him a glove.

Joker put on the glove, shoved through, and he was right. The kid was as big as his hand.

But she seemed so fragile, he hesitated to touch her. Instead, he pressed his finger to her palm.

And when he did, her fingers curled right around.

Tight.

"Told you she'll be good," the nurse muttered.

Joker stared at the baby girl, feeling something soak into him through his fingertip.

Then, gently he pulled his finger away and his hand out of the hole.

He nodded to the nurse and walked to the door. He took off the shit he'd put on and walked back into the hall.

"Do not fuck with me on this," he growled to Lee.

"Woman came in, had the kid, took off. She barely hit recovery before she vanished. No one's seen her since," Hank told him. "It's been a week and a half."

Joker glared at him.

"She was high when she came in. Deserted her baby," Hank went on.

"And how many people out there are in line for this kid?" Joker asked.

"None," Hank stated.

"Mixed race," Lee said quietly, and Joker narrowed his eyes at him, knowing that didn't mean dick to people who wanted a kid. "Born preemie, addicted, serious shit, Joke. And all systems are go now, but no one has any clue what's gonna happen with that kid. How she'll grow up. How she'll develop. There could be problems down the line, and those problems and their likelihood, those in line have backed off. That little girl needs someone special who can suck it up and don't give a fuck what they'll face, long's they got a kid to love. Now, if we don't find people who got it in 'em to give her a beautiful life anyway, she grows up in the system."

"So what you're sayin' is, you want me to go to my high school history teacher who's been through the wringer with his wife and offer up a kid with issues and a mom that's disappeared?" he asked.

"You think for a second they'll say no, then no, I don't want that shit," Lee returned.

"My guess, they won't blink at the kid. But the mom has disappeared. She comes back—"

"She won't come back," Hank stated.

"If she comes back—" Joker started again.

"She won't come back," Lee said firmly.

Joker stared at him.

Then he asked, "Dad?"

"Dad's out of the picture," Hank said.

Fuck.

They knew the dad.

They also knew the mom.

They knew everything.

Fuck.

"How out of the picture?" Joker pushed.

"*Very*," Hank told him.

Joker looked between the both of them.

Then he clipped, "I get their hopes up, shit goes south, we got a problem."

"There won't be any problems," Lee replied inflexibly.

Joker took a beat.

Then he said, "You gotta give me twenty-four hours."

"Why?" Lee asked.

"'Cause I gotta talk to Carissa," he told him.

"Good call. She can back you up with your teacher," Hank muttered.

Actually, he hadn't thought of that. But he'd pull her in on that too.

What he'd thought of was little fingers curled around his own.

Tight.

"Yeah," he agreed. "But gotta talk to her mostly because, they say no, I gotta know if she's good takin' on a baby who might have problems down the line."

Lee's head jerked, and Hank stared.

Joker walked away.

*   *   *

The next day, standing in the Compound, Carissa at his side, her hand tight in his, Joker stared at Keith Robinson, who stood, head bent, hand lifted and wrapped around the back of his neck.

They were the only ones in the room.

They waited.

He took his time.

Finally, he dropped his hand and looked at Joker.

"I can't put my wife through it again."

Joker nodded.

He'd given him the info, and he wasn't surprised at his decision. The man loved his wife. Carissa went through what Keith watched his wife go through, Joker would make the same call.

"Then Carissa and I are takin' her on."

Keith blinked before his face changed.

"That's honorable Carson," he looked to Carissa, "Carissa, honey," back to Joker, "but believe me when I say that if things turn, you fall in love in an instant, and hearts break very easily."

"I've been assured by people who can do that that things won't change," Joker told him, repeating something he'd already shared.

"You think that and then—"

"Keith, you don't get me," Joker cut him off quietly. "These people would not have approached me if they didn't *know* things would not change."

Keith stared into his eyes.

Joker let him.

Carissa squeezed his hand and leaned into his arm.

"Maybe I should talk to my wife," Keith whispered.

Carissa made a sound like she was fighting tears.

"Maybe you should," Joker replied. "No pressure. Either way, that little girl will have a home. But you got my number. We'll be at the hospital."

Keith nodded and didn't waste time after his handshake for Joker and letting Carissa touch her cheek to his before he took off.

"Do you pray?"

Carrie's quiet question made him look down at her to see she was looking after Keith.

"No," he answered.

Her gaze came to him.

"Start," she whispered.

He looked in her eyes.

Then he started.

*   *   *

Joker was leaning his shoulders against a wall in the maternity ward at Children's Hospital, watching Keith Robinson walk into a room with a physician and a CPS officer.

Carissa and Keith's wife were suited up and in a room with the incubator, holding Keith's new daughter.

The door closed on Keith, and when it did, Joker felt a whisper up the back of his neck.

He turned his head and instantly braced.

At the end of the corridor stood Knight Sebring.

Next to him was a woman Joker knew. She'd been on Chaos's patch often. He'd ousted her a few times himself. She was a mouse, a flake, and an addict. She had no business being in the life. She was too weak. That life was going to chew her up, it was only a matter of time.

He hadn't seen her in months, and he'd thought the life had chewed her up.

Now he saw she looked frail and tired, and was wearing a bulky hoodie and baseball cap pulled low over her forehead.

Knight tipped his head to the side.

Joker jerked up his chin.

Knight nodded.

The woman put her hand to her mouth and her body bucked as her face collapsed.

Knight put a hand to her back, turned her, and they disappeared.

So this wasn't Lee's deal.

It was Knight's.

Which meant that woman had just *disappeared*, she did it safe, she'd do it clean. Knight was giving her a new life plus the knowledge her kid would be loved.

Joker drew in breath.

Then he looked at his boots and let it out.

*   *   *

Carissa sat next to him in his truck as they drove from the hospital.

"You know I love you?" she asked quietly.

"I know you love me, Carrie," he answered the same way, squeezing her hand he held on his thigh.

She squeezed back.

They rode in silence.

She broke it with, "I want another one."

"I know, Butterfly."

"Soon," she whispered.

He'd do soon. He would have planted one in her that night, but he'd been declared clean (something, for her, she'd already thought of, considering her ex had replaced her, and it was something that came as a matter of course through her care while having Travis) and she was now on the Pill.

"We'll do soon," he promised.

That got him another squeeze.

"You want Las Delicias?" he asked.

"I do, but that's our family place, you, Travis, and me," she answered, and he felt his chest get light. "Why don't we get a burger or something?"

"Whatever you want, Carrie," he muttered.

She squeezed his hand again.

He drove her to My Brother's Bar for a burger.

And after, he took her to Dairy Queen for a Blizzard.

* * *

"Joke!"

He turned his head at Lenny's call, and at what he saw, Joker muttered, "'Scuse me," to the photographer he was talking to.

Then he smiled as he walked through the garage to Carissa, who was wearing a sweet tank with shiny shit stitched on the front, sweeter jeans, and the high-heeled black ankle boots he'd fucked her in the night she keyed his father's car.

She also had big hair, lots of makeup, and a huge, bright smile. The whole package meant Joker was fighting his dick getting hard as he made his way to her.

When she got close, she made that a more difficult struggle

because she immediately wrapped her arms around him, pressed tight, and tipped her head back.

In return, he dipped his and slid his fingers into the back pockets of her jeans.

"I'm dressed as biker babe just in case Henry Gagnon happens to get a shot of me," she announced. "I don't want to let down the side."

She couldn't do that even if she was wearing that butt-ugly nightshirt he had thankfully not seen since he asked her to lose it.

"In other words, you couldn't stay away," he replied.

Her eyes sparkled as she pressed closer. "*Wilde and Hay* here to instigate their fabulous spread on my manly man biker and his brethren? No way."

He grinned.

She kept talking.

"And I have *two* pieces of good news I had to share *immediately*," she told him, saying the "two" and "immediately" on squeezes.

"Yeah?"

She launched in, "First, Megan called. She and Keith get to take Isadora home today."

It had been just over two weeks since the decision had been made. They needed Isadora to gain weight, learn how to suck so she could feed, and have her blinders taken off.

Guess all that happened.

"Great news, Butterfly," he murmured his understatement.

"Yes, *amazing*, and *get this*," she went on. "Aaron called me."

Joker's body got tight.

"Say again?" he demanded.

She shook her head, still grinning. "I'll say I was a little freaked when I saw his name on my phone, because he's not supposed to call me unless there's an emergency with Travis. There wasn't. He's fine."

"So why did that fuck call?" Joker bit out.

"Because," she was still smiling, "he has a date!"

Joker frowned down at her. "And he thought you gave a fuck about that because...?"

"Because Aaron asked that, instead of his mom and dad looking after Travis while he takes this woman out, maybe you and me would do it."

It was then Joker stared down at her.

"I said yes, of course," she continued. "He's bringing him over tomorrow night."

"You're shittin' me."

She kept smiling but did it shaking her head, her hair brushing her shoulders, giving him a show he really liked. "Nope."

The guy did have a soul.

And he was moving on.

And the biggest surprise of all that shit, he was finally demonstrating he wanted to give Carrie what she actually wanted, a copasetic relationship between all of them for Travis's sake.

Maybe he did love Carissa.

But this kind of love, Joker could deal.

His relief was so great he dropped his head so his forehead was resting on hers.

"Yeah, sweetie. This is *awesome*," she whispered, staring into his eyes.

"Yeah, Carrie, it is, baby," he agreed.

"Joke, brother, I get Carrie's ass in those jeans demands a man's hands in her pockets, but shit's happenin'!" Boz shouted.

Joker watched Carissa's eyes smile.

Then he felt her lips brush his.

He went in and made the kiss deeper and wetter, but he couldn't make it longer.

When he broke it, he asked, "You're gonna hang?"

"Wouldn't miss this," she whispered.

He grinned at her.

Then he kissed her forehead and let her go.

*   *   *

Joker pulled the stroller out of the back of the truck, shook it out, and shoved his foot down on the pedal that locked it.

The second he was done, Carissa was right there, planting Travis's ass in it.

But she was doing this being sassy.

"I cannot *believe* you're taking us to the mall."

"You wanted a burger. We got your boy, can't go to a bar, and Johnny Rockets is here," he reminded her.

She looked up at him as he scanned the parking garage, making sure it was safe before he started pushing the stroller.

She fell in beside him and declared, "Just to say, Gunther Toody's is more fun *and* it isn't in a mall."

"I'm hungry and that's further away," he muttered.

"By, like, five minutes," she retorted.

He ignored that, maneuvered the stroller down some stairs with Carissa spotting, and then she dashed forward to open the door.

"And just to say," she went at him again when they were inside, "you couldn't have parked further away. Johnny Rockets is all the way at the other side."

"Seein' as I mighta been here once, but I don't remember if I have because I blocked it, I don't have it memorized."

This was true.

Mostly.

"Whatever," she said but he could hear her smile.

He could also feel her thumb in his belt loop.

Which meant, when they'd moved through the mall and he made his turn, she had to come with him.

"Jo—"

She cut herself off and he knew why.

She couldn't miss the store they were in.

Since he'd scoped it out, he didn't waste time and guided her right where they needed to be.

Silently, Carissa followed him.

While Travis babbled and kicked his feet, Joker positioned the stroller sideways against the display case so the kid had a view before he hooked Carrie's waist and pulled her close.

"Hello," a salesperson greeted them. "Is there something I can help you with today?"

Since he'd scoped it, Joker pointed immediately to the case and answered, "We wanna see that one."

He heard Carrie suck in a breath.

"Of course. It's beautiful. Fabulous choice. One moment," the salesperson said, keys jingling.

He heard Carrie start breathing heavily as well as felt her body start shaking.

A velvet mat was put out on glass and then the Tiffany engagement ring was set on it.

"There you go," the salesperson said.

Joker nabbed it, grabbed Carissa's hand, and slid it on her ring finger.

They'd need another size. It was too big.

But for now, the gesture would do.

He looked into her eyes, which were on the ring, just as a tear escaped one and slid down her cheek.

He felt that.

And he loved how it felt.

"How's that for a promise ring?" he whispered.

Another tear slid down her cheek as her fingers curled around his hand and her gaze locked with his.

"It's perfect," she whispered back.

"Joe joe kah!" Travis shouted.

Carissa's eyes got huge one beat before she burst out laughing at the same time she burst into tears.

Joker pulled her into his arms, took her laughing, sobbing mouth in a long, wet kiss, and through it, he heard the salesperson murmur, "I love my job."

*   *   *

The front door opened and Joker looked that way to see Carissa walking in.

"Yo," Boz called from beside him at the dining room table.

"Carrie," Snapper greeted, also at the table.

"Babe," Roscoe, at his other side, said.

"Hey, Carrie," Rush, at the foot, called.

Hound grunted.

Joker just kept his eyes on his woman and smiled.

She smiled back, calling, "Hey," to the men at the table drinking beer and playing poker.

But she came right to him.

Putting her hand to his jaw, she bent in and kissed him lightly before repeating a much softer, "Hey."

Like always.

Right in his dick.

"Hey, baby, how was girls' night out?" he asked.

"Good. But...um, can I talk to you a sec?"

He tried to read her face, saw something he couldn't put

a finger on, didn't like that, so he nodded and didn't waste time putting his cards facedown on the table.

"Be back," he told his brothers.

"Time for fresh ones," Roscoe announced, pushing back in his seat.

Joker got up and Carissa took his hand.

She walked him down the hall, asking, "Are you winning?"

"I haven't lost the house," he said by way of answer.

She tossed him a grin as she moved them into their room. "Hound's kicking your booty again."

Joker didn't return the grin, he was still trying to read her, but he did reply, "The man's a poker savant."

Her grin turned into a smile and she asked, "Can you close the door?"

Joker closed it then gave her his full attention, begging, "Please tell me that you and your bitches didn't decide tonight was the night to light my father's house on fire."

She burst out laughing.

He watched, hoping that was a no.

She sobered and informed him, "No. And actually, this is a show not a tell."

Carissa giving him a show.

He thought of Roscoe getting fresh ones.

Then he thought none of his brothers would be too concerned they had to slam them and get the fuck out because he might not tell them he was going to get a show, but they could guess, and they wouldn't be brothers if they were the kind of men to stand in the way of that for a game of poker.

So he crossed his arms on his chest and ordered, "So... show."

"To preface this, I'll say I like my promise ring."

Joker shook his head but did it grinning.

He knew that. In the week since she'd got it, he'd seen her

staring at it. She'd even made a habit of rubbing the diamond against her lower lip more than occasionally.

If he caught that last and was in a position to do so, he put her in a position of using that lip in a different way, among other things.

"And also," she went on, "this is the culmination of what Elvira calls a 'wild hair,' something I'm told happens when cosmo two turns into cosmo three."

"Butterfly, get on with it."

She slid her hands down the skirt of her cute dress, her eyes on his but his eyes dropped to her hands.

"Also, it should be said that Tyra's in the know about practically everything," she informed him.

Joker didn't say anything. He was watching her pull up the skirt of her dress.

She shifted to the side, telling him, "Including where the brothers get their tats."

His chest got tight because he saw panties and under them, at the top right corner of her ass, in from her hip, down from her waist, a bandage.

Carefully, she pulled her panties down over the bandage as he stood immobile and watched.

Still silent and watching him, she peeled the bandage away.

"I got a ring," she whispered. "This is your promise."

Without moving a muscle, Joker stood there staring at the gooed-up red flesh in which, smaller but fucking magnificent, was the card he'd designed for his tat guy to ink on his chest.

But it was on his girl's heart-shaped ass.

"I'm not a tattoo person but I thought... Joker?"

She ended on a call to him because he'd dropped his arms and turned on his boot.

He threw open the door and yelled down the hall, "Party's over! Get out!"

He heard a "What the fuck?" and a guffaw but that's all he heard before he slammed the door and turned back.

"Sweetie, that was rude...oh!"

She cried out because he was stalking.

She was backing up.

She had a hand up and was looking at him closely as she moved.

"Does this mean you like it?" she asked.

He didn't give her an answer verbally.

But a while later, when he was not doing his usual watching her pussy take his dick but instead his eyes were locked to his card on her ass as she took his fucking on her knees, her whimpers muffled by the covers where her face was pressed, he figured she got the message.

*   *   *

He figured she also got his message when she sat next to him, babbling about wedding plans, co-workers at LeLane's, her and her girls' predictions of when Malik would pop the question, as he laid back in the chair, the buzz sounding as his tat guy worked at his chest.

Like the joker card, it was his design, so he could change the deck to whatever the fuck he wanted it to be.

So the card the guy was inking slanted over his heart next to the joker was the queen of hearts.

And butterflies.

*   *   *

The back door flew open and Carissa flew in carrying the handles of a LeLane's paper bag in one hand, a massive stack of magazines tucked in her other arm, her purse over her shoulder, and wearing her khaki's and LeLane's polo, Converse on her feet.

Joker was at the stove.

Travis was unsteady on his feet as he ran to her, shouting, "Moomah!" then he took a header, landed on his hands and knees, tipped his head back and giggled.

"Googly," she greeted, dumping bag, magazines, and purse and cutting her eyes to Joker. "Please tell me you're browning the ground beef."

"Seein' as I got a text five minutes ago tellin' my behind to do that and I'm standin' at a stove...yeah."

She smiled at him, bent, scooped up her kid, gave him kisses, tickles, and snuggles, then put him down again and came right to Joker.

Her eyes were shining.

"Did you see it?" she asked.

He nodded. "Tyra bought twice as many as you got over there." He jerked his head to the counter where she'd dumped her shit.

"Did you read it?" she pushed.

"Uh...yeah," he answered.

"It...is...*amazing*!" she cried. "So amazing. So cool. So *you*! And the brothers. I'm framing it. Every page!" she declared.

"Figure you will, bein' a goofball," he muttered, fighting his smile.

"Don't make me annoyed when I'm this happy." She jumped suddenly and yelled, "I have to change! Be back! There's ice cream in that bag, toss it in the freezer, sweetie, will you?"

Then she didn't wait for him to answer. She pursed her lips and blew him a kiss, which he thought was cute, and he usually loved it when she did that, but not so much right then when she just got home and he would prefer something a fuckuva lot different.

He didn't get it.

She raced out of the kitchen.

Joker turned down the meat, bent, nabbed Travis, and planted him on his hip.

"Joejoekah, loo lah, kah kah."

"I hear you," Joker muttered as he walked to the bag, took the ice cream out (three tubs), and put it in the freezer.

Then he went to the magazine, grabbed the top one off the stack, set it to the side and flipped it open.

He got to the page and whispered, "There it is, boy."

"Dah, noo, fah, lah," Travis replied.

"That's what I think," Joker said.

He stared down at the picture.

It took up both pages. One of his builds, a bike, purple, fucking brilliant pinstriping, and even he had to admit the framing was inspired.

In big writing at the top it said, *Custom Cool* and under that, smaller, it said, *Denver's Chaos Motorcycle Club, led by design mastermind Carson "Joker" Steele, takes custom rides to the next stratosphere.*

The brothers were gathered around the bike in the garage. All of them. Joker at the front wheel, arms crossed on his chest, Tack next to him, arm slung casually over Joker's shoulders, his boots crossed at the ankles.

The back wall was behind them, their tool chests and equipment lined up at the bottom against it, a massive Chaos flag stretched across the wall above.

Boz was smiling like a lunatic, but the rest of his brothers were staring at the camera natural, looking badass.

It was a fucking great picture.

He flipped the page to a better one.

Top right corner, a side shot of Joker in Carissa's arms, his hands deep in her back pockets, their attention focused on nothing but each other.

They were smiling.

Under it, it said, *You can't have bikers without biker babes. Steele with his fiancée, Carissa.*

"Moomah," Travis mumbled and Joker looked to the kid to see his eyes on the magazine, his fingers twiddling his lip.

"Yeah, son, that's your momma."

Travis looked to him. "Moomah."

"Yeah, boy."

Travis took his fingers from his lip and curled them around Joker's. "Joejoekah."

"Yeah," Joker whispered. "I'm your Joker."

The boy wobbled a second then dropped forward and landed a sloppy, open-mouthed kiss on his hand and Joker's mouth.

He wobbled back.

"Love you too, kid," Joker whispered.

Travis giggled.

Then he twisted and reached to the floor.

Like he would do if he could do it for as long as he could do it, Joker gave Travis what he wanted and put his ass on the floor.

*   *   *

"This shit fuckin' *rocks*," Boz declared, scooping up his third helping of Carissa's chili and dumping it on a bed of chili cheese Fritos.

Watching his brother do that, Joker thought it was good his woman had made a vat.

He went to the fridge, nabbed a couple of cold ones, popped the tops, and walked them out, going straight to

Linus, who, in the crush of people, was standing by the window in the dining area, Candy perched on his hip.

Joker handed a beer to his friend and got a mumbled, "Thanks, Car."

"No probs," he replied, turning to the room where all his brothers, their bitches, and Chaos friends, including Elvira and Malik, Lawson and his family, Lucas and his family, Delgado and his family, and both Nightingale brothers and their families, with the additions of Linus's family, Mrs. Heely, and Keith, Megan, and Dora Robinson, were shoved in his and Carissa's house.

Luckily, some of them were shooting the shit in the kitchen and others were out in the cold on the back deck, or there wouldn't be enough room.

Even if there wasn't room, the shit-ton of kids currently in their pad found ways to run around, which they were doing.

Joker felt something light touch his shoulder.

He turned and saw Candy doing a lean his way.

He looked to Linus as he took her weight, heavier than he was used to, and settled her on his side.

She wrapped her arm around his neck and rested her head on his shoulder.

"My baby's got a crush," Linus said under his breath.

Joker turned his head and grinned at him.

"Excellent spread in that magazine, Car," Linus said louder. "Kamryn bought five of 'em. She wants you to get your brothers to sign them."

Hearing this, Joker wondered if there was a copy left in Denver, considering any women remotely associated with Chaos were hoarding them. Stacy had bought ten (and made the brothers sign them). Elvira had bought twenty (and bossed the brothers into signing them).

"Proud," Linus whispered.

Joker lifted his beer and took a swallow, but didn't look at him.

"All I'm gonna say but that runs deep, Car," Linus kept at it. "And not just because you're famous."

With all he was feeling, the only thing Joker had to give he gave.

He nodded.

Linus, as always, took what he had to give happily and clapped him on the back.

Joker felt that light in his chest as he felt something else.

His eyes moved to the couch and he saw his girl sitting close to Mrs. Heely, Indy Nightingale, and Gwen Delgado, all of them gabbing like they weren't being crawled on by kids or casually dodging toys flying.

But Carissa's eyes were over the back of the couch and she was looking at Candy.

Her gaze shifted to him.

"Soon," he mouthed.

She smiled.

The most beautiful thing he'd ever seen.

She pursed her lips and blew him a kiss in a way, with their house chock with people, he'd accept.

And then that was the most beautiful thing he'd ever seen.

She turned away quickly when Suki Nightingale landed in her lap.

He heard her laughter as he watched her do it.

His chest got even lighter.

Because that was when *that* was the most beautiful thing he'd ever seen and he knew he'd get that again and again and again.

Easy.

Steady.

Beauty.

She gave him what she'd promised he'd have.

A beautiful life.

The best part?

He got to give it back.

EPILOGUE

Oh Yeah

THERE WERE MILES of cream, pink, and peach streamers twisted and stretched from Ride the store to Ride the garage.

There were tents set up. At their corners, ribbons were waving from under big, shimmering peach and pink butterflies.

There were tables under the tents covered in cream plastic cloths that glinted with sprayed on glitter. On top were pink plastic cake plates and peach plastic forks, and down the middle, bouquets of cream, pink, and peach roses with scrolled and twisted bits of green spiraling around the blossoms, little glittery butterflies sticking out.

Suddenly, when the background music of Godsmack doing their cover of "Rocky Mountain Way" ended, a rough voice sounded over a loudspeaker, saying, "Carrie, your biker wants your ass on the dance floor."

That was when a woman in a strapless lace dress with what looked like diamonds sparkling all over walked toward the dance floor. The full, poofy skirt that went almost to her ankles swayed against her legs over high-heeled peach sandals.

She had a diamond on a chain around her neck. Her

honey curls were pulled back in a loose bun at her nape. She had pearls in her ears.

But she had little butterflies stuck in her hair.

She also had a small baby bump at her belly.

She was smiling at a man with black hair that was cut short at the sides and was a mess at the top. He had a thick beard. He was standing on the dance floor wearing a pair of jeans and a cream shirt.

He was smiling back.

She lifted her hand toward him when she was a few feet away.

He took it when she got close.

He wasted no time pulling her into his arms, and the woman didn't quit smiling at him as he did it. In fact, her smile got so big, it near on split her face.

Then the opening strains of Louis Armstrong singing "What a Wonderful World" started playing.

The woman threw her head back and her peal of laughter could be heard over the music.

It was laughter even if it also sounded almost like a sob.

The man watched her and the white of his teeth that shone through his beard didn't disappear as he did.

Then she tipped her head forward and buried her face in his neck as she wrapped her arms around his broad shoulders.

He rested his jaw against the side of her head and swayed her in his arms.

A group of people moved, and Jefferson Steele could no longer see his son dancing with his new wife at their wedding reception from where he stood at the fence.

It was time to go anyway.

He didn't even know why he came, except for the fact that for the first time in years, he ran into fucking Linus

Washington and the man wouldn't shut up about Carson and his girl Carissa, telling him all about them getting married.

He turned to head to his truck that he had to park a fucking million miles away because Broadway was lined with cars, trucks, and bikes.

But he stopped dead when he saw a salt-and-pepper-haired, goateed man standing there with his arms crossed on his chest.

"You got that." His voice was low, gravelly, and hostile. "Now do not ever come back."

Jefferson Steele took one beat to consider the idea if he could take this asshole down.

It only took a beat.

Then he nodded, shifted around him, giving him a wide berth, and walked to his truck.

Tack Allen walked to the fence and looked into the forecourt of Ride.

All he could see over the crowd was the side of Joker's head, his face obscured by Carissa's honey curls.

He scanned and caught sight of his woman.

Tyra had his grandbaby tucked in her arm, but she was smiling down at Travis, who was standing on his pudgy little kid legs and pounding on her thigh.

Elvira got close and swooped him up.

Travis giggled so loud, Tack could hear it.

He felt his lips curl up and he shifted his eyes back in the direction of the dance floor just as Louis sang *oh yeah*.

Tack walked toward the party, agreeing.

Get lost in the Chaos!

Kristen Ashley's captivating series continues …

Please see the next page for a preview of

WALK THROUGH FIRE.

I Never Would

I SHOULD GET a salad.

I should have gone to Whole Foods and hit the salad bar (and thus been able to get a cookie from their bakery, a treat for being so good about getting a salad).

I didn't go to Whole Foods.

I went to Chipotle.

So, since I was at Chipotle, I should get a bowl, not a burrito.

I had no intention of getting a bowl.

I was going to get a burrito.

Therefore, I was standing in line at Chipotle, trying to decide on pinto or black beans for my burrito, telling myself I was going to have salad for dinner (this was not going to happen, but I was telling myself that, something I did a lot).

And in the coming months, I would wish with all my heart that I'd gone to Whole Foods for the salad (and the cookie).

It was lunchtime. It was busy. There was noise.

But I heard it.

The deep, manly voice coming from ahead of me in the line.

A voice that had matured, was coarser, nearly abrasive, but I knew that voice.

I'd never forget that voice.

"Yeah, I signed the papers. Sent 'em. Not a problem. That's done," the voice said.

I stood in line having trouble breathing, my body wanting to move, lean to the side, look forward, see the man attached to the voice, *needing* that, but I couldn't seem to make my body do what it was told.

"Not set up yet with a place, don't matter," the voice went on. "Got a condo in the mountains for the weekend. Takin' the girls up there. So I'll come get 'em like I said, four o'clock, Friday. I'll have 'em at school on Monday. I'll sort a place soon's I can."

I still couldn't move, and there was an even bigger reason why then.

Takin' the girls up there.

I'll have 'em at school on Monday.

He had children.

Logan had kids.

Plural.

I felt a prickle in my nose as my breathing went unsteady, my heart hammering, my fingers tingling in a painful way, like they'd gone to sleep and were waking up.

The voice kept going.

"Right. You'd do that, it'd be cool. Tell 'em their dad loves 'em, I'll call 'em tonight and see 'em Friday." A pause, then, "Okay. Thanks. Later."

The line moved and I forced myself to move with it, and just then, Logan turned and became visible in front of the food counter at Chipotle.

I saw him, and my world imploded.

"Burrito. Beef," he grated out. "Pinto. To go."

I stared, unmoving.

He looked good.

God, *God*, he looked so damned *good*.

I knew it. I knew he'd mature like that. Go from the cute but rough young man with that edge—that dangerous edge that drew you to him no matter how badly you wanted to pull away. But you couldn't stop it, that pull was too strong.

I knew he'd go from that to what was standing in front of the tortilla lady at Chipotle wearing his leather Chaos jacket.

Tall. His dark hair silvered, too long and unkempt. Shoulders broad. Jaw squared. I could see even in profile the skin of his face was no longer smooth but craggy in a way that every line told a story that you knew was interesting. Strong nose. High cheekbones. Whiskers (also silvered) that said he hadn't shaved in days, or perhaps weeks.

Beautiful.

So beautiful.

And he once was mine.

Then I'd let him go.

No, I'd pushed him away.

I turned and moved swiftly back through the line, not making a sound, not saying a word.

I didn't want him to hear me.

Out, I needed *out*.

I got out. Practically ran to my car. Got in and slammed the door.

I sat there, hands hovering over the steering wheel, shaking.

Takin' the girls up there.

I'll have 'em at school on Monday.

He had kids.

Plural.

Girls.

That made me happy. Ecstatic. Beside myself with glee.

I signed the papers. Sent 'em.

What did that mean?

So I'll come get 'em... I'll sort a place soon's I can.

Come and get them?

He didn't have them.

Signed the papers.

Oh God, he was getting a divorce.

No. Maybe he'd just gotten one.

I'll come and get 'em...

He was a father.

But was he free?

I shook out my hands, taking a deep breath.

It didn't matter. It wasn't my business. Logan Judd was no longer my business. He'd stopped being my business twenty years ago. My choice. I'd let him go.

And clearly it didn't happen, where I'd thought he was heading, where I'd thought his Club was heading. What I'd expected would happen hadn't.

He was in line at Chipotle, not incarcerated.

He had that scratchy voice, so obviously he hadn't quit smoking when he should have (or not at all). But he seemed strong, tall, fit.

I didn't see him top to toe from all sides, but what I saw was what I'd hoped.

I'd hoped he'd find his way to happiness.

He'd said his order was to go.

Oh God, I needed to get out of there. It wouldn't do for me to escape him inside only to have him see me outside in my car, freaked out so bad I was shaking.

I pushed the button to start my car, carefully looked in all mirrors and checked my blind spots, reversed out, and headed home.

I had no food at home but a bin of wilting baby spinach and some shredded carrots.

This was because I thought grocery shopping was akin to torture. I did it only when absolutely necessary, which was infrequently considering the number of options available for food that did not require a stocked pantry.

Conversely, I loved to cook.

I just didn't do it frequently because I hated to shop for food.

I had good intentions. Practically daily I thought I'd change in a variety of ways.

Say, go to the grocery store. Be one of those women who concocted delicious meals (even if they were only for one), sipped wine in my fabulous kitchen while listening to Beethoven or something. There would be candles burning, of course. And I'd serve my meal on gorgeous china, treating myself like a princess (since there was no one else to do it).

After, I'd sip some fancy herbal tea tucked up in my cuddle chair (candles still burning) reading Dostoyevsky. Or, if I was in the mood, watching something classy on TV, like *Downton Abbey*.

Not what I normally did, got fast food or nuked a ready-made meal, my expensive candles gathering dust because they'd been unlit for months and not bothering even to dirty a plate. I'd do this while I sat eating in front of *Sister Wives* or *True Tori* or some such, immersing myself in someone else's life because they were all a hell of a lot more interesting than mine.

Then I'd go to bed.

Alone.

To wake up the next morning.

Alone.

And spend the day thinking of all the ways I would change.

Like I'd start taking those walks I told myself I would take. Going to those Pilates classes at that studio just down the street that looked really cool and opened up two years ago (and yet, I had not stepped foot in it once). Driving up to the mountains and hiking a trail. Hitting the trendy shops on Broadway or in Highlands Square and spending a day roaming. Using that foot tub I bought (but never took out of the box) and giving myself a luxurious pedicure. Calling my friends to set up a girls' night out and putting on a little black dress (after I bought one, of course) and hitting the town to drink martinis or cosmopolitans or mojitos or whatever the cool drink was now.

Seeing a man looking at me and, instead of looking away, smiling at him. Perhaps talking to him. Definitely speaking back if he spoke to me. Accepting a date if he asked. Going on that date.

Maybe not going to bed alone.

Every day I thought about it. I even journaled about it (when I talked myself into making a change that day and being together enough to journal).

But I never did it.

None of it.

I thought all this as I drove home, then into my driveway and down the side of my house, parking in the courtyard at the back. I got out and went inside, stopping in my kitchen, realizing from all these thoughts something frightening in the extreme.

I was stuck in a rut.

Stuck in a rut that began twenty years ago on the front stoop of Logan's and my row house, watching him leave because I'd sent him away.

Walk through fire.

The words assaulted me, and the pain was too intense to bear. I had to move to my marble countertop, bend to it to rest my elbows on it and hold my head in my hands.

Then it all came and blasted through me in a way that made my head feel like it was going to explode.

You love a man, Millie, you believe in him, you take him as he is. You go on his journey with him no matter what happens, even if that means you have to walk through fire.

His voice was not coarse back then. No abrasion to it. It was deep. It was manly. But it was smooth.

Except when he said those words to me. When he said them they were rough. They were incredulous. They were infuriated.

They were hurt.

Walk through fire.

The tears came and dammit, *dammit*, they should have stopped years ago.

They didn't.

They came and came and came until I was choking on them.

I didn't make a salad with wilting spinach and the dregs of shredded carrots. I didn't hit my desk and get back to work until all hours of the night, trying to catch up.

Instead I pulled my phone out of my bag, struggled to my couch, collapsed on it, and called my sister.

I couldn't even speak when she picked up.

But she heard the sobs.

"Millie, what on earth is wrong?" she asked, sounding frantic.

"Dah-dah-Dottie," I stuttered between blubbers. "I sah-sah-sah-saw *Logan* at fu-fu-fucking *Chipotle*."

Not even a second elapsed before she replied, "I'll be over. Ten minutes."

Then she was over in ten minutes.

She took care of me, Dottie did.

Then again, my big sister always took care of me in a way I knew she always would.

The bad part about that was that I never did any of those things I said I was going to do.

I never pulled myself out of my rut.

I never fought my way to strong.

When I lost Logan, I lost any strength I might have had.

That being him.

He was my foundation. *He* was my backbone. *He* made me safe. *He* made life right.

Hell, *he* made life worth living.

Then he was gone, so I really had no life and commenced living half of one.

Or maybe a third.

Possibly a quarter.

Likely an eighth.

In other words, I was the kind of sister who would always need to be taken care of.

I knew I should wake up one day and change that.

I knew that just as I knew I never would.

*   *   *

At a party, in a house, twenty-three years earlier...

"Hey."

"Hey."

He started it. He'd been checking me out since he got there ten minutes earlier and he didn't hide it. He came right to me and started it.

I liked that.

I also liked that he approached, not wasting a lot of time.

But mostly, I liked how incredibly cute he was.

Cute and edgy.

Holding my cup of beer in hand, I stared up at him.

God yes, he was cute. *So* cute.

But cute in a way that my mother would not curl up at night, safe in the knowledge her daughter had excellent taste in men. In other words, talking to a well-dressed guy who I would soon learn had a life mission he'd decided when he was a boy, this being astronaut or curer of cancer.

Cute in a way my mother would despair, pray for, and live in terror of and my father would consider committing murder (one of the various reasons my mother would be living in terror).

But looking into his warm, brown eyes, for once in my life, I didn't care what my mother and father thought.

I just cared about the fact he was standing close to me at Kellie's party, he'd come right to me and he'd said "hey."

"Name's Logan," he told me.

God, he even had a cool name.

"Millie," I replied.

I watched his eyes widen a bit before he burst out laughing.

That wasn't very nice.

I swayed a little away from him, feeling hurt.

He kept chuckling but he noticed my movement and focused intently on me, asking, "Where you goin'?"

"I need a fresh beer," I lied.

He looked into my full cup.

Then he looked at me, smiling.

Oh God, *yes*. He was *so* cute.

But he was kinda mean.

I mean, my name wasn't funny. It was old-fashioned but it was my great-grandmother's name. My mother had adored her, and Granny had lived long enough for me to adore her too.

I liked my name.

"You got Millie written all over you," he stated.

What a weird thing to say.

And more weird, it was like he knew what I was thinking.

"What?" I asked.

"Darlin', all that hair that doesn't know whether it wants to be red or blonde. Those big brown eyes." His smooth, deep voice dipped in a way that I felt in my belly. "That." He lifted his beer cup with one finger extended and pointed close to my mouth so I knew he was indicating the little mole that was just in from the right corner of my top lip. "Cute. Sweet. No better name for a girl that's all that but Millie."

Okay, that was nice.

"Well, thanks, I think," I mumbled.

"Trust me, it's a compliment," he assured.

I nodded.

"What're you doin' tomorrow night?"

I felt my head give a small jerk.

Holy crap, was he asking me out on a date?

"I...nothing," I answered.

"Good, then we're goin' out. You got a number?"

He was!

He was asking me out on a date!

My heartbeat quickened and my legs started to feel all tingly.

"I...yes," I replied then went on stupidly, "I have a number."

"Give it to me."

I stared at him then looked down his wide chest to his trim waist then to his hands. One hand was holding his beer, the other one had the thumb hooked in his cool-as-heck, beaten up, black leather belt.

I looked back to his face. "Do you have something to write it down?"

He gave a slight shake of his head and an even slighter (but definitely hot) lip twitch before he stated, "Millie, *you* give me your number, do you think I'm gonna forget a single digit?"

Okay, wow. That was *really* nice.

I gave him my number.

He repeated it instantly and accurately.

"That's it," I confirmed.

He didn't reply.

I started to feel uncomfortable.

And nervous.

I'd just made a date with a guy I didn't know at all except I knew my parents wouldn't approve of him and then I gave him my number.

Now what did we do?

"You come with someone?" he asked.

It was weird that he asked that now, after he'd asked me out.

After I thought it was weird, I thought that maybe he thought I was on a date and then made a date with him *while* I was on a date and then he'd think I was a bitch!

"No, just some girlfriends," I told him quickly.

He gave me another smile. "That's comin' with someone, darlin'."

Oh.

Right.

I bit my lip.

"Who?" he asked.

"Justine," I answered, tipping my head toward the kitchen table where there were four guys and two girls sitting. When he turned his head to look, I expanded my answer, "The brunette."

And right then, Justine, my friend the pretty brunette, drunkenly bounced a quarter on the table toward a shot glass, missed, and grinned. Two of the guys and one of the girls immediately shouted, "Shot!" Thus, she unsteadily grabbed the glass and threw it back, some of the vodka in it dribbling down her chin.

She finished this still grinning.

"You ain't ridin' back with her," Logan growled and my gaze shot back to him. "Fact, she ain't drivin' anywhere."

Oh man, I could love this guy.

Oh man!

That was crazy!

How could I possibly think I could love this guy just from him saying that?

"She isn't, and I'm not," I shared. "We're staying the night here."

"Good," he muttered right before he got bumped by someone precariously making his way to the keg.

"You wanna get out of here?" I found myself asking and got his swift attention. "I don't know. Sit out on the back deck or something?" I finished quickly so he didn't get any ideas.

"Fuck yeah," he whispered, his brown eyes locked to mine, and the way he said that, the way he was looking at me, I felt a shiver trail down my spine.

"Okay," I whispered back.

He leaned in and grabbed my hand. His was big and rough and felt warm and strong wrapped around mine.

Okay.

Oh God.

Seriously.

Seriously.

It was true. It was crazy and *totally* freaking true.

I could fall in love with this guy.

And I knew that just from him wanting me to be safe and the feel of his hand around mine.

Oh man.

He led me out to the deck, straight to the steps that led to the yard, and we sat on the top one.

I was nervous in a way I'd never known before, but it felt good as I stared out into Kellie's parents' dark yard.

"So, Millie, tell me what we're doin' tomorrow night," he ordered.

I turned my head to look at him. "What?"

"Whatever you wanna do, we're doin' it," he stated. "So tell me what you wanna do."

I tipped my head to the side, intrigued by this offer.

"How about we fly to Paris?" I suggested on an attempt at a joke.

"You got a passport?" he asked immediately, not smiling, sounding serious.

My heart skipped a beat.

Though, he couldn't be serious.

I mean, Paris?

"Do you?" I returned.

"Nope, but that's what you wanna do, I'll get one."

I grinned at him. "Not sure you can get a passport in a day, Logan."

"You wanna go to Paris, I'll find a way."

I shook my head, looking away.

He was good at this. A master at delivering lines.

I liked it. It showed confidence.

But they were still just lines.

"And he says all the right things," I told the yard.

"Babe, I'm not jokin'."

My eyes flew back to him because he still sounded serious.

And when they flew back to him, the lights from the house illuminating his handsome face, he *looked* serious.

"I don't wanna go to Paris," I whispered. "Well, I do,"

I hastened to add. "Just not tomorrow night. I don't think I have the right thing to wear on a date in Paris."

He grinned at me. "Well, that's a relief. Coulda swung it by the skin of my teeth but it'd set me up for a fail on our second date. Not sure how I'd top Paris."

He was already thinking of a second date.

I liked that too.

But I liked his words better because it was cool to know he could be funny.

I couldn't help it and didn't know why I would try.

I laughed.

He kept grinning while I did it and scooted closer to me so our knees were touching.

"So tell me, Millie, what d'you wanna do?" he asked when I quit laughing.

"I wanna see what you wanna do," I told him.

"Then that's what we'll do."

I looked into his eyes through the dark and felt something strange. Not a bad strange. A happy one.

Comfortable. Safe.

Yes, both of those just looking into his eyes.

"So, do *you* wanna go to Paris?" I asked. "I mean, one day."

"Sure," he told me. "Though, not top on my list."

"What's top on your list?"

"Ridin' 'cross Australia."

"Riding?" I asked.

"On my bike."

I felt my eyes get big. "You mean, the motorcycle kind?"

He put pressure on my knee as he gave me another grin. "I'm the kinda guy, Millie, who doesn't acknowledge there *is* another kind of bike."

Absolutely for *sure*, my parents would not approve of this guy.

And absolutely for *sure*, I so totally *did*.

"So you have a bike?" I pushed.

"Harley," he told me.

"Do I get to ride on it tomorrow?" I went on, not bothering to filter the excitement out of my question.

He stared into my eyes.

"Absolutely," he answered.

I smiled at him and I knew it was big.

His gaze dropped to my mouth and when it did, my legs started tingling again. But this time, the tingles emanated from the insides of my thighs, out.

I looked away and took a sip of beer.

"Millie," he called.

I kept my gaze to the yard and replied with a, "Hmm?"

"Safe with me."

My attention cut back to him.

"Never won't be, babe," he went on softly. "Not ever. Yeah?"

Again, it was like he read my thoughts.

And he knew. He knew he was exactly what he was: that guy parents would freak if their daughter ever said yes to a date with him.

But I knew something else, looking at him.

My parents were wrong.

"Yeah?" he pushed when I just stared at him, not feeling tingly.

Feeling warm.

"Yeah," I answered.

He pressed his knee into mine again and looked to the yard.

"So, you wanna go to Paris," he noted. "What else you wanna do?"

I looked to the yard too and told him.

We stayed out there, sitting on the steps of the deck, our knees brushing, for what felt like minutes and yet at the same time seemed like hours, talking about nothing that felt like everything. The guy he came to the party with stuck his head out the back door and called, "Low, ridin' out."

To that, he told me he had to go and we both got up.

He didn't kiss me.

He walked me into the house straight through to the front door.

There, he ordered somewhat severely, "Your girl is totally shitfaced, so you go nowhere with her and you let her go nowhere. Hear?"

I nodded. "Staying here, Logan," I reminded him.

He nodded.

Then he lifted a finger as his eyes dipped to my mouth and he touched my mole.

More thigh tingles.

He looked back at me. "Tomorrow, babe. Call you."

"Okay, Logan."

He grinned and walked away.

I watched him, feeling a crazy-giddy that had nothing to do with beer, strangely not disappointed he didn't kiss me.

He'd touched me in a way that felt way sweeter than a kiss.

And the next day, he called me.

Can't get enough Kristen Ashley?

Please see the next page

for an exclusive bonus chapter,

"MORE PLEASURE THAN PAIN."

Tabby

I LAY IN BED, fully clothed, tangled up with my man (who was also fully clothed), staring at the poster-sized picture of us on the back of his bike that was on the wall over our dresser.

"It's time, sugar," he whispered.

It was. It was actually time five minutes ago.

But I wanted this. I wanted these few minutes that were the last of the best of us before we became even better.

"Just a couple minutes longer," I told Shy.

"Whatever you want, Tabby," he murmured, pulling me closer in his arms.

I already knew the answer to the question that the test that was sitting on the bathroom counter brewing was going to provide.

And that answer was what I wanted. That answer was what *we* wanted. In fact, I had a feeling Shy wanted it even more than me, considering all he'd lost and how much it meant to him. He wanted to rebuild that. He wanted it for himself. For me. For his brother. And in honor of the memory of his parents.

And we were going to have it.

But now, I just wanted these last moments of just him and me.

So I lay tangled up in Shy, my cheek to his chest, my eyes on that picture hanging on our bedroom wall.

As I stared at it I thought what was in that picture was us and always would be. We would always have that no matter what. No matter what we added. How we grew. When we grew old.

That picture of me wrapped around Shy on the back of his bike would *always* be us.

"We should get a dog," I blurted.

I heard the smile in Shy's voice when he replied, "Sounds good."

"A mutt. A rescue," I decided.

"Okay, babe."

"We should get him before."

"Probably smart."

I tipped my head back until my nose was pressed to the underside of his jaw.

I felt him. I smelled him.

He smelled good. He felt great.

"Do you know how much I love you?" I asked.

The smile was gone from his voice. It was quieter, rougher, when he said, "Got a fair idea."

"Take that fair idea and times it by ten thousand and there you go."

He slid me up and onto his chest so we were eye to eye.

I looked into his green eyes, saw his messy dark hair, and fell in love even more.

God, my man was gorgeous.

"Let me go look," he whispered.

He couldn't wait.

"You want this," I whispered back.

"Yeah," he said.

"Me too," I told him, but he already knew that. We'd talked about it. This was not unplanned.

"Then let me go look."

"Whatever you want, baby."

Those green eyes told me things I loved to see before he slid his hand up into my hair and pulled me down to kiss me.

It was not a quick peck. It was long and lazy and wet and sweet.

I knew he was almost done when he rolled me to my back before he broke the kiss. But he didn't leave me immediately. He kissed my chest and the underside of my jaw before he again looked in my eyes.

"Be back," he said.

"Okay," I replied.

He slid away.

I looked back to the picture of us.

The beginning of our now started in Shy's bed in the Compound, him holding me, me crying and singing a sad song.

The conclusion of our now ended in a bed that was ours, both of us wearing the other's ring, with that kiss.

I'd take that.

Happily.

I kept my eyes to the picture until Shy took my attention by rounding the bed to come back. His gaze was on me as he moved, and he kept hold when he moved in, putting a knee to the bed then shifting in over me, covering me with his long, lanky, loose-limbed biker body, most of his weight on a forearm.

When he was right where he belonged, he ended our now.

And opened our future.

We'd had beautiful.

But the best was yet to come.

"We're pregnant, baby," he whispered.

I said nothing. Just watched his eyes start to shine with happiness.

I suspected mine were doing the same.

And not just because I had my husband's baby inside me.

But because him knowing that we were going to be a family made him happy.

*   *   *

"I'm gonna be an uncle?" Rider shouted. "That's crazy! I'm too young to be an uncle!"

"I think it's awesome!" Cutter announced loudly. "That means I'm not gonna be the youngest anymore, and I get to boss someone around!"

We had the family over at our house for dinner. Dad and Ty-Ty, Rush, Rider and Cutter. We hadn't let on that there was a purpose for this, and since we got together often, no one thought anything of it.

But Shy and I had just shared our news.

I was grinning at my little brother when I felt strangeness coming at me. I looked in the direction it was coming and saw Dad throw his napkin down, push back, and get up from the table. He then promptly walked out of the dining room.

I looked first to Shy, whose gaze was on where Dad had disappeared.

Feeling my look, Shy gazed at me.

"It's okay," Tyra said, and I tore my attention from my man to look to her. "He just needs some time."

"Some time for what?" I asked, confused and a little freaked. "I thought he'd be happy."

"He is, honey," Tyra said softly. "He just needs to have a second to wrap his head around it."

I didn't get that and began, "Shy and I have been married awhile, and he knows that we planned—"

"He knows," Tyra cut me off to say. "That doesn't mean the reality isn't something different."

"It's 'cause he's old," Rider shared with authority. "And now he's gonna be a granddad, which means he's even more old."

"Your father will never be old," Tyra told her son.

This was true. Dad was the kind of man who would be vital even if he lived to be one hundred and five.

Though, Rider wouldn't get that, or all the goodness it meant to him considering he was of Dad's blood, for probably ten years.

"You should go talk to him," Shy said. I looked at him. When I did, he jerked his head to the door.

He was probably right, but the person who would know that to be true needed to weigh in.

I turned to Tyra. "Should I?"

"Being with you in this moment?" She smiled a gentle smile and said no more.

That meant I should.

I pushed back my chair and got up, moving around it to follow Dad.

I got two steps in before I was stopped because my big brother was standing in my way.

I looked up into his eyes. Mom's eyes. My mom had not been a good mom, but she'd given Rush and me one good thing. She gave her son her eyes that were beautiful in Rush's face.

And I got to look at them.

"I'm gonna be an uncle," he said, and the way he said it, it sounded like it was unbelievable.

Unbelievable in the sense that he just got the news he won the Mega Millions lottery.

My eyes started stinging.

"Yeah," I confirmed.

"I'm gonna be an uncle," he repeated.

"Rush," I whispered.

He yanked me into his arms and wrapped them tight.

I returned the gesture.

His voice sounded funny, thick, choked, when he said, "Happy for you, Tabby."

I pushed in closer to my brother and drew in a deep breath before I replied, "Me too." I paused then finished, "Uncle Rush."

His arms got even tighter.

I fought back a sniffle.

We held on awhile before he gave me a squeeze and muttered, "Go. Be with Dad."

I nodded against his chest then tipped my head back to again catch his gaze. "Love you, bro."

"Same, Tab."

I grinned at him, and he grinned back before he leaned in, pressed his jaw against the side of my head for a beat, then let me go.

I glanced again at the table, which, in a few months and through the years, would change. There'd be high chairs. Then there'd be booster seats. More place settings. More noise. More food. More laughter.

Shy and I would create that like Tyra and Dad had. Then Rush (I hoped) would add to it.

And Dad gave us this. Dad found Tyra, and they gave us Ride and Cut. This would be what we had forever, and this would be what we'd teach our children to build.

Because Dad made what we had beautiful and safe so we could give the same.

On that thought and one last glance at my husband, I went in search of my father.

I found him on the back deck, hands to his hips, head tipped back, eyes to the starry sky.

Silently, I moved in beside him, gave it a second, then said softly, "Hey, Daddy."

At my words, his arm shot out and hooked me around the neck, yanking me forcefully his way so I slammed into his side, his hold tight.

Other than that, he didn't move.

My eyes started stinging again as I wound my arms around his middle.

"That's who I am, Tabitha," he declared, his gravelly voice rougher than normal. "No matter what, girl, that's who I am to you."

He was not wrong.

He would always be my daddy.

And I would always be Daddy's little girl.

"I'm happy," I told the side of his chest, the words were heavy like a blanket, warm and snug.

"I'm glad," he replied.

"Shy's over the moon," I shared.

"Knew somethin' was up the minute we walked in, so he ain't hidin' that, darlin'."

That made me grin.

"I love him," I went on, telling him something he very well knew.

He confirmed he knew.

"I know you do."

I drew in breath and my grin died. "Thank you for giving me this."

At that, his arm got even tighter, curling me into his front as his other arm stole around so he could hold me with both.

I felt his lips come to the top of my hair.

"That was my line."

I made the noise right before the tears flowed, and I held on to my dad as he held on to me and let me cry.

"Always wanted this, just this for my girl," he whispered into my hair. "However that came about, you bein' happy. Findin' someone to love. Findin' someone who loves you back just as deep. Buildin' your life. All I wanted for my girl."

I drew in a deep breath and his head came up when I tipped mine back.

"Well, you got it."

He stared at me through the dark with his deep blue eyes. My eyes. I got to look at a piece of my dad that was beautiful every time I looked in the mirror.

Another gift.

"Why'd you leave the table?" I asked when he didn't speak.

"Maybe you'll get it one day, Tabby. Don't know what a woman goes through, so don't know if you ever will, but 'spect it'll happen. Do know, a man, his daughter, I had to give you up to give you to Shy. You bein' a mom, gotta give up a little bit more."

He was so very wrong.

"You don't have to give me up," I said firmly.

He shook his head. "Shy's job is to take care a' you. Your job is gonna be takin' care of your babies. Those two things are gonna be your life, honey." He gave me a squeeze. "This is not a complaint. Pleased as fuck you got that. But in that equation, I'm not there."

Wrong again.

"You're always there," I retorted.

"Not the way I'm used to bein'," he returned then lifted a hand to curl it where my neck met my shoulder, effectively silencing me when I opened my mouth to speak. "There's more pleasure than pain, Tab. I just gotta get used to the idea that I give that part up but I get back. When I gave you to Shy, it took time, but it finally hit me that, outta that, I got Shy as a new son. Now," he grinned, "it won't take near the amount of time to get used to gettin' what I'm gonna get now, givin' up another piece a' you. That bein' my first grandbaby."

I wanted to grin back but all he was saying was making me think.

And what I thought came out of my mouth. "I hope we don't have girls. If we do, Shy's gonna have to go through the same thing as you."

"You don't have girls, you'll have boys, and that means *you* givin' up the same thing as me."

I hadn't thought of that.

God!

We were screwed either way!

Contemplating this heretofore unconsidered idea, I looked to Dad's shoulder.

"Tab," he called.

I looked back.

I knew he knew what I was thinking even before he confirmed it by speaking.

"Darlin', like I said. You don't get it," he told me. "You will. And like I said, there's more pleasure than pain. It's life, honey. Sometimes the beauty of the journey is unexpected and hard to recognize. That don't mean it isn't still beauty."

Okay, I guess he wasn't wrong.

He was right.

Time to move on.

"Are you better now?" I asked.

"Got one of my two best girls in my arms. No way I can't be."

That made me plant my forehead into his chest and feel wet again in my eyes.

God, I so totally had the best dad in the world.

Dad moved his hand to the back of my neck and held it, warm and snug.

"Love you, baby girl," he whispered into the top of my hair. "Proud as fuck a' you."

"Love you too, Daddy," I whispered back.

We held on.

We did this too long.

We'd know this when we heard the sliding glass door open and Cutter shout, "Dad, Tab, you gonna be out here forever or what? You're holding up dessert!"

I tipped my head back and caught Dad's eyes.

I was grinning.

He was looking beleaguered.

"Sure you wanna do this?" he asked.

I burst out laughing.

My baby brother shouted, "Jeez! Dessert is pudding parfaits! My favorite! And we've waited…like…*forever*! *Come on!*"

And at that, I laughed harder.

*   *   *

I felt a release and heard bawling.

I slumped.

"You want the honor?" my OB asked.

"Fu…yeah," Shy answered.

I heard this but I was concentrating on the bawling, my eyes darting around seeing people but wanting one thing.

Then the nurse turned and I got what I wanted. She plonked a weight that was surprisingly light on my chest, considering what it felt like tugging on my spine and resting on my bladder the last three months.

I looked down and all I saw was a mess of wet, dark hair.

"Ten fingers, ten toes, healthy lungs, all good," the nurse murmured, barely to be heard over the bawling.

My hands went to the weight.

He had something wrapped around him that the nurse was using to wipe him off.

I didn't feel that or her movements.

The skin of my fingers hit the skin of his little body and I was lost.

Gone.

Gone for my baby boy.

He rolled a bit and I pushed up a bit so I could get a better view.

And I saw him. His pissed-off face. His scrunched-up eyes. His teeny balled-up fingers. His pumping little legs.

Oh yes.

Gone.

Gone for my baby boy.

"Shy," I whispered.

"Right here, sugar," he whispered back and then he leaned in so deep he was almost in the bed with me, his face so close to mine our jaws were touching, his hand snaking up to hold our son's tush. The nurse wrapped him up and left him where he was so she could do other things.

"Shy," I repeated.

"Right here," he did the same.

"Look at him," I ordered.

"Lookin', baby. He's gorgeous. You did good, Tabby. You did so fuckin' good, baby."

I felt him kiss my jaw.

"Look at him, Shy," I demanded.

Our boy kept howling, and I held him to me as Shy lifted a hand to his cheek and slid his finger down the soft, red skin.

I watched, thinking I'd never seen anything so beautiful, Shy's long, handsome finger trailing down that soft, red skin.

"I see, Tabby."

"He's perfect."

Shy cupped our son's tiny head in his big hand. "He is, baby. Top to toe."

I tore my eyes away from my baby to look at my man.

"He's perfect," I repeated, my voice cracking in the middle.

Shy looked from our son to me, and his green eyes flared before they warmed.

"He is, Tab. Top to toe," he whispered and dipped in closer, his gaze holding mine. "You're gone, aren't you?" he asked.

"Totally," I whispered back.

"Yeah," Shy replied, his eyes now smiling before he went in for a light kiss on my lips.

When he moved back, he said, "You did so good, sugar. So fuckin' good."

I looked down at our son, who was still bawling and squirming on my chest.

"I did," I agreed. "We did." I said as I felt my son squirm and tightened my hold on him. "We did so *fucking* good."

*   *   *

I watched Dad take my sleeping boy from Shy.

I listened to Tyra's soft crying as she pressed in close to her husband in order to get a good look at Shy and my baby.

And I saw it when Dad settled my boy in the curve of his arm and lifted his other hand to curl his finger around Kane Landon Cage's throat.

I knew what he felt. I'd done it myself the first time I had the chance.

The pulse was strong.

Dad's eyes came to me. His gaze warm too.

And happy.

"See?" he asked quietly. "More pleasure than pain."

I got him.

I *so* got him.

Then again, Kane "Tack" Allen, my dad, was never wrong.

Fall in Love with Forever Romance

POWER PLAY
by Tiffany Snow

High-powered businessman Parker Andersen wears expensive suits like a second skin and drives a BMW. Detective Dean Ryker's uniform is leather jackets and jeans...and his ride of choice is a Harley. Sage Reese finds herself caught between two men: the one she's always wanted—and the one who makes *her* feel wanted like never before...

RIDE STEADY
by Kristen Ashley

Once upon a time, Carissa Teodoro believed in happy endings. But now she's a struggling single mom and stranded by a flat tire, until a vaguely familiar knight rides to her rescue on a ton of horsepower...Fans of Lori Foster will love the newest novel in Kristen Ashley's *New York Times* bestselling Chaos series!

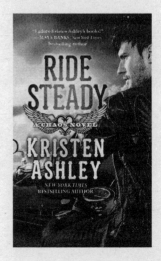

Fall in Love with Forever Romance

SUMMER AT THE SHORE
by V. K. Sykes

Morgan Merrifield sacrificed her teaching career to try to save her family's bed-and-breakfast and care for her younger sister. So she can't let herself get distracted by rugged ex–Special Forces soldier Ryan Butler. But her longtime crush soon flares into real desire—and with one irresistible kiss, she's swept away.

LAST CHANCE HERO
by Hope Ramsay

Sabina knows a lot about playing it safe. But having Ross Gardiner in town brings back the memory of one carefree summer night when she threw caution to the wind—and almost destroyed her family. Now that they are both older and wiser, will the spark still be there, even though they've both been burned?

Fall in Love with Forever Romance

A PROMISE OF FOREVER
by Marilyn Pappano

In the *New York Times* bestselling tradition of Robyn Carr comes the next book in Marilyn Pappano's Tallgrass series. When Sergeant First Class Avi Grant finally returns from Afghanistan, she rushes to comfort the widow of her commanding officer—and ends up in the arms of her handsome son, Ben Noble.